The
Space
Between
Us

MEGAN HART

The Space Between Us

HARLEQUIN®

entertain, enrich, inspire™

Recycling programs
for this product may
not exist in your area.

ISBN-13: 978-0-7783-1308-3

THE SPACE BETWEEN US

Copyright © 2012 by Megan Hart

For questions and comments about the quality of this book, please contact us at
CustomerService@Harlequin.com.

www.Harlequin.com

Printed in U.S.A.

This book is dedicated first to Superman, who can't dance worth a damn but who's always willing to give it a shot.

To my family and friends, of course and as always, because without you I would never have any stories to tell.

To the BootSquad, for reading this and helping me make it better.

To my bestie, Lauren Dane, who sometimes sends me links to horrific porn.

Everyone has a story.
Here's how this one ends.

Charlie's mouth.

That's what I want on my body now. His hands and mouth. Tongue, teeth, fingers. I want the crush of him on top of me, the silken brush of his hair against my flesh, the whisper of his lashes as he closes his eyes when he kisses me.

I want Charlie's mouth, and yet something makes me turn my face when he moves in close. Charlie sighs and presses his forehead to mine. His eyes shut, but I can't seem to close mine. I have to see him, even this close. Every hair and pore, every scar. Every blemish and flaw that make Charlie so perfect.

"If I'd known," Charlie says. His hands are heavy, one on my shoulder, the other on my hip. His breath smells of whiskey and smoke. He looks like Charlie, but he doesn't smell like him.

I don't want Charlie to wish he'd made a different choice.

Please, Charlie, I think. *Please don't tell me you wish you'd missed all of this.*

Charlie sighs. "It's just…there's this space between us. This big wide space. And I don't know what to do with it."

We fill it, I want to tell him, but say nothing. The words won't come. If I can't kiss him, how on earth could I possibly tell him that I love him? That it doesn't matter where Meredith's gone or if she's coming back. All we need is right here. The two of us will find a way to make things work. That it will all be okay.

I could tell him that, I think, as Charlie pulls away. His back is toward me. His shoulders slump. The jutting lines of his shoulder blades urge me to reach and touch, but my fingers curl in on themselves instead. I touch myself because I won't touch him. I could tell Charlie it will all be okay. It will all work out. But though I can't say I've never told a lie in my life, none of them have been to Charlie. I'm not about to start now.

"I'm sorry," Charlie says again in a low hoarse voice. He doesn't sound like Charlie now, either.

"I'm not," I say finally. "I'm not sorry about any of it, Charlie."

And that, at least, is the truth.

Chapter
1

Everyone has a story. That was Meredith's schtick. How she got us talking. Sometimes she asked about our favorite childhood candy, our biggest fears. What we'd dreamed about the night before. She asked, we answered. I never thought to question her about why she wanted to know, just like it never occurred to me to wonder why we all wanted to tell her.

Today it was about crazy.

"So, Tesla, tell me. What's the craziest thing you've ever done?" Meredith said this with gleaming eyes and lips wet from where she'd licked them.

Unlike some of the other times, I didn't have a ready answer for her. "Haven't I told you enough stories?"

She shook her head, her sleek honey-blond hair falling just so on the shoulders of her soft, pale blue cardigan. "Never enough. Carlos here already told me about how once he got caught jerking off to old people porn."

I paused, jug of coffee in my hand, and looked at them both. "Whaaaat?"

Carlos is a writer. We get a lot of them in Morningstar Mocha because we offer a bottomless refill for under two bucks, and free Wi-Fi. Carlos was in there every day, tapping away at his keyboard with his earbuds in before he headed off to his day job. Today he'd succumbed to the seduction of Meredith's charm and actually closed the lid of his laptop. *That* was pretty crazy.

Meredith came to the Mocha to use the free internet and drink coffee like the writers did, but she wasn't a writer. Meredith sold things—candles and cookware and jewelry, all from those home-party companies. She wasn't annoying about it the way Lisa, who sold Spicefully Tasty products, was. Meredith would be happy to sell you a pair of earrings or a fancy-smelling jar of wax if you asked her to, but she never pushed her stuff on anyone. She knew how to be subtle.

Well, mostly.

"Porn of old people fucking," she said. "You know. Like lemon party."

I didn't even know what that was, but Carlos made a face, so I guess he did.

"I was young. It was all I could find." He shrugged, barely embarrassed.

I laughed, put the full jug on the counter and lifted the empty one. "No offense, but that doesn't sound too crazy to me. I mean, who hasn't looked at gross porn at least once or twice."

I paused, just to give him a little bit of a hard time. "Can't say I've ever buffed my muffin over it or anything."

Carlos laughed and rolled his eyes. "Like I said, I was young."

"I told you." Meredith reached across their tables to poke him. "Our girl Tesla's a wild child."

I got that a lot. Maybe it was the Doc Martens, which I refuse to believe will ever go out of style, or my short-cropped hair. It was platinum-blond at the time, and that day I'd tied a cute Strawberry Shortcake bandanna around it, very 1940s Rosie the Riveter. Well, except that I was frothing milk and filling coffee jugs instead of fixing airplanes. If crazy was retro clothes and lots of eyeliner I might qualify, but not because of my day-to-day life.

I made a little wiggling gesture with my fingertips. "Yeah, o-o-oh. I'm s-o-o-o wild. And cra-a-azy! Watch out, I might just do something really nutty like wipe up the crumbs on your table."

"I meant it in the best way," Meredith said.

"Thanks." I started to say more, but my boss came out from the back room and shot me with the death-ray lasers of her gaze. "Talk to you later, when Joy's not breathing down my neck."

"Did you refill the self-serves?" Joy asked, and continued without waiting for me to answer. "I need you to pull all the baked goods today at four instead of five. Someone's coming from the women's shelter to pick them up. And listen, that panini on the menu? We're taking it off at the end of the week, so push it hard so I can get rid of that avocado."

We had half a dozen panini sandwiches on the menu, but at least the bit about the avocado tipped me off. I gave Joy my best and brightest, if dumbest, smile. Made sure to add the blank doll eyes, too, just because I knew how much she loved feeling superior. Hey, everyone's got a hobby, right?

Hers was being a bitch. Mine was letting her think she was getting away with it.

"Sure thing. No problem." I settled the empty jug near the coffee machine.

"Don't fill that now—it'll be off temp when it's time to replace it." She said that as if I hadn't worked here for almost two years already.

I didn't bother arguing. There are just some people in the world you can't please except by not pleasing them. And life's too short for making drama, you know? Sometimes you just gotta play nice, even when someone else is trying to grind your Play-Doh into the rug.

But then she floored me.

"I'm leaving at twelve-thirty, and I'm taking the rest of the day off."

"Are you okay?" It was the first question that rose to my tongue.

Joy took most weekends off, her privilege as manager, but that meant she never took days off during the week. And leaving early? No way. Privately, I thought this place was the only thing she had in her life.

Her sour expression showed me I'd stepped out of line. "What? Of course! Please don't tell me I need to stay, Tesla. I mean, you can handle this, right? Do I need to call Darek to come in earlier?"

Her tone made it clear she had about as much faith in me handling the shop as she would if the mop in the corner came to life and started grilling up paninis. "Yes. Of course. Have fun."

"It's an appointment," she said. "Not fun."

I shut up after that and got to the business of serving coffee and pastries and pushing panini sandwiches on poor, unsuspecting squares who didn't know the reason I raved about the turkey avocado club was because we were trying to get rid of it before the end of the week. By the time Joy was about ready to leave, the line of customers stretched all the way to the front door. That happened every day, though. I wasn't worried.

"I called Darek," Joy said. "He'll be here in twenty minutes. I can't really wait for him…."

I liked working with Darek. Still, the fact she'd needed to call him in early twisted my nipples a little. "It's fine, Joy. You go. I can handle this."

"With one hand behind her back," said the next customer in line, Johnny D., without being prompted. I love that guy.

You can't work in any sort of job dealing with the public and not get to know the people who come in day after day. Regulars. Well, I have regulars and then I have favorites.

Johnny Dellasandro was definitely a favorite. He's older than my dad, but has the most adorable little boy I've ever seen. He's made of fabulous, that guy, always with the smile and the wink. A dollar in the tip jar. A girl notices those things. He likes flavored coffee and sweet things, and he likes to sit with his newspaper in the booth closest to the counter. Sometimes he comes in with his girlfriend, Emm, sometimes with his little boy, sometimes with his much older daughter and his grandson.

Joy never gave him a sour look. She shot me another one, though, as if it was my fault she had to leave. Then she shrugged into her coat and left.

"Where's your little dumpling?" I asked Johnny when she'd gone.

"With his mama today."

"Must be nice to be a man of leisure," I teased. "Swanning around coffee shops and whatnot, being all pretty and stuff."

Johnny laughed. "You caught me."

"What can I get you?"

"Chocolate croissant. When you getting in those peppermint mocha lattes again?"

"Not until closer to Christmas," I told him as I pulled out the biggest croissant from the case and settled it on a plate for him. "We have the pumpkin spice, though. I can get you one of those."

With Johnny served, I moved on to the next customer. One at a time, that was how to do it, making sure to listen carefully to the orders so I didn't make mistakes—it was no good being fast if you were sloppy.

Eric was an emergency room doc who liked a pot of tea while he sat at a table in the front window and wrote list after list on yellow legal pads. Lisa the law student always had a jalapeño-cheese-stuffed pretzel and an iced tea while she studied. Jen was a regular I hadn't seen in a while, and we chatted about her new job for a minute. I spotted Sadie the psychologist at the back of the line and gave her a wave. Sometimes Sadie came in with her husband, another tasty bit of eye candy, only Joe was the kind of man who never even looked sideways at another woman. Today she was alone. Sadie waved back with the hand not on her hugely pregnant belly.

"Hot chocolate, extra whipped cream, and…" I tilted my head, looking Sadie up and down when she got to the counter. "Bagel with lox spread. Am I right?"

She laughed. "Oh…I was going to be good, but you've convinced me."

"If you can't indulge when you're pregnant, when the heck can you?" I tipped my chin toward the front of the shop, where Meredith had snared some other regulars into telling stories.

Laughter rose and fell. "I think there's something exciting going on up there. Grab a seat. I'll bring it over."

Sadie huffed a sigh. "Thanks. I swear, I used to be fit. Now just the walk from home to here has me winded. And my feet hurt."

"No worries." While she waddled to a table in the sunshine coming through the large front windows, I set to work toasting the bagel, steaming the milk, adding the chocolate syrup.

"The queen's holding court," Darek said as he moved behind me to hang up his coat and put on his apron.

I looked up at the sound of Meredith's laughter floating toward the back of the shop. "Doesn't she always?"

I'd known her only a few months, uncertain of when she'd gone from a regular to a favorite and then to a friend. It might've been the day Joy went into one of her raging shit-fits and Meredith had calmly but coolly put her in her place by reminding her "the customer is always right, or this customer goes someplace else to spend four-fifty on a mocha latte."

Since then Meredith had weaseled out most of my life history over coffee and sandwiches. I guess I'd had a crush on her from the moment she'd walked through the front doors of the Mocha with her oversize handbag and complementary dark glasses, her shoes that matched her belt, her perfectly styled blond hair. Meredith was the sort of woman I thought about trying to be sometimes, before ultimately accepting it took a lot of money, effort and desire I mostly didn't have. She'd become a part of our little coffee shop community even though she didn't live anywhere close to the neighborhood. More than that, she'd become a part of my life. She thought I was crazy. Wild. And she meant it in the best way, whatever that meant.

She really didn't know me at all.

The crowd waiting for food and coffee dwindled, though

most of the tables remained occupied. The Mocha's a popular place all day long. Sadie left. So did Johnny and Carlos, my regulars. A few of Darek's came in, but he took care of them. With Joy gone for the rest of the day I had time for a break, and I took my oversize mug of chai to Meredith's table.

She looked up from her computer when I sat. "You missed some good stories today. You still haven't told me yours, though."

"Haven't I told you enough crazy stories?" I'd told her plenty, most about my summers as a kid in the commune. "What, The Compound wasn't wacky enough for you?"

"Those were about a place you were, not things you did. There's a difference."

I sipped chai and looked her over. "Do I look like someone who does crazy things?"

"Aren't you?"

I shrugged. "I don't even have any tattoos."

Meredith waved a dismissive hand. "Every sorority girl has a tattoo these days. Piercings all over the place. They wear nipple rings like it's something special." She eyed me. "When I said you were our wild child, I didn't mean because of the way you dress or wear your makeup."

"What, then?" The mug warmed my hands better than the sunshine slanting through the glass. Early October in Pennsylvania can be glorious, warm and fragrant with the scent of changing leaves. This year, it was getting cold early.

Meredith shrugged, so graceful and artless that jealousy slivered through me. I could practice for a million years and never look that elegant. "Let's just say there's something about you."

"There's something about anyone, isn't there?" I lifted a fingertip to point discreetly toward Eric, sitting alone with legal pads and lists. "Check out Dr. McSexypants over there.

What's he doing with all that stuff? Every time he comes in here, he's writing on those legal pads. Why don't you ask him about a story?"

Meredith laughed, low and throaty, not the same laughter that had earlier filled the shop. This was just for me. "Because he won't tell anyone about them. Still waters run deep and all that shit."

"Maybe I have still waters, too."

She shook her head, playful. Charming. "No, honey, you're more like a waterfall."

"Because I rush a lot?" I asked with a wink.

"Nope. A thing of natural beauty with some treasure hidden behind it. C'mon, Tesla. Tell me. The craziest thing you've ever done."

There was no trying to deny her. What Meredith wanted, she'd have, and she made me want to give it to her. "I don't think anything I've done is crazy. Crazy's like…I dunno. Putting a dead bird in your locker at school so you can bury it later. Lighting stuff on fire."

"Okay, not crazy. Wild, then. Free? Unique?" She paused, thinking. "Unencumbered."

"Ah. You mean sexual."

Meredith wore a huge diamond and a gold band on her left hand. She talked sometimes about her husband, but only in the vaguest of ways. I knew his name was Charlie and that he was a teacher at some fancy private school. They had no kids.

"Yes-s-s," Meredith hissed with glee. "Sexual. Tell me, Tesla. What's the wildest sex thing you ever did?"

I wasn't surprised she wanted to know my wild sex secrets. She liked to talk about sex a lot. Well. Who doesn't?

"Hmmm." I turned my mug round and round in my palms,

the ceramic sliding on the tabletop. "The craziest thing, huh? I'm not sure I can beat old people porn."

"Did you know Sadie was married to someone else before Joe?" Meredith said quietly.

"No. She was? Huh." I shrugged. "Was that the craziest thing she'd done? Got divorced?"

Meredith shook her head. "Oh. No. Her first husband died."

I frowned, thinking of pretty Sadie with her big belly and gorgeous husband. "Gee, that's too bad."

Meredith shrugged. "It happens."

It wasn't the first time I'd heard her sound a little bored by the pain of others. She liked hearing stories, but mostly only the funny or exciting ones. Sad stories didn't melt her butter.

I looked up to the counter, but Darek was busy flirting with one of his favorites. Nobody else was waiting. I still had time—and half a mug of chai. "Fine. Crazy things. You go first."

She shook her head and licked her mouth again. I couldn't help watching her tongue move over her lips. Meredith has a mouth like Angelina Jolie. Full, soft lips. Pillowy, I think some people call them. She has a smile full of teeth, the kind you can't help but smile back at. Meredith's mouth is the sort that would break your heart if you saw it frowning.

"I haven't done anything crazy. I'm married."

I laughed at that. "So? Were you a virgin when you got married? Don't married people get up to crazy shit?"

Her eyelids lowered for a moment, as if she was remembering something. "No. Not really."

"You must have something crazy to tell me." I sat back when Eric got up to help himself to a refill from the jugs on the counter next to us.

"Tesla," he said, and nodded at Meredith. "Hi."

"Hi, Eric." She didn't flutter her lashes or anything contrived like that. Meredith didn't have to. "How's tricks?"

"Putting Houdini to shame," Eric said, though he didn't have quite the same easy flirting tone with Meredith that he had with me. He looked at her sort of warily, keeping his distance.

She made sure to ogle his ass as he walked away, then turned back to me. "I would bang that man like a screen door in a hurricane."

"If you weren't married."

"And if he didn't look at me like he was afraid I might bite him instead of kiss him," Meredith said with a touch of scorn.

I looked away from where Eric was again looking at his lists. "Oh, c'mon. He didn't."

Her smile lifted a bit. "He never looks at you like that."

"Because I'm not a moron and because I give him sugar and caffeine," I said with a laugh. "Eric's a good guy."

She shot him another glance, then dismissed him with a wave. She lifted her mug and drank, her eyes never leaving mine. She licked her mouth again.

"I kissed a girl," Meredith said.

"And let me guess. You liked it?" I swallowed hot tea.

She shrugged. "It was okay. It wasn't much of anything, really. It was in college. We were just fooling around."

"To see what it was like," I offered. I'd heard that story before, too many times.

"Sure. Lots of people do it. You do it," she added.

"Sometimes." It wasn't something I considered crazy or wild, and obviously she didn't, either, since she already knew about it and was still teasing me into telling something else.

"And you like it."

"Well…of course." I laughed. "I wouldn't do it if I didn't like it."

"See? That's what I mean. You do what you want to do, what you like to do, whatever turns you on." Meredith paused. "I admire that about you. I envy it, I guess."

As if she could really envy anything about me, a chick who worked in a coffee shop, drove a piece-of-shit car, didn't even live on her own. Besides, it had been ages since I'd kissed anyone, girl or guy.

"You don't answer to anyone," Meredith said.

"Tell that to Joy."

"C'mon, Tesla. I see it in your eyes. You have some good stories."

I laughed. There was really no resisting her. I'd seen her work her wiles on everyone from other customers in the Mocha to the cop she'd talked out of giving her a ticket. Even Joy warmed to Meredith, though she always reacted afterward as if her friendliness unnerved her, and was even more impossibly horrible for hours, as if she were trying to scrub herself free of any taint of kindness.

"I fucked brothers once. Twins." I didn't say this smugly or with any sense of pride, though by the way Meredith's eyes widened, I saw she was impressed.

"At the same time?"

I hesitated for just the barest second. She *had* asked for the craziest thing, and though I personally didn't think anything I'd ever done could qualify as crazy, clearly Meredith had her own set of standards. Well, most people do. "Yes."

She breathed out, long and slow. "Wow."

"It wasn't—" I began, but she held up a hand. I went silent.

"Tell me about it."

I hadn't told anyone about it, ever. So why tell her, now?

For no other reason than, just like the Billy Joel song, she had a way.

"Tell me," Meredith urged me.

So I did.

Chapter
2

Chase and Chance Murphy had never been separated. I was new to the district, but everyone else had gone to school together since middle school, some even since kindergarten. The boys' mother, the formidable Mrs. Eugene Murphy—if she had her own first name, and she must've, nobody ever used it—was something like a force of nature in the school, where her sons were both first-string on the basketball and soccer teams. "The twins," she called them. She made a unit of them, not recognizing them as individuals.

Maybe that was why it was so easy for me to fuck them both, or rather for them both to fuck me, at the same time. They were really good at sharing. I'd bet it wasn't what their mother had ever intended for them, but then I'm pretty sure Mama Murphy hadn't thought ahead to the years when the twins would get hair on their chins—and on their balls.

We were all seniors, me the new kid still finding my way, Chase and Chance popular boys despite their mother being such a legendary pain in the ass. They were tall, lanky, athletic. They were completely identical, though they'd stopped dressing alike by then. Later I discovered I could tell them apart by the slight curves of their cocks. One to the left, the other right. Mirror images. They were popular, good students. They'd been altar boys. They were going off to college.

Me? I was small and wore thrift-store clothes, but unlike Molly Ringwald in *Pretty in Pink,* this only made me poor, not quirky. I had no Duckie to adore me, but at least I wasn't all hung up on the rich boy from the other side of the tracks. No Andrew what's-his-face for me, thank God. Unfortunately, no James Spader, either. I'd have hit Spader like the fist of an angry God back then. Hell, probably even now.

I was smarter than the Murphy boys and just about everyone else in my class when it came to math, and their mother, determined they'd maintain their eligibility for sports teams— because sports apparently built character, something you'd never have guessed she believed, given her own unathletic state, or that of their dad, a dentist who wore thick glasses and had buckteeth that could've benefited from some of his own expertise—hired me to be their tutor.

That's right. Mama Murphy paid me to divest her darling twins of their virginity. It didn't start out that way, of course. I mean, I had every intention of teaching them calculus. I needed the money and wasn't afraid to insist that Mrs. Eugene Murphy pay me twice the normal rate because I'd be teaching two instead of one, even though she tried to convince me that it wasn't the cost per individual that should count, but the total amount of time spent.

"And since you're teaching them both at the same time," she had reasoned, "I should pay you the regular rate."

"They're not the same person," I'd pointed out to her, standing my ground.

"But they're twins!"

I'd only raised an eyebrow, as I recall. She'd taken in my long denim skirt, the black, knee-high Doc Martens, my dyed-black hair. I guess to her I was sort of scary looking.

"You did come highly recommended by the school guidance counselor." She'd sounded doubtful.

"I'll make sure Chase and Chance pass their finals with A's, or your money back."

It was done. She paid me every week. I made good on my promise.

It didn't start out as a fuckfest. If anything, the brothers were pains in the ass to teach. They didn't like calculus. Worse, they didn't care about it. They were both doing poorly enough that it was threatening their place on the school team. They still didn't care. Calculus was for douche bags, according to the brothers Murphy.

But like I said, I needed the money. There was no way I was going to let them get away with anything less than what I'd promised their mother. I could never have paid her back—I'd already spent everything she'd given me on clothes and books and music, the necessities of life.

"If you learn this—" it was the first offer I made them "—I'll blow you."

This stopped their stupid scribbling and wiggling around in their seats like puppies that couldn't be made to sit. Both of them had looked up at me, eerily simultaneous. They weren't the same person, but they did have a way of moving or saying the same thing at the same time. They were connected, no doubt about it.

"Get the fuck out," Chase said.

"No fucking way," Chance said.

"I will blow you both," I told them, putting my hands flat on the table and leaning over it to look them in the eye, one at a time. I can't remember which one I looked at first. I didn't think it mattered then, but it would. "I will make you both come so hard you see stars."

I would never be a teacher, had never even dreamed of it as a career, but one thing I'd learned about teaching was the effectiveness of positive reinforcement.

That was how it started. They finished their work in record time, and, aside from a few simple mistakes, correctly. As with most things in life, getting the Murphy boys to learn calc was a matter of simple motivation. I wanted them to get A's, and they wanted my mouth on their dicks.

It wasn't until they both dropped trou that I started thinking I might actually be getting the better end of the deal. I'd never thought much of Chase and Chance as boyfriend material. For one, they seemed sort of a package deal, despite my insistence to their mother they were two separate people. Two, they were a real pair of Weasleys, my very own Fred and George. Dark auburn hair with the pale skin to match, dark brown eyes. The freckles on their noses might've seemed a little Howdy Doody, but when Chase and Chance both pushed their jeans and briefs around their ankles, the only wooden puppet I thought about was the stiff, thick branches of their not-quite-identical cocks. I didn't know at the time they'd never been with a girl before. All I saw was beauty.

And I was greedy for it.

I made them stand shoulder to shoulder, hip to hip. I got on my knees in front of them. The carpet in their parents' finished basement was thick and soft, a perfect cushion. I took them each in a hand. I slicked them with my spit. I took the first one in my mouth, and then the other. I do remember who was first, because I was looking up at him when I did it. He was looking down.

It was Chase, though it should've been his brother, since I picked him totally by chance. Later it would make a difference, but at the time I don't think any of us cared. I slid his thick, pretty cock as far as I could into my mouth, and sucked, while I used my hand to stroke up and down his brother's prick.

Both of them groaned at the same time. They sounded the same. They looked the same. In another second I discovered they tasted the same, too.

If I could've taken them both in my mouth at the same time, I'd have done it. As it was, they had to be satisfied with my equal but back-and-forth attention. And at the end of it, wanting to watch them both when they came, I left off the use of my lips and teeth and tongue to lean back and finish them with my hands. They shot within seconds of each other, spurting onto their flat, rippled bellies. Both of them had closed their eyes, heads bent. Mouths I would later learn were talented with kissing and licking and sucking were lax and open with their moans.

Chase was the one who looked at me first. His hand, which had been gripping the table behind him, the one on which we'd spent hours scribbling equations, loosened its grasp and stroked along my hair. His thumb passed over my lower lip, which felt swollen and wet. He blinked slowly, as if waking from some dream he didn't want to leave.

"Fucking hell," Chance had said, breaking the moment. "That was awesome."

That was just the first time.

Chapter 3

"Wow," Meredith said when I'd finished. "That is…"

I didn't really want her to say crazy. It couldn't dilute what had happened, couldn't make it something it wasn't, but still. I didn't want her to say it like that.

"Fucking supernova hot," Meredith said.

I flushed, heat creeping up my throat and down lower. I hadn't told her the rest of it, but I thought I might, if she asked me. All about that long fall with the brothers Murphy, the three of us graduating from simultaneous blow jobs to cunnilingus and every combination of fucking that two cocks and a pussy can get into. It was over by Christmas.

"It's absolutely not what I thought you'd say," she told me with a shake of her head. "Wow. Not at all."

"What did you think I'd say?" I'd finished my chai and

break time was over, but I was curious exactly what she'd thought she knew about me.

"I told you. Hidden treasures."

I blinked slowly under the heat of her gaze. She'd kissed a girl, sure, but what did that mean? Nothing.

There's never any point in flirting with straight girls, you understand. Not even the "curious" ones. Straight girls have come to the conclusion that it's perfectly okay to make out with their bestie on the dance floor as a way to get guys' attention, or because they're drunk, or because it's trendy. Straight girls know that unless you eat pussy you're just experimenting, and even if you do go down on another girl it doesn't mean you're a dyke.

I'm not a straight girl.

I'm not a queer girl, either. I guess you could say I'm sexually fluid. Love comes in all shapes and flavors, and I just want to be able to taste them all. But if there's anything I learned from working at Morningstar Mocha, where the coffee flowed like Niagara Falls and waistbands expanded just by coming within a few feet of the dessert case, it's that wanting and having are two different things.

"It was a long time ago." I sounded lame.

"Can't have been that long ago," she pointed out, sounding wry. "You're barely out of high school."

I laughed. "Hardly. I'm twenty-six."

"A baby," she said, but fondly. "An experienced baby."

Age didn't mean much to me. "I have to get back to work. Darek's giving me that desperate look that means someone's ordered a drink he doesn't know how to make."

"Tesla to the rescue. You'd better go help him then. Anyway, I need to get going. I have some things to do." Meredith gave another of her low, sultry laughs that made the hairs on the back of my neck rise.

We both stood at the same time. She'd been coming in here for months, but today was the first day she'd ever hugged me. For the first few seconds, standing startled in her embrace, I didn't know what to do. She'd moved closer, and the smell of her was exotic and expensive and subtle. Her arms went around me, pulling me closer. Her sweater was soft on my skin, her hands warm on my back between my shoulder blades. We stood chest to chest and crotch to crotch for the span of half a heartbeat.

By the time I'd relaxed into her touch, closed my eyes and breathed in the deliciousness of her, it was over, except for the lingering heat in my ear from her breath where she'd whispered a goodbye, and the tingle in my cheek where I might've only imagined she brushed her lips.

"Tesla?" Eric said this from his place in front of the self-serve station, shaking me out of what must've been quite a show of shock. Meredith had already left the shop, the bell on the door jingling behind her. Eric cocked his head to give me the once-over. "You okay?"

"Oh, sure. Fine. Of course." I held out my hand for his empty mug. "You finished? I'll take it up for you."

He looked amused. "Nah. Gonna have another, if that's okay with you."

I laughed, embarrassed that I was so out of sorts by something so simple as a hug that had lasted less than a couple of seconds. "Of course. Drink away. If you don't, someone else will."

"Isn't that always how it goes?" He lifted the mug at me.

Then he turned to fill it with another round of coffee, Darek meeped out a cry for help up at the counter, and I got back to work.

Chapter
4

When I got home from work, the house was unusually silent, with no sign of anyone else. Normally I'd have sent out a not-so-quiet little hoot of bliss—I loved the people I lived with, but also craved having, and hardly ever got, the house to myself. Tonight, though, I was totally bummed to come home with not even the porch light left on to welcome me. No dinner, either, and that was worse. I made myself a tuna sandwich with a side of mac-n-cheese, because there really is nothing better than that. Unless it's hot dogs with mac-n-cheese, and sadly, we were out of hot dogs.

I couldn't help wondering what they'd gotten up to, those Murphy boys. The memory of them was a small, sore spot in my brain I worried once in a while the way I'd have done with a slice in my gum from flossing too hard. But my thoughts of Chase and Chance hadn't been close to the surface in a long time. Time has that funny way of smoothing out the rough edges of things, even ones that hurt a little bit. Or a lot.

"You're a user, Tesla," Chance had said to me the last time we'd been together. "Nothing but a user."

It wasn't true—I was more than a user. I was a lot of things we were too young and dumb to understand. And when he'd said it to me, I'd turned my back and walked away, burning with the self-righteous fury of being maligned. Now, with time and distance and experience between us, I understood why Chance had felt that way.

I hadn't heard anything about them in years, though it would've been easy enough to find out what they'd been up to. My brother, Cap, three years younger, would prob-ably know. I'd had friends; Cap had been popular. Football player, stage crew, homecoming king, voted Funniest in the yearbook. He'd had a good enough time in high school that he kept in touch with buddies from back then. Not that he'd been friends with the Murphys, but he could find out.

Calling my brother to get intel on a pair of guys I'd had sex with was right up there with walking in on your parents fuck-ing. I mean, that had happened to me, but it wasn't something I either wanted to think about or dwell on. Cap was probably the only other person who knew about me and the Murphys, but just because he'd known about it back in the day didn't mean he'd be down for discussing it now.

So, because even monkeys have been known to use tools, I turned to what I had on hand. The internet. My laptop had crapped out on me a few months ago, and I hadn't seen the way to buying a new one. Not until I'd saved up enough to get the biggest, fastest, sweetest Mac I could afford, which was going to take me a long time unless I could get over my ad-diction to cute retro clothes and glittery eyeliner. That didn't seem likely. Until then, I checked email and stuff from my phone and used the ancient desktop upstairs.

I'd set up my own user account on the desktop not so much because I wanted to look at things little kids shouldn't see, but to prevent them from messing up anything I'd saved. At four, Simone could expertly wend her way through the labyrinth of online kiddie games, but she also had a quick-draw delete finger. I'd lost documents and important emails more than once. Her brother, Max, at two and a half, was more likely to simply pound a bunch of keys, making the computer perform any number of wacky functions we had no idea it could do, and that it probably wasn't meant to.

Since nobody had come home yet, I didn't have to worry a lot about being pestered to look at videos of cute pets or play an educational game with colors so bright they made my eyes bleed. I didn't have to be careful about little eyes watching over my shoulder as I glanced through the pictures posted to my Connex friend feed. Meredith had been wrong when she said I didn't have to answer to anyone. I lived with four other people, one of whom would hand my ass to me on a plate if I exposed his kids to junk they shouldn't see.

Stalking people on Connex is supereasy if they're not concerned enough to make sure they tick off all the appropriate privacy controls. I don't have my account on lockdown because I never upload any pictures or anything too private that I don't want the world to see. Besides, I want people to be able to find me. That's what it's for, right?

I found the brothers Murphy with only a few keystrokes. They both belonged to a fan group for our graduating class. I hadn't joined. In their profile pictures they looked less alike than they ever had. Still tall and lanky, but time had put weight on them both, and it suited them.

Chance was married. Two small kids. I surfed his photos, feeling only vaguely creepy about it. He was living in Ohio, working for some accounting firm. He had a beautiful family and appeared happy. My cursor hovered over the Add Friend button, but I didn't click it. I was happy to see Chance looked like he had a good life, but I didn't feel any need to be even a peripheral part of it.

Chase wasn't married.

And he looked damned fucking fine, I won't even lie. He had lots of pictures uploaded. Albums of him hiking, biking, boating. Lots of shots with his shirt off, belly all ridged, arms buff. Lip-smacking good. He also had a lot of pictures of him with the same guy. Over and over, arms slung casually over shoulders. Laughing. I scanned Chase's profile information, which just said single, but it was clear to me there was a reason for this other man being in all his photo albums. Maybe Chase hadn't chosen to announce it to the whole world on Connex, but there was no hiding it.

I didn't friend him, either. I wanted to. I wanted to send him a message, ask him if he was happy. If the reason he hadn't wanted to be with me was because he was into guys, not because he didn't love me the way I'd loved him. I wanted to ask him a lot of things, but in the end I didn't. There'd be no point in picking at that old scar.

I distracted myself surfing the Apple website, yearning for what I wanted and couldn't have. It seemed to be the theme of the day. I imagined I smelled Meredith's perfume clinging to me, felt the softness of her sweater against me. With a low, muttered groan I twirled around in the desk chair with my head tipped back and only my feet moving. Round and around, the ceiling twirling above me until I dug a toe into the carpet.

I stopped. The room kept moving. If I stood, I'd stumble, probably fall. It was not quite enough to make my stomach sick, though in retrospect the tuna hadn't been the best idea. As I turned back to the computer, my eyes still trying hard to focus on one unspinning thing, I heard the front door open and the sound of little shoes on the tile entryway. Then voices. Simone, shrieking at her brother, who was giggling like a lunatic. Their mom, Elaine, admonishing them without much force. Then the diversion of the noise from the den, up the stairs and presumably toward the bathroom, where the kids would be bathed, toothbrushed and pottied before being put into their beds.

I closed down my windows and cleared my history before logging out, and was just turning in the desk chair to face the doorway when he came in. "Hey, Vic," I said.

"Hey." He looked tired. Kids could do that to you. Vic pressed the heel of his hand against his eye, then focused briefly on the computer. "Didn't think you'd be home."

"Not everyone has a blooming social calendar like you," I teased.

His smile quirked faintly on one side. Just the one. "We took the kids over to Elaine's mom's house for Nancy's birthday. If I'd known you were going to be home I'd've told you."

"It's okay. I had stuff to do." Elaine's mom and sister had never been mean to me, but they'd never gone out of their way to be nice, either. We had a policy of neutral ground when it came to family events. If they came here or we met someplace else, we treated each other distantly but politely, never really delving too much into my place in their son-in-law's life. I simply never went to their house.

He nodded. "I'm going to help Elaine with the kids. You up for some Resident Evil 4 in a bit?"

It was our favorite video game, especially played on Vic's Wii with the special guns that attached to the controllers. "Hell, yeah. You guys need some help?"

"Nah." He shrugged and yawned. "We got it covered."

"How's she feeling?" Elaine was pregnant with their third and didn't have morning sickness. She had all-day sickness.

"Like shit." He shrugged again, a man bewildered by the complications of women's bodies, though not unsympathetic.

It was enough to make me determined never to get pregnant. Like, ever. Well…maybe if Christian Bale was donating, I could be persuaded. But other than that, probably not. "I'll set up the game for when you're ready."

There was no reason for me to have told Vic I'd been thinking about looking up Chase and Chance Murphy. It still felt like a lie, one that weighed heavily enough on me that I couldn't quite keep my concentration on the game. Since it was single-player, Vic and I took turns at it, switching when one of us died. I died a lot.

"What's up with you, Tesla?" Vic took the gun controller from me as the red ooze dripped across the screen, showing I'd kicked it again.

"Long day at work, I guess." I got up. "I should go to bed. Early morning tomorrow."

"Yeah. Me, too." But Vic didn't get up. He leveled the gun at the screen again, starting the next level. "'Night."

The rest of the house had gone quiet hours ago, Elaine and the kids in bed. It was just Vic and me, sitting in the dark, killing zombies. The flickering light from the TV made shadows move on his face, giving him expressions I knew he wasn't making.

He caught me looking and paused the game. "What?"

"You should go to bed. You have to get up early, too."

"Thanks, Mom," Vic said.

I shrugged. "I'm just saying."

"Yeah, I know what you're saying. I just want to finish this level, that's all. You go to bed. I'm fine."

Since Vic often got up even earlier than I had to for the morning shift, I knew he wouldn't be fine. "You look tired—"

"I'm a grown-up, Tesla," he interrupted through tight jaws, his eyes steady on the waves of zombies coming to kill Leon S. Kennedy, until he flicked a gaze at me. "I can decide for myself when to go to bed."

I stepped back, tossing up my hands. "Fine. You're right. Good night."

"'Night," I heard him repeat as I left the den and headed for my bedroom.

He was right, of course. I wasn't his mom, perish the thought, and I wasn't his wife. But that didn't mean I didn't have the right to worry about him, did it? Vic worked hard, long hours at the garage and used-car lot he owned. He had two kids and a pregnant wife. He had me living in his basement.

Showered and in bed, I heard the faint sounds of zombie deaths through the door. Then, as I was drifting to sleep, silence. Then the comforting creak of the floor in the kitchen, the living and dining rooms. Vic was making his rounds. Checking the doors and windows, making sure everything was locked and we were all safe.

His footsteps on the basement stairs sent me staring, wide-eyed, into the darkness. I heard him moving around the perimeter of the basement, doing what? Checking the windows down here, too? They were too small and awkward for anyone to get through. I heard the rattle of a toy being kicked, the mutter of a curse. Then the metallic squeak of my door-knob being turned slowly.

A square of lighter darkness appeared as my door opened. I couldn't make out his silhouette, but I could hear him breathing. I heard the soft scuff of his feet on the carpeting, and I closed my eyes tight. Stifled and slowed my breathing so there'd be no way he could think I was awake.

I tensed when Vic leaned over me. But instead of touching me, all he did was press the lock on the high, narrow window above my bed. Then, assured all was well, he left the room, closing the door with a soft click behind him.

I let out my breath in a whoosh and burrowed deeper into my pillows. Chill sweat had broken out all over me, and I was breathing hard. Warmth filled the cave I'd made, but it took me a long time to stop shivering.

And when I did, when I slept, I dreamed.

I don't know what Vic does when he's not at The Compound, but when he is here, he works on cars. Some people here, like my parents, for example, drive Volvos or BMWs the rest of the year, but during the summer they ride around in beater cars. Old Jeeps, dinged up and rusted muscle cars, stuff like that. Because The Compound's not about money or status, it's about getting along with people and raising vegetables and flowers or some shit like that, I don't know. I've been coming here my whole life, and all I know is that this summer I've been bored out of my mind.

There's not much to do for me here. I could hang out in what they call the crèche, helping with the little kids, but the stench of cloth diapers gets to me after a while. I could help in the gardens, weeding and stuff, but it's the hottest summer on record for like, twenty years, and it's just brutal out in the fields. And for what? I don't even like tomatoes.

I'm like that girl in the song in that movie, the one about the family that sings while they escape from the Nazis. I'm sixteen, going on seventeen, and I don't have a TV, a computer or a phone, and there are tons of younger kids here and lots of adults, but there's only one other girl my age and we don't get along. Her parents live here full-time, and she acts like that makes her better than me, when really I think it should be the other way around. She thinks Adam Ant was in Culture Club, and I know that's a little old school for some kids, but still.

So I spend my time hanging around the garage. It's loud in there with the clanking of tools, but Vic's got a radio he tunes to classic rock. My little brother, Cap, hangs out here, too. He's better with cars than I am. Well, fact is, Cap's kinda fucking brilliant. I can replace a windshield wiper, that's my accomplishment of the summer, but Cap can practically rebuild an engine.

Vic never acts like I'm in the way, though. He's patient, showing me what parts go where and how they all fit together. He's got grease in his knuckles and under his nails, even when he wipes them with the scraps of T-shirts he keeps in a big box on the workbench. Sometimes, when he uses the back of his hand to wipe his face clear of the sweat, he streaks his face with grease, too.

Today Cap's gone swimming with some younger kids over at the gross pond that's full of algae. They took a picnic. Healthy foods like hummus and pita and cucumbers grown in the gardens here. I'm dying for a cheeseburger, milk shake, fries. I'm wasting away here this summer, frying in the heat, mind numbed from all the smiles everyone has. I want to scream.

So I do. Really loud and hard, my fists clenched, eyes closed. I stomp my feet, one-two, in the dirt outside the garage. And I kick it. I stub my toes inside my old black Chuck Taylors against the barn siding. And then I lean forward to rest my head against the splintery wood and think about how there's only a few more weeks left. How usually I'm sad to leave The Compound, but this year I can't wait.

"C'mon. Can't be that bad." Vic's leaning in the doorway, a wrench in one hand and some grease along his forehead.

"I'm fucking bored."

Vic shrugs. "I'll put you to work, Tesla. You know I will."

That's the reason why I came here. Because he'll put me to work. And because maybe he'll take his shirt off when he gets too hot, and I can watch the sweat run down his back, between the dimples just above his ass. Vic wears his jeans low on his hips and cuffed above his big black motorcycle boots.

Vic makes me lie awake in my bed at night, shifting restlessly in the sticky summer air.

I know all about sex. Everyone here does it with everyone else. Nobody talks about it, but it's no secret. And if you think it's gross to think about your parents doing it with each other, try thinking about them doing it with other people. Sometimes more than one at a time. Along with peace and love and organic veggies, there's a whole lot of fucking going on at The Compound.

I know all about it, but I've never done it. Boys in my school don't appeal to me. Too young, too immature, and besides, I go away for the whole summer. That's prime boyfriend-girlfriend time. The one time last year I tried going out with a guy, I came back to school in the fall to find out he'd spent the summer dating his way through the entire cheerleading squad. First of all, I'm so not a cheerleader. Second, I guess

I couldn't blame him. A girlfriend who disappears for three months isn't much fun.

I work next to Vic all that long, hot summer afternoon. We're fixing an old Impala that doesn't look like it'll ever run. He does take his shirt off, and I pretend I'm not staring, but we both know I am.

"Fuck." He growls the word when the wrench he's holding slips and clangs against the metal.

I use that word all the time, but something about it freezes me now. I'm standing too close to him, at his side, our hips touching as we lean over to watch him twist something with the wrench. He says it again, lower.

"Let's take a break," Vic says.

In the small back room there's an ice chest full of cold beers and a couple of Cokes. Vic takes the beer and hands me the soda. I think for about half a second of asking him for a beer, since even though I'm underage, stuff like that mostly goes unnoticed at The Compound. But I hate the taste of beer and wouldn't be able to drink it, anyway.

"We'll get it working. We're a good team, you and me." Vic tips the beer in my direction.

I care about a thousand things more than I give a damn about that car. One of them is the way Vic looks at me. Or doesn't look at me, which is closer to the truth. I don't want to be on a team with him. I want him to notice me.

From outside in the garage, the Rolling Stones start singing about painting a door black. Vic's fingers thrum against his thigh as he lifts the bottle to his lips and tips back his head to swallow. The bottle sweats, wetting his fingertips. His throat works.

I want to lick the hollow of his throat. I want to run my tongue along the curve of his collarbone. His shoulders.

Suddenly, I want.

This time, I don't glance away when he looks up to see me staring.

Vic licks his lips.

He could easily push me back when I cross the short distance and stand between his legs. It would've crushed me. Probably made me unable to make the first move again for the rest of my life. But he doesn't push me away when I stand, my calves pressed against his, then my knees on the inside of his thighs.

It's hot in this room. Stifling. Sweat sheens Vic's upper lip, and I don't think about anything but leaning forward and tasting it. My tongue slides over his salty flesh, and my lips brush his.

It's too much, I know. I've made a mistake, gone too far. Vic's older than me. Has never even flirted with me. And I've kissed only a couple boys, nothing like this. Bold and free and wild.

Vic doesn't stop me. His mouth opens under mine. His hands go to my hips, just above the waistband of my jean shorts and below the hem of my T-shirt. At the touch of his fingers on my bare skin, a soft sigh slips out. I'm sure then he'll push me away. Maybe laugh.

I end up on his lap. We kiss for a long, long time. His tongue strokes mine. It's better than I thought it would be. Under my butt, I feel him getting hard. My heart pounds faster than it ever did while I watched him work with his shirt off.

I'd do anything for Vic right now. His zipper's undone, my hands inside his jeans, before I even know what I'm doing. Then he stops me with a hand on my wrist. Not pushing me away, just holding me still.

"Tesla." His voice is low and growling, the way it was earlier when he cursed at the wrench.

I don't want him to tell me we should stop. I shift against him, my fingers curling around the unfamiliar thickness of his dick. I ache to stroke him, even though at the same time, I'm afraid I won't know how.

He groans when I move my hand.

That's the first time I understand the power of giving someone else pleasure.

I move again, exploring his length as best I can with his jeans in the way. The couch creaks and complains beneath us as we shift, until somehow we're stretched out side by side, Vic's hand at the small of my back the only thing keeping me from falling onto the dirty concrete floor.

We kiss harder. Our teeth clash. Somehow, I manage to get his prick out from his jeans. I'd put it in my mouth if I were brave enough, if I could figure out how, but for now I'm satisfied just with moving my fingers up and down. When I touch him, Vic shudders. He tastes like sweat and beer, and somehow I don't mind the taste when it's on his tongue.

I'm so caught up in figuring out how to jerk him off, I don't notice at first that Vic's got his hand down the front of my shorts. But when his fingers stroke over the front of my panties I discover exactly why he shuddered. His hand moves. One fingertip circles slowly, slowly, pressing against me through the cotton. Then faster, until I gasp into his mouth.

I know about sex, but I don't know about this. All I know now is that the hot, thick feeling I get when I watch Vic work with his shirt off is building up between my legs, in my nipples. Crazily, in the soles of my feet.

We're not even naked. We don't even get that far. Vic and I kiss and kiss and kiss. My grip stutters on his dick, but his doesn't falter against me. When he slips his fingers inside my panties, directly on my skin, I think I might die. A couple minutes later, when he pushes one finger down inside me, then up again, when it moves in slippery circles on my clit, I do.

Or at least I explode, which I imagine might feel the same. It feels so good I shake and push my hips against him, needing something but not sure exactly what. Vic knows. His fingers move a little faster. Then faster still.

And I…I am surging along on this wave of pleasure that's so strong I can't decide if I never want it to end or if I can't stand another second of it.

When it's over and I can focus again, when I can breathe, I blink up at him. My hand is sticky, lying flat on his hard belly. His fingers have stilled between my legs, though my clit is thumping with the beat of my heart. I'm not exactly sure what happened, but I know that whatever it was, I can't wait to do it again. Looking down at me, Vic licks his lips and smiles. Despite my earlier fears, he doesn't laugh.

But I do.

Chapter
5

I woke up laughing and coming at the same time. I hiccupped, my eyes flying open, my fingers clutching the tangled mess of my sheets that told me I'd had a rough night. I cut off the laughter by sealing my lips together, but nothing stopped the surge of pleasure that ripped through me, not entirely unwelcome.

A wave of guilt followed it.

I hadn't thought of Vic in that way for a long time. Now everything was turning upside down and sideways. My body ached from being twisted in the sheets, and it was still a few hours before I had to get up and take care of some things before it was time for work.

I'd only just closed my eyes and started to drift when the two small bodies pounced on me. It wasn't unexpected, but it was alarming. I shouted before I could hold it back, then fell onto my pillow with a groan and a hand clapped over my eyes.

"Guys, please," I begged. "Go away."

"Turn on 'toons? Peeze," said Max, who had good manners only when it suited him.

His sister, who fancied herself far more mature at four than any baby two-year-old could ever be, poked him. "Please and thankyouverymuch!"

"Thankyouverymuch," her brother said. He smelled of wet diaper, a stench that reminded me too much of crèche duty at The Compound. "'Toons?"

I shifted, bunching the cushions and pillows so I could sit up. "How is it that the two of you can operate every electronic device in this house, but not the television set?"

"The memote," Max explained patiently. "Mama says don't touch the memote."

Of course their mother didn't want them messing around with the remote—it was a complicated and expensive thing that operated all their dad's complicated and expensive audio-visual equipment, including the television, the TiVo, the sound system and the Wii. It was supposed to make everything easier because you needed only one piece of equipment to operate everything in the rec room, but it was for adult use only. And since I was the closest adult, I was the one the kids came to.

"What's Mama and Daddy doing?" I was afraid to look at the clock, but the light shining through my window meant it was at least past six. "Getting ready for work?"

"Mama's in bed," Simone said, self-important with this knowledge. "Daddy said to leave her alone so she can sleep."

Max had something to say about this, too, accompanied by a sour look that said exactly what he thought of the situation. "Baby."

"Just give me a few minutes, okay?" I begged as they bounced on me. "I'll turn on the cartoons in a minute. Can't you play with your toys or something?"

They had plenty of them, spread all over the floor in the very places I usually wanted to walk in my bare feet when the lights were off. I'd been lamed by Legos so often I'd taken to shuffling along the floor with each step, much the way they tell you to walk along the sand where there are stingrays so you can push them out of the way rather than step on them. That was what my life had become—shuffling to avoid the sting.

They could play with their toys, but it turned out the screeching that went along with the game was worse than the mindless blather of cartoons. No more sleep for me, then. I scrubbed at my face and turned everything on for them, settled the remote high on the shelf where they couldn't be tempted to reach for it, and made my careful, shuffling way up the steep and uncarpeted stairs to the kitchen.

Which was bright. Too bright. I flung a hand up against the glare and blinked fast, but tears still burned in my eyes, so I had to rub them again. My vision blurred and cleared.

"Rough night?" Vic asked from his place at the stove, where he was cooking what I assumed to be eggs, since that was what he had every morning. "You look like shit."

"Feel like it." I slumped in one of the hard wooden kitchen chairs and put my head in my hands. The ends of my hair tickled my nose until I pushed them back, and I looked up to see him laughing at me. "Fuck you, Vic."

He turned back to the skillet. "Want some eggs? I'm making toast for Elaine. You can have some."

He shoveled scrambled eggs onto a couple plates and added toast as it sprang up from the toaster, then put both on the table and took a seat across from me. He'd forgotten forks, which was typical Vic, so I got up to grab them. It was my turn not to look at him.

He didn't ask me any questions, and I offered no answers. We ate in companionable silence broken only by the ticking of the wall clock and an occasional burst of excited laughter from the rec room downstairs. Vic finished and took his plate to the dishwasher, then spread the extra toast with a thin layer of butter. He added a can of ginger ale and a straw to the plate, but I stopped him before he could leave the kitchen.

"You go ahead. I'll take it to her."

He looked again at the clock. Though he has a couple of good guys working for him, he still does a lot of the mechanic work himself. He likes to be open for people who need to get in before work, and he likes to leave early to spend time with his wife and kids before bedtime. Vic is an awesome husband and dad.

"Thanks." He grabbed his jacket and shouted a goodbye down to the rec room, waited the few minutes while his kids pounded up the stairs to grab him around the knees and burrow against him. He tousled their hair, squeezed and kissed them, then pried loose their clinging fingers and sent them back down to rot their brains with animated mayhem.

For me, Vic had no kiss, no hug. We got over all that a long time ago. It didn't affect how we were now, didn't make it awkward or anything like that. It wasn't a secret from Elaine. But we never spoke of it, and anyone who didn't know would never have guessed that Vic and I had once sort of been lovers.

In their bedroom the shades were drawn, but Elaine had turned on the nightstand lamp. The base of it was shaped like a ballerina, her head obscured by the shade, which was patterned with toe shoes. It was a really ugly lamp, but I guess Elaine loved it.

"Brought you some toast."

She let out a sigh. "Thanks, hon."

I sat on the side of the bed and gingerly handed her the plate, which she balanced on her belly, just beginning to mound. She looked pale, her eyes shadowed and her hair lank. I was pretty sure I looked the same, if not worse, and I didn't have a sea monkey in my belly to blame.

She nibbled a bite of toast. "Kids watching TV?"

"Yes."

"Vic off to work?"

I nodded. Elaine grimaced, and I handed her the ginger ale with the straw. She sipped at it and sighed again.

"Pregnancy," she said, "sucks."

"I believe it. I've seen you through it two and a quarter times, remember?"

She sipped again, her throat working, and looked at the toast but didn't take another bite. "I know it'll pass in a few weeks. Or a month. And then I'll have a few months of being able to eat whatever I want."

"And then you have that labor to look forward to," I said without even cracking a grin. "Bet you can't wait for that."

Elaine managed a small smile. "At this point, maybe the kid'll just slide out."

"I think that doesn't happen at least until kid number four, if not five or six." I smoothed the comforter between my thigh and the edge of hers.

"Bite your tongue." She looked aghast, but since I knew she'd already said if they were going for three they'd have to commit to trying for four, the look had to mostly be fake.

Elaine was planning to have this kid the way she'd had Max and Simone, at home. Here in this bed, as a matter of fact. Without drugs. She was going to have a doula and a midwife, the same ones who'd delivered the other kids, and she'd already started putting together all the supplies she needed for her birth plan.

Personally, I thought she was nuts. Give me the sterile green walls of a hospital room, a masked doctor with a needle, and a full-on epidural the moment the first contraction hit.

"So, why do *you* look like shit?" Elaine said around a bite of toast. Some color was coming back into her cheeks. She might actually keep it down.

"Someone's kids woke me up too fucking early." I pinched the bridge of my nose. "Have a headache. Want more sleep. You need more reasons?"

"I guess that's enough. Sorry about the kids. I'm sure Vic sent them down. I'd have told them to play in their rooms."

I laughed at that and we shared a look. "Ri-i-i-ight."

She laughed, too, but as if it pained her. "What time do you have to go in to work?"

"Not until three."

"You can nap before then. I'm taking them to playgroup around lunchtime. You'll have the house to yourself."

"Ahh, sweet freedom." I tapped my chin with a finger. "Should I run around naked first? Or drink milk right from the carton? Or both?"

I was glad to make Elaine laugh, especially if it kept her from feeling sick to her stomach. If my feelings for Vic had always been and would always be complicated, I had no issues about my love for Elaine. She was the older sister I'd never had—the sort I tried to be, though I figured I'd never get the hang of it the way she did.

"Did you put your list by the phone?" she asked with another sip of ginger ale, another bite of toast. The first piece was almost gone and she was looking even better. "I'm going to the store later."

"I can go if you want. Run out before work."

"Could you?" She appeared relieved. "I hate to drag the kids with me."

"I know you do." She always came home with junk cereal and sugary snacks when she took Max and Simone with her, and though I was a fan of Marshmallow Mateys myself, I liked it much better when my financial contributions to the household budget came home in the form of food that didn't add to the bulges I worked hard to get rid of. "I'll go. No problem."

Elaine reached for my hand, surprising me. "I'm so grateful you're with us, Tesla. You know that, right?"

There are a lot of women who wouldn't have opened their homes to some girl their husband had finger-banged on a grimy couch, much less treated her the way Elaine has always treated me. If anyone was grateful, it was I. Without Vic and Elaine, I might've been on the street. No, not might've. Definitely would have.

Still, I shrugged off her compliment because I recognized the sheen of tears in her eyes. Elaine was superemotional, more so when she was pregnant. I didn't want to start the day with tears. I was feeling a little too fragile myself.

"Slave labor," I told her. "Live-in babysitter. Toilet scrubber. What's not to love?"

She squeezed my fingers, knowing me too well to be offended. "Well. We do love you, Tesla Martin. Don't forget it."

I couldn't forget it and wouldn't have wanted to. I untangled my fingers from her grip and held out my hand for the plate. "Done?"

She sighed heavily and nodded. "Can you check on the kids for me? I'm going to get up and get in the shower."

"No problem."

My phone was beeping with a missed text message by the time I got back downstairs and made sure the bratlings hadn't destroyed anything too badly. It was simple, two words: *Call me.*

I thumbed in the number as I kicked dirty laundry into a pile. "Cap. What's up?"

"Vic leave yet?"

"Yeah. Maybe half an hour ago. Why?"

"Some lady's here, says her appointment was for seven, but—" My brother broke off. "Shit. Oh, well, never mind, Vic's here. She's going to chew him a new one."

"Vic can handle it. Hey, do you think you can take a look at the Contour sometime this week? It's still making that weird noise."

"Which one?"

My car was so old, held together with dreams and diarrhea, as our dad would've said, that it made any number of weird noises on a regular basis. But this one was really strange. I imitated it. "It's like a wah-h-hm wham-m-m. Like the Tardis. Fuck you, Cap."

My brother had burst into laughter. "What's it sound like again?"

"You heard me the first time." I was laughing, too. I love and hate that about him, how he always makes me laugh. "Can you? I forgot to ask Vic."

"Duh, of course. Bring it in whenever."

"Sure, I can do that," I said, "but I don't have time to wait around all day for it."

"Jesus, Tesla, you're a pain."

"If I have to leave it, I'll need something to drive."

Cap made a strangled noise. "Of course you will."

I grinned into the phone. "So?"

"You can borrow my car. *If* you have to," he added quickly, "which I'll make sure you don't."

Cap has a sweet ride, a restored 1978 Mustang that growls when you hit the gas. He's spent more time and money on that car than he's ever spent on a woman, which is probably one reason he's single. Or maybe it's the fact he's in love with his roommate—who's a woman, by the way, but who seems totally oblivious to the fact that my brother thinks she walks on water. Which is his own fault, since he won't tell her.

But then, who am I to give anyone advice about relationships?

"I'll bring it in," I told him. "And later I'll bring you some chocolate cake from the coffee shop. How's that?"

"Not a great trade. But okay."

"Later," I told him, and hung up.

Chapter
6

I fucked the Murphy brothers for about a month and a half before I discovered something important. I loved having two cocks to suck and stroke, one in my pussy and one in my mouth—though never up the ass. They didn't ask, and I surely didn't offer. I'm not certain any of us thought such a thing existed outside of porn movies, anyway, and we were so gorged full on everything else we were doing that adding that forbidden thing didn't even seem necessary.

More than just the physical aspects, the bonus of two sets of hands and tongues, I discovered I enjoyed the attention of two. If one boyfriend was good, two would be better, right? Except it wasn't like the three of us could go sashaying down the halls in school, all of us holding hands or making out at our lockers the way everyone else did.

"Pick one," Chase said. He was in an old recliner in their

parents' basement, feet flat on the floor, his hands on either side of my head, his dick in my mouth.

I gave his cock another long suck before taking it in my hand and sitting back on my heels to look up at him. His brother was sprawled on the sofa next to us, idly stroking his own boner. "What do you mean, pick one?"

Chase, typical boy, put his hand over mine to rub his dick across my mouth, but I pulled away just enough that it couldn't reach my lips. "Pick one of us, Tesla," he repeated.

I laughed, thinking he was joking. "For what?"

"You know," Chance said.

I looked back and forth at them. I'd never be able to see the twins as anything but two separate people ever again, and yet I couldn't imagine them as anything but part of a unit. "I don't want to pick just one."

"She wants us both. I told you," Chance said.

His brother shifted, his young, thick cock not wilting even the slightest bit. "You have to, Tesla."

"Why?"

Chase was the firstborn brother. Nobody had told me; I could just tell. If there were decisions to be made, he was generally the first to make them. Chance was more likely to wait and see what happened. Now Chase tangled his fingers in my hair, and I tensed, thinking he meant to pull my face forward again.

"You don't have to stop fucking us both," he said. "Just pick one of us for public."

"Oh." I stroked his dick, twisting my palm around the head in the way that made him shudder. "That."

The truth was, I didn't really feel the need to go public. I already had the advantage of being a little exotic. I wasn't the only girl who wore Docs or dyed her hair colors that were deemed "distracting" by the school. I wasn't the only one with piercings or what seemed like a permanent weekly appointment with the guidance counselor. I was just different because none of them had known me their whole lives. Or because I didn't seem to need their approval.

"Who says I want to go public?" I leaned forward to lick him, then took him in my mouth again. I closed my eyes to concentrate on the sensation of all that hot, hard flesh on my tongue.

Chance made a low noise, though it was his brother's knob in my mouth. I slitted open my eyes to look at him, smiling around Chase's dick as I sucked and stroked. I didn't want to make him come like this. I wanted to fuck him first. I wanted to fuck both of them. I wanted them both sweating and groaning, working inside and against me. I wanted the spiraling crescendo of orgasm to rip through me. Basically, I wanted to get in, get on, get off, get up, get dressed and get out.

Even at the time, I was pretty sure that wasn't the way the rest of my schoolmates operated. They were concerned about being seen together, all the accoutrements of "going out," like class rings or hickeys. Things that marked them as belonging to someone. The thought of belonging to any one person was not only foreign to me, but more than slightly distasteful. When I thought about picking one of those Murphy boys to parade around with in front of everyone to somehow legitimize this, what we did here in the basement in secret…well, my lip curled as if I'd put my hand in something rotten.

Whatever conversation those brothers had intended to have with me, and I had no doubt they'd discussed it at length beforehand, I was able to get them to forget about it. Especially when I reached to take Chance's dick in my fist while I sucked his brother, and when I dipped my head down low to mouth Chase's balls.

When I lifted up the pleated plaid skirt I'd bought from the Catholic thrift store, someone's leftover school uniform, to reveal I'd already slipped off my panties and wore only a pair of knee-high socks, it was a good guarantee both those boys would lose their powers of speech. And I didn't need them to talk. I urged Chance to move behind me. I was on the pill, but I made them use rubbers anyway, not because I thought either of them were screwing around with anyone else, but because there was less mess to clean up after if they shot into a condom.

They hadn't known a lot about female anatomy when we first started, but now Chance knew just where to slide his fingers, right along my already rigid clit. He filled me a little too fast, bumping me forward against his brother's lap. Chase's cock went down my throat too far and would've choked me if I hadn't held him so firmly by the base—but by now I'd learned to anticipate Chance's clumsiness. I liked it, actually, how eager he was to get inside me. How his hands gripped my hips hard enough to bruise, sometimes, those faint blue marks on my skin a better reminder to me of what we'd been doing than any suck mark on my neck or collarbone could've been.

Chance fucked into me from behind. I sucked Chase's dick and rubbed his balls. It was all good and getting better. Faster, harder, in and out, my pussy slick and tight. Full.

I came before both of them. I think they never understood how easy it was for me; how it wasn't their skill that got me off. Chance came next, and that was also usually the way it happened. With his brother still inside me, I peered up at Chase. He was looking down. I pressed my finger against his asshole and he exploded into my mouth with a hoarse shout that made me smile because it sounded...just a little...like my name.

"If you had to pick one," Chance said after I'd used the tiny bathroom and come out with my face washed, mouth rinsed, hair brushed, panties replaced, "which one of us would you choose?"

Chase had already gone upstairs. Chance was the one who would wait and walk me to my car, the beat-up piece of junk that I still drove now, nine years later. Chance was the one who put his hand on the driver's side door so I couldn't open it, who peered down at me with a solemn look. Chance was the one who really wanted to know.

"I can't choose," I told him, even though I knew it was a lie. "I'm into both of you."

"Yeah, but..."

I stood on my tiptoes to kiss him, thinking, as he probably wasn't, that his brother's taste still lingered on my tongue despite the rinsing. "Not into the boyfriend scene, okay? It's all cool. Right?"

He nodded. What else could he do? He was getting regular, slightly freaky sex. Was he going to turn that down just so we could hold hands and go to football games together? Maybe homecoming, and later, the prom?

"Not my thing," I told him, and meant it.

He didn't move his hand even when I gave it a pointed glance. "Why not?"

I didn't have an answer for that. I couldn't explain to that nice boy whose mother was still way too attached to him all my reasons for not wanting what every other girl I knew seemed to want. So I didn't give him an answer. I kissed him again, and when I pulled away he put his hands on my hips to hold me closer to him.

Later, I would break that boy's heart and not care, because
my own would have already been shattered. But we didn't
know that then. At that moment, we were sneaking kisses in
the turning-cold fall air.

I thought about them now as I pulled into the parking lot
of Capriotti's Auto Sales and found a space for my car. I got
out, still thinking about it. I was looking for Cap, but found
Vic instead.

"Hey. What're you still doing here? Where's Cap?"

Vic looked tired again. The garage closed at seven, but the
car lot stayed open until nine. I didn't see Dennis, the sales
guy who usually had the later shift.

Vic shrugged and yawned. "Had to send him out on a run
for some parts that didn't come in on time."

"And Dennis?"

"Went home sick. Upchucked all over the men's room."

I grimaced. "Yuck."

Vic smiled. "Yeah, well, that's what happens when you eat
someone else's lunch and don't bother to check how long it's
been in the fridge. Maybe next time he'll learn."

"Still, gross." I tossed him my keys. "It's the clunking again,
left front end."

Vic nodded and pocketed my keys. "Can't do anything
about it until tomorrow. You got a ride to work?"

"Cap said I could use his car. He'll get a ride from Lyndsay or walk."

"Cap's letting you use his car?"

I laughed wickedly. "Bwahaha! Of course he is. He loves
me."

Vic snorted. "He's easily manipulated."

"Is that what you think of me?" I said with a frown. The
words came out sounding catty. Snide, even. "Nice."

Vic gave me a surprised blink before frowning himself. "Huh?"

"Never mind." The dream had unsettled me. It wasn't Vic's fault, though maybe he'd prompted it by his unexpected little drive-by through my room. "Listen. What's going on with you?"

"What? Me? Nothing. Why?" He sounded genuinely confused.

"You're not sleeping," I pointed out, adding, before he could jump in, "and yeah, I know. I'm not your mother. Or your wife. Old news. Your mother doesn't live with you, and poor Elaine's so exhausted she'd have no idea if you were in bed next to her or not. So I'm the only one who knows you're up at all hours of the night."

"It's not all hours."

"I hear you walking back and forth. I hear the floor creaking." I paused, thinking about whether or not to mention him being in my room. "What's going on?"

"Insomnia."

"Uh-huh." I gave him a narrow-eyed glance. "That doesn't sound like you."

Before he could defend himself or agree, my brother came into the office on a cloud of cold air and the faint smell of oil and gasoline. He stopped short at the sight of us. Then he sighed.

"Damn, he already gave you the keys, huh?"

I gave Vic another look, but the moment had passed. "Yep. No wrestling them away from me now."

"Can't you just hang out here and wait while I take a look at your car?" Cap asked.

"With Dennis gone I could use an extra set of hands," Vic interjected.

He couldn't have known, of course, about the dream I'd had. Or how it had made me feel. "Nah. Errands to run before I get to work. I promised Elaine I'd go to the store for her. Apparently we're out of a lot of stuff."

"Can you pick me up some stuff, too?" Cap asked.

I raised a brow. "Like what?"

"Toaster pastries. Half-and-half."

The other brow went up. "Really? What the hell for, Captain?"

My brother winced at the use of his full first name. "Lyndsay likes it in her coffee, and I like them for snacks."

I laughed, trying to get at him to poke his side, but he was so much bigger he fended me off without a problem. "You want me to pick up stuff for your—"

"Don't say it," Cap warned in a fierce enough tone to keep me from continuing. "She's just my roommate."

I was pretty sure that despite their every action designed to prove otherwise, Cap and Lyndsay were fucking like bunnies. No, not like bunnies. Like ninjas, all secretlike and only in the dark. I tempered my laughter. "Sure. I'll drop it off here. Without Dennis around, it should be safe in the fridge. Hey, Cap…listen, you want to check out that new zombie flick sometime next week? *The Risen,* or whatever it's called?"

"How come he gets to go and I don't?" Vic asked, only half listening as he texted something.

"Because he's single and you're an old married fella with a pregnant wife at home, duh." I turned to my brother. "You up for it?"

"Yeah, sure." Cap shrugged his broad shoulders.

I paused, deciding how deep to stick the shiv. "You don't have to ask Lynds first?"

Too far. Cap scowled. I backed off, hands up, an apology

on my face and tongue, but not really in my heart. He'd have to own up to it sometime—that he was crazy in love with his roommate and she wasn't so far from looney for him, too, even if neither would admit it.

"I'll pick you up tomorrow, then."

"In my car," Cap said, with a resigned sigh that made Vic laugh.

"Unless you fix mine sooner." I managed to get in a poking pinch my brother could've easily batted away, but allowed because I was older than him.

"It'll be fixed," he promised.

I punched his shoulder and waved at Vic, but he was too engrossed in his phone call to pay attention. In the parking lot, I revved the Mustang's engine a few times just to get Cap all worked up. I refrained from spinning the tires or doing a doughnut, though, just to prove I didn't have to be a total dweeb. By the way he flipped me off as I left the lot, I figured he wasn't that impressed.

At the grocery store I pushed my cart through the aisles and tried to remember what was on the list I'd left on the kitchen table at home. I wasn't paying close attention to where I was going, which was why I nearly ran over a little kid who was spinning out of control in the candy section.

I recognized a tantrum in progress and meant to steer my cart past him, but stopped when I saw his mother. "Mandy?"

She turned. "Oh, my God! Tesla? Wow. Long time, huh?"

Mandy had been one of my best friends in Lancaster before my parents dropped their mutual basket and my life had spun into something else. I hadn't seen or heard from her in years. To find her here now, with a child, was surprising—but good, I discovered, when she clung to me in a hug that left her kid staring with goggle eyes.

"You look fantastic!" She beamed, taking me in. "You haven't changed at all. Wow."

"You have." I grinned, pointing at the boy now clinging to her leg. "Yours?"

She lifted him, pride all over her face. "Yep. This is Tyler. Say hi."

Tyler buried his face in his mom's neck. I wasn't offended. "So…you live around here?"

"Yep. My husband and I moved here a few months ago. He's working for the state. And I stay home with the kiddo here. How about you?"

"I work at Morningstar Mocha. You probably don't know it."

"Sure I do! Sure. I'll have to stop in sometime. Are you still living with…?" She let the question trail off.

"Vic? Yeah. And his wife, Elaine. Their two kids. Cap moved out, though."

"Oh, Cap." Mandy laughed. "How's Cappy doing?"

"He's doing great. Really great." It was hard to believe that once we'd spent almost every day blabbering each others' ears off, and now we were reduced to chitchat in front of a display of candy bars. "Listen, stop in to the Mocha. Really. It would be great to catch up with you."

"I'll do that," she said, even as I think we both knew she probably wouldn't.

Time had passed. Life had changed. She had a husband and a kid, and I was still single. Stuff like that gets between people, even if the years hadn't.

"I have to run. This one's about to melt down. You take care, Tesla. So good to see you."

"You, too." I watched her go.

I'd never wanted what Cap and I had always called "the

front door," from that old Adam Ant song "A Place in the Country." The front door was marriage, kids, a mortgage, a dog. But there was envy again, that funny thing. It can creep up on you without warning, hit you over the head with a snow shovel. Envy can taste like the candy you buy because you suddenly crave something sweet.

Chapter
7

Here's a story I never told Meredith.

At the end of my junior year of high school and Cap's eighth grade, our father walked in on our mother fucking one of her colleagues from the college where they both worked. Apparently, even in an open marriage you can still be cheating if your partner doesn't know what you've been up to, because my dad promptly packed up his stuff and left without telling any of us where he'd gone. With no more Compound to retreat to in the summer, my mom decided to take a cross-country camping trip with her new lover in an ancient Volkswagen Rabbit.

While Cap and I had no problems with her new boyfriend, there was no way we were going to subject ourselves to traveling across the United States in the back of a Rabbit. My mom, who could certainly have been called a free spirit or even flighty, was nevertheless the more responsible of our parents and wasn't about to leave us living alone even though at seventeen and fourteen we were capable of taking care of ourselves. She insisted we go with them. We insisted we didn't want to. So I did what any red-blooded teenage kid would do when faced with what promised to be a certain kind of hell.

I ran away.

I didn't have to go very far, and I took my brother with me. I knew how to find Vic. I hoped I could count on him. We showed up on his doorstep with little more than the clothes on our backs and a couple hundred bucks I'd pinched from my mom's dresser.

As it turned out, I could. Cap and I moved in with Vic, who might've been surprised to see us but didn't let that stop him. My mother ended up staying in California when her lover's car broke down. She still lived there. My dad turned up in Brazil, of all places. He'd found another community like The Compound where he could live full-time while teaching English in a nearby town.

Vic had been there for me when I needed him. It had nothing to do with sex—not unless he'd fooled around with Cappy, too, and I was one hundred percent positive that had never happened. It had everything to do with the sort of guy Vic had always been.

And I envied him.

Meredith had told me I went for what I wanted. That I had to answer to nobody and could do whatever I liked. In a way, she was right. I mean, I had my job, and my responsibilities as part of Vic and Elaine's household. I had bills and debts. But I didn't have convictions, not really. Nobody would ever come to me when they were in trouble. Hell, I was twenty-six and still living in a basement, not because I couldn't get out and live on my own but because staying there was easier than moving out.

Not exactly a picture of someone wild.

When I got to work, Meredith was convincing people to tell stories again. I knew it the second I walked in the front door and saw her sitting at her favorite table with her head tipped back in laughter. I knew most of the others by face, not necessarily by name, but everyone looked as if they were having a grand old time.

She waved at me. "There's our Tesla!"

I lifted a mittened hand in response to the raised coffee cups. Meredith's smile made the cold outside seem faraway, but I didn't stop at her table. She was busy talking; I had to get busy working.

"What is it about her, anyway?" Darek said when I rounded the counter.

I pretended not to know what he meant. "Who? Meredith?"

"Yeah. Queen Meredith, sitting over there with her…what do you call them?"

"Subjects?" I offered, shrugging out of my coat and hanging it on the rack in the hall leading to the storage room.

Darek shook his head. "Minions."

"That makes her sound like some sort of evil overlord."

"Yeah. What is it about her?"

I paused, thinking. "I don't know. She's just… I don't know. Sometimes you don't, Darek."

He made a noise instead of an answer. I looked across the room at Meredith, whose laughter had trilled to catch my attention. She ran perfectly manicured fingers through her honey-blond hair and it settled just right.

Again, envy.

With the late afternoon sun slanting through the glass, she

was so beautiful it made my heart hurt. Not just pretty. Not just sexy, though she was surely that with that mouth, those eyes, that laugh. She was like something set up high on a shelf, made to be admired and adored. Coveted, but never gained.

I must've sighed, because Darek gave me a sympathetic look. "You're into her."

I slanted a glance his way but wouldn't gaze at him full-on. "Look at her."

"Oh, I am." He put his hands on his hips. "She wants people to look at her."

"Who doesn't?" I tied the strings of my green apron tight around my waist and took a few minutes to run my fingers through my hair to stand it on end after it had been flattened by my knit cap. "I mean, don't we all want people to notice us?"

"I guess so."

I stared at her, then at him. "Don't you like her?"

"I like her just fine." He grinned. "Married ladies are my specialty. But you saw her first."

I laughed. Darek was a lot of talk. In all the time we'd worked together I hadn't known him to have a single fling with a married lady. "We're just friends. She's not...you know."

"And you are?"

I shrugged and checked over the desserts in the case, noting which would need to be pulled later if they didn't sell. "Sometimes. Once in a while. Discriminately."

"How many?"

I turned. "What?"

Darek appeared way too intrigued. "How many girls?"

"This place," I told him with just the barest sourness in my tone, "has really become, like, this hotbed of prurience."

"Whose fault is that?" Darek asked, with a lift of his chin toward Meredith's table.

"Pffft. You can't blame her for everything. You're the one grilling me on my sex life! I already told Meredith—"

"Yeah?" Again, he seemed too interested, all lolling tongue and wide eyes.

I put one fist to my mouth, the other at my cheek, and made a cranking motion. "Roll up your tongue. It wasn't about girl-girl action."

Darek appeared only faintly disappointed before perking up again. "Then what was it about?"

I wasn't going to tell him about the Murphys. Dredging up that past stuff had already wreaked a bit of havoc on my brain. "None of your business. God, do I grill you about your sex life?"

"You could," he said. "So…I'm just curious, Tesla, that's all."

"About my lesbian history?" I had to laugh at him, so typical male. "I had one serious girlfriend. We dated for about four months before she dumped me for a guitar player in a folk rock band who wore wife-beaters all year round and had a tattoo of the feminine symbol on her twat."

His look said it all.

"Yeah," I said. "That's what I thought, too."

Darek made a face. "That's it? That's all you got?"

"Look," I said, suddenly disgruntled. "What did you think I had? Some long and lurid inventory of lesbian dalliances I'd trot out for you like a laundry list, complete with descriptions? A 'Desperate But Not Serious' sort of thing going on? Who with and how many times?"

He totally failed on the Adam Ant reference. "Huh?"

I sighed. "Never mind."

"Sorry." Darek frowned. "I just, you know. Thought maybe it was more exciting than that."

I sighed again, this time in exasperation. "Why?"

"Because you just seem like you've had an exciting life, Tesla, that's all. Jesus. I'm sorry!"

Wild child. I touched my throat, felt the pendant in the shape of a rainbow with a star on the end. Today I wore a black shirt with a picture of the cover of the Rolling Stones' *Sticky Fingers* on the front—some dude's crotch. Black leggings with rainbow leg warmers. Black ballet flats. I had glitter in my hair, but so what? Unconventional, maybe, but not that exciting.

"Well," I said, "I'm really not."

Darek looked over the front counter to the group of laughing customers. "Maybe you should tell her that."

"Tell her what?" I frowned and wished for someone to come and order something, or for Joy to pop out of the back to yell at us. Anything to keep this conversation from continuing. "Oh, that. Well. It's just a crush. It's not like I haven't had them before. They go away, Darek."

"I wouldn't know."

"You've never had a crush?" I rolled my eyes. "Please. I see how you look at that girl who comes in here, the one with the red hair."

"Yeah, she's hot. But it's not a crush."

"Whatever." I waved a hand. "You gonna tell her you like her? Ask her out, maybe?"

"She has a boyfriend."

"So you get it," I told him. "It's better just to crush in silence."

He didn't look happy about that, but he didn't argue with me, either. Then finally one of Meredith's admirers broke off from the group long enough to come up and order a slice of pie and another latte, so both of us had something to do and we didn't have to talk anymore.

The rush helped, too, leaving both of us so busy we didn't have time for deep and soul-searching conversations about the sad state of our love lives. By the time we'd gone through that, I figured Meredith would've left, but when I took a break to make the rounds of the shop, clearing away crumpled napkins and left-behind mugs, she was still sitting in her spot.

The sun had moved, and she was alone. She was still beautiful. Something pensive in her face as she tapped away at her keyboard made me pause. She'd pushed her hair behind her ears, in which she wore simple and elegant pearls I knew had to be real despite the size. Not Jangle Bangles, either. She might sell that stuff, but she didn't wear it. She had faint lines at the corners of her eyes and mouth, but they didn't take anything away from her beauty.

She caught me staring. "Hey."

"Oh. Hey. You're still here. Can't get enough of the caramel crunch, huh?" I gestured toward the row of self-serve carafes.

"I'm fully caffeinated." She showed me her empty mug. "But I got my money's worth today, I'll tell you that."

"Joy's going to charge you rent," I said with a glance over my shoulder to the counter. Joy was serving Eric, actually giving him a bit of a flirtatious smile. "Jeez, that guy can make even Joy tingly."

Meredith closed her laptop. "It's all in the smile. I think he makes everyone a little tingly."

"Yeah," I said fondly, watching Eric take his plate and mug to his favorite table and lay out his paper.

"You missed some good stories today." Meredith leaned

back in her seat. "The things people get up to, you'd never believe it."

"I'm sure I would. Want me to take that for you?" I pointed to her empty mug and the plate beside it. "How was the apple crumb?"

"Tesla," she murmured.

I stopped with my hand halfway to the table, caught like the Tin Man with his ax up. "Hmm?"

"We should do something."

I forced myself to take the dishes, though they rattled when I lifted them. "Like what?"

"Something fun. Out of this place." She twitched her fingers in Joy's direction. "Without your boss hovering over us."

"Sure. That sounds great." I picked up her napkin, too, faintly imprinted with her lipstick. It crumpled in my fingers. I didn't want to throw it away.

"What time do you get off tomorrow?"

"I work early, so three."

"How about we grab some dinner or something? Maybe hit a club?" She paused. "It's a Friday night. You don't have a date or anything, do you?"

"Me? Oh. No." I laughed.

"Good," Meredith said, as though everything had been settled. "You do now."

Chapter

8

"You look pretty." Simone watched me carefully as I applied eyeliner and shadow. "Can I have some?"

"You want some pretty?" I turned from the mirror to look at the kid. With her blond hair and big blue eyes, there was no question who she belonged to: Elaine all the way. But she had something of her dad in the set of her mouth when she wanted something. I held up the square box of eye shadows in one hand, my angled brush in the other. "Green or blue?"

"I like the sparkly."

I eyed the tube of liquid glitter eyeliner. "That might be a little too much for you, kiddo. It's messy and…"

Her baby brother could really put on the waterworks, but Simone wasn't much of a tantrum thrower. She could throw a mean pout, though, and now that rosebud mouth turned down with such skill there was no way I could deny her. I sighed. "Your mama might be mad at me."

More likely it would be her daddy who gave me the lecture about tarting up his four-year-old, but Vic wasn't any better at denying Simone when she wanted something. She sighed, tiny shoulders shrugging. The pout stayed put.

"Fine. C'mere." I put down the shadows and pulled out the glitter liner. "But you have to promise, promise, promise me you'll take a shower later and without complaining, you hear me? Because it's really important you wash off all your makeup before you go to sleep, anyway."

"So you don't get zits," Simone said, with the sort of happy grin a kid gets when she's having her way.

"Yep. No zits." At twenty-six I thought I should've grown out of zits, but I usually had a sweet monthly reminder that that wasn't the case. "Sit up here."

She hopped up on the edge of my sink, her little feet banging against the cabinet beneath until I gave her a stern look and she stopped. I told her to close her eyes, then outlined the upper lids with the glitter liner. It was just cheap stuff, marketed to tweens, using the face of some ditzy pop idol, but as with all things glittery and sparkly, I loved it. So did Simone. She hummed happily as I painted a design on her cheek using a different color of liquid liner—surely her dad couldn't complain about that, right? It was like face-painting at a carnival.

"There. What do you think?"

She twisted to peer in the mirror, brow furrowed. She looked more like her dad when she did that. Critical. Then she grinned. "I like the flower!"

"Good. Now," I said, lifting her down and patting her on the rear, "scram, kid, I gotta get ready."

"You're going on a date," Simone crooned in a sing-song voice. "Right? That's what Daddy told Mama."

"Oh, did he?" It was my turn to frown then. Just a little. I glanced at myself in the mirror.

"Yep." In the glass, Simone's reflection shrugged, barely interested.

"Well…sure, I'm going on a date."

"Are you gonna kiss him?"

I turned to look at her. "Where do you get this stuff?"

"TV," Simone said blithely.

"You should read more," I muttered, which was ridiculous, since the kid wasn't even in preschool. "Now go on. Get out of here. I'm busy, kid."

She did reluctantly, my date preparations apparently more interesting even than the television. From upstairs I heard the pounding of small feet and the cries of welcome—Vic was home. I'd probably have to face him, too, before I went out.

Sure enough, I found them all in the kitchen when I emerged from the basement. Elaine, her belly leading the way as she moved from the pot of mac-n-cheese on the stove to the table, gave me a once-over, but said nothing. Vic, on the other hand, snorted softly and shook his head. But he didn't say anything, which told me a lot—there were times in the past when he'd have been unable to keep his mouth shut. Marriage had mellowed him.

"Have a good time," Elaine said as she plopped a spoonful of yellow noodles on Max's plate. "Be careful."

I laughed. Just going on this "date" felt like the opposite of careful. "I'll be home late. Don't wait up."

"We'll leave the light on for you," Vic said.

"Oooh, you and Tom what's-his-face from Motel 6." I paused to squeeze Vic's shoulder. "Thanks."

"Cap said your car will be ready tomorrow." Vic held up his plate for his own portion of macaroni and gave me a long, steady look. "I can give you a ride to the shop in the morning, if you want."

It was his way of asking if I planned on coming home. Number one, it wasn't really his business. Number two, I doubted I'd have a different offer. Three, I had my brother's car anyway, so I just smiled and winked at him, a response guaranteed to drive Vic batty. Elaine laughed, though. For someone who loved him enough to marry him and have his babies, she surely did like to tease.

It was good for him, to be teased like that. And to be loved.

"Later, gators," I said, and was out the door before any grubby hands could streak my clothes.

Meredith had called it a date, and I assumed she'd meant it whimsically. Still, I'd dressed accordingly. My heart beat faster, my palms a little sweaty, and I felt as much anticipation as if it were a date. Maybe more.

We'd agreed to meet at The Slaughtered Lamb because, according to Meredith, they had a shepherd's pie to die for, and live music. Some Irish band I didn't know. It was tucked neatly off a side street and not part of the Second Street strip of bars and clubs, so while I'd been there once or twice, it wasn't a place I hung out in regularly.

Meredith did, apparently, based on the way the guy at the door greeted her and the waitress smiled when she showed us to our table. Meredith settled into her seat and pulled off her leather gloves with the sigh of a woman grateful to be out of the cold, while I thought seriously about leaving my mittens on to disguise the sudden trembling of my fingers.

"Hello, gorgeous," Meredith said when the waitress had handed us our menus and left. "I love the scarf."

It wasn't anything fancy, just a strip of teal silk I'd tied to one side of my throat above the boat neckline of my peasant blouse. I touched it, though, when she admired it.

"Very fifties French sailor," she said. "Very Audrey Hepburn."

That had been the sort of look I was going for, with makeup to match. "Thanks."

And after that, it was fine.

Most of it was her way. How easy she made it to be with her. She was different here than she was in the Mocha. A little less bright, a little softer, her voice more a murmur, so that I had to lean across the table to catch what she was saying, though I never had any trouble hearing her laughter.

I liked making her laugh.

"See," she said, when I'd finished describing to her the situation with my brother and his roommate. "You have a great talent for telling stories. I don't know why you're so hesitant to join in at the Mocha."

"I don't want to share my secrets with strangers. Then they wouldn't be secrets anymore."

"Why's it have to be a secret?" She smiled.

I drew my fork through the mashed potatoes left on my plate. She'd been right about the shepherd's pie. "I have to face those people every day at work. I don't want them knowing about my sex life."

"We don't only talk about sex. We talk about lots of things." Meredith had eaten only half her food, and now she pushed her plate away with her fingertips.

I wiped my mouth with a paper napkin and thought of how she'd left the imprint of her lips behind on the one I'd eventually tossed in the trash. "What is it about secrets and stories you like so much, anyway?"

She shrugged. "I don't know. I've always liked knowing things about people. I guess you could say…I'm a collector."

"Of what?"

"People," Meredith said. "Interesting people."

"How do you do that?" I asked, meaning to sound light, but realizing I was leaning closer again.

"I watch them for a while, see if they look interesting. You can't always tell at first."

I nodded. "Of course not."

"So I talk to them. See if they don't seem stuck-up. If they're cool, I get them to tell me about themselves. People like talking about themselves, Tesla." She paused. Smiled a bit reproachfully. "Most people do, anyway."

I thought of the group she gathered around her at the Mocha. I was probably my least interesting at work, where Joy managed to suck the life out of any attempts at creativity. "Did you collect me?"

"Doing my best," Meredith said, with another of those smiles that turned me inside out. She cocked her head. "I'm not a stranger, am I?"

I wasn't quite sure what she was, but it wasn't that. "No."

She looked around the bar, which had become steadily more crowded as the evening went on, but still offered us a lot of privacy. "And you're not at work."

"Thank God."

Meredith was the one who leaned, this time. "So, Tesla. Tell me something."

"What do you want to know?"

She pretended to think, in such an exaggerated way I was

sure she'd already thought of what she wanted to hear before she'd even asked. "What's the best sex you've ever had?"

"You go first." I made the same offer I'd made the last time I told her a story, but again, she put me off.

"The best sex I've ever had is always the last sex I had," Meredith told me. "Otherwise, what's the point?"

"Lucky you," I murmured.

She leaned closer. The table was just large enough for our two plates and glasses, and since I'd already leaned in a bit myself, she got pretty close. Her pupils had gone wide in the dim light, giving her a look of innocence completely at odds with the tilt of her mouth.

"So. Tell me," she said, and again, I did.

Chapter
9

Her name was Melissa. She was two years older than me, and unlike the other partners I'd had, she came on to me first. We were camping, of all the crazy things to be doing in the late fall, but the leaves were turning colors, the rates at the state park campgrounds had gone down, and I was friends with a bunch of people who liked to go out into the woods and get liquored up and rowdy.

She had dark, dark hair that fell to her ass in long, straight lines. Her hair was heavy. Even now I can remember the weight of it against me, how when she slept next to me her hair would cover me, warm as a blanket. She had dark eyes, too, tilted at the corners, and she wore eyeliner to emphasize them.

We had mutual friends and had met a bunch of times before, but we weren't quite friends ourselves. When we got to the set of matching cabins we'd rented for the weekend, people started pairing off—some of them couples, some friends who'd already decided they were going to bunk together. I didn't mind sharing with a guy, but I didn't want to share a room with Shawn, who had some personal hygiene problems. Kent had a nervous laugh and bad acne, which wouldn't have been an issue except that rumor also had it that he had the hots for me—and I didn't feel like fending off his advances and ruining the weekend for all of us by turning him down. I hadn't met the other three girls, Cindy, Dee and Tina, before, so when Melissa asked me casually if I wanted to room with her, I said sure.

"We got the room with only one bed," she said, as if she was surprised, and I like to think she was. "Hope you don't mind sharing."

I didn't care. We dumped our things and headed out to the campfire, where there was plenty of beer and marshmallows. And if she sat a little closer to me on the downed log that served as a bench, well…there were a lot of people and not many places to sit.

I didn't realize Melissa liked me romantically until we were taking a hike along one of the trails toward what was supposed to be a "pretty bitchin' waterfall," according to Scott, one of the guys who'd organized the trip. When she took my hand, linking her fingers casually through mine, I must've looked startled.

"Is this okay?" Her palm was warm on mine, her fingers strong.

"Sure." And it was, actually. Before that moment I couldn't have told you if, my crush on Marilyn Monroe aside, I liked girls. Not definitively, anyway.

I'd put the Murphy boys years into my past, Vic even further back than that. I'd had a few boyfriends in between, nobody serious. Nobody who'd made me feel as thrilled as Melissa did when she took my hand.

We slept together in the same bed that entire weekend, and though I lay awake listening to the sound of her breathing as she fell asleep, and waiting for her to touch me, Melissa never did. She didn't move fast like that, she said seriously on our last morning there, when we'd both rolled over to stare into each other's eyes.

"I'm not in this for giggles," she said. "I want you to be sure this is what you want."

By that point, I wanted it. I wanted her. It had grown from a kind of giggly curiosity into full-blown desire, hot and aching in my blood. But I didn't know how to make the first move on a girl. I wasn't afraid she'd turn me down, but it was like I was a virgin all over again. I had no idea where to put my hands, which way to tilt my head to go in for a kiss.

We saw each other for two more weeks before she kissed me. It seemed longer than forever. And then when she did, her mouth was so soft, so different from a guy's, that I could only sit there with my eyes closed and let her do it.

"You can kiss me back." She was amused.

So I did.

I closed my eyes again and opened my mouth, and kissed Melissa with everything I had. I lost myself in the taste of her. Strawberry lip gloss. In the perfume of her shampoo and the weight of her hair against the backs of my hands when I buried them in it. And most of all, her softness.

Her belly, smooth and curving, firm but not muscled. Her arms, the skin like satin. The column of her throat without the lump of an Adam's apple to distract me. Her smooth cheeks, no beard stubble. Everything about her was smooth and soft and sweet, and I soaked it all in as we made out for hours. She took her time with me, and I didn't quite know how to handle it.

"Relax," Melissa breathed against my mouth. "We have all night."

We used all of it, too. I'd been happy to demand multiple orgasms from the guys I'd slept with in the past, but since they only ever got that singleton climax, when they were done, so was the fucking. It wasn't like that with Melissa. With her mouth and her hands she built me up until I was close to the edge of coming, then eased me off.

Melissa was the first person to make me come just with her tongue. I went up, up and over into bliss. Then again, until I broke with it. I wasn't in the habit of crying during sex, but I wept a little at how good it felt.

That amused her, too. So did my clumsy attempt at going down on her—I was willing enough, and I had a good idea of what would work on women, since I could imagine what worked on me. But I was too hard, too fast.

"Too focused," she told me, holding my face in her hands as I looked up at her from between her legs. "Think butterfly, not bee."

Eventually, I figured out how to make her clit pulse under my tongue, her pussy to clench my fingers. I learned to make her come, then come again with barely a pause, come so hard the bed shook and she cried out.

"And that," I said to Meredith, "was the best sex I've ever had."

Chapter
10

I'd embellished the story—not lying, but deliberately putting in details I might otherwise have left out because, I'll admit it, I wanted to see what she'd do. I'd felt a little pressured by Meredith in her quest for stories. And I'd felt a little put out by her bragging that she'd kissed a girl.

But mostly, I wanted her to know that I was a woman who knew how to make another woman come. I went all the way.

"What happened?" she asked.

I laughed, rueful but not without humor. "Oh. Well. Four months into it, she dumped me."

"For another woman?"

"Oh, hell yeah. Melissa didn't go for guys. Not ever."

Meredith looked sympathetic. "Why'd she dump you? What a bitch."

I'd thought as much at the time.

Melissa had been blunt, I could give her that. "Seriously, Tesla, do you think you can imagine spending the rest of your life with me? Having kids, all that? Because when I'm in it, I want it to be for the long haul. With someone like me."

Since she said this just after I'd finished giving her three orgasms in a row, using tricks she'd taught me, I'd been appropriately affronted. "What's that supposed to mean?"

"You know what it means," was all Melissa had said, and that was that. The end of it. She took up with someone more like her, whatever that meant.

"The last I heard they were still together. Two kids," I added. "I guess she found what she was looking for."

"So…what did she mean?" Meredith asked. "Someone like her? Someone more…gay?"

I shrugged and lifted my glass to drink. It left a wet circle on the napkin, and when I put the glass down, I fitted it exactly to the outline, then looked up at Meredith. "I guess so."

"Eating pussy didn't make you gay enough?" she mused, sounding as if she didn't really expect an answer.

"I'm not gay. I'm not straight." I pointed this out because it was important. "And I'm not wild, either."

"You've done so much," Meredith said, as if I hadn't even spoken. "And I've done…nothing."

I laughed. "You kissed a girl. And you liked it."

Her eyes gleamed. Did I imagine she looked at my mouth as she licked her lips? Maybe not.

"That was nothing," she said.

"You wanted a story," I told her with another shrug. "It's not a secret. But it was the truth."

"That story was worth the price of dinner."

I hadn't known my words could have such value.

Meredith reached across the table to cover my hand with

hers, fingers squeezing. "Tesla, baby, don't worry about it. Besides, the person who asks for the date is supposed to pay, right?"

She gave me a twinkly-eyed grin to show she wasn't serious. Not about the date part, anyway.

She didn't have to try too hard to convince me to go dancing. I worked the evening shift the next day, which usually sucked on Saturdays but for which I'd be thankful when I didn't have to work Sunday morning. By the time we got to the Pharmacy, the line was already spilling out onto the sidewalk. With dollar drinks and a band downstairs, and two floors of dance music above, it was a popular spot. We showed our IDs and pushed our way inside.

Meredith wasn't interested in the lower level. She glanced over at the bar, where a college-age guy who already looked wasted had been settled into a barber chair, a scantily clad server hovering over him, with a bottle ready to pour into his mouth, and a belt to spank him with—if he was sober enough, after, to stand up and bend over for it.

Meredith rolled her eyes and pointed to the stairs. Conversation was worthless here. I made to follow her through the crowd, but a pair of giggly bachelorette party girls in tiaras got between us. I knew where Meredith was headed; it was no big deal. But she looked back to see if I was there, and frowned at the intrusion. She reached around them, pushing them subtly to the side, and grabbed my hand. Our fingers linked, twisting as she turned toward the stairs again.

This time, I had no trouble keeping up with her.

It didn't mean anything, that hand-holding. Nor did the way she let the contact linger when we got upstairs, where the dance floor was less crowded, when she could have easily let me go. I knew better than to expect any interest from her. Not like that, anyway, whether she'd once kissed a girl or not.

"Want a drink?" She said this directly into my ear, her breath hot, the whisper of her lips against my skin enough to make me shiver.

She smelled expensive and delicious. I shook my head. She pulled away enough to look into my eyes, her head tilted, the red and blue and green and gold lights of the dance floor dancing across her face like sunshine through stained glass. She hadn't let go of my hand. Her fingers squeezed. She leaned in closer as someone passed behind her.

"Sure? A beer?"

"No, thanks." I gently took my hand from hers and feigned an interest in the crowd. "You go ahead."

Shit. I should've offered to buy her drink, since she'd paid for my dinner. But Meredith was already scouting the bar, and nodded toward an older guy leaning against it, a beer in his hand. He was scouting, too.

"He'll buy it for you," she told me. "I can get him to."

I had to laugh at that. I had no doubts Meredith could get that stranger to buy us both whatever she wanted him to. "I'm good."

She was gone in the next second. I watched her make magic with the guy at the bar. She was so good at it. She tipped back her head, laughing, shaking her long hair. She even held up her wedding rings and flashed them, giving the guy a playful "no-no" wag of her finger, though the look she shot me said she had him right where she wanted him. She'd be making him think the drinks were his idea.

Sure enough, she came back across the room with a mojito in one hand and a beer for me in the other. He watched her the whole way, not quite with the lolling tongue of a cartoon dog…but close. Meredith didn't glance back, not once. She pressed the cold bottle into my palm, and her eyes gleamed when she grinned at me.

"Drink up," she said. "And then let's dance."

Tonight it seemed as though all the men were interested in observing the cultural phenomenon of the bachelorette party. True, those women were making quite a scene. At least three different groups, with matching T-shirts or tiaras or penis necklaces, had sort of taken over the place. There wasn't much room for men on the dance floor with all the cavorting and circle dancing going on.

Somehow, though, Meredith made her way in. Not into the circle. That she looked at with great disdain, rolling her eyes at me in a way that would've made me laugh even without that last beer. She imitated one bride-to-be's sorority girl shuffle with a straight face. Not even the woman's friends noticed their home-girl was being mocked.

Meredith cast another glance as the second group surged closer. This was the penis-necklace group, and they were slightly more obnoxious than the other two parties. They were playing the "buck-a-suck" game, in which they offered up candy necklaces to men who'd bite off one of the pieces for a dollar. It seemed like an easy, if sloppy, way to make a few bucks.

Meredith was clearly not amused.

"Sluts," she said into my ear, drawing me away from them and toward one of the cages on the outer edges of the dance floor.

Her derision made me laugh again. "They're just having a good time. Didn't you have a bachelorette party?"

"Oh, sure, with a male stripper and everything. But that

was private." Her lip curled as she peered over her shoulder. "Christ, look at them. Now they're fake grinding."

I looked. Two of them were writhing to some song that was supposed to be sexy, and might've been, had they been dancing to the beat instead of off it. I laughed. "They're having fun."

"They're being ridiculous." Meredith scowled.

I thought her real problem was that they were taking all the attention, with none left for her. I bet that didn't happen often in her life, at least not that I'd ever seen. Meredith turned heads wherever she went.

At the rising sound of catcalls, we both turned. The girls who'd been grinding together were now ass-to-crotch, the one in front bent over as her friend behind slapped at her butt with one hand and made cowboy lasso motions with the other. They were both nearly falling over from laughter or too much drink.

"They're not even trying to be sexy," Meredith said. "Bunch of dumb cunts."

"They're a couple of twat-whistles," I agreed, "but so what? If you don't want to dance, Meredith, we can go someplace else."

Or go home, I thought, stifling a yawn with the back of my hand. Unlike Meredith, who could sleep in as long as she pleased, I was guaranteed to be woken earlier than I wanted.

"Buck a suck!" shouted out one of the obnoxious girls as she yanked the bride forward by the wrist. "Hey, everyone! A buck a suck!"

"I'd give them ten to get their fat asses off this dance floor," Meredith said, and before I could reply, she'd turned. True to her word, she held up a ten-dollar bill. "What do I get for a ten-spot?"

Those girls were giggling like crazy, some still gyrating as if someone had unhinged their hips. The one tugging at the bride's hand snatched the ten from Meredith and waved it in the air. The crowd whooped in approval.

"Buck a suck? You'd better get ready," I thought Meredith said, but the music was so loud I could've been mistaken.

That poor girl had no idea what hit her. Meredith put her hands on the bride's hips, pulling them belly to belly as she slid a thigh between her legs. The idea of the game was to lip at the candy necklace the bride-to-be wore, and bite or suck off the individual candies, but Meredith, who'd paid for ten, was making sure she got her money's worth.

That girl-on-girl action that had been going on earlier? Nothing compared to what was happening now. Those other girls, those straight girls who thought a little dirty dancing or some fake kissing was the way to get guys to notice them, couldn't begin to compete with Meredith when she turned it on. Meredith skimmed her lips over the necklace, not bothering with the candy, and found the bride's throat beneath. Her hands gripped tighter as she pressed her thigh against the other woman's pussy. Their bodies moved and melded.

I thought the future Mrs. Whoever-the-fuck-she-was would push Meredith away. I think all of us watching did. But she must have been too drunk, too horny or simply too surprised, for all she did was tip her head back and let Meredith mouth her neck.

And then Meredith kissed her.

Full-on, openmouthed, tongues twisting together like snakes. Meredith's hands slid up the other woman's front to cup her breasts through her pink and sparkly T-shirt. They weren't dancing, really, just grinding and tongue-fucking each other's mouths. Her girlfriends looked on, agape.

The men surrounding us exploded into a frenzy of catcalls, whistles and whoops.

Meredith looked at me, and though her lips were still fused to that hapless bachelorette, I saw the curve of a smile. She broke the kiss abruptly, her lips still wet from it. The future bride stumbled back, looking stunned, her mouth slack, eyes glazed. Her nipples were hard, too, poking at the front of her shirt. Her friends surrounded her in the next minute, closing her in, reaching to support her because it looked as if she might just keel over.

We were very popular after that.

Not with the bridal parties—they gave us a wide berth. But the men who'd been watching that display? Oh, they couldn't get enough. They all wanted Meredith, of course, but I got the overflow. Too bad I wasn't interested in dancing with any of those guys.

I spotted the bride whose world Meredith had rocked. She looked pretty drunk, dancing with her hands up, twirling around and around. Someone had given her a handful of blinking cock necklaces, and it looked as if she'd finally had all her candy bitten off. I didn't think she was going to last much longer, and for her sake I hoped her wedding wasn't for a few days at least, because she looked pretty fucking rough. She also couldn't stop staring at Meredith.

I knew how she felt.

Here's the worst thing about crushes you know are unrequited. You'd think it would be better when you know that the chief reason your crush isn't interested in you "that way" is because their door just doesn't open in your direction. It should be easier to deal with that burning, that ache, when you know it's not your fault, but the simple setup of nature or nurture or whatever it is that turns us into what we are.

Let me tell you, though, it isn't.

It had never bothered me to know Meredith was married. I'd never been jealous of her husband, that nameless, faceless man who'd put a ring on her finger and never seemed to care where she went or with whom. I wasn't jealous of the men she was flirting and dancing with, the ones buying her drinks. But I wanted to reach across the room and smack that candy necklace slut right across her drunken face.

"I need to go," I told Meredith, when the man behind me had grabbed my ass one too many times.

"What?" she cried, too caught up in being freaked by not one, but two dudes in striped shirts, and clouded in a miasma of cologne.

"I gotta go!" I shouted, and bumped the ass bandit off me with a hip. He tossed up his hands and backed away when I glared. "I'm wiped out!"

"N-o-o-o!" Meredith abandoned her admirers and came after me to take both my hands. "Tessie, it's early!"

My given name's bad enough. Being called Tessie is like having a sliver of bamboo inserted oh-so-gently under the fingernail. I grimaced and kept backing up, bumping into whoever got in my way, and not caring. Suddenly the room was too hot, the extra beer had settled none too happily in my gut, and I wanted to dive into a cold shower and cry my eyes out.

On the street, I took in gulps of chilly air as gooseflesh humped up on my arms—the only humping I was likely to get tonight—and my nipples peaked in sympathy. Meredith came out right behind me. She linked her arm though mine.

"Hey, girl, hey." Her voice was too loud even for the street full of traffic and people. She softened it. "Hey. What's wrong?"

"Nothing. Just tired, that's all." It wasn't a lie, but I couldn't look her in the eye when I said it.

Meredith pulled me a little closer. That was the problem with her. She was a hugger, a social kisser. She thought nothing of squeezing and smooching and smoothing. I'd taken it as part of her personality, but just now it was too much.

"I'm starving!" she declared. "Come to Tom's Diner with me first. Let's get eggs. And bacon. And toast. C'mo-o-on, Tesla. You know you wanna."

She gave me that smile that slayed everyone, including me. "Meredith…"

She sidled closer to tuck her arm through mine, our hips touching. In her four-inch pumps she was a good few inches taller than me, but she bent to press her chin into my shoulder. "Please? Please, please…?"

I wasn't hungry, and though normally it wouldn't have mattered, I shook my head anyway. "Can't. Really. I'm about to fall over. My feet hurt."

She looked at my shoes. "You can sit. Take your shoes off."

In most of my life, I'm not pliable the way I was for her. It wasn't just me—I'd seen her work her magic on lots of people. Knowing I wasn't special made it worse, not better, but what could I say?

"Nah. Really. I need to get home. It's late," I pointed out, though certainly we'd each been out later than this before. "And I have stuff to do tomorrow before work."

She nodded, but reluctantly. I wondered, not for the first time, how often Meredith didn't get her way. She held out her arms for a hug I could think of no graceful way to decline, but instead of pressing against me and letting go, Meredith lingered.

I loved the way she smelled. Loved the whisper of her breath against my cheek and the low, slow seduction of her chuckle. I tried to let her go, but my arms closed naturally around her waist, my hands flat on the bony parts of her shoulder blades poking up beneath the silky fabric of her top. I closed my eyes, pathetic, wanting something I knew I wouldn't get.

"Tesla, Tesla," Meredith murmured into my ear. "There's something I want you to do for me."

It shows you what sorts of scenes go on in downtown Harrisburg that nobody even gave us a second glance. Two women embracing on the sidewalk, both dressed to impress. I guess the two guys shoving each other across the street or the girl who tripped and went down, too drunk to get back up even when her friends tugged her by the arms, were more exciting to watch. Meredith hugged me, and she whispered in my ear, and I thought I'd like to stay like that for a very long time.

"What's that?"

She turned her head slightly, her lips brushing my earlobe and sending sparkling shimmers of pleasure all through me. "I'm afraid to ask you."

My heart thumped as I tried to breathe. She'd kissed that girl on the dance floor and made it about power, not seduction, but that didn't stop me from imagining what it would be like for Meredith to kiss me, instead. I thought of it every time I saw her. I turned my head, too.

"Just ask me," I said, hoping she wouldn't ask. Hoping she'd just...do.

She moved against me, then pulled away enough to look into my face. My lips parted, waiting. My hands slid to her hips.

Meredith smiled, and once again I was lost in the curve of

that mouth. The flash of her eyes. She leaned in, and so did
I. Waiting.

"I want you to fuck my husband," Meredith said.

Chapter

11

"You took a cab here, right? Let me drive you home." Meredith ran her hand down my arm, then clutched lightly but briefly at my wrist. "Let's talk about this. Okay?"

She seemed nervous as she pulled out of the parking garage, tapping the steering wheel too rapidly to match the beat of the music. She had her iPod hooked up, and I lifted it to see what she was playing. A song I didn't know, something slow and syrupy. It reminded me of slow dancing and the heavy scent of flowers, tiny twinkling white lights strung through mosquito netting. That sort of thing. Sexy music.

I wondered if she'd picked it on purpose or if it was coincidence. When the next song came on, something much the same, I figured she'd made a playlist. I put the iPod back.

In the light from the dashboard, Meredith's eyes flashed.

She kept them on the road, after giving me the quickest of glances. "I need directions."

"Across the Market Street Bridge to Nineteenth Street, near the library. I'll show you."

She sighed. Her fingers rap-a-tapped. We rode in silence except for when I gave her directions, until she pulled up in front of my house. When she turned off the car, the music didn't stop but the dash went dim. We sat in the dark and listened to a woman sing about longing.

I said nothing.

When the song ended, Meredith pushed the button to turn off the stereo. The silence was louder than the music had been. So was the sound of her breathing. She turned to face me, and her perfume wafted toward me in the close space.

"Charlie and I have been talking about this for a while, but it's hard, you know. To find someone."

"I bet it's not so hard."

Her laugh sounded nervous, too. I found the Meredith who didn't know what to do with herself charming and sweet and a little disconcerting. "Not if you don't have standards."

"I'm glad to know I meet your standards," I said in a low voice.

"But you don't want to do it?"

"I haven't even met him, Meredith."

"You could meet him first. Of course." She leaned a little closer, into the small bit of light shining from the streetlight. She paused, smiled. "You haven't said no."

I hadn't decided to say no. "I want to know why."

"Why you?"

"Why you want another woman to fuck your husband, first of all."

"Because I think he'd like it," she said.

"What about you?"

She glanced at me with a tilt of her head and an assessing look. "I want to watch him with another woman. It's a fantasy, okay? Can you understand that?"

"Sure. Of course." Probably better than she could've known. "You're not worried?"

"About what?"

"That it'll cause problems. A lot of people can't handle watching someone they love with someone else. They think they can, but they can't."

"We've talked about it. I'll be fine." She sounded confident again, not nervous, and the smile had crept back to her mouth. "I want to watch him go down on a woman and make her come. I think it would be hot."

My throat went a little dry. "Okay, then. So why me?"

"Because you're sexy as hell. Because I think you'd be up for it, without making it too weird."

"Because I'm wild."

"Because you know what you want, and you take it, Tesla."

"You've talked a lot about it, I guess. With Charlie?" I didn't know how to feel about that. Flattered? Maybe wary. More than a little turned on.

Meredith's husband fucked her. And fucking him, well, that might be as close as I could ever get to knowing what she tasted like. But still I couldn't quite manage to outright agree.

"And now I'm talking about it with you." She leaned even closer, and the waft of her scent drifted across my face, getting inside me with every breath. "Tell me you're not freaked out about this, Tesla."

It took a little more than a proposition to freak me out, of course, but it touched me that Meredith was worried. "I'm not freaked. Just surprised, that's all. And flattered, I guess."

Her smile got a little bigger. She said nothing, and the silence grew in the space between us until I felt compelled to break it with something witty or clever, if only I could think of something to say. There was nothing I could give her except a smile in return, but Meredith didn't seem to mind.

"It would be fun," she said. "I promise."

I'd heard that before.

Chapter
12

"It'll be fun," Chance told me. "I promise."

In my short experience with the brothers Murphy the promise of fun could be counted on if you considered illicit sex and sneaking around fun, which I guess I did at the time. Chance's promises, on the other hand, weren't quite as reliable. It wasn't so much that he was deliberately false, just that he was easily distracted. He was trying to get me to agree to go to the Christmas dance with him.

Just him.

Chase would be going with Becka Miller. She was on the girls' basketball team, was a good six inches taller than me and wore her bland, brown hair cropped short in a style that was in no way half as cute as a pixie cut. I'd never said more than a couple of words to her and frankly, that was the way I wanted to keep it. Becka Miller was a jock who could pound me into next week if she wanted to, and since her temper was as ugly as her haircut, I wasn't going to risk giving her a reason to want to.

Also, really, the Christmas dance? I couldn't have thought of anything I wanted to do less than put on a semiformal dress and buy a dead flower to stick on the front of his sport jacket, then go to dinner at the IHOP and dance to music that would surely suck while couples who were "in love" gyrated all around us.

Not with Chance Murphy, anyway.

To my surprise, because he wasn't the sort of guy I'd ever thought would care about dumb shit like that, Vic told me I should go. He was at the stove, mixing up some instant stuffing to go with the pork chops we were having for dinner. I'd made up some of those instant biscuits that come in a tube, and Cap was off somewhere doing Cap stuff, like lifting weights or possibly deconstructing string theory, who the hell knew with him. We had a little, unconventional family, but even so, I wasn't expecting Vic to offer me paternal advice.

"You might have fun," he said.

"That's what Chance said." I put out the butter, some forks and plates.

Vic turned, stirring the stuffing with a wooden spoon that probably harbored an army of bacteria. "And you don't believe him?"

Of course, I hadn't told Vic about what was really going on before and after the tutoring sessions, and all the times I told him I was going to tutor them and didn't even crack a book. So now I carefully didn't look at him as I finished setting the table. "Not sure."

"Tesla," Vic said, but stopped.

I still didn't look at him. I pretended I didn't know he was

THE SPACE BETWEEN US

staring at me as I rummaged in the fridge for some salad and drinks. But he was still staring when I finally had to close the door and turn around.

"It might be good for you," Vic said.

I greeted that with a curled lip. "What—the Christmas dance? Are you kidding me? Really?"

"Going out with a guy, having a good time. Doing something...normal."

The bottle of ranch dressing clattered on the table as I finally faced him. "I'm not normal, Vic. Me and Cap, not normal. You, not normal." I gestured around the kitchen. "None of this is normal. And you're really the only one who seems to have a problem with it."

His face got hard then, and while most of the time Vic's gaze was guileless, now it was scary fierce. He slammed the pot of stuffing on the table hard enough to make the plates jump. I jumped, too.

"What, that's a shitty thing for me to want? That you and Cap should have a normal life, after—"

"Nothing bad happened to me there!" I shouted.

Vic had crossed the small kitchen to me faster than a blink, and gripped my upper arm hard enough to bruise. "No, but it could have!"

He was hurting me, but I wasn't going to give him the satisfaction of knowing it so he could feel guilty about it later. Caught flat-footed, I couldn't get close enough to Vic to look in his eyes and with the table behind me, I couldn't back up. All I could do was wait for him to realize what he was doing.

With a muttered curse, Vic dropped my arm and backed away. First he scraped a hand over his face. Then he put his hands on his hips, head hanging, shoulders hunched. A vast and painful silence filled the space between us. I hadn't wanted to cry when he grabbed my arm and hurt me, but I had to swipe away tears now.

"It wouldn't have been your fault if it did, Vic. Nothing that happened there was your fault." Even at eighteen, I knew that it didn't matter. Vic blamed himself, maybe because it was easier to feel guilty for failing rather than admitting that no matter what he'd done, he'd have been unable to succeed.

"It could have," Vic said again in a lower, broken voice.

"But it didn't." I didn't reach to touch him. "I'm okay. Cap's okay. And that *is* because of you, Vic."

"You should go to that dance with that boy." Vic went back to the oven to pull out the pan of pork chops, which he put on the table along with the small pot of green beans from the stovetop. "Get a pretty dress, take your pictures. Have fun with friends your own age."

That was the key, right there. Friends my own age. I'd gotten over our summer fling, but Vic had not—which didn't mean he was still hung up on me, or yearned for me, or anything like that. In fact, I'd have been more likely to suggest a renewal of our sexual relationship than Vic, who seemed uncomfortable remembering it. And certainly never spoke of it.

"What's going on? Dinner ready?" That was Cap, back from wherever he'd been. He had dirt on the front of his shirt and grass stains on his knees. The rest of his jeans were soaked.

"What the hell were you doing?" I asked.

"Flag football," he said.

"In the snow?" I rolled my eyes.

At sixteen Cap had finally started growing into the promise of his huge feet and hands. He ate constantly, slept like the dead and took showers so long the rest of us were left with icy water. He scored off the charts on standardized tests, but got solid Cs in school, not because he didn't understand the material but because he couldn't seem to remember to turn in his homework.

Now he gave me a blank look. "Yeah?"

"Wash your hands, sit down and eat." Vic let his eyes skate over me. "You, too."

We did eat, Cap putting away more than Vic and me combined. After, we told Cap he had to do the dishes since we'd made the meal. Vic headed off to the den to watch television. I had homework, but instead of going upstairs to my room to do it, I followed him.

"I'll make you a deal," I said from the doorway.

He'd settled into his recliner, feet up, beer in one hand. He didn't even turn to look at me. "What's that?"

"I'll go with Chance, if you go out with Elaine."

Vic half turned his head. "Who?"

"Elaine," I said patiently, knowing he knew exactly who I meant. "Red Ford Probe, comes in for an oil change every couple of months whether the car needs it or not."

Vic didn't protest or try to pretend he didn't know who I meant. "Why would I ask her out?"

"Because she's totally into you and you like her, too." That was the truth. I never saw Vic laugh so much as when Elaine was sitting in the waiting room at the shop. "She's pretty, she's smart, she's not a psycho."

Silence.

Then, "Fine."

"Fine," I said, as if that was that, even though I thought I was getting the worse end of the deal. Not that Vic had any idea of why or how complicated the situation really was. But I didn't want him worrying about me anymore, and I didn't want him sitting around the house night after night doing nothing but watching TV.

Vic deserved a life, too.

So I went to the dance with Chance, and I watched his brother make out with Becka on the dance floor, and some part of me died inside because until that moment I hadn't known or wanted to admit I loved just one of the brothers Murphy, and it wasn't the one I was there with.

Chapter
13

Forget love making the world go round, it's all about the sugar and the caffeine, baby. We had three different specialty drinks that changed every week, along with the normal coffees, and fresh-baked desserts that had arrived that morning, including rich fudge brownies with inch-thick icing, chocolate muffins, and a truly stellar apple-crumb muffin that liked to call my name.

And then…there was Meredith.

I'd been half hoping she wouldn't come in that day. Worried that she wouldn't. I shouldn't have been concerned. She breezed in the way she always did, with a smile for everyone and an extra special one for me.

"What's good today? Other than your pretty self?"

In the past I'd blown off her flirting as fake, given it back to her in a way she couldn't construe as anything but a joke.

Today I didn't quite have it in me. "We have the pepper-mint mocha lattes, early this year. Back by popular demand. They're good."

"Sugar-free?"

"Sure." I gestured at the menu board, though of course she'd been in dozens of times and probably could've recited the items on it as well as I could. "The caramel macchiato's good, too. But we don't have that in sugar-free—we ran out of the syrup. Sorry."

"I'll take a peppermint, then." She leaned over the counter. "And come see me when it's ready."

My boss could be ten kinds of a cranky bitch, but today Joy was in the back placing stock orders, or maybe plotting new ways to make life miserable. I mixed up Meredith's latte the way she liked it, adding an extra pump of syrup without charging her because I liked to do that for my favorites even when they didn't know about it.

She'd taken her usual seat between the front window and the self-serve coffee station, and she was staring out the glass when I put the cup down in front of her. Her smile took a few seconds to follow her eyes. She wrapped her hands around the cup with a sigh. "Mmmm."

"Taste it. Make sure it's okay."

"I'm sure it's great." She sipped anyway, saying "mmmm" again, this time with a low, breathy sound, almost like a moan.

I paused in refilling the napkin canister to look at her. The Morningstar Mocha had emptied, though the evening rush meant that would change soon enough. Meredith made eyes at me over the rim of her mug.

"Sit down with me, Tesla."

I gave a quick glance around first. I shrugged and pushed the napkin holder back into place. "I can't."

"I need to talk to you."

"I'm listening." I bent to pull open the cupboard to check for more packets of sweetener. "But I have to work, too."

"Have you thought any more about what I asked you?"

The bell over the front door jangled and Carlos came in, with a nod for me and a wink for Meredith before he slid into his favorite seat. Sometimes watching the customers in here was like overseeing an elaborate ballet—this one liked this seat and was out of it by a certain hour so another could come in. Woe to the person who overstayed his time or messed up the seating chart. Carlos preferred the table closer to the right front window, because it was near an outlet for his computer and also, strangely (so he said) didn't pick up the internet as well. Less temptation to distract him.

I, on the other hand, could've used a distraction from this conversation. "Carlos, you need anything?"

"Gonna need a bottomless in a few. But I can grab a mug for myself."

Only if Joy wasn't there to see him. She had some lame rule about customers not helping themselves to mugs, even the regulars and even though, like the seats, they all tended to use their favorites from the purposefully mismatched collection. Some of them even brought in mugs to donate.

"Carlos, you love the bottomless," Meredith called over to him, and they both laughed. To me she said, "Sit for just a minute."

I shook my head. "I should get behind the counter."

"Tesla. We have to talk about this."

"Not here," I told her.

"Fine." She sat back in her seat. "But sometime. I'm not going to let this fuck up our friendship."

"Like fucking your husband wouldn't?" I whispered fiercely.

She didn't pull away, didn't scowl, didn't frown. Her brows didn't even knit on that perfect forehead. "Not if I asked you to, it wouldn't."

"And you're asking me to."

"I'm inviting you to, yes." She smiled, one brow lifting just so. "I don't ask just anyone."

Something twisted and jerked in the vicinity of my heart. "You ask a lot of women?"

Now she appeared concerned, and reached for my hand. I turned my body so that even if Carlos looked up, he wouldn't necessarily see us holding hands like moony high school sweethearts. I didn't pull away, though.

"No. You're the first."

Her gaze flicked behind me. I heard the sound of sneakers squeaking on the tile floor—Joy's distinctive tread, and then the long-suffering sigh that told me she was gearing up to complain about something. I put away the extra sweetener and napkins so she couldn't complain about me, and crumpled up the paper wrapping from the containers I'd emptied the supplies from.

"I've thought about it," I said.

Meredith smiled and settled back in her seat. "And?"

"I haven't decided yet."

"You could just come and meet him. He'll like you, Tesla." She paused. "And I know you'll like him."

I sighed. "He knows about this?"

"Of course he knows. C'mon. Come out to dinner with us tonight. We'll talk about it."

I didn't say no.

Chapter
14

"You should get yourself one. Then you don't have to drive Cap's." Vic jerked his chin toward the window and the parking lot beyond, where I'd parked the Mustang.

I shrugged. "Meh. The Contour has to do it for me for a while. Unless you'll give me a good trade-in...."

He laughed. Vic had sold me the car originally. "On that piece of—"

"Uh-huh. See how far friendship gets me? Nowheresville, man." I shook my head in mock sorrow and tossed him the keys to Cap's car. "What was wrong with it?"

Vic shrugged, pocketing them. "Don't know. Cap tightened some things. Changed your oil and stuff, too. Why do you wait so long for that?"

I fluttered my eyelashes and put my hands beneath my chin

to look winsome. "Cuz I don't have a big stwong man to do it for me?"

Vic made a face. "You have your brother. And me. Hey, listen, I have to run some errands. Cap's coming in, but he's late. Can you hang until he gets here?"

I'd done my share of shifts at the garage, but waiting on my brother could take forever. "Actually, I have plans. How late is he?"

Vic looked at the clock. "Ten minutes. He should be here soon. I think I pulled him away from a project or something."

"That would explain it. Yeah, sure, I can wait for him. What are you doing?" I asked for curiosity's sake, not to be nosy, but Vic's expression immediately shut like a door in my face.

"Errands. What are *you* doing?"

"Uh…well, it's sort of a date."

This pulled him up short. "Another one?"

"Yeah. Surprise, surprise, someone digs me enough to go out with me twice," I said a little sourly. "Christ, Vic. Way to stroke my ego. Anyway, it's just sort of a date. Not really a date."

"What makes it not really a date?"

I hesitated, trying to think if I wanted to explain. Or how. "Well…it's with my friend Meredith. And her husband."

Vic looked confused. "How does that work?"

I laughed. "So far it doesn't work like anything. It's just… you know. A date. Sort of."

Vic knew I'd dated girls and had never said much about it. Now he gave me the side-eye. "So who's the date with? Your friend? Or her husband?"

"Um…both of them."

Vic seemed pained. "Tesla."

I snorted softly. "You asked."

He made a face and waved his hands at me. "I'm sorry I did. I have to get going. Sure you're okay until Cap gets here?"

"I'm fine, unless he's really late, and then I'm locking up and leaving."

Vic nodded. "Fair enough. See you at home."

All dressed up, I didn't really want to sit in the chair at his desk, but the ones in the waiting room weren't much better. I settled for filling a paper cup with water from the bubbler and looking over Vic's collection of vintage pinup calendars. No bare boobies—he was careful about stuff like that where kids could see. But plenty of pretty girls with Bettie Page haircuts and high heels. I was just getting ready to call my brother and tell him to get his ass to the garage when lights swept the lot and a car pulled in. I went to the door.

"Hey." Cap got out of the passenger side, leaned in to say something to the driver, then shut the door and thumped the roof before the car drove off. He turned to me. "What're you doing here?"

"Glad to see you, too. Vic had to go. I brought your car back. Safe," I added, when he automatically looked for it in the lot. "I only scratched it with a Brillo pad a little bit all over."

Cap winced. "Don't even."

With him there, I could head out, but I paused. "Hey, listen. Has Vic said anything to you lately?"

Cap, my tall, broad-shouldered brother, was handsome enough to turn heads, but though I knew he was smart, he often did his best to hide it. "About what?"

"Anything."

"Vic doesn't talk to me about much beyond cars, Tesla." Cap shrugged.

"You look tired."

He yawned. Shrugged. Cap wasn't much of a talker.

I glanced in the direction the car had gone. "Lynds gave you a ride? How's she doing?"

Another shrug.

I sighed. Whatever was going on with Cap and his roomie had been happening for long enough that I knew better than to ask him about it when I had someplace to go. It could take him hours to reveal the tiniest piece of information. Instead, I stood on my tiptoes to kiss his cheek and hug him, hard. I punched his chin lightly.

"Giant little brother," I said.

This earned a smile. "Tiny big sis."

"Gotta go." I backed up toward my car, and my brother's voice stopped me as I pulled open the door.

"Heard you had a date."

I stopped to look over my shoulder. "What? Who told you that? And when?"

"Vic called to ream me for being late, said you were waiting."

"I thought he didn't talk to you about anything but cars."

Cap smiled. I smiled, too. But I didn't offer any details. If my brother could keep silent about whatever monkeyshines he was getting up to with his roommate, I could hold my tongue about a first date.

We left it at that.

Chapter

15

I'd agreed to meet Meredith and Charlie at the Firehouse, one of the nicer restaurants downtown. Waiting for them in the parking lot, pacing back and forth alongside my car, I wished I smoked. It would've given me something to do with my hands besides chew my fingernails. When they pulled up in Meredith's familiar black Saab, I did think about turning tail. Just…running. But it was only a date, after all. It wasn't a lifetime contract.

Instead, I took in a deep breath, straightened my skirt and held off from running my fingers through my hair again. It was already ruffled and spiked, the fringes splayed artfully (or so I hoped) against my cheeks. Touching wouldn't make it look any better, and probably worse.

Meredith got out first, as put together and beautiful as always. She waved, her smile familiar but not exactly setting me at ease. "Tesla! Hi!"

Charlie didn't look anything like I thought he would.

He was gorgeous, of course. I shouldn't have expected anything less, for a woman who looked like Meredith. I'd expected athletic, bronzed, blond and blue-eyed, the Ken to her Barbie. Charlie was something else altogether.

He stood about five-ten, still a good five inches taller than me and a few more than his wife. His dark hair had glints of silver at the temples and was brushed off his forehead, trimmed neatly around his ears and the nape of his neck. He had dark eyes with a few lines at the corners. Smile lines, too. He wore a teal shirt beneath his dark suit jacket, his tie a swirl of colors. He'd dressed up…for me?

"Tesla?" He moved forward, a hand out to take mine. The other closed over it, both his hands wrapping mine with warmth. "Meredith's told me so much about you. Nice to meet you."

For one long minute we stayed like that, the possibilities of what might lie ahead somehow palpable between us. Like something solid I could touch, if only I could make myself remove my hand from Charlie's. He was grinning, I saw that much, before I realized I was also smiling like a fool.

He didn't drop my hand, but released it gently, and I'm not going to lie, it sort of felt like it floated back to my side rather than fell. Every part of me felt a little bit like I was floating just then. Silly and giddy. It didn't occur to me to mention that while his wife might've told him a lot about me, she'd barely said anything about him.

"Let's go inside," Meredith suggested.

Both of us followed her without a pause, and I don't know about Charlie, but I was glad to be led so that I didn't have to think about where to put my feet. She kept up the familiar rattle-tatta-tat of her constant conversation all the way, stepping aside without missing a beat to let Charlie open the door for her—and for me. He ushered us in, one hand alighting briefly on the small of my back, there and gone so fast I might've imagined it if everything about this night wasn't already permanently engraving itself in my brain.

Charlie pulled my chair out for me.

Now, I was no stranger to good manners. My parents, despite their fairly free and easy ways, had been sticklers for "please and thank you." But pulling out chairs went beyond their casual attitude. I froze for a second while Meredith settled into hers, and Charlie gave me a curious glance.

"Thanks," I said.

He smiled. "Sure."

"I'm starving." Meredith grabbed up the menu. "What do you want, honey? What are you hungry for?"

"I don't—" I began.

Then stuttered to a stop as Charlie said "I think I—"

It was Meredith who bridged the moment with laughter, making this okay. I liked the way Charlie ducked his head shyly, and covered his eyes with his hand for just a moment before he looked at me. He gestured for me to go first. A gentleman.

"I've never been here before. What's good?" I studied the menu to hide the rising flush in my cheeks.

"I like the T-bone steak," Charlie said. "Oh…unless you're a vegetarian, Tesla."

It charmed me suddenly that he seemed as nervous as I felt. "God, no."

"Oh, our Tesla likes meat." Meredith gave me a slow wink that made my cheeks heat further. "Don't you?"

By then the waiter had come to see what we wanted to drink. Meredith urged Charlie to pick a wine, and they both argued amiably over which bottle to buy, while I sat and watched them be in love. Envy had no taste this time; envy was just a breath threatening to push me over.

"Tesla?" Charlie said at last, while the waiter looked on with barely concealed disdain. "What would you like?"

I knew nothing of wine, but they were both gazing at me expectantly. "Whatever you guys like, I guess."

"Charlie," Meredith said with the slightest edge to her tone, "order the merlot."

He looked at her. "Sure. Okay. We'll take the merlot."

It was the only edge during the dinner. The rest of the time, the three of us laughed and carried on like the best of friends. Charlie had a terrific sense of humor and was what my mother had always called "wicked smaht" in that slight Boston accent that she hadn't passed along to my brother or me. And he was sweet, too, making sure our glasses were filled and that we lacked for nothing.

"Tell Charlie about your summers," Meredith urged as the waiter put our desserts in front of us.

"Oh. My summers." I paused, fork hovering over the piece of chocolate cake. "What do you want me to tell him?"

"He'll be fascinated," Meredith said.

Charlie smiled. "Will I?"

"I spent most of my summers in a commune." I poked the top of the cake with my fork but didn't scrape off a bite. "My parents were both college professors at Franklin and Marshall College. They had this share in a place in upstate New York called The Compound. A real holdover from the sixties, though most of it was built in the seventies. It was really...umm...well..."

What could I say about The Compound? Just as the stories Meredith had asked me to tell didn't sound crazy to me until I said them out loud to someone else, nothing about The Compound seemed interesting or exciting until I started telling stories. Which was why I usually said nothing to anyone who wouldn't understand.

"Creative," I managed to say. "My parents and their friends were creative."

"They named you Tesla," Charlie said. "I'd have guessed that."

I laughed. "Yeah, after Nikola Tesla, not the heavy metal band."

"What?" Meredith looked up from her crème brûlée. "I thought it was for the band."

"Nope. Nikola Tesla, the father of commercial electricity." I lifted my fork, heavy with the weight of chocolate and cream. "But I got off okay. I have a brother named Captain, and you'll never guess who he was named for."

"Captain America," Charlie said.

"He wishes. No. Captain Ahab." I snorted laughter, shaking my head. "He goes by Cap. And you can't ask him about his name—he'll deny it. He'll answer to Captain, but he'll never tell you about the Ahab bit. He thinks our parents were morons."

"Wow. So this compound place. It was full of what, hippies?" Charlie poured more hot water from the small pot over the teabag in my mug. He and I were drinking tea; Meredith had coffee.

"Old hippies. The worst kind. Some of them who'd have been hippies if they'd been old enough in the sixties, but instead sort of had to live out their fantasies during summer break." I paused. It had come out sounding more bitter than I'd intended. "They grew their own food. Lived communally, mutual finances, the works—at least during those three months."

I didn't mention the other communal living, the crèches where the babies and toddlers lived, cared for by whatever set of adults had drawn the duty for that day. The coed dorms for the teens, where we were encouraged to "explore" ourselves…and each other…in ways most parents were actively trying to restrict. Drugs and booze, nothing hard-core. Beer and weed, mostly. I didn't mention the way the adults lived, either. Forming pairs and clusters regardless of the legality of marriages. They didn't call it swinging. They called it "free living."

"Sounds fascinating," Charlie said.

"Told you!" Meredith waved her fork in the air.

When I was younger I thought it was amazing, like the summer camps a lot of my friends talked about, though my parents had always made it very clear we weren't supposed to talk about the stuff that went on there. What we did on our summer vacations was filed under "stuff we only talk about at home." And as a matter of fact, we didn't really even talk about The Compound when we were at home.

Every fall, after three months of indulgence and orgies and who knew what else had gone on, my parents packed up me and Cap and took us back to our suburban development with the fenced-in yard of mostly green grass, the television, our socks and shoes. Hell, our clothes in general, which was always quite a shock after The Compound's lax policy on clothing. We'd spend the winter doing the stuff every family seemed to, but come the end of school in the spring, I could see my parents getting edgy.

This wasn't always a bad thing; anticipation of the summer

ahead made my dad laugh more, leave off the lectures he was prone to give on behavior and grades and the expectations of society, and how we should (or shouldn't) conform. With my mom it could go either way. She could either be slightly manic, packing up the house and singing while she worked, or she could snap and scream at the least provocation that she had "too much to do and not enough time to do it!" Later, I'd figure out it was because my mom didn't love The Compound the way my dad did, and that she had very valid reasons. But back then all I knew was that our lives changed every summer in ways none of my friends' ever did.

When I was still older I'd watch *The Howling* at a friend's Halloween party. While everyone else was jumping and screaming at the scary bits, I was consumed by the atmosphere of the place in the mountains the lady reporter goes to—The Colony. Okay, so The Compound didn't have shape-shifters, but it did have wolves in human clothes. Worse than the dude digging that bullet out of his brain or the lady reporter turning into that cute little kitty-wolf at the end.

Nothing bad had happened to me at The Compound. Nothing to scar me, nothing I'd need therapy for. It had happened around me, before and after me, but not *to* me.

I shrugged. "It was definitely not the sort of childhood you see in Disney movies."

"Well, who the fuck has one of those?" Meredith shrugged and licked her fork. "I mean, even Bambi's mom got shot by a hunter."

"Shortly after my last summer there, The Compound was raided. Big drug bust. A couple people died."

This stopped them both. I hadn't meant to say it, especially not on this, our first date. But it had come out anyway, and I couldn't be sure why.

"Mary Jane?" Meredith asked, perking up.

I shook my head. "Poppies."

She looked confused, but Charlie let out a low chuckle. "Heroin?"

"Opium," I said. "You can harvest it from the flowers and smoke it in that pure state without doing anything to it."

Meredith shook her head. "Opium? Who smokes that?"

"Apparently," I said drily, "wannabe hippies who want something a little stronger than marijuana."

"Wow." Charlie leaned forward a little. "How did that affect you?"

It was a kind question. But before I could tell him that I hadn't been affected at all, that though I knew about the gardens with the flowers, I hadn't even been at The Compound when the raid happened, Meredith interrupted.

"What's it like?" she asked, leaning even closer than Charlie had. "Opium, I mean."

I had to laugh. "Umm…I don't know. I never smoked it."

She looked disappointed. The conversation turned to other things, Meredith mostly leading it, but I caught Charlie gazing at me now and then. He didn't glance away when I caught him. Neither did I.

By the end of the night, I'd figured out this was one of the nicest dates I'd ever had, no matter how unconventional. Maybe that was what I liked about it. The fact that there were two of them. With their attention on me.

Like Chase and Chance, Meredith and Charlie were a unit. Husband and wife, but more than that. Clearly friends. Comfortable enough with each other to know in advance where to laugh at the jokes, or to pass the cream and sugar without being asked. Yet also like those boys from my past, they were individuals, clearly told apart.

In the parking lot, I waited for them to ask me if I wanted to go home with them. I could see the question in Meredith's eyes, though I didn't know Charlie quite well enough to read his. I put a hand on the handle of my car door, pausing coyly, giving one or both of them the opportunity to make the offer.

I still wasn't sure what I'd say.

"This was great, Tesla." Charlie moved forward first.

I tipped my face, but instead of kissing my lips, his mouth brushed my cheek. His hand squeezed briefly on my hip, then withdrew. He took two steps back. I might've been embarrassed that I'd offered a lover's kiss and been granted one from a friend, except that nothing about Charlie ever felt like it could make me embarrassed.

That was when I knew that when the time came, I was definitely going to say yes.

Chapter
16

At four in the morning it's hard to be perky even if you're a morning person, which I've never been. Some people I knew would just be rolling in to bed—my brother, for example, might even have still been out and about. I, on the other hand, had to get to the Mocha by five so I could open at six. There could be a riot if those doors didn't open on time.

When I came upstairs, the dark form huddled at the kitchen table startled me into a terrified squeak. I stumbled back, barely keeping myself from tumbling down the stairs again by grabbing the edge of the door frame. For several agonizing seconds my heels hovered in empty space. *This is it,* I thought, strangely calm. *Look out below, I'm gonna eat it.*

But then I managed to right myself, overcorrect and trip forward over my feet. I dropped my purse, spilling the mess inside all over the linoleum. I knocked into the round table hard enough to shift it.

"Nice," said the voice I knew, even if darkness obscured the face it was coming out of.

"Dammit, Vic! You scared the shit out of me!" I put a hand on my heart, the other on the back of a chair. I really thought I just might faint before I forced myself to breathe. Shakily, I went to the sink to draw a glass of water.

I didn't want to ask him why he was sitting there in the dark. Like a coward, I didn't want to talk with him about it, and that wasn't fair. Vic had done his share of being my shoulder. If he needed someone to listen to him, I of all people shouldn't forsake him.

"Sorry," he said quietly. He got up, went to the fridge, pulled out a beer. He didn't crack the top. Just tapped it a few times before rolling it between his palms.

I could see this because my eyes had adjusted to the dim light. I turned, leaning against the counter, and drank my water. I'd be drinking coffee or tea all day long at work, and wanted to get something else in my system. Still, it was too early for beer, even for me.

"You're up early," I said. "Or maybe it's late."

"Max had a nightmare about half an hour ago. Got up with him so Elaine could sleep. Couldn't get back to sleep myself."

"Ah." There wasn't much more to say about it than that, but I tried. "Warm milk?"

This got a laugh from him, which was good. "Um, no. Gross."

"I have to get to work. But…" I drifted closer to let my hand squeeze his shoulder, just once. Once was always more than enough with him. "You okay? You need…something?"

He looked up at me. The square of glass over the sink had

lightened. Day was coming. I could see the faint outline of his eyebrows, the bridge of his nose and shadow of his mouth. I loved this man in complicated ways neither of us understood and probably never would. But for now, all I could offer him was the squeeze of my hand.

"No. No, I'm good. Hey," Vic said too casually, so my chin went up immediately, my shoulders squared in preparation. "How was your date?"

"Fantastic," I told him, without even pretending not to grin like a fiend. "Best I've had in a long time."

Vic's brows rose. "Huh. Really."

"Yes. It was awesome." I punched the air, one-two. Did a little dance, my Chucks scuffling on the worn linoleum. "Awesome."

Vic let out a low chuckle. "Okay. Well. Good. What's his name again?"

I saw right through that one, but told him anyway. "Charlie."

"Charlie what?"

"Stone," I said, after half a second.

"Charlie Stone. I'll keep that in mind."

"Jesus, Vic," I sighed. "Don't Google him. Please? Leave the cyber-stalking to me."

"Everyone Googles, Tesla."

I held up a hand. "Vic, I swear to you…"

He laughed then, a real one, loud enough to wake the kids if he wasn't careful. "You're so easy to get riled up."

I punched him in the biceps. Hard. "Shut up. Jerk."

From upstairs came the creak of floorboards and the murmur of voices. If we were going to get out of here without being swarmed by Vic's children, we had to leave now. We shared a glance, both of us thinking it at the same time and sharing a guilty grin in the gray light of dawn. He grabbed his keys. I took my purse. We were out the back door and heading for the alley, giggling like lunatics as we leaped the concrete back steps and hit the sidewalk.

He reached his car first. I got to mine a minute later. We raised our keys at each other in a mutual salute that made me laugh.

He was totally going to Google Charlie.

Chapter
17

They took me to the movies next, Meredith and Charlie. He sat between us and passed the popcorn we all shared. It was a romantic comedy, one of those movies with half a dozen subplots that somehow all tie up together at the end. I'm sure it was funny and sweet and romantic and possibly even sexy, but I was so distracted by the shift of Charlie's thigh against me, the brush of his fingers on mine in the popcorn bucket, I couldn't have even said who was in the film, much less how it ended. There was something I did know by the time the final credits rolled.

I wanted him.

I wanted to know if he tasted as good as he smelled. How he kissed. I wanted to know how big his cock was, if it was as pretty as the rest of him. What he could do with those strong hands.

They were practically offering me Charlie on a platter. No worries about if he liked me or not. What he'd want from me...or not. Sure, there were plenty of worst-case scenarios I could think up if I were the sort to spend a lot of time brooding about what-ifs and might've-beens. But that was my brother's schtick, not mine.

In the parking lot, Meredith linked her arm through mine and tugged me close, to say into my ear, "So...?"

Charlie had gone ahead of us when we'd lingered in the bathroom. He was in their car, the overhead light on, looking at something on his phone. I liked the way the light slanted over him. I liked that he had a fancy phone. I liked that he'd worn a shirt with buttons and a vest with jeans and a thick black belt to go to the movies, and I liked the way his hair was short enough to stay out of his eyes.

"So...what?" I said, just to tease.

Her grip tightened on me a little, and she turned me to face her. "So, do you want to come back to our house with us?"

She must've seen something in my face I didn't even know was there, because a shadow passed over hers. Meredith pulled me a little closer, and for one breathtaking moment I thought she meant to kiss me. But she just leaned in to whisper into my ear, "I don't want to force you."

I breathed in her perfume, and as always, it sent tendrils of arousal all through me. "I'm not forcible. Don't you know that by now?"

Her laugh moved over me. "So come on. Come with us."

And I did.

It was sweet, Charlie's hesitation. I'd forgotten he'd met me only twice, that the easy friendship I'd built up with his wife had grown during months of chatting over coffee. It was sweet and simple the way he waited for me to make the first move.

Actually, it was Meredith who made it. She put a hand on the small of my back, urging me forward inch by inch until Charlie and I stood face-to-face. I'd worn heels for this date, and their height put me closer to eye level with him. Mouth level, too.

"Tesla," she said. "Meet Charlie. Charlie, Tesla."

His lips curved into a smile and he drew in a breath that lifted his shoulders. "Hi."

"Hi, Charlie." With Meredith behind me I could smell the scent of her perfume and feel the heat of her hand, but it was only her husband's face I could see.

His gaze flickered past me, over my shoulder, and whatever he saw there must've given him some courage, because he put a hand on my hip. We moved a little closer. I slid my hands up the front of his shirt.

Neither of us moved.

Not until the pressure of Meredith's hand on me moved me toward him. My head angled. I was already opening my mouth when I kissed him. His hand tightened on my hip, and Meredith, perhaps feeling her job had been done, let go.

Then it was just the two of us, spinning in the magic of a first kiss.

It didn't last long, and he was the one who broke it with a small sigh. His eyes were still closed when he pulled slightly away. Under my palm I felt the hard and sudden beat of his heart, the subtle tremor of his muscles. I didn't want him to be afraid.

I slid my thigh between his, pressing upward just enough to make him give another sigh. I kissed him again. I moved one hand to the back of his neck, where his hair wasn't long enough to sink my fingers into. I kissed him hard, then harder, and this time I was the one to break it. To pull away. And this time, Charlie's eyes were open when I did.

"We should go upstairs," Meredith murmured from behind me, her heat against my back, though she was no longer touching me. "C'mon, baby. Let's take Tesla to bed."

Upstairs, she pushed open the door to their bedroom. It smelled like her. The four-poster bed was huge and made up as though it were going to be photographed for a decorating magazine. Smooth, elegant comforter in shades of pale green and gold, a mountain of matching pillows.

It struck me then, what this meant. Asking me to fuck her husband was one thing, but to do it here in the bed they shared somehow made this all more important and intimate. And I stuttered at that intimacy, though Meredith was murmuring low, encouraging words and Charlie was holding back to let me walk ahead of him into the room.

I stopped halfway to their bed and looked back at the doorway, where he lingered. My shoes had left marks in the thick, cream-colored carpet that had obviously never suffered the presence of a child or even a pet. It still bore the crosshatch marks of a recent vacuuming, unmarred by anything but the trail of my steps.

Meredith had been the one worried about forcing me, but Charlie was the one who seemed to notice something was wrong. "Tesla?"

I gave myself a little shake and looked at both of them. "I'm just…this is…"

In three long strides, he crossed the room. He put his hands on my upper arms, his eyes searching mine. Charlie wasn't smiling, and somehow that made it easier. That he didn't seem to be taking this lightly.

He kissed me. Long, sweet, slow. Kind. His hand came up to cup the back of my head, and when we both pulled away, I was breathless from it. Somehow we'd moved to press against each other, his hand on my ass holding me to his crotch, where I felt the totally shiver-making thickness of his cock through his jeans.

"Your mouth tastes so good," Charlie said, never moving his gaze from mine. "Can I taste the rest of you, too?"

I nodded, incapable of words with my mouth gone so dry. I found my voice enough to sigh when he slid slowly to his knees in front of me, his hands resting lightly on the backs of my knees where my skin dimpled. He looked up at me, those blue eyes still so serious, but then his mouth quirked. Just on one side. And he closed his eyes when he turned his face to kiss my bare thigh just below the hem of my skirt.

He kissed me there the way he'd kissed my mouth, sweet and slow, sucking gently on the soft flesh of my inner thigh before nudging his nose a little higher against my panties. I'd dressed in anticipation of getting naked, glad now I'd picked this lacy pair that let his breath and the wetness of his mouth reach me through the material. I swallowed the murmur of his name, which, like the great big bed, seemed too intimate for this first time.

I looked at Meredith, who'd crossed to the bed and pulled the comforter away to reveal plain white sheets. She smoothed them with her hand as she pushed the pillows aside. She unbuttoned her blouse and shrugged out of it to stand in her skirt and a black satin bra. Watching us, she unhooked it at the back and hunched her shoulders to let the straps fall forward, though she held the front of the bra with one hand so it didn't come off.

Charlie moved his hands from the backs of my knees up

my thighs, fingers hooking in my panties to pull them down my legs. I stepped out of them, looking at him. My skirt covered me, but I could still feel the air on my skin. He pushed my skirt up, slowly revealing me to him, his eyes on mine until the last moment, when the material gripped in his hands bunched at my hips. Then he returned his face between my thighs, and I felt the pressure of his lips on my clit.

I bit back a cry, one hand going involuntarily to his head as my hips bumped forward. The wet swipe of his tongue against me made my eyelids flutter, my feet shift apart, my pussy tilt toward him so he could access every part of me. Charlie made a low, satisfied noise, muffled against my flesh.

I couldn't stop myself from looking at Meredith. She'd tossed her bra to the side, and her breasts were high and round, with cherry nipples standing up hard and tight. I wondered what sort of noise she'd make if I sucked them as sweetly as Charlie was working my clit. The thought forced swirling heat all through me, fierce enough to spin the world a little bit.

I didn't say a word, but Charlie looked up at me. He licked his lips, then got to his feet. "Come to the bed."

Meredith had slipped out of her skirt and lay on those clean white sheets in nothing but a pair of tiny black panties. Her fingers idly stroked her clit through the satin. She reached for my hand.

"Come here, Tesla."

I'd thought fucking the Murphy boys had prepared me for this. I'd figured the few times I'd gone to bed with girls would make this easy. I'd believed my crush on Meredith, the fact that her husband was sweet and handsome, and I was horny, meant I was ready.

I was wrong.

Oh, how I was wrong.

I shook when Meredith took my hand and linked her fingers through mine. I shivered when Charlie slipped my blouse over my head and unhooked my bra, then covered my breasts with his hands from behind, the heat of him all along my back and his cock nudging my ass. I got up on the high bed next to her on my hands and knees. The sheets were smooth and clean and crisp under my palms and against my shins.

"I want him to make you come with his mouth. I want to watch," Meredith murmured.

I looked at Charlie, his mouth still wet, his face flushed and eyes bright. His hair had finally become mussed. He'd loosened his tie and undone a few buttons at his throat, but was still fully dressed. He looked at his wife when she spoke, then used the back of his hand to wipe his mouth.

"Do you want me to?" he asked me.

It was Charlie who made it easy.

In answer, I rolled onto my back and hooked my thumbs in my waistband to push my skirt down. My head rested just next to her bare, smooth thigh. I spread my legs, offering myself to him.

Charlie smiled. Our eyes met. Something wordless but completely understood bridged the space between us, made the distance disappear. He crawled up on the bed and settled on his knees between my legs. He ran his hands up my legs, over my belly, no longer looking at my face but exploring every inch of me with his gaze.

I shifted just enough to look up at Meredith, but she was watching her husband as he ran his mouth along my shin and knee and thigh. When he reached my pussy, her eyes fluttered closed just for a moment. Her hand moved up to cup her breast, to tweak the tight, red nipple. Her mouth opened and the tip of her tongue snuck out to touch the center of her top lip.

At the heat of Charlie's mouth on my clit it was hard to keep my eyes open, but I managed. I didn't want to miss any of this, not a single second. Charlie had been kneeling, but now he eased his body down flat on the bed. He slid his hand beneath my ass, lifting me just a little.

"Oh, baby, that's so good." Meredith's eyes were open now. She watched him, not me. Her hand caressed his hair. "That's right, baby, lick her clit. Make her come."

Charlie's mouth was working magic, no doubt about that, but I wasn't even close to coming. I had an instant of alarm—I could get to orgasm swiftly enough, but I'd been with lovers who thought women's bodies were like machines. Push the button, get the prize. It would take me a little more than that.

I got up on my elbows to watch Charlie eat my pussy. Meredith sank her fingers into Charlie's hair. She pressed him closer, too close. Too hard. She shifted his head—not the way I liked it.

I put my hand on hers.

We all stopped.

Delicate business, this dance of three. It takes more than choreography; it takes sensitivity. She'd said she wanted her husband to make me come. Maybe she thought she was helping. I tugged her hand up to my mouth and licked the pad of her forefinger, then took the tip inside my mouth and sucked enough to wet it. Then I used her finger to circle my nipple and get it hard.

I wanted her to kiss me, but she didn't. Her fingers pinched gently on my nipple, then she pulled away. She shifted onto the pillows without a word. The finger I'd licked slipped inside her panties, and her head tipped back with a sigh.

Charlie hadn't moved from between my legs, though he'd paused in his licking and sucking. "Meredith?"

"Make her come," she said in a dreamy voice.

He looked up at me. I put my hand on his hair, not tugging or pushing the way she had. He surprised me when he rolled us both so that he was on his back and I straddled his face. My palms skidded on the soft sheets, but Charlie's hands on my hips kept me steady. His seeking mouth found my clit.

I laughed. This seemed to startle them both. Meredith looked at me. Charlie's tongue paused in its delicious rhythm.

"Tesla?" Meredith said.

"Surprised me. Feels good, though, Charlie. Don't stop."

"Feels good?" Meredith smiled. The bit of weirdness passed. She looked like her old self. Her fingers circled, circled inside her panties, and her thighs dropped open as her hips shifted. "Good."

I wanted to move between her legs, to sip and lap at her pretty pussy the way Charlie was so thoroughly pleasing mine—but in this position I couldn't reach without shifting around. Also, though it seemed as if Meredith was into me— at least so far as she was getting off on watching her husband eat me out—I still wasn't so sure she was really into girls. Besides, Charlie had found the pace and pressure that was hitting me just right, and it was hard to concentrate on anything more than how good it felt.

I wasn't going to fuck this up. I had a handsome man between my legs whose oral talents were pretty damn stellar. And though I'd have gladly extended the favor toward Meredith or even Charlie, had he taken off his clothes and made it possible, nobody was asking me to do anything but relax and enjoy it. What else was there to think about, really?

As far as I was concerned, not a damn thing.

When I rocked my clit against his tongue, Charlie let out another of those sexy, helpless-sounding sighs. Instead of laughing this time, I eased my breath out in a moan that Meredith echoed. She shifted, her knees falling wider apart as she worked at her pussy. Her back arched.

I couldn't help kissing her knee. Pleasure had filled me to overflowing. I was going to come soon. I wanted my mouth on something. My hands.

Her skin was soft, the fine hairs she'd missed shaving a little prickly on my cheek. Ticklish on my lips when I mouthed her skin. Meredith twitched when my mouth touched her. She shifted, the bed rocking as the three of us moved, and I couldn't tell if she pulled her knee away on purpose or if it just happened.

She did move a few moments later, getting behind me. I looked over my shoulder to watch her work at Charlie's belt buckle, then pull his pants down. His cock sprang out into her hand. She took him into her mouth.

Twisting in this position hurt my neck, so I turned back the way I'd been. Then nothing mattered but the fact that I was tipping up and over and into this great, swirling whirlpool of pleasure. I gave in to it, thinking of nothing but Charlie's tongue on my clit. The press of his fingers into my pussy and the way they spread me in just the right way.

I couldn't see if Meredith was still using her hand on herself, or even if she was sucking Charlie's cock with as much enthusiasm as he was giving my pussy, but by the way he started licking me faster, I thought she probably was.

He moaned against me. Meredith gave a stuttering cry. And I came on Charlie's tongue, my hips bucking. My fingers dug into the sheets, the mattress dimpling under my touch.

And after, I laughed again, my face pressed into the soft

coolness of expensive fabric. Charlie moved from under me so I could collapse, belly down, onto the bed. His hands drifted over my bare ass and thighs, and I twisted so I could look at him. He'd pushed up onto his knees and stared down at me, his lips parted as though he meant to join me in laughter.

Meredith was always beautiful, but she looked so lovely in the aftermath of her pleasure that it took my breath away. Her gaze went to Charlie first, then to me. She grinned. She grabbed his tie and pulled him forward to kiss him.

"Mmm. God, baby, that was amazing." Her gaze flickered toward me. "I can taste you on him."

With my orgasm still running like heated silver through every inch of me, I was feeling more than a bit liquidy myself. I ran a hand up Charlie's back and leaned into him. "Is that a bad thing?"

Meredith slid her tongue across her lower lip, then caught it in her teeth, denting the soft flesh. She tilted her head to study her husband. "What do you think, love?"

Charlie shook his head. "No. I don't think so."

"I'm starving," she said suddenly, and bounced off the bed. Meredith grabbed a robe from the chair and was all the way to the door before she paused to look over her shoulder at us. "C'mon. Food."

Charlie and I glanced at each other. We laughed at the same time. I'd have kissed him then, but he was already getting off the bed. He zipped up, then held out his hand to me. "C'mon, Tesla. Food."

"So…not only did you just give me some incredible head," I said, following, "but you're gonna feed me, too?"

He looked at me, eyes lingering on mine, though his gaze spent more than a few seconds on the rest of my naked body. "Yep. Apparently, Meredith wants food."

I picked up my panties and stepped into them, but settled for pulling my T-shirt over my head without a bra. "And let me guess...you do everything Meredith wants?"

I'd said it lightly, teasing, but Charlie only gave me half a smile. "Well. She is my wife."

"Yeah," I said. "I guess she is."

Chapter

18

I didn't sleep over, for a few different reasons. I hadn't told Vic and Elaine I'd be out all night, and felt bad that they might worry if I didn't come home. I had to work in the morning and didn't have any extra clothes with me. But the main reason was even simpler than all that: they didn't ask me.

Meredith walked me out to my car, though. She'd shoved her bare feet into boots and pulled on a parka over her undies, and her teeth chattered as she danced in place to keep warm while I unlocked the driver's side door.

I thought and hoped she might kiss me, but instead she pressed her cheek to mine and gave me a squeeze. "Mmm, this was great."

"Yeah." I'd forgotten my mittens and tucked my fingers into my armpits to keep them warm; my keys dug into my side. "Did you...was it...okay?"

"Of course it was. It was great!" She beamed as she danced. "You're fucking amazing, you know that?"

I wasn't quite sure about that, but it was still nice to hear. "So…will I see you tomorrow? Or later today, I guess. At the Mocha."

I was babbling, but Meredith didn't seem to notice. "Oh. I'm sure, of course. Why wouldn't you?"

Because I just fucked your husband while you watched, I thought. Because he'd gone down on me like the *Titanic* after hitting an iceberg. Just because.

"Silly Tesla," she said, and gave me another hug, then backed up the sidewalk toward their front door. "Drive carefully. Text me when you get home, okay? The roads look icy."

I had so much else to say and no words to say it. So instead I nodded and got in my car and drove home. I texted her from the driveway; there was room in the garage for only Vic and Elaine's vehicles, and I wasn't quite ready to brave the cold between my car and the front door. As it turned out, I was smart to gather up those few extra moments of warmth, because when I got to the front door, I couldn't get in.

"Shit." My fingers were already getting numb as I fumbled with the key, which didn't fit neatly into the lock the way it should've. It was nearly three in the morning, everyone was in bed, and Vic had obviously made his rounds.

I tried it again. This time, it broke off in the lock. Shit.

I had my phone in my purse. Elaine wouldn't appreciate it if I woke them all up by calling the house phone. I could send Vic a text, but he wouldn't like being woken an hour before he had to get up. And that was if he even heard the ping of the message coming in. I slept with my phone next to me on the nightstand, but Vic often left his downstairs next to his wallet and keys, so he wouldn't forget it when he went off to work.

"Shit," I muttered again, and took two steps off the square of concrete that made up the front porch.

Vic's house was on a nice residential street with decent lighting from the streetlamps, but around the side and back of the house, along the screened porch, it was all darkness. Our neighbor had a motion-activated light I set off as I walked around the house, but it shone mostly into his own backyard and made his dog bark. It didn't do much for me. I settled for using the flashlight app on my phone, which meant exposing my already frozen fingers to the air.

Which meant I dropped my phone into the bushes along the side of the porch. And into the puddle that ran off from the gutters and hadn't yet frozen. I wasn't sure which was worse, the splash of water or the crunch of plastic on concrete.

"Fuck! Fuck, fuck..." I grabbed at it, found it, but couldn't see if it had been permanently damaged. I clutched it to me with a silent prayer to the gods of technology that I wouldn't have to replace it.

Then, determined, freezing and more than a little pissed off, I yanked on the porch door hard enough to pull the small hook-and-eye lock out of the wood. The hook dangled, still in the eye, and when I closed it behind me I took the time to shove the screw end back into the door. Vic had fixed it a dozen times, but the wood was old and soft, and too many people had yanked the lock loose.

Vic had winterized the windows with large plastic sheets, but it wasn't any warmer inside. At least the furniture was all stacked neatly and covered with cloths, so I didn't have to worry about barking my shins or tripping over something. I had only the smallest hope that the back door, which led to the den, would be unlocked. It wasn't. Which left the small, narrow windows set just above the floor. One peeked into the rec room, the other the basement storage room. Both were just wide enough for me to get my shoulders through, although if my hips would fit was anyone's guess, and I could only hope I'd be able to make it without ending up like Pooh stuck in Rabbit's doorway.

I'd never had a curfew since I'd come to live here with Vic, so had never sneaked into the house this way before. But I had learned how to work the window free of its frame and get out through it in case of a fire. Vic was big on drills for things like that, and since I slept in the basement, he'd put me through all the steps of what to do if the house was burning.

Of course, unlatching the window from its frame on the inside, and pulling it out the way it was manufactured to do, was totally different from wiggling it from the outside. Being unable to feel my fingers didn't make it any easier, either. Cursing, and close to frustrated tears, I finally worked my fingertips into the small ridges on the sides of the window frame. I pushed, then pushed harder. Metal squealed, and the window came free so fast I fell forward and smacked my face against the rough brick around it. But total bonus, I didn't drop it.

I managed to hold on to it with one hand and lower it down inside, to the couch directly under the window. Then I put my head and shoulders through, sucking in my belly as it scraped the frame. I had to shift sideways to get my hips through, which left me hanging upside down, and wondering why in the hell I hadn't gone through feetfirst.

But finally, after much maneuvering, I was able to lower myself onto the couch, and contort myself so that when my legs finally made it all the way through, I wasn't falling and breaking the window or anything.

None of that mattered much when I rolled off the couch onto the carpeted but still hard-as-concrete rec room floor.

Or when a pair of strong hands grabbed me by the back of the neck and one arm, and hauled me upright before shoving me facedown into the carpet again.

I was too surprised to scream, so I kicked instead. Thrashing wildly, I got in a couple good blows before my assailant picked me up again and hurtled me down—this time onto the couch. And the window. Which shattered against my elbow, thankfully protected by my thick pea coat. Then I was thrown back onto the floor, this time with a knee in my back.

I finally managed to scream. Not very loud, since I had no breath and my face was smashed into the carpet. I was a mass of pain. I had glass in my hair; I could hear it crunching against the carpet.

"Tesla?"

The weight on my back disappeared. The hurting, grabbing hands turned kind, helping me up before leaving me to sit woozily. The lights came on.

"Shit. Oh, shit, Tesla. What the fuck were you doing?" Vic crouched in front of me, grasping my upper arms gently. "Oh, honey. What the hell?"

It must've been really bad for him to call me honey, an endearment he used only when the kids or Elaine were hurt or sick. I drew in a breath, thinking to yell at him, and found no voice. My elbow throbbed, but I didn't think I was cut. My face hurt, my back and shoulders ached and even my knees felt scraped raw.

Vic stroked my hair off my forehead with his fingertips, looking into my eyes. "I'm sorry. Christ, you're lucky I didn't shoot you."

I hadn't noticed the gun. A SIG Sauer pistol, strapped to his belt in a leather case. I'd seen it hundreds of times before, of course. Had even shot it a few times on the range. I knew what sort of damage it could do, and yet I still couldn't quite wrap my mind around why Vic would have used it on me.

"I heard someone trying to get in," he said. "Then the dog barking next door. Someone at the back door. I didn't know it was you. Dammit, Tesla, why didn't you just knock? Or, Christ, call me? I'd have let you in!"

"I didn't want to wake you," I managed to say. My mouth felt numb, my lips swollen. I realized I could taste blood. I'd bitten my tongue.

"What the fuck were you thinking?"

"What was I thinking? What were *you* thinking, playing Rambo? Why didn't you turn on the lights first, see who it was before you jumped me? God, Vic, did you really think it was someone breaking in?"

"Yes," he said flatly. "I did."

I swallowed blood and pressed my fingers to the inside corners of my eyes. "Shit, I broke the window."

"Are you cut? Bleeding?" He started probing my arm. "Your coat's ripped."

"Great. That was my favorite coat. Son of a bitch, Vic."

"I'll buy you another one." He flexed my elbow. "It's not broken. What about the rest of you? Take this off. Let me check you out."

I jerked away from him and got to my unsteady feet. "You've done enough."

Vic stood, too. "I said I was sorry. Jesus, Tesla. I'm supposed to apologize for wanting to protect my family? I thought someone was down here. I thought maybe he'd go after you... hurt you...."

My anger was fading, replaced by bruises. I couldn't stay mad at him. It had been pretty dumb of me to try coming in through the window. And his concern touched me enough that tears welled up.

"Shit," Vic said miserably. "I'm sorry. Don't cry. Don't, please?"

I swiped at my face. "I think I need some ice."

"C'mon. I'll help you." And he did, up the stairs into the kitchen, where he made me sit quietly at the table while I took off my coat and we examined my elbow.

Vic handed me an economy-size bag of frozen peas. "Here. The kids won't eat these, anyway."

I put them on my face over my right eye, the one that had been most mashed into the floor. "Thanks."

He made us both tea, taking the kettle off the burner before it could whistle, then sat across from me with his mug in his big hands. We didn't say much. I was really starting to ache, and didn't want to say anything, since complaining would make him feel bad.

"You should call off work," Vic said. "Maybe even go to the doctor."

Calling off work was a definite. I didn't think I could keep my eyes open for my shift, much less be perky. Or deal with Joy. "I don't need a doctor. Just sleep."

"I'm sorry," Vic said again.

I put the peas on the table between us so I could sip at the hot tea. Once again we were sharing time in the dark, waiting for the sun to rise while the house slept all around us. It seemed as good a time as any, so I asked, "What the hell is going on with you?"

He didn't say anything. He turned the mug around and around until the whisper of the porcelain against the wood had me reaching over to put my hand on his wrist. He stopped. He still wore the gun on his belt, though I couldn't see it below the edge of the table. But it made me realize something else.

"You have your clothes on."

"Yeah? What?"

My frown hurt my mouth. "I mean, you weren't wearing pajamas."

"I put these on when I got up. When I heard someone trying to break in."

"Which was me." I sipped hot tea and winced at how it burned my bitten tongue. I glanced over at him, caught his eye. Knew something at once by the shifty gaze. "Liar."

"Fine. I was already up."

"Because you hadn't gone to bed yet? What were you doing?"

"Putting together the crib in the baby's room. Making sure it was all good. Meets the regs and all that." Vic twisted the mug in his hands again, but stopped when he saw my look.

"You couldn't wait to do that until the morning? The baby's not coming tonight, Vic." And even if it did, it would sleep in the bassinet in their room with them for the first few months.

"I was maybe doing some stuff on the laptop, too."

This was completely out of character for him. Vic hardly ever used the ancient desktop, having given it up to the kids and sad-sack me when my laptop died. He'd bought Elaine a laptop to use on the days her pregnancy sickness kept her in bed. She could watch movies on it, check her email, pay bills and shop. I'd never known Vic to use it, but apparently that didn't mean he didn't.

"In the baby's room?"

"Elaine was sleeping." He sounded defensive. "I had to look up some stuff about how to put the crib together—stupid instructions were missing. And some other stuff."

Here's the thing about Vic—he's a magnificent liar. It makes him an excellent card player, and he never gives away what he bought you for your birthday. He can look you in the eye and tell you a flat-out, even outrageous, lie without blinking, and have you so convinced he's telling the truth you'd go to court and swear it in front of a judge. The fact I knew he was lying now wasn't due to any special skill on my part, no supernaturally close bond we shared. If he was letting me see the lie, it was because, for some reason, he wanted me to see it.

"You're going back to it. Thinking about it, anyway. Aren't you." I didn't want any more tea, but I drank some to give me some nonchalant action to add to my deliberately casual tone.

Again, Vic said nothing, which was more than enough of an answer.

"So…why the big secret?" I asked. "It's nothing to be ashamed of, Vic."

"Elaine doesn't know."

"That you're thinking of going back to your old job?"

"That I used to have an old job."

Stunned, I sat back in my chair. "What?"

"She doesn't know," Vic said in a warning voice. "And I'm not sure I want her to know. Not yet."

"You can't…this is…" Again, words failed me. I shook my head, which made it ache. I put the peas back against my eye. "You have to tell her."

"Of course I have to tell her," he snapped. "Especially if I go back. Which I haven't decided yet."

"Where is all of this coming from?" The peas were getting warm, but still felt good on my eye. They had the added benefit of blocking part of my vision, so I didn't have to look him in the face while all this was going on. I wasn't sure what my expression looked like.

"A buddy of mine called me up. Said they needed some good guys on this new team he was setting up here in Harrisburg. Said he could guarantee me a great starting salary. Benefits. In case you didn't notice, Tesla, I have another kid on the way."

This time, his words hurt more than my frown. "Wow, that's a shitty thing to say to me. Like I don't live here, too. Like I wouldn't notice something important like that."

He sighed. "I'm sorry."

"You've said you were sorry more tonight than you've said to me for the entire time I've known you." It was an exaggeration that felt true. "Stop it."

"The hours would be kind of shit, but on the other hand, I'd be able to be more flexible."

"Sounds like you've already decided." I got up to put the peas in a plastic freezer bag, pulling a marker from the junk drawer to scribble "DO NOT EAT" on them in big block letters. As if that were a worry.

"I can't decide until I talk to Elaine."

"No shit, Sherlock." I faced him, the counter at my back, my hands gripping the edge. "I just don't understand why you never told her before."

"She only ever knew me as a guy who fixed cars. Sold cars. She never knew me as a cop, Tesla. And by the time we got together..." Vic's voice lowered. "I didn't want her to know me as that guy. That's all."

My lips pressed together. I probed a cut on the inside of my cheek with my sore tongue. Neither pain kept me from speaking. "You say 'that guy' like you have a reason to be ashamed."

He looked at me. "Don't I?"

"No." I wanted to cross the small distance between us and take his face in my hands. I wanted to gaze into his eyes and force him to see how wrong he was. If getting on my knees in front of him would've convinced him, I'd have done that. Instead I stayed where I was, as did he, the way we'd grown so accustomed to doing.

He shook his head. "I messed up. Did shit I shouldn't have."

"You mean me."

"No. I mean…shit. No, Tesla, you're not shit. That's not what I meant."

I gave him a steady stare. "What, then? You mean the rest of it? You mean taking what you knew back to your boss so he'd have enough reason to send in people to raid The Compound? You were doing your job."

"People died," Vic said tightly.

"You need to tell her, Vic. It's a job. It's not the end of the world." I paused. "She already knows about The Compound. About me. It's not like any of that was a secret. I don't get why the rest of it was."

But I did know. I saw it on his face. Because he was ashamed of what he'd done. No matter what had come after, how he'd done more good than bad, Vic still felt guilty.

"You wish you'd never fooled around with me," I said. In all the years I'd lived with him, we'd never talked about the fact we'd once made each other come.

"Tesla…"

I held up a hand, moving past him toward the basement. "I get it. I just thought we were both past it. It happened. And I don't regret it, but you do. So maybe every time you look at me you think about how you can't believe you fucked around with me—"

"I should never have done it!" he said in a muted shout.

From upstairs, I heard the creak of floorboards.

"Because I was too young. Because you were there working. Because, because, because." I'd have spat the words, except it hurt my mouth too much. So I settled for whispering fiercely. "Here's the fact, Vic. I came on to you. I wanted to fuck you. I wanted you. And here's another little piece of information for you to fret and mutter over. I loved every single second we were together. I loved making you come, and I loved how you made me come, and I love that I know what I know about sex because of what you taught me. Okay? I don't regret anything about it, because I love you."

He made a noise in the back of his throat.

"I'm not *in love* with you," I added quickly. "I love you, I love Elaine, I love your kids. I love that we are a family. I love that you took me and Cap in when our parents were too fucked up with their own shit to do right by us. I love that you are a good and decent man who protects the people he loves with everything that he has. I love you despite the fact we messed around and not because of it, Vic, which is a little bit of a mess, I know. But if I can get past it, if your wife, for fuck's sake, can get past it, I think you should be able to get past it, too. And I hate that you can't. I hate that you allow what we did—what we both did, by the way, not just you—to make everything we have now somehow dirty. I hate that."

I didn't wait for him to answer, just went down the stairs.

Chapter

19

I must've sounded truly awful on the phone, because Joy didn't even give me a hard time about not making it in to work. She did ask if I'd be in the day after, since she had another appointment and she didn't want to leave Darek in charge, which was stupid since he was just as capable of running the shop as I was. Anyway, I assured her I would be, and I spent the day holed up in my room watching old movies and playing board games with the kids so Elaine could spend the day in her own bed.

I didn't want to tell her I knew something she didn't, and I wasn't happy that Vic had put me in that position. Avoiding her was easier. I didn't think she noticed, since it was one of her rough days and she was just grateful to have me there to keep Max and Simone occupied.

We even baked cupcakes toward the end of the day, when

my aches and pains had finally started fading. I'd expected a bunch of bruises, but I guess I was tougher than I'd thought, because despite the soreness, very few had shown up.

"Tesla, I love you," Simone told me matter-of-factly as we spread thick chocolate icing on top of the cupcakes, which had come out of the pan a little misshapen but still delicious.

"I luff you!" Max added. He was completely covered in icing and was busily licking more from his fingers.

"I love you guys, too." I used the rubber scraper against the side of the bowl to take my own fingerful of goodness. "Mmmm."

Apparently having decided declaring her love aloud wasn't enough, Simone put her arms around my stomach and squeezed as hard as she could. For a little girl, it was pretty hard. Added to the already sore bits and pieces I had, I admit I was less than thrilled by this, but I managed to hug her back without too much agony or getting icing in her pale blond hair.

She tipped her face to look up at me. "You won't ever leave us, will you?"

"Umm…" I wasn't a believer in lying to kids, Santa and the Tooth Fairy excluded. "I don't have plans to leave you anytime soon."

"Cappy left." Simone scowled at this.

Since Cap had moved out on his own before Max was born, I wasn't sure why this so affronted her, but it made me laugh. "Yeah, well, he wanted his own place."

"He lives wif Lynds," Max said. "Not hims own place."

"Sure, but before he lived with Lynds, Cappy had his own apartment." He'd asked me to move in with him, but I preferred Vic's basement to the crap-hole apartment my brother had found for himself.

"But you wanted to stay here with us!" Simone beamed as if I'd done it as a personal favor.

The truth was, I'd thought about moving out many times. Life with babies, especially ones that aren't your own, isn't exactly all sunshine and roses. Nor is living in a basement, for that matter. Sure, I wanted my own place. I could afford one, maybe even without a roommate. But I had stayed because living in Vic's house felt like home. His wife and kids, family. Not conventional, sure, but that felt more normal to me than anything else would've.

"Because you luff us," said Max.

"Sure. Because I love you. All of you." I kissed the top of Simone's hair and pushed her gently away so we could finish the cupcakes.

"You love Mama. And me. And Max. And Daddy, too." She reached for the small plastic container of candy confetti shaped like dinosaurs, and began adding them liberally to the cupcakes.

"Yep. All of you." It was true, but after last night's conversation with Vic, it somehow felt like maybe I wasn't allowed.

"Does Cappy love Lynds?" Simone asked.

I looked down at her. "I think so."

"Will he marry her?" Simone licked some icing thoughtfully.

"I don't know, hon. You guys go downstairs and play so I can clean up the kitchen, okay?"

Max was off the chair and down the stairs in seconds, but Simone lingered. She wouldn't be much use in the cleanup, since she wasn't tall enough to reach the sink to help wash the bowls and pans, but I didn't chase her away. She had something to say. I could see it in the set of her small face.

"'Sup, pup?"

"Are you going to get married?"

I laughed. "Not anytime soon. Maybe never."

"How come?" Simone tipped her face to look up at me.

"Oh...I don't know." I put the mixing bowls in the sink and ran the hot water, squirted some soap. "Haven't found anyone I like enough, I guess."

"I bet someone would like you enough, Tesla."

I turned to face her, then got on my knees to hug her close with my sudsy hands. "Thanks, kid. Thank you."

She squeezed me back. "I love you, Tesla."

"Love you, too, kid. Now beat it, I need to get this stuff cleaned up." I patted her butt to get her moving, but what she said lingered with me the whole time.

Chapter
20

I don't think any of the three of us thought it would last. What ever lasts in high school, you know? Relationships spring up overnight like mushrooms, and some are just as poisonous. What I had with Chase and Chance wasn't supposed to become serious.

But it did.

Something had changed after the Christmas dance. Just as I'd promised their mother, the brothers were getting A's in calculus. As a celebration, the next time I came over to help them with their "homework," their mom invited me to stay for dinner.

Mrs. Murphy actually wore an apron to cook in, and she held up one thickly cushioned oven mitt for emphasis. "We're having meat loaf and mashed potatoes."

"Sure," I told her brightly. "I'll stay."

"Do you have to call your parents and get permission?"

At Vic's house, we'd be having leftover pizza from the frozen section in the supermarket, not even takeout. He'd probably have a beer or two in front of the television before going off to bed. If I was lucky, he'd tell me about his day and ask about mine. Cap would make us laugh. We might play a game of cards or something. Vic might slide me some cash across the scarred kitchen table, enough to buy groceries for the week or pay a few bills. But he wouldn't kiss me. Wouldn't even touch me. In fact, he'd barely look at me.

"No. I don't live with my parents."

Mrs. Murphy's eyebrows met her hairline. "You don't? Oh, I didn't know. Sorry."

"It's all right." There was a lot to the story, none of it her business, but I could tell she was dying to ask. "Anything I can help you with in the kitchen, Mrs. Murphy?"

She seemed pleased I'd offered. It was no big deal to me. When I'd lived at home my parents both worked weird hours, leaving the cooking of meals to me and Cap, who was helpless at it. At The Compound I'd taken my share of days in the kitchen. And of course at Vic's house mealtime was haphazard, depending on what else was going on.

I didn't mind helping her, even if I didn't necessarily like Mrs. Murphy. I thought she babied her sons too much and was too involved with them. She was the type of mother I was glad I didn't have, and never wanted to be. As we worked at setting the table and mashing the potatoes, I discovered she had a pretty decent sense of humor that didn't get its full share of her time.

Chance, as it turned out, wasn't at dinner. He'd gone to a friend's house, something that shouldn't have surprised me. I mean, it wasn't like I didn't know the brothers had friends, or that they sometimes did things with those friends separately from each other.

And actually, I was glad. I wanted Chase to myself. I'd wanted it ever since the Christmas dance, watching him with that behemoth Becka Miller. And it wasn't that I didn't still like having Chance fuck me from behind while I sucked Chase's dick, or having both of them shaking and shuddering and muttering my name, because I still did. It was all the rest I wanted with Chase instead of his brother. Holding hands while we walked between classes, wearing his letter jacket—yes, even a rockabilly girl like me could be swayed by the status of wearing a boy's letter jacket.

After dinner, the Murphys left to run some errands and Chase and I went downstairs into the rec room to "study." By this point I should've felt doubly bad about taking Mama Murphy's money. Her sons didn't need me to tutor them anymore. But if I gave up tutoring, I'd have no excuse to come over and fuck them, and at eighteen I wasn't too proud to have an excuse that had nothing to do with what I actually wanted. I'm not sure I'd be too proud now.

"I already did the homework," Chase said. "We have a test tomorrow."

"Want me to quiz you on it?" I was already unbuttoning my shirt, the heat of arousal gathering in my belly and lower.

"Nah." He shook his head. "I got it."

When I moved to kiss him, he turned his face at just the last second so my lips landed at the corner of his mouth, not on it. I didn't pull away at first, and he didn't move, so for an eternity of seconds we stayed like that with his subtle rejection between us. When I did draw back, the heat in my stomach turning to ice, he caught my wrist to keep me next to him on the couch.

"You don't want to kiss me?" I asked in a low voice.

"Sure. Sure, I want to kiss you. But maybe…" He trailed off, looking uncomfortable.

I'd never seen Chase look anything less than confident, even when he was failing calc. I sat farther back on the couch, my wrist still imprisoned in his fingers. "But maybe what?"

"Maybe we should wait for Chance to get back."

The gears in my brain whirled, stuck, whirled again. "Why?"

Chase wouldn't look me in the eyes. "Because he's a part of this, right? He's always been a part of it."

A squicky feeling stole over me. "You can't do it without your brother here? Or you don't want to?"

"No!" Chase cried, lip curling. "It's not that."

I moved a little closer. Our knees pressed together. "What, then? I mean…yeah, I like being with both of you. I told you that before. Besides, he's not here. You are."

Chase's fingers tightened on my wrist, pulling me closer. He kissed me then, long and thoroughly. Lingering. His tongue stroked mine. He was a better kisser than his brother.

Always before, the fact we were three instead of two had made the sex a little frantic. So had the possibility of being caught by their parents. Tonight, with Mr. and Mrs. Murphy gone and only one twin to focus my attention on, things felt different. There was the same familiar licking, stroking and sucking, but for the first time since I'd started this with the Murphy brothers, it felt like something other than fucking. It felt like making love.

It was still pretty fast. We were still teenagers, eager to get to business, and mindful that though the Murphy parents had gone out, they'd still be home at some point. We were totally naked within minutes, something we'd never done with the

three of us, since it had always been important to make sure
we could get dressed in a hurry if we had to.

Chase seemed nervous being naked in front of me, though
I'd seen his cock dozens of times already. He seemed even
more nervous looking at me fully naked. I wasn't nervous
at all. We'd never done it face-to-face before, but without
his brother between us, there was no reason not to fuck the
old-fashioned way. Chase lay me back on the rec room carpet—oh, the luxuries we're willing to do without when we're
teenagers! Kissing me, he put on a condom from the box he
and Chance had cleverly hidden under the couch. When he
pushed inside me, we both groaned.

Blinking, Chase pushed himself up on his arms to look
down at me. I reached for him. Pulled him down to kiss me.
And kissing me, he began to move.

I'd come with him before, and with his brother, too. I'm
a greedy slut for orgasms and even back then saw no point in
not getting mine when I had the chance. But this time was
different. This time I didn't have to use my own hand to get
off while I used my mouth on one brother and the other one
fucked me. I didn't have to steady an overeager hand or slow
the pace of one of them fingering me. This time, we just
moved together and the pleasure built up and up until I was
digging my fingernails into Chase's back and hooking my heels
around the backs of his thighs to push him deeper inside me.

It was like the difference between riding an old wooden
roller coaster and getting on the zero-to-seventy loop-de-
loop coaster. We were doing the same things, but it was better this time with just the two of us than it had ever been with
both brothers. Chase kissed me, his hips moving faster, and
mine rose to meet him. I was already coming when he drew
in a breath and groaned. He opened his eyes and looked into

mine. We came within seconds of one another—yet another first. He collapsed against my neck, and I stroked his hair as I blinked and tried to catch my breath.

"I'd pick you," I told him, unable to stop myself from telling him the truth, and so caught up in the afterglow of that ridiculously great sex that I had no filters.

Chase shifted, still inside me, and pulled out. He knelt between my knees, one hand still on his dick to keep the condom from slipping off. "You went to the dance with Chance."

I pushed up on my elbows, aware suddenly of how sweaty we both were. How the air smelled like sex. I needed to pee and wanted a drink of water, but I was still so languorous I couldn't rouse myself to move, even to relieve the pressure of the nubby carpet on my ass. "Yeah, well, he asked me. You didn't. And you went with Becka. But I… If I had to choose…"

I paused, this truth a wall between us I wanted to knock down. "If I had a choice, it would just be you."

In the Murphy basement, there was a long closet that extended along the entire back wall of the space. I didn't register the creak of the closet door opening right away, but Chase did. He was up and away from me in seconds, pulling the condom from his limp dick and wrapping it in a wad of tissues he pulled from the box on the end table. I didn't have time to do more than sit up before I saw Chance in the closet doorway, and even then I didn't get it. Not at first.

"You're a user, Tesla," Chance said in a high, wavering voice not like his usual tone at all. His face was always pale, but now two spots of red highlighted his cheeks. He was shaking. "You're nothing but a user!"

It seemed like a good idea to get dressed, and I found my discarded clothes as fast as I could. I was in my panties and hooking my bra before I found any voice to answer. "I thought you went to Brett's house."

Neither of them answered me. I stepped into my skirt, leaving off my tights for the moment as I buttoned myself into my blouse. The euphoria of making love with Chase had vanished completely, leaving me cold and as shivery as Chance looked. I glared at them, back and forth.

"What the hell's going on? What were you doing in there, Chance? Watching? You were watching us? Sicko!"

"I told you," Chase said, refusing to look at me. He was getting dressed, too, his back to both of us and his shoulders hunched. "I said you didn't really want to know, Chance."

"Oh, I did want to know. I'm glad I know." He sounded anything but glad.

Chase pulled on his sweatpants and T-shirt. I didn't see what he'd done with the rubber. I waited for him to stand next to me, even as a bigger part of me understood that was never going to happen.

"Did you plan this?" I demanded. "Chase?"

"I…he wanted to know…."

"Wanted to know what?" I sat on the couch to start pulling on my tights, and because I suddenly felt as if I might fall over.

"Who you'd pick," Chance said. "And now I know. Shit, I can't believe I took you to the fucking dance. I bought you flowers, Tesla. I took you to dinner, and I paid for it! And the tickets!"

"But…you wanted to." I didn't know how to react to this. It was a betrayal, but I wasn't sure who'd done the betraying. I found my shoes and shoved my feet into them, doing up the laces so I'd have something to look at instead of either one of them. "It's not like I begged you to take me or anything. Christ."

"If Chase had asked you, would you have gone with him?"

I stood. I faced Chance. "Yes. Of course. But he didn't, and you did. So I went with you."

"But you'd rather be with him." Chance sounded miserable.

I got it, then. I hadn't set out to be a heartbreaker, but that's what was happening. I frowned, unable to deny it, but not wanting to say it out loud again.

"He doesn't want to be with you," Chance said.

I looked at the place on the carpet where we'd just had sex, then at Chase, who was still not looking at me. "No? So what was that we just did?"

"We wanted to see if you'd do it." Chase's voice didn't edge up an octave or shake like his brother's had. His had gone low and rough, a preview of what it would become in a few years, when he finished growing, became a man.

Chance cleared his throat and, to my alarm, seemed to be fighting tears. "Without me. And you did."

"You set me up?" The afterglow had vanished completely. I wasn't quite angry, not yet. That would come later, when I thought about how shitty everything had turned out. But just then, all I could think of was that I'd been had. "Why would you do that?"

That's when Chase looked at me. "Because we wanted to know."

The three of us could've made a circle, soft and smooth, but what had happened made us into a triangle with sharp, stabbing points. I had nothing to say to either of them. I'd hurt Chance without meaning to, but what they'd done had been on purpose. It was all I could do not to burst into angry, devastated tears, a reaction I refused to give them.

"Well," I said. "Now you know."

I didn't wait for them to answer. I left them both in the

basement, and when I saw them in school the next day I didn't even turn my head as I passed them at their lockers in the hall. That at least wasn't new, or different than anything we'd ever done before. I returned Mrs. Murphy's final check to her with a note saying I couldn't tutor them anymore. They didn't need me, anyway.

Chase Murphy hadn't wanted me. Melissa had dumped me for someone more like her. Vic cared about me, but was so wrapped up in his guilt over it that it would almost have been better if he didn't.

I'd had boyfriends, girlfriends, one-night stands. Nothing had lasted, and I'd told myself that was the way I liked it. But now, with Simone's question lingering in my mind, all I could think about was Meredith and Charlie bickering over wine.

Why couldn't I have that, too?

Chapter

21

Sundays are the best day at the Mocha. Not just because Joy takes the day off, but because most everyone who stops in isn't rushing to get somewhere else. Even having to get up early to be there to open isn't so bad on Sundays.

This Sunday, Eric was one of the first through the door. As usual, he had rumpled hair, a leather bag and a legal pad. He looked as tired as I felt.

"Rough night?" I asked as I handed him a mug for his bottomless cup.

"Night shift at the E.R. is never pleasant," he said with a grin, and took the mug. "How about you?"

"I didn't have to give anyone stitches, so I guess I had it better than you."

"No doubt." He lifted his mug and took it to his table.

I watched him for a few minutes. Meredith had said everyone has a story, sometimes more than one. I wondered about his.

"Feeling better?" Darek asked, then took a step back to look me over. "You okay? What happened?"

Though most of me still ached, the only visible evidence of my encounter with Vic was a small bruise high on my cheek. I'd covered it with foundation, but anyone looking hard enough would still see it. I touched it lightly.

"I'm fine. It was an accident."

To my surprise, Darek scowled, fists clenching. "Who did it? Some fucker hit you? Who was it?"

I blinked, then laughed. "Oh…it was the guy I live with. Vic. But it really was an accident. I mean, he didn't hit me on purpose, Darek. Thanks, though."

Darek didn't look like he believed me. "Don't fuck with me. I mean it. If someone hit you…"

I couldn't really explain the whole situation to him and make sense. "Really. I'm fine. You think I'd let someone hit me and get away with it?"

He softened his stance, still looking angry. "I don't know. I guess not. Sorry."

"Don't be sorry. It was totally sweet." I fluttered my lashes at him. "Didn't know you cared, actually."

That got him to laugh. "I'd be some kind of major dick not to care if one of my friends was getting beat up."

"You're not a major dick." I busied myself separating the carrot cake muffins. The cream cheese icing had a tendency to stick them together.

"Joy thinks I am. But she's a bitch, so I guess we're even." Darek leaned against the counter. "She ripped me a new one yesterday."

I looked up at him. "Isn't she always ripping someone a new one?"

"This was above and beyond. Reamed me out in front of the whole shop. I was pissed." He paused, still scowling. "I almost quit. And I swear, the next time she lays into me, I will."

Wow. That was serious. "I'm sorry."

He shrugged and looked up when the bell jangled with new customers coming in. "Shit happens. But she's gonna be sad if she keeps giving me shit, that's all I'm saying. Hey, Johnny D. You want him?"

"Of course." I left off the muffins to lean across the counter and give Johnny a big grin. "Morning."

"Hey, Tesla, how you doin'?" His accent's just the cutest thing. He didn't bother scanning the menu, just gave the dessert case a quick glance. "Gimme one a them carrot cakes and a bottomless, will ya?"

"Good choice."

"I like the little carrot on the top," he told me, and handed me enough money to cover the bill, plus dropped a buck in the Tips Appreciated canister. "Don't spend it all in one place."

"Thanks." I laughed and gave him his change, which he also put in the canister. "See you later."

In my flirtation with Johnny, I hadn't noticed the customer behind him. I broke into a broad grin when I saw who it was, though. "Meredith. Hi."

She didn't smile at me. "You're here today."

"Well…yeah." My smile faded a bit as I studied her. "Why wouldn't I be?"

"You weren't here yesterday. I thought maybe you were avoiding me." She didn't look around to see if anyone was listening to us, but I did.

"Of course not." I paused, smiling tentatively. "You could've called me, you know. I mean, I'm glad you missed me."

"I just thought, you know, I was worried. That you'd be weird about what happened."

"No. I had a great time." We stared at each other. I felt more awkward about this conversation than I did about fucking Charlie. "A really great time."

This seemed to please her, because she finally gave me a smile. "Good. Thank God. I didn't want to have to tell Charlie you were going to bail on us. He'd have taken it hard."

"Really? Peppermint latte?" I added, already moving to make it the way I knew she liked it.

Meredith nodded. "Yeah. He's like that."

He hadn't impressed me as the supersensitive sort, but what did I know? "I'm not going to bail." I held the cup beneath the steamer to froth the milk. "So…does this mean you want to do it again?"

Her smile got bigger; how anyone could ever deny her anything she wanted, I didn't know. "Yes. Definitely. I told you it would be fun, didn't I?"

I finished up the latte and handed it to her. "You did."

Our fingers touched as she took the cup. She handed me a ten-dollar bill and pointed at an apple crumb muffin. "One of those, too."

I gave her the muffin and her change. I didn't want her to walk away just yet. "So…when?"

"Tonight, of course," Meredith said. "Tomorrow night, too. The day after that…"

"Stop." I laughed, shaking my head. "You're being silly."

She gave me an arch look, tossed her change carelessly into her purse and hung the strap higher on her shoulder. "So. Not tonight?"

"No, tonight's fine." I couldn't stop the smile. "It'll be great."

"Oh, I know that." She winked at me and moved off to her favorite table at the front, where she opened her laptop and started doing whatever it was she did for hours. Darek moved behind me, startling me a bit when I backed up a step and bumped into him. I laughed. He didn't.

"So, you and her?"

Apparently our smiles hadn't been secret enough. "What about me and her?"

"You're going out with Meredith?"

I gave him a curious look. "Sort of. Why? I mean…"

A sudden, horrid thought struck me. I'd never thought of Darek as dating material and had been pretty sure he didn't think it of me, either. We had each other's phone numbers and were friends on Connex, but never socialized outside of the Mocha.

"She's married," he pointed out.

"Well…yeah." It wasn't any of Darek's business what I was up to with Meredith and Charlie, even if I was the sort to spread my business. Which I'm not.

Darek shrugged and moved around me to get to the toaster, so he could put in a bagel. I didn't really want to talk about it with him, so when we got a little rush of customers I was happy to take care of them instead of discussing my dating life with him.

By the time I had a chance for a breather, Meredith had gone. I tried not to be disappointed, and didn't manage very well. She'd left something for me, though. Another napkin, this one deliberately imprinted with a lipstick kiss and one word scrawled on it.

Tonight.

Chapter

22

Cue the trippy montage set to something bouncy, like an old Partridge Family song.

I saw Charlie and Meredith ten nights out of fourteen over the next two weeks. We went to dinner or the movies, we sat in little clubs and listened to live music, we made out in the parking lot and had breakfast in a diner at three in the morning. Charlie called me five minutes after I left them, and we talked for another hour on the phone. Meredith came into the coffee shop and sent me naughty texts while she sat only a few feet away. Me and Charlie, Charlie and Meredith (though never me and Meredith)—we kissed and touched and stroked and sucked and fucked.

We glutted ourselves with each other.

I'd had a crush on Meredith since the first time I saw her, but Charlie...oh, he was something else. Generous, amiable and not easily ruffled, unlike his wife, who tended to go off on tangents and get worked up about things that left me and Charlie sitting back, silent and watchful, until she turned to us and broke into laughter. He was kind. Thoughtful. Polite. He had a dry but exquisitely tuned sense of humor. Two weeks isn't a long time in terms of a relationship, but it didn't take me long to feel like I knew Charlie.

Meredith was out at one of her home parties, this time for Jangle Bangles, but had told me to go to their house after work and wait for her to get home, since she planned on being back by early evening. This left me and Charlie alone for the first time since this had all started, and though I'd spent hours talking with him on the phone, actually being with him without Meredith between us felt new and awkward and unbearably exciting.

I'd brought something to read and occupy myself with while we waited for Meredith to get home. Charlie kissed me at the door, but then settled in on the couch with his stack of papers to be graded. I sat on the other end, my feet tucked beneath me. We were silent together for a good fifteen or twenty minutes before he looked up with a yawn.

"Whatcha reading?"

I held up the worn paperback I'd been rereading. "It's called *Boy's Life*."

"Is it good?"

"One of my favorites." I showed him the cover. "Robert McCammon. Have you read him?"

Charlie shook his head. "No. I'm a big King fan. Koontz, Barker. Clegg. I mostly read horror and science fiction."

I laughed. "You'd like McCammon, then. This one's a weird sort of Bradbury kind of story, but he's written some excellent horror stuff. You like scary movies, too?"

"My favorite. Not that torture porn stuff," Charlie warned. "But a good psychological horror, or paranormal. I love zombies."

"Me, too! *28 Days Later?*"

We beamed at each other, connecting on yet another whole new level that had nothing to do with our crotches.

"Yeah, that one. Have you seen *A Tale of Two Sisters?* It's Korean." Charlie shuddered. "Scared the living shit out of me."

"N-o-o-o-o," I breathed. "But I love Asian horror, all that black hair all over the place, and it's so creepy and horrifying! I'd love to watch it. I'll have to rent it."

"Oh, I have it on DVD. We could…" Charlie hesitated just for a second. "You could borrow it. Or we could watch it together. I mean, I'd feel like a real jerk if I sent you home with it and you had to watch it alone."

"I'd like that, Charlie."

We shared a smile.

"Like what?" Meredith, laden with her purse and the suitcase she used to transport her jewelry samples, had come in, unnoticed, from the garage.

"Horror flicks. Tesla loves horror." Charlie got up to help her with the suitcase.

She shot me a look as she let him take it. "Does she? How nice that you have something in common."

"You don't like horror, huh?" I jumped up to greet her. "How come?"

She shrugged and kissed Charlie, then hugged me. "Just don't. Mmm, you smell good. What is that?"

I paused to sniff my wrist. "Oh, it's a perfume oil I picked up at the farmer's market. It's called Steam Dreams."

She leaned closer, breathing deep. "I like it. It smells like you."

"I guess that's good, since I'm wearing it."

She gave me a look I'd seen her give Charlie many times. "Smart-ass. Are you both ready to go? Just give me a couple minutes to change, let me get rid of this crap."

She jangled one of her bangles, already unclipping it from her wrist.

Charlie glanced at the couch. "I have a few more papers to grade. I need about another hour, maybe?"

She frowned. "I thought you were going to be done by the time I got home."

"I'll help you, Charlie. I can grade papers with you while Meredith gets ready," I offered.

He seemed surprised. "Really?"

She was already leaving us, glancing over her shoulder. "Good. Kick him into gear, Tesla, I'm going to take a quick shower and stuff, too, since it looks like I have time."

When she'd gone, Charlie looked at me. "You don't have to."

"Hey, it ain't no thing." I shrugged. "I guess if I can't correct some third-grade papers, I'd better be ashamed of myself, huh? Unless maybe it's social studies—is it? Because, I'll be honest, I'm shit with remembering the names of the conquistadores and stuff."

"Nope. Spelling sentences. I think you can handle it."

I grinned. "Do I give extra points for creativity?"

Charlie's fingertip traced the edge of my bangs, along my forehead just above my eyebrows. Featherlight, a whisper of a touch. It sent shivers all through me. We shared another smile, something secret, just for us.

"You should," Charlie said.

Chapter
23

Meredith said she had a surprise for us. I wasn't sure about Charlie, but I knew I was surprised where she took us. Samantha's was classier than I'd expected. When she said strip club, I pictured neon lights and women who looked like maybe they'd been hit one too many times in the face with the ugly stick. Instead, we walked into a classy, dark-wood-paneled room with tastefully erotic portraits on the walls and a nice bar surrounding a stage setup with two poles that reached all the way to the super-high ceiling. The room also had small, separate areas set back from the stage with comfy-looking couches and booths.

"I'm starving," Meredith said as she linked her arm through mine. "What do you want to eat?"

"They serve food here?"

"They serve anything you want here," she told me with a

laugh, and nudged me with her hip. "But the burgers are really good. Let's sit at the bar. Charlie, c'mon."

He had been hanging back just a bit to adjust his belt, which he'd taken off to step through the metal detector at the front door. Now he caught up with us. "What's that?"

"The bar. Let's get a seat at the bar." Meredith sounded a little impatient. "And order some food."

"Sounds good to me." Charlie shot me a grin and linked my other arm with his. "What does Tesla want?"

"Tesla wants a burger," I told him. "And a beer, I guess."

Meredith snagged us three seats along the bar. "And to see some naked titties."

"Well, who doesn't want to see that?" Charlie said.

The waitress who slid a set of coasters in front of us was young, pretty, a little chubbier than I'd have expected, but with enormous breasts surging out of the corset she wore tight enough to give her an hourglass shape. She also wore cute boy-cut shorts and fishnet stockings and a pair of those curve-bottomed sneakers. Not at all like I expected. She gave me a wink as she handed the three of us menus.

"Mixed drinks are on special for the next twenty minutes," she offered. "Food's listed there on the menu, along with our cigar list and beers on tap."

"Hey, burgers," Charlie said, and waved the menu toward Meredith.

My stomach rumbled a little. "She said they were good."

Charlie looked across me to his wife. "Are they?"

Her attention was focused on the stage, where a woman had just arrived. Meredith barely looked at her husband. "Huh? How would I know?"

"You said—" I began, and stopped when she shot me a look.

"I heard they were good. That's all." Meredith turned back

to the stage, where the woman had shimmied out of her long mesh dress and begun a spinning routine on the pole. "Impressive. Look at that."

There was no mistaking her envious tone, and I had to admit I felt a little the same. In the dim light it was still easy to see the stripper had a few wrinkles, a little bit of cellulite, but she was amazing on that pole. She'd climbed halfway up to the thirty-foot ceiling, then hung there just using her thighs. Her hair fanned out as she spun.

"The pole's spinning, not the girl," Charlie commented. Then, quieter, "I hope she doesn't fall."

Meredith snorted soft laughter. "Leave it to Charlie to worry about safety. Focus on her boobies, honey. That's what you're paying to see. Speaking of, give me that stack of dollars. I've been collecting them for weeks," she told me, and handed me a few from the stack Charlie passed her. "Here. Crumple them up and toss 'em."

That seemed sort of rude, but it was what everyone else who wasn't sitting within G-string tucking distance was doing. Crumpled dollars and wolf whistles filled the air as the dancer loosened her grip on the pole and slid down, stopping just as the tips of her long blond hair brushed the floor. Then she arched her back and flipped herself over to land on her five-inch platform shoes.

"God," Meredith muttered. "Would you just fucking look at that."

I was happy to look. I didn't have to be a connoisseur of strippers to appreciate her talents. When she turned to send a smile our way, I was happy to toss her a crumpled dollar bill. It bounced off her bare breasts, and she caught it neatly in one hand, then dropped me a wink and bent to pick up her mesh dress before sashaying off the stage.

"I wish I could do that," Meredith said.

"Pole dance?" Charlie peered around me to look at her. "I bet you could. We could set one up in the living room."

I knew he was joking, but Meredith rolled her eyes. "That would go great with our decor, right?"

More and more girls started coming out. Two got up on the stage to do pole work, while the woman who'd already danced started mingling with the customers. Some other dancers came out, too, more than one of them wearing fancy gowns I'd have expected to see at a cocktail party, not a strip club.

"Hey, I'm Donna. How you all doing tonight?" The woman who'd been dancing a few minutes before had changed from the mesh dress into a tiny plaid skirt with a buttoned-up shirt left half open, the hem tied over her tan belly. Her breasts spilled out, helped along by a really great push-up bra I envied. Her gaze slid over me and Charlie, snagged for a moment on Meredith, then moved back to me. "Hey, darlin'. Cute top."

"I was just thinking the same about yours. And the skirt, too." I didn't really love it, but there's never any point in being mean. She worked hard for the money.

"This old thing?" She winked again and leaned casually against the bar next to Charlie. "So, is this your first time here?"

"Yes," Charlie said.

Her gaze went to him, her smile a little broader. "Well, handsome, just so you know in case they didn't tell you, private dances are twenty a song, and I'll do a special for couples. Two for one."

She looked at me, I guess because I was sitting next to him. "Whattaya say, honey? Want to treat your husband to something special?"

"He's my husband," Meredith said, though not with malice. I think she liked surprising people. "And does your special go for triples?"

You'd think strippers would be hard to surprise, but the woman's eyebrows lifted before she looked again at me. "Can't say I've ever done three at a time before, but…sure. Why not? Tell you what, you pay for three songs, and I'll do the three of you. How's that?"

Charlie hadn't said much this entire time, though he didn't seem to mind the dancer's arm brushing his or the way her hip nudged him when she shifted. "What a bargain."

She glanced at him. "What can I say? I like a challenge."

Meredith hopped off the bar stool and stood, her eyes gleaming in that way I'd come to know so well. "Good. Let's go."

Charlie and I exchanged looks. I was up for it, and I couldn't think of any reason why he wouldn't be. Yet he hung back with more hesitation than simple politeness. His hand went to the small of my back as we followed Meredith and the dancer through the crowd, which had doubled since we came in. Our seats at the bar were quickly taken.

"You sure about this?" he murmured in my ear as we moved toward the back of the bar, down a short hallway past the restrooms and into a smaller room with a bouncer at the door.

I paused to face Charlie, though Meredith had already followed the dancer into the room. "Sure. Why…aren't you?"

"I've never had a lap dance before." He looked adorable almost all the time, but just then I wanted to eat him up.

Meredith stuck her head out from the doorway. "What are you doing? C'mon."

Charlie's fingers tightened in mine. "Better not keep her waiting."

"No. She doesn't like that." I tugged him. "C'mon, Charlie. Let's pop your lap dance cherry."

"Have you had one?" he asked as we went past the bouncer and the cashier just inside the doorway, where Charlie pulled out his credit card for her to swipe.

I shook my head, looking over the room, which featured about ten of the same booths that were out in the main area, except these had even higher backs and sides to provide for total privacy from the ones next to it. "Nope."

"So we're both popping our cherries tonight." Charlie signed the slip and tucked his card and the receipt in his wallet, then put it in his pocket. He leaned to brush his lips against my temple, then tugged my hand. "C'mon."

"Tesla, you sit between us." Meredith wriggled on the velvet seat and patted it. "Charlie, you sit there."

She was orchestrating us, as usual. We sat as Donna watched us, looking amused. She toyed with the crisscross-tied hem of her shirt. When we were settled, she unbuttoned it swiftly and shrugged out of the bra, leaving herself in the tiny skirt.

"I can take this off or leave it on," she offered, turning to show us how the skirt flipped up to show off her ass in a lacy thong. She looked at us over her shoulder and wiggled her hips from side to side. "Your choice."

"Off." Meredith clapped her hands and bounced on the seat, shaking me against Charlie.

I had to laugh at her. "I dunno, I sort of like it on."

"Charlie," Meredith said. "Tiebreaker."

I thought he'd choose what she wanted, so it surprised me when he said, "On. I like it. It's sexy."

Meredith looked surprised, too, and not that happy, but she shrugged. "On, then."

Donna glanced toward the cashier and held up three fingers, getting a nod back that probably signified Charlie had indeed paid for three dances. The music started a few seconds later. She'd danced to something fast earlier, but now a slow and sexy song filtered through the speakers. "No Ordinary Love" by Sade.

"One of my favorites," Charlie murmured, before he had a faceful of giant breasts and a lapful of stripper.

It can't have been easy, dancing for three, but God bless her, Donna did her best. She moved back and forth, sitting on each of our laps and rubbing her ass along us, then turning to press our faces into her ample boobs. She smelled good. Her skin was soft. I liked the weight of her on my lap, and I liked when she sat on Charlie's lap next to me and arched her back so that her face was pressed alongside his and her tits pushed up to the ceiling. She ground against us, one at a time, then added in the stroke of a hand or a flirty look to make sure that even as she pressed against one of us, another still got some attention.

I gave myself up to the pleasure of being seduced by a pretty woman who knew how to give us our money's worth. I liked the way she made eye contact, letting it linger, and I liked how she made Charlie blush a little when she rubbed her ass on his crotch.

When the third song ended, Meredith stood before Donna even had time to back up a few steps. "Thanks. Great job."

Donna smiled as she slipped her arms through her bra straps and hooked it in the front. "Thanks. Glad you had a good time."

Meredith didn't look at her twice, though she gave both me and Charlie a narrow-eyed look. "I'm going to the bathroom."

She left us there without a second glance.

Donna appeared concerned. "Is she okay?"

"I'm sure she's fine. I'll check on her." I stood on tiptoe to whisper in Charlie's ear, "You should give Donna a nice tip."

I patted him on the ass and headed for the bathroom, where I found Meredith just coming out of the stall. She washed her hands, then patted wet fingertips at the back of her neck and on her throat. She looked at me in the mirror.

"Let's go home," she said.

I shrugged. I hadn't been the one to suggest we come here, and though I was having a good time, I wasn't married to the idea that we stay. "Sure. You okay?"

"I just don't see the point in tossing money away to pay for what we can do at home for free." Meredith faced me, her fingers skimming up my arms. "And better."

I laughed. "You want to give Charlie a lap dance at home? Okay, I'm down with that."

"Not just Charlie. You, too." She pulled me a little closer, nuzzled briefly at my throat, then my cheek. Not quite a kiss, but the promise of one. She pulled away just enough to look me in the eyes. "I'm horny as fuck, aren't you?"

I hadn't been before, but now I was. Her touch. That look. The quick rise and fall of her shoulders as she breathed and the rapid throb of her pulse at the base of her throat. These were things that turned me on.

I wanted to be the reason why all that happened to her.

"Yeah," I said. "Let's go to your place."

"Sit there, baby. Let us take care of you." Meredith pulled a chair from the dining room table, through the arch into the living room, and turned it around with a twist of her wrist. "Let us show you what we've got, Charlie."

He sat willingly enough, already tugging at his tie to loosen it, then the button at his throat. "Ladies, I'm all yours."

"And you don't even need any dollar bills," I told him from the corner as I scrolled through the playlists on Meredith's iPod to find something suitable. I plugged it into the speaker dock and pushed the Play button.

Charlie laughed. "Awesome."

Meredith spun in a circle, then stopped, pointing the toes of one foot against the thick carpet. Her hips swayed. She threw me a glance over her shoulder. "C'mon, Tesla. Let me see you rock Charlie's world."

I was already dancing, bouncing on the balls of my feet, but I went obediently enough. I added a bump-n-grind, a pelvic thrust. I ran my hands up my body to cup my breasts. It was a joke, really, but my nipples got hard anyway.

Charlie let his legs sprawl out as he leaned against the back of the chair. He pulled a little harder on his tie and I captured the end of it. Pulled until it came free in my fingers and slipped through his collar. I hung it around my own neck, over my blouse.

Behind him, Meredith's hands slipped over Charlie's shoulders. Her fingers worked at his shirt buttons, slipping inside to stroke his skin and tweak his nipples. I straddled him, bumping our crotches together, but slid off his lap before he could anchor me against him with his hands on my hips.

"No touching," Meredith breathed into his ear.

The music swelled around us as we took turns wiggling and writhing around Charlie. He made the perfect audience, because while he'd seemed to have a good time at the strip club, here he was having an even better time.

His cock thickened in his pants as I mimicked one of Donna's moves, sitting on Charlie's lap and rocking my hips back and forth as I arched my back to press my cheek close to his. And though we'd told him no touching, I took his hand and slid it up beneath my skirt to stroke me through my panties before I pushed away, laughing, to give Meredith a turn on his lap.

"I thought you were the ones supposed to be stripping," Charlie complained good-naturedly as Meredith worked open the rest of his buttons and took his shirt off.

She tossed it to the side and looked at me. "Good idea."

We'd all been drinking, though I didn't feel drunk on anything but passion as I unbuttoned my blouse and took it off, twirling it around my head and letting it fly onto the couch. I wasn't wearing a push-up bra and my boobs weren't as big as Donna's, but I was wearing a cute little skirt. I spun in a circle so it flew out around my hips, flashing my panties at them both.

"Look at her," Meredith said. "Look at our pretty, pretty Tesla."

I gave up to the music, letting it fill me, no longer mimicking the stripper's moves but making up my own. Dancing, just dancing, letting the beat make my heart pound and my feet move. I shook what my mama gave me like a tambourine and gave myself a whistle.

Charlie, shirt off and belt unbuckled, had his cock in his hand as he watched. Meredith pulled another chair from the dining room and set it up next to his. She'd stripped down to her bra and panties and sat in the chair to watch me.

So I danced for both of them.

It was a little silly. I did the cabbage patch and the running man and the lawn mower. Charlie laughed, but his stroking hand didn't slow, and Meredith's eyes gleamed as her tongue swept across her mouth.

I took off my bra and thumbed my nipples while they watched. I licked my fingertips and stroked them down my belly, under my skirt, inside my panties. Dancing, I moved forward and put one foot up on the edge of Charlie's chair so he could run his free hand up the inside of my thigh, but when his fingertips skimmed the lacy edge of my panties, I danced away again.

"No touching," I told him with a shake of my finger, then did the same to Meredith.

She didn't try to touch me, but she arched her back a little when I put my foot on her chair. She slipped her fingers into the front of her panties the way I did. Rubbing, rubbing.

I turned back to Charlie, leaning in close to kiss him. I put my hand over his, fingers curling around his dick. I took over the stroking while he shifted to push his pants down his hips. I looked down between us, then at Meredith. She put one hand on Charlie's thigh, her other still busy on her pussy.

We didn't really have to shout out directions; I moved and Charlie moved with me down to the floor. I pushed him gently onto his back and stroked his cock a few more times before bending to add a long, slow lick to his balls.

I loved the way it made him groan, but there were three of us here. I held out my hand to Meredith, who linked her fingers through mine and got on her knees beside him. She kissed his mouth. I kissed his cock.

Sex can be great even without a lot of gymnastics. I moved naturally between Charlie's legs while Meredith straddled his face. He got the best of everything, a hot mouth and hands on his dick and a face full of pussy. And the sounds she made as he worked her closer and closer to coming were so hot I had no trouble getting close myself.

Just as I'd lost myself in the dancing, now I lost myself in the pleasure from my hand rubbing my clit and the thickness of Charlie's delicious cock. Actually, I wanted to ride it, but since I didn't feel like leaving off what I was doing to hunt up a condom, I satisfied myself with slipping my fingers deep into my pussy. Not a substitute for Charlie's cock, not completely, but it was good enough to make me come.

Climax spiraled through me, making me shudder. I took Charlie's cock deep into my mouth. It jerked on my tongue. He was getting close, too. When Meredith cried out, a wordless groan of pure pleasure, Charlie came.

Minutes later the three of us were on their living room carpet. I heard the soft mutter of Charlie's snores, and giggled, though my own eyes were closed and I'd stifled a yawn or two. Meredith sighed.

I opened my eyes and rolled on my side to look at her. "Hey."

She passed a hand over my hair. "Hey."

"We should wake him up."

She smiled. "We could just let him sleep down here all night."

"You wouldn't. That would be so mean." I curled my legs a little, pushing against her touch, lazy like a cat. "Though this carpet is as nice as some beds I've slept in."

"What was it like, really? The Compound? I picture it like summer camp, with bunks."

"Yeah. It was like that. There were dorm-style buildings for the teenagers. Little cabins for the adults. Everything was kind of old and run-down. Shabby, I guess you could say. Furnished with castoffs people brought from home to donate." I yawned again and captured her stroking hand to pillow it beneath my cheek. Her palm was warm.

"Was it great?"

I was having a hard time keeping my eyes open, but I managed so I could look up at her. "Was what great?"

"Living there. Just…the freedom of it. Every time you talked about it, it sounded great. Was it like a real hippie commune?"

"When I was a kid, I thought it was great. Sure. There was a lot of freedom, yeah. We sort of ran wild all summer. It made it hard to adjust to the rest of the year. And…" I yawned again. "Honestly, Meredith, the people there were crooks. I mean, they cheated on their taxes and grew drugs for profit. They let their kids run rampant all summer so they could fuck around on their spouses. One summer my brother had to shave his head because he couldn't get rid of the lice."

"It still sounds like a great experience."

"It wasn't all bad, no."

I snuggled against her hand. Charlie's thigh was warm against my knees. I could fall asleep right there, except I knew eventually we'd get cold, and at the very least, I needed to get up and pee.

"You work early tomorrow?" Meredith asked.

"Hmm? Yeah. I should get going."

She shifted nearer to me so that when I opened my eyes we were so close I could see the white flecks surrounding her irises. "You know, if you stayed here you wouldn't have to leave."

I smiled. "Whoa. That's so deep. Is that like 'wherever you go, there you are'?"

Charlie hadn't moved, though his snores had gotten a little louder. I ran my hand lightly up his thigh, over his hip. I touched his belly and he wiggled a little but didn't wake.

"Charlie has to get up early in the morning, too. And I didn't bring anything with me to stay over."

She sighed and rolled her eyes, then got up. "Fine. I get it."

I stood up, too, looking for my clothes, and shot her a grin as I scooped up my panties. "I'll plan better for next time, okay?"

Her gaze slipped over me, not missing an inch. "Next time. Mmm."

At the front door, I leaned to kiss her goodbye and caught the corner of her mouth. Meredith hugged me close, her bare breasts pressing sweetly against the front of my blouse. She squeezed my butt, but it was a friendly sort of pinch, not terribly lecherous.

"Drive safe," she said, and shut the door behind me.

Chapter 24

"You sit." I pointed a warning finger at Elaine, who'd been struggling to move from stove to fridge and back again without tripping over Max and Simone. I pointed at them, too. "You two. Out!"

"We're h-u-u-ungry," Simone whined, turning on the pout that would usually have won her what she wanted—from her mama or daddy, at least.

I wasn't so easily won. "Out. You just had yogurt twenty minutes ago and neither of you finished it. Go play in the rec room, and stay out of my room."

Max shuffled in his footie pajamas toward the doorway. "Tum on, Simone, we tan pway twucks."

His sister let out a long-suffering sigh and gave me another practiced look. "Can we have some cheese crackers?"

I had to bite back a laugh at her efforts, but passed that one on to their mother, who was also trying not to giggle. Plastic cups of crackers in their hands, the kids went downstairs. I turned to Elaine.

"Okay. Dinner. Spaghetti?"

"Sure," she said wearily. "Everyone will eat that without argument. We can slice up that Italian bread you brought home, and make garlic bread."

I dug in the bread drawer and pulled out the loaf, handed it to her with a knife and cutting board. Then the butter and crushed garlic in the jar from the fridge. "Here, you handle that. I'll make the sauce."

Growing up, all I'd ever eaten was premade pasta sauce from a jar or can, but Elaine had taught me how to make "fresh" sauce using crushed tomatoes, olive oil and spices. I took the ingredients from the pantry and set to sautéing some onions and garlic, opening jars and digging up the oregano and basil from the spice cupboard. It could simmer on a low heat until Vic got home or we gave up on him and ate without waiting.

"Thanks, Tesla." Elaine spread butter on the small slices of bread and ladled minced garlic on top. "Can you hand me the—"

I was already passing her the flat cooking stone we used for everything from pizza to cookies. And garlic bread, too. I laughed at her expression. "What?"

"I'm so glad you're here," she said.

This set me back a step, though I tried not to show it. Elaine was naturally affectionate and always had been to both me and Cap. For some reason, though, her statement hit me harder than it should have. I busied myself with stirring the oil, garlic and onions.

"I am," she said quietly. "You're so great with the kids, I

don't know what I'd do without the extra set of hands. You've spoiled me."

"I love your kids." I added some spices to the pot and stirred that, too, so I didn't have to look right at her. "And if you or Vic need help, I'm happy to give it."

Elaine snorted a small, unamused laugh. "Oh. Vic. Does he ever need help?"

I closed my eyes for a second, not wanting to have this conversation and not seeing any way to get around it. I switched the burner to low and covered the pot, then turned to the counter to open the cans of crushed tomatoes. "Of course he does."

"He won't ask for it." Elaine put the butter knife on the table with a sharp rap of the metal blade on the wood. "He won't accept it. I know something's going on with him, Tesla. He leaves early, he comes home late. He's on that stupid laptop all the time when he is home, and he won't tell me what he's doing."

The can opener was old, the cans a little dented around the rim. I struggled to twist the handle that turned the gears that cut the metal, then, sighing, took a break for a minute to look at her. "He's an asshole sometimes. I mean, you knew that."

Other women might have taken offense to someone calling their husband an asshole, but Elaine only laughed. "He's opinionated. And overprotective."

"That, too." I finally forced both cans open and dumped the contents in the pot, where everything sizzled briefly and sent up a cloud of steam. "Mmm, smells good."

"I just want to know what he thinks he's protecting me from. That's all."

I didn't want to look at her, afraid she'd see in my eyes that I knew exactly what Vic was hiding from her. I kept my focus on the stove, stirring the sauce that didn't need any more attention. I heard her sigh.

"Tesla. Please. I know you know something."

I sighed, too, and turned to pull down the big pot from the rack. I filled it with water as I answered. "He's been acting strange lately. That's for sure."

"But why? I thought everything was going great with the shop. We're not behind on any bills or anything. We even have some money set aside so he can take time off after the baby comes. I've tried to think of all the things that could be bothering him and I just can't." She sighed again. "Does he talk to you?"

For the first time ever, in all the years I'd known her, I heard the edge of jealousy in her voice. In that moment, I hated Vic for putting me in this place between them. I didn't want to know things about him that his wife did not. I didn't want to be the one he confided in, not even if it was because he trusted me or because he loved her more.

"Vic and I don't always see eye to eye on stuff. You know that." I glanced toward the pantry, but it wasn't time to put the pasta in the water yet. I had to face her instead. So I put on my big-girl panties and did. She looked sad, and it broke my heart. I hated him a little harder.

"But does he talk to you? Has he been talking to you? I feel like…" She lifted her hands and dropped them helplessly against the mound of her belly. "He's always been close-mouthed about stuff. But lately he's not just taciturn, he's secretive."

I pulled out the chair opposite her and sat to help with the garlic bread. I thought of a thousand different ways to tell her he was considering going back to his old job, but since apparently she didn't even know he'd had an old job, I was stuck.

She'd always known where Vic had met me and Cap. We spoke only rarely about The Compound, but we did talk about it. I'd never realized we never said what Vic had really been doing there. I didn't want to be the one revealing to her that he'd been lying by omission for the entirety of their marriage.

"Have you asked him?" I stacked some buttery, garlicky slices on the stone. "Flat-out asked?"

"I've asked him if something was wrong. He says no." She frowned. "I don't believe him."

"Stress at work?" I offered. "Dennis has been out a lot, and working with Cap has to be a challenge."

That earned a laugh, thank God. "Your brother is the sweetest guy alive."

"He's the dumbest smart guy alive, you mean. I know he drives Vic crazy sometimes. And with the baby coming and stuff, I'm sure Vic just wants to work as much as possible so, like you said, when the baby comes he can take time off."

I felt like shit even though what I'd said was no more a lie than Vic saying nothing was "wrong." Elaine lifted her hair off her neck and twisted it, securing it with a ponytail holder she pulled from her wrist. She briefly touched the spot between her eyes as if it pained her. When she looked across the table at me, I hated seeing the sheen of tears in her eyes.

"If something was wrong and you knew about it, Tesla. You'd tell me. Right?"

"Of course. Of course I would." It tasted like a lie, though I meant it to be the truth.

The back door opened and caught us looking guilty, like we were the ones keeping secrets. Vic came in, stamping off the slush from his boots, and paused in the doorway. He looked first to his wife, who got a faint smile from him, then to me.

I got a frown.

THE SPACE BETWEEN US 193

"What's up?" he asked.

Elaine heaved her bulk from the chair and went to give him a kiss. "How was work?"

"Fine. Closed early, had no appointments and Cap was on about something having to do with what it would take to launch an iPhone into space or something like that."

I laughed, and Vic shot me another frown. "Did he have diagrams?" I asked.

"Yes." Vic rolled his eyes and looked over Elaine's shoulder to the stove. "Spaghetti?"

"Yes. It'll be a few minutes." She hugged him close.

I looked away from their intimacy, not because it embarrassed me, but because I didn't want to see Vic's face when he hugged the woman he was lying to. The pounding of feet up the stairs alerted the three of us to the kids before they hurtled through the door to attack their dad, and I took the opportunity to finish the bread, then start the spaghetti. Vic played daddy for a few minutes, then went to take a shower before dinner.

Elaine let the subject drop, but it still hovered between us as we both set the dining room table and put out the food. My phone rang just as Vic, head wet and clothes changed, came down the stairs. He looked as if he was going to say something to me, but I held up a hand to hold him off while I answered.

It was Meredith. "Hey, sugar pie."

"Hello, crumb cake," I answered, just to be sassy.

She laughed. "What's going on?"

"Getting ready to eat." Phone in one hand, I snagged Max by the back of the pants with the other as he ran by. He yelped, I giggled.

"Sounds crazy over there." Meredith herself sounded the opposite of crazy—calm and amused. "It's a circus, huh?"

"Yeah, a circus. With monkeys." I picked Max up in one arm, ignoring his wiggling protests, and took him into the dining room to hand him to Vic. "It's pretty much always a circus here. What's going on with you?"

Frowning, Vic took his son from me. I ignored his glare, not interested at the moment in his judgment, since he had no justification for it as far as I was concerned. He narrowed his eyes; I widened mine innocently and turned my back.

"I wanted to take you out to dinner," Meredith said. "See a movie. Whisk you away from your dreary, humdrum life and give you something magical."

"Magical, huh? Sounds exciting." I looked over the table, Simone and Max in their places and most of the food set out. Elaine looked up curiously as she placed the bowl of pasta and sauce, already mixed, in the center. "Where do you want to take me?"

"What are you hungry for?" A shuffle sounded in the background, then her distinctive giggle. "Charlie says he has something nice for you to eat."

Charlie's voice muttering a protest came through next, though I couldn't quite hear what he said. I laughed at the mental picture of him laid out on a table. Naked. "Mmmm."

"Let us come and pick you up. We can be there in fifteen minutes. Is that enough time to get ready?"

I laughed again at that; Meredith was the one who took forever. "I'm a wash-and-go sort of girl. You know that."

"Good." She paused. More shuffling, something muttered. "Charlie says wear something sexy."

Apparently that wasn't what he'd said, because I heard him retort, loud and clear, "I said tell her to come hungry!"

"He says get ready to come," Meredith said.

I was giddy and giggly, listening to their exchange. Tingles in my toes. Cheeks a little flushed. It must've been obvious because when I turned to face the others at the table, they were all staring. "I'll be ready. See you."

I disconnected the call. "What?"

"Who was that?" Vic asked suspiciously.

Elaine smiled. "I bet I know."

"Santa Claus!" Simone shouted.

"No, not Santa," I told her. I didn't answer Vic and spoke instead to his wife. "I'm actually not going to eat here. I got invited out."

Elaine's smile got bigger. "Woo, woo!"

I picked up the plate we'd set for me, and tickled Max as I passed, then ruffled Simone's blond curls. "Catch youse on the flip side."

"What's the flip side?" Simone asked, twisting in her seat to look up at me.

I touched her nose. "It means later, gator."

I took my plate and fork to the kitchen before I left, and when I turned, Vic was standing so close behind me I let out a surprised squeak and had to step back so I didn't bump into him. "Christ, Vic, what the hell?"

"Don't you think you're being a little selfish?"

I could only stare, drop-jawed.

He gestured toward the dining room. "Dinner's all ready, and you're going to dump us so you can go out with someone else?"

I held up a hand. "Slow your roll."

"Slow my…" His expression transformed from irritated to infuriated.

"Yeah. Slow your fucking roll, Vic." I kept my voice low to keep the kids from hearing me curse, because I'm not a totally insensitive twat. "Back off. And it's not any of your business, anyway."

"It's completely my business."

"Since when?" I demanded.

"Since always."

My jaw dropped again, and I actually made that noise cartoon characters make when they're flabbergasted. *Boing-oing-oing-oing.* "Are you fucking kidding me?"

"Elaine worked hard to make that dinner in there. I think you shouldn't be a self-absorbed little brat, but get back in there and eat it with us."

It was like someone had reached down my throat and torn out every single word I'd ever uttered. I couldn't form a sound to save my life. All I could do was stare.

Well, stare and blink away the rapidly rising tsunami of red fury that had begun crashing over me.

"First of all, I made the dinner. Most of it." Saying it that way made it sound like a complaint, which it wasn't. "So I doubt Elaine really cares if I don't eat it."

Vic's mouth worked. A smart man would've stepped back. After all, he knew me. We'd gone at it with hammer and tongs enough times for us both to know when to stop pushing the other one's buttons. But he didn't.

"When's the last time we all ate together? Maybe instead of rushing off with your friends you should spend some time with your family."

I didn't like the way he said "friends."

"Is that your issue? That it's with them? What if I were meeting someone else—would that matter?"

"Didn't you learn anything from what happened with your parents?" Vic said tightly. "Jesus, Tesla. I thought you'd be smarter than that."

"This is nothing like that. It's not like anything in The Compound." I meant it as the truth, but it came out sounding defensive. Like a lie.

"You should stay here with us."

"I've had more dinners here with your wife and kids in the past three weeks than you have," I pointed out coldly. "I'm not the one off fucking around."

"I'm not…" Vic stopped to lower his voice. "I'm not fucking around. Jesus, Tesla."

A sound in the doorway made us both turn. Of course it was Elaine, face drawn, expression bleak. "What's going on?"

"I think Tesla should eat dinner with us tonight, not run off."

"Since when do you care where Tesla eats dinner?" she asked quietly.

Vic looked caught. "It's just that we… She…"

Elaine gazed at me. "She has a right to her life, Victor."

I'd hated so much about this day already, and this added one more thing. I didn't want Elaine to have to defend me to her husband. I didn't want them fighting. Not about me, not about anything.

"So, I'm the asshole again?" Vic scowled. "Great. Fine. I just thought—"

"She's right. She has eaten dinner with us more often than you have lately. She's been here to give the kids their baths and help me put them to bed, Vic. She's been here, and you haven't. So why don't you tell me the truth about what's going on?" Elaine lifted her chin and crossed her arms over her belly. Her gaze didn't waver and neither did her voice.

I didn't want to be here during this standoff, but Vic was between me and the door to the basement. I was going to disappoint Charlie, I thought randomly. I'd totally lost my appetite.

"I've been working." Vic said this so steadily I could tell he was keeping something back. Not a lie, not exactly. But not telling all the truth.

If I knew him so well from our long acquaintance, surely his wife knew him even better. The corners of Elaine's mouth turned down, but she kept her eyes on him. "At the garage?"

"I…" Vic stopped himself and gave me a furious look. "What have you been telling her?"

I held up both my hands and shook my head.

"She hasn't said anything. Is there something she should say?" Now Elaine flicked a glance at me, her disappointment evident.

My heart sank. The only good that could come of this was going to be wrapped up in a whole lot of hurt. I didn't want to be part of it, but I was tangled as tight as a ball of yarn in a thorn bush.

Vic scowled at me again. "Jesus, Tesla. I thought I could trust you."

"Trust me to do what?" I found my voice at last. Found my balance, too, and pushed past him to get to the basement. But he snagged my elbow hard enough as I passed to spin me toward him. "Let go of me."

"Tesla?" Elaine asked, and I couldn't keep it inside anymore.

"He's thinking of getting a new job," I spat. "He wants to go back to being a cop, because he thinks the world's such a big, bad place full of horribly scary things and he's the only person in the whole wide world capable of taking care of it. That's what he's been doing, Elaine. Not just working late at the garage. He's been getting back into detective work. Undercover."

It spilled out of me, words tumbling like rocks in a river. I shuddered and clamped my mouth shut. I jerked my elbow from Vic's grasp, and his suddenly loose fingers couldn't hold me.

"Getting back? I don't understand." Elaine looked at Vic. "What's going on?"

"Tesla needs to learn to keep her mouth shut, that's all."

"And you need to learn to talk to your wife," I retorted.

Silence, broken after a few seconds by Elaine's stifled sob. Vic turned to her in dismay, but she backed up a step with a shake of her head. That left his anger to come back at me, but I was ready for it.

"No," I said before he could speak. "Don't even. If you're going to give me shit for anything, just…no. I'm not having it, Vic. I'm going out with friends, and it had nothing to do with you before, but it sure as hell does now."

"You live in my house. The least you could do is show some respect," he said.

He knew it was a mistake the moment the words left his mouth; I could see it in his eyes. But he wasn't much for apologies.

"Really? You're going to throw that 'not under my roof' shit at me? Really?" I shook my head, heading for the basement.

"Mama?" Simone appeared in the doorway, her pouting mouth ringed with sauce.

We all froze.

"Go back into the dining room," Elaine said.

Simone didn't go.

"Now!" Vic shouted.

His daughter burst into tears and ran from the kitchen. I slapped a hand to my forehead. "Nice."

"You," he said, pointing, "don't get to judge my parenting skills."

"That's right," I said, pointing back. "Because you're not my father."

Elaine and I both jumped when Vic slammed his hand into the side of the fridge. She squeaked in surprise; I backed up a step. He looked instantly ashamed.

Decisions we make in haste aren't always ones we'll regret. Watching Vic and Elaine struggling in front of me, I knew I could no longer be a part of it. I'd been here too long already.

"I'm going out with my friends," I said into the suddenly quiet kitchen. "And I'm probably not coming home."

"Tonight?" Vic asked.

I gazed at him steadily, but said nothing.

He looked at Elaine. "What's this shit?"

I thought she'd be the one to try and convince me to stay, but she only gave me the same steady sort of look I'd given Vic. The disappointment in her eyes broke me even more— I'd never wanted to lie to her. She cleared her throat before replying, but her voice was as steady as her gaze.

"She's saying she's going to move out, Vic. And I think…I think that might be for the best."

"What?" he cried, but neither Elaine nor I looked at him.

We stared across the kitchen table, where only an hour or so ago she'd told me how happy she was to have me here. And where I'd said I'd tell her if I knew something was going on with her husband, but hadn't. I didn't really want to go, not like this, but I could see no good way to stay.

"No. Tesla, you don't have to do that," Vic said.

I ignored him and went downstairs to gather up some things I'd need for the next few days. I looked around the room he'd built for me down here. Vic had given me shelter when I'd had no place to go. He'd made me a part of his life and part of his family.

I loved him for that and many reasons, most of which I'd never be able to untangle. But it was time for me to go.

Chapter

25

Dinner and a movie. Nothing kinky or extraordinary about that, right? Not unless you consider that it's two women and one man on that date, and that the three of them are going to end up in bed together.

Not that anyone watching us would've known it, of course. But *we* did. And that gave everything we said a little extra element of anticipation. At least it did for me—or maybe I was just trying so hard to forget about the fight with Vic, and thinking about what I was really going to do, that I focused too much on what would happen when I went back with Meredith and Charlie to their house.

"God, that movie was the worst ever." Meredith tossed her purse on the counter. Kicked off her shoes. She left a trail of clothing, coat, hat and gloves as she headed for the living room, where she bent to rummage in the liquor cabinet.

"I've seen worse." Charlie had taken my coat and hat from me and hung them in the hall closet before hanging his own.

I blew on my fingers. I'd worn my mittens, but the temperatures had dropped so fast that the short walk from the theater to the car had left them like ice cubes, and the car ride home hadn't been quite long enough to warm them.

"Still cold?" Charlie took both my hands in his and chafed them gently, then lifted them to his mouth and blew on them.

I shivered for reasons unrelated to my chills. "Thanks."

He kissed my hand and smiled. "No problem."

"Who wants a mojito?" Meredith stood in the arch between the living room and kitchen holding a bottle of lime-flavored rum. "I have fresh limes."

"It's a school night," Charlie reminded her with a glance at the clock. "And it's getting late."

Meredith pouted, and I was reminded with a pang of Simone. I hadn't even said a proper goodbye to the kids. I was a shitty pseudo auntie.

"And I guess you have to work early?" Meredith said to me.

"Yeah. But I brought some things. So I can stay over…if you want me to." I wasn't sure what I'd do if one of them said they didn't want me. Where I'd go. Cap would be happy to put me up, and Lynds wouldn't mind, at least short-term. But I didn't want to go there.

"Don't be dumb. Of course we do. Right, Charlie?" Meredith put the bottle on the counter and came over to hug me. "Mmm. Tesla."

She nuzzled my neck, which felt nice, but then stepped back too fast for me to really enjoy it. "No drinks?"

"Not for me. I'm going to take a shower," Charlie said. "I'm tired."

Meredith frowned again and looked at me. "Charlie…"

He paused. Glanced from her to me and back again. "What?"

She put her arm around my waist so we stood hip to hip. "I can't believe you're going to just abandon us."

The last thing in the world I wanted was for Charlie to feel pressured into fucking me. As much as I wanted to lose myself in the physical, I could sympathize with him being tired. Not only that, but I was still caught up in everything else.

"It's fine," I told her. "I'm tired, too."

She let go of me. "You want to go to bed?"

Charlie and I exchanged a look. He held out his hand and I took it. Then he took his wife's.

"We can all go to bed," he said. "How's that?"

She didn't seem that happy about it, but shrugged. "Fine. Party poopers."

"When you have to get up at five in the morning," Charlie said, "we'll see how perky you are at eleven at night."

In their bedroom, he undressed in front of me without any hint of self-consciousness, then went into the bathroom. Meredith turned on the flat-screen TV hung on the wall, and made space for me beside her on the bed, though she relaxed on the pillows and I sat more upright, feeling a little awkward.

"I can't believe him," she said after a few minutes of mindless reality programming had passed.

"Who, Charlie?" I rolled onto my belly to face her. "Really, it's okay."

Clearly, it wasn't. She sighed and wriggled deeper into the pillows. She brushed her fingers over the tips of my hair. I'd kept it blond but added some dark streaks at the ends. "I like your hair."

I laughed. "Thanks."

"I'm serious. I do." She sat up and looked over at the mirror on the dresser as she ran her fingers through her own shoulder-length waves. "Maybe I should get it cut."

"If you want. But I love your hair the way it is." I sat up to shift closer to her. I touched it, curling one long strand around my finger before trailing my fingers over her shoulder. When I leaned in to kiss her neck, though, she moved away just enough to stop me.

"But yours seems so easy to take care of. You never have to fuss with it. Mine takes forever to look good." Her eyes met mine in the mirror.

In the reflection I saw two women, both blonde, though my hair was platinum and hers honey. She was full-breasted and flat-bellied; I had curves in my hips and thighs and ass. I saw two women sitting close enough to touch, but with a canyon-size space between them nonetheless.

"Your hair is beautiful," I told her.

A slow smile curved her mouth. "You're just saying that."

I shook my head. In the bathroom, the sound of the shower stopped. I heard Charlie humming. In the mirror, Meredith's eyes never left mine.

"I…I had a fight with Vic. A pretty bad one. I told him I wasn't coming back tonight."

"What's his problem?"

I shrugged, not wanting to discuss it. "It was time for me to get out of there anyway."

"You're moving out?" Meredith pursed her lips.

I shrugged again.

Her mouth parted. The pink tip of her tongue peeked out, just barely, touching the center of her top lip before disappearing. "You should stay here."

"Tonight," I said.

"You could stay longer than that, Tesla."

"What about Charlie?"

"Charlie adores you."

"Yeah. When I'm sucking his cock." I figured there was no point in sugarcoating it. "Living here's a totally different thing. For you, too, Meredith."

"It would be great. We'd see so much more of you. And what could be bad about that?" She gave me the smile that got her what she wanted every time.

"Having a third person living with you isn't the same as having a guest. Your house, your kitchen, your washing machine. Your things." I ticked off the list on my fingers. "There's a share of utilities to consider. Who buys groceries? Where would I sleep?"

"You make it sound so complicated." She touched my hair again, toying with the fringe against my cheek.

"If you don't talk about this stuff up front…" I took a breath to keep my voice steady. "You told me you talked about me with Charlie before you asked if I'd join you."

She had a blank look for a second. "Yeah?"

"You had to, right? To make sure everything was set up? So that nothing went wrong, nobody got hurt or jealous. Right?" I thought that's what they'd done. It was what I'd have done.

"I thought you liked being part of us." Meredith frowned and the crease appeared between her eyes.

I took her hand and brought it to my lips. I kissed her knuckles. "I do. I like it a lot."

"What, then?" She shifted closer. "What's the problem?"

"I like being with you. Both of you. And I adore Charlie." I deliberately used the term she'd used. "That's the thing, isn't it? Being with you? Both of you," I added. "But I'm really not."

She frowned but didn't look away from the mirror. "What's that mean?"

"It means that I'm with Charlie, and Charlie's with you, and you're with Charlie. But you're not with me." I brushed my lips over her shoulder, not lingering. "And I need to know if that's going to change."

She kissed me.

After all the months of imagining it, fantasizing about the softness of her lips and how she'd taste, this kiss nevertheless caught me completely unawares. I drew in a breath, startled, and she put a hand on the back of my neck to hold me still. It didn't last long, that kiss, but it was long enough to promise something more.

She drew back just enough to look me in the eyes. "I made the offer. Think about it."

"About what?" Charlie asked, entering the room with a towel around his hips. He went to the dresser, not the one with the mirror, and pulled out a pair of pajama bottoms.

"Tesla moving in with us."

I could see him in the reflection, too, as he turned. I didn't want to tell them I'd already decided. That in fact I had almost no choice, at least in the short term, until I could find something else. That I was flattered and grateful she wanted me, afraid he didn't, worried about how it would all change. Or not change.

"Oh?" Charlie asked.

Meredith and I didn't look away from the reflection as he crawled onto the bed behind us. She leaned back a little toward me. He moved to her other side.

"But Tesla has some issues with how things have been going between us, Charlie."

He let out a slow breath, appearing confused. This was between us, the women in the mirror. I gave my head the tiniest shake.

"I don't want you to do anything you don't want to," I told her. "But if you kissed a girl…"

Charlie gave her a slightly startled look.

"And you liked it," I added, "I'm just wondering why you don't want to kiss me."

"We never talked about that." Meredith glanced at Charlie in the mirror's reflection. "We talked about him being with you."

I nuzzled her shoulder again. "Like you said, there's always something to talk about."

"I thought you didn't want to, that's all," Charlie said. "I never wanted you to think I'd have a problem with it, Meredith."

"Do you?" I asked him.

We looked at each other face-to-face. Without the mirror bridging us. Charlie shook his head.

"No. Of course not. Hell," he admitted with a sheepish grin, "it would be hot. You know, what guy doesn't want to watch two women together, right?"

From this angle I could see Meredith only in the mirror, but I thought that made it easier somehow. That distance. She shivered when I touched her.

"I guess I have to ask the question. Why do you want me to move in with you? What would make that better than what we're doing now?"

That earned a smile from her. "You need a place to stay. And we have a good time together. Don't we?"

"Sure." Charlie rubbed my back. "I do, anyway."

I smiled. "Me, too. But living together is a big step."

Meredith relaxed, leaning back against me. "You spend so much time with us already, I just thought it would be easier. And fun."

I put my chin on her shoulder, my hands on her belly. "I just want to be sure, before I say yes...."

"Say yes," Meredith said.

Charlie's rubbing hand slowed and came up to cup the back of my neck. "Say yes, Tesla."

"I want to know if you want me, Meredith." Said aloud, the words weren't scary. And if she said no, at least we'd have it out between us. "Because I'm never sure where to go with you."

She drew in a slightly stuttering breath and put her hand over mine. The three of us sat very still. Charlie's fingers squeezed my neck gently before sliding down my spine again, and he moved away from us, back against the pillows.

"How about all the way?" Meredith said finally.

Tension that had coiled in my gut got a little tighter. "Are you sure?"

Her lips parted and the pink hint of her tongue appeared, delicately touching her top lip. "I guess we'll find out."

I grinned and pressed my mouth to the nape of her neck as her fingers linked with mine. "It's only kinky the first time."

She laughed then, relaxing even more against me as she leaned her head on my shoulder. "Charlie?"

"Yeah, baby."

"Do you want to watch me and Tesla make love?"

"Um, yeah, of course." In the mirror, he grinned, his hand already rubbing at the front of his pajamas.

She moved my hand lower, our linked fingers skimming the waistband of her skirt. In the reflection, her eyes never left mine. She slid our hands down her thigh and up again, bringing her hem up, too. My fingertips whispered on her tights and discovered the heat between her legs. She pressed my hand against her pussy.

Shifting, I moved so my knees pressed on either side of her

hips, my front against her back. I kissed her neck, slow and sweet and careful. I breathed in the scent of her and let my tongue flick out to taste her skin.

Meredith let go of my hand to use both of hers on the buttons of her blouse. She had them undone in half a minute, her shirt gaping to show off the pretty, hot-pink demicup bra that revealed just the barest hint of her areolae. I pushed my hand inside her tights and panties and found the soft brush of her curls. Lower, the slippery heat of her pussy and tight button of her clit. I pinched it gently, so gently between my finger and thumb, and was rewarded with her low cry. The shift of her hips. She arched against me, her gaze never leaving mine.

Two women still in the mirror, though now only one could be fully seen. Behind us both, Charlie's reflection watched. He'd pulled his cock out, stroking it. I slipped a finger inside Meredith's pussy, then out to circle on her clit.

Sitting this way, my pussy against her ass and my knees cradling her, it was sort of like we'd become one person. Kind of like I was touching myself. I knew so well how good it felt to push one, then two fingers deep inside myself, curling them against the slight roughness of my G-spot. How it felt to coat my fingers in my arousal and use it to slide over my clit. To jerk it like a tiny little cock. I knew how fucking delirious it made me to press against the hood of my clit and shift my hips against my hand the way Meredith was doing now, instead of using my hand to press on my clit.

She cupped her breasts, pushing down the bra, showing her tight pink nipples. She licked her fingers, using them to wet her nipples. Make them harder. She rocked her pussy against my hand as her head fell back farther, against my shoulder.

She turned her head and kissed me.

Our tongues met and danced, slow at first, then faster. I

heard Charlie groan, and wanted to make the same noise my-self. Meredith broke the kiss with a small gasp.

"Oh, God," she said. "Oh, my fucking God."

In the mirror, she watched my fingers play against her pussy. She watched me watching. Still looking, she hooked her fingers in her tights and panties and lifted her ass so she could get them down and off her feet. With her skirt pulled up, her pussy completely revealed, she pressed back against me and offered me everything.

I slowed the pace, letting her watch my fingers slide inside her. Then up. From this distance it was hard to see the details, but I had no doubts she felt everything. My breath caught at her shudder and the jump of her inner muscles against my fingers. I shot Charlie a glance in the mirror and found him con-centrating, a little grim-faced, his cock in his fist. But when he saw me, his grin lit up the room.

I was doing this as much for him as for her or myself. In this position I couldn't really touch myself, but for the mo-ment that was fine. It was arousing enough to watch her face and feel her thrusting against my fingers.

Meredith put her hand on mine, stopping me. She swal-lowed, her voice rough. "I want your mouth."

She didn't have to ask me twice. We turned on the bed, scooting up closer to Charlie. She kissed him, their tongues sliding against each other. She stroked his cock and cupped his balls. Then she turned on her back, thighs tipped open.

I knelt between her legs and undid the button on the side of her skirt. Eased it off her. She was bare now but for the open blouse and her bra, but I liked the way she looked, wanton and disheveled, so I didn't take those off her.

I moved my mouth over her thigh. Her belly. I listened

for her soft sighs and moans. Her hand found my hair again, ruffling it.

When I found her clit with my tongue, she cried out. Her hips jerked. I slid my hands beneath her ass and used my thumbs to open her. Her clit, perfect, tight and hard, twitched beneath the flat of my tongue when I licked her.

There's one secret to making a woman come: consistency. It can be difficult to find what works, but once you do, don't switch it up.

Meredith liked long, slow swipes of my tongue. She liked the press and slide of my fingers inside her. And she really, really liked it when I used my fingers to press just above her clit as I licked her.

Charlie groaned again. In the next minute, he moved, getting on his back so that his face was under my pussy. His mouth found my clit; his hands grasped my hips. I rocked against his lips and tongue, the brief press of his teeth.

We came within seconds of each other, me and Meredith. She shook with her orgasm, but bit back her cries. Mine were muffled against her flesh. I pressed my lips to her clit as it pulsed, and felt mine echoing it almost exactly.

Something that can take so long to achieve is over so soon. I rolled onto my back and caught my breath. Charlie moved against me, one hand resting on Meredith's hip. She didn't stir.

Then she said, "The room at the end of the hall can be yours, so you'll have your own space. And we'll expect a third of the electricity and other utilities, including groceries. You can cook, I'll clean up—I'm shit with cooking. Charlie takes out the garbage and I do the laundry, but you can do the vacuuming."

She pushed up on one elbow to look at me cuddling with

THE SPACE BETWEEN US

her husband. She wet that lovely mouth with her tongue. She kissed me. Then him.

"There will always be stuff to talk about," Meredith said. "But is that enough for now?"

I'd been pretty sure before coming over tonight that it would be, but now I stretched, lazy and sated, and pulled her down to snuggle with us. "Yes."

And that was how it began.

Chapter

26

"We either go with her or we have Thanksgiving here." The dishes rattled in Meredith's hands as she moved them from dishwasher to cabinet. "That's just how it's going to be, Charlie. Or you go to your sister's by yourself. Whatever. You think I care if I miss her dried-out turkey breast and baked spaghetti? Who the hell serves baked spaghetti at Thanksgiving, anyway? Oh, that's right, the sort of person who doesn't serve mashed potatoes."

I paused in the upstairs hallway, not meaning to eavesdrop but unwilling to go down into the kitchen once I'd heard them arguing. Well, Meredith was arguing. Charlie was his usual amiable, softer-spoken self. I heard him say something, but couldn't catch the words.

Another cupboard opened and closed. Hard. "She lives with us. You agreed to it, and the last time I checked, you were having a great old time. She's part of us, Charlie. And so, what? Because you don't want to tell your family, you're going to tell Tesla she has to stay home by herself? Fuck that noise."

My heart sank. I didn't want to be the reason Meredith and Charlie fought. This was a complicated business, being a third of a relationship instead of half. It made it hard when we went places together because someone always had to sit in the backseat. I could only imagine what a commotion it would cause if they took me to Charlie's sister's house as something other than a roommate. After all, I'd been living there only a few days. It was unlikely Charlie's family even knew he had a roommate.

Honestly, it would've been fine with me if they left me home. I didn't really want to go to his sister's house for Thanksgiving. I had to work the Friday after, so going to my mom's in California was out, even if I'd wanted to make the trip to see her. I'd figured I'd get Cap to cook me something, since Lynds was going to be out of town with her family, and we'd watch old movies all day long.

I'd been back to Vic's house once to get my things and say goodbye to the kids. Simone had refused to talk to me. Max hadn't seemed to understand. Even though Elaine hadn't protested my moving out, she'd told me I was welcome to go to her mother's house with them. When I asked her what Vic thought about that idea, all she'd been able to say was, "The kids and I would like you to be there." I believed her, but I still couldn't go to Thanksgiving at her mother's house.

"You can't just expect me to tell them the truth." Charlie sounded reasonable. He always did. "You're my wife. I'm not supposed to have a girlfriend, too."

More rattling and slamming. "News flash. You do."

"I'm not sure how I feel about asking my sister if I can bring a stranger to Thanksgiving dinner—"

"She's not a stranger. She's Tesla. You might remember better if your face was buried in her pussy."

Even I cringed at that. Yet I heard Charlie laugh. I figured it was time to make an appearance. I made it loud enough that both of them would have to turn. Strangely enough, it was Meredith who looked as if she'd been caught at something.

"Honey, come here." Charlie beckoned and I went to him willingly enough. He put an arm around me and then around a reluctant Meredith, who suffered his embrace for only a second or two before pushing away from him to finish unloading the dishwasher.

"I can make plans with my brother," I said, before Charlie could dive into the embarrassing explanation of why he wasn't going to invite me to eat turkey with his family. "Really, Charlie. It's cool."

"It's not cool." Meredith shot the remark over her shoulder.

"If Tesla wants to spend Thanksgiving with her family—" Charlie began, but she cut him off.

"That's not what this is about, Charlie, and you know it. It's about you not wanting to admit what's going on, because God forbid your family figure out you're kinky."

He drew me a little closer to him, though he was looking at her. "It's none of my family's business what I do in my house or in my bedroom. But it is their business what I bring to their house."

"I'm not a thing to bring anywhere," I said to them both.

They looked at me.

I stepped out a bit from Charlie's hug, though not so far he couldn't reach for me if he wanted. "I'm not a bone for you two dogs to fight over, okay? Really. Meredith," I said, facing her. "The fact is, there's a reason why it's called a couple. Couple is two. Not three."

"Nobody tells me how I should live my life. I'm not going to be ashamed of it, or conform to what society—" she began, but it was my turn to interrupt.

"I'm not ashamed. Charlie's not, either," I added, hoping that was true. "But…you have to live in the real world. We all do. I love being with you. Both of you. But it's not something we can just go flaunting around to everyone and expect the rest of the world to understand. Like Charlie said, it's not anyone's business."

She frowned, her brow creasing, and crossed her arms. She looked as beautiful being stubborn as she did acquiescing. "If we were dykes we'd have parades to march in. But what, because we're three…?"

I reached for her hand and, when she let me take it, tugged her closer to me and Charlie. "Baby, I don't really care. I don't need to go with you for Thanksgiving."

"But I want you there," she said.

"I want her there, too." Charlie slipped his arm back around my waist and kissed the top of my head when I snuggled closer. "But I can't just bring her in and tell them all the truth. I won't subject Tesla to that, Meredith. You can call me a coward if you want, but I'm thinking of her, too."

I stroked my fingers along the back of her hand, but she wouldn't join our hug. "And you. They'd give you a hard time, too," I said. "Or maybe pity you, thinking Charlie's got himself a side piece."

She glowered. "Anyone who knows me would not pity me. Ever. For anything."

Charlie laughed. "No, but they'd talk about you behind your back."

"You think I care?" she said, but her anger was softening. She sidled a little closer and hooked a finger through Charlie's belt loop. "Fine. We could just say she's our roommate. Let them think we made some bad investments or something and need the income. Though your sister's not dumb, Charles. She'd totally see right through all of it, unless you can keep from looking at Tesla like you want to eat her right up. Which you can't."

"Probably not," he admitted, and kissed me again. "And I don't want to have to."

"It's better if I don't go with you. Next year," I offered boldly, since next year was something we'd never even talked about, "we can have it here and nobody needs to explain anything."

Finally, Meredith moved toward us. Her hand slid over the ass of my fleecy sweatpants, cupping my butt. Her other hand did the same to Charlie. She pushed up on her toes to kiss his mouth briefly, then gave me a slightly longer smooch.

"That's our Tesla. So smart." Her forehead pressed mine.

So close I couldn't focus, her face blurred, but her eyes stayed clear. She blinked and kissed me again. Her tongue slipped inside my mouth, delicately probing.

"You sure you'll be okay? I hate the thought of you spending Thanksgiving alone." She put her head on my shoulder.

"I don't have to be alone. Cap needs someone to hang out with, anyway. I should spend the day with him. It'll be fine."

Charlie's hand made circles on my back. "Hey, let's stream a movie on Interflix. Just relax tonight."

I liked the sound of that. "I'll make popcorn. Real butter. Salt. It'll be awesome."

"All those calories?" Meredith said without real heat. "Guess we'll just have to work them off."

"I like the way you think." Charlie kissed her.

He kissed me, too.

The three of us eased apart, Charlie to head into the den to find something to watch, Meredith with the last of the dishes. I went into the pantry to pull out the plastic container of popcorn kernels and then to the fridge for real butter. I was reaching into the cupboard for salt when Meredith moved behind me to put something in the drawer. We bumped into each other and, laughing, she put her arms around me.

She kissed me again, backing me up against the counter. Her hands fit neatly on my hips. Her tongue stroked mine as her thigh pressed between my legs.

"Mmm," I said into her mouth. "What's going on with you?"

"What do you mean?" She paused, her hands on their way to my breasts, but stopping just beneath. She frowned.

I didn't want a frown. I wanted smiling and sultry Meredith. Playful, not pouting. "Nothing. Never mind."

I leaned to kiss her again, but she pulled away enough to keep me from reaching her mouth. "Why should something be going on with me?"

I didn't want to point out that she rarely, if ever, initiated anything with me like that. Flirty caresses and a kiss here and there, yes. But she'd kissed me the way she kissed Charlie, and that was unusual. Because I liked it, though, I didn't want her to feel self-conscious.

I pushed my crotch lightly against her thigh. "It shouldn't. I liked what you were doing. Don't stop."

She drew in a breath, her shoulders lifting. She tilted her head, looking over my face. Her hands moved up to cup my breasts, her fingers tweaking my nipples before moving away. "Charlie's waiting."

I smiled. "You think he'll mind if we start without him?"

"He might mind if we finish without him," she said, and kissed the corner of my mouth before moving away. "Besides. I want some of your insanely fattening popcorn."

I caught her before she could move too far. "Meredith, you're gorgeous. You know that, right?"

Sometimes I wasn't sure she did, even though now she tossed the fall of her perfect golden hair over her shoulders and gave me a look worthy of any silent screen vamp.

"Of course I am." She winked and moved toward the door to the laundry room that led to the garage. "Getting a soda. You want one?"

"Sure." I pulled down a pot from the rack and set it on the burner. "Thanks."

Twenty minutes later we were all settled on the big over-stuffed couch with bowls of salty, buttery popcorn on our laps and cans of soda in front of us. Charlie had picked a horror movie I hadn't seen, and though Meredith had curled her lip, she hadn't insisted we watch something else. Set up between them, I could laugh when she jumped and hid her eyes, and discuss the plot points with Charlie.

In that moment, I knew how that third bowl of porridge felt, that third chair, the third and final bed Goldilocks had tried. I wasn't too hot or too cold, too hard or too soft. I was just right.

The movie ended. I held up a handful of popcorn for Charlie to take from my fingers. He lipped at my palm, his tongue swiping along the flesh in a way that made me shiver. When I looked up at him, those dark blue eyes dug right into my soul.

I kissed him because I could. Because here in this place, on this couch and in this house, Charlie belonged to me in a way that had nothing to do with rings or ceremonies. Behind me,

Meredith's breath caressed my neck before I felt the warm, wet press of her lips on my skin.

Upstairs we went to their room by unspoken agreement. We'd fallen into the habit of bed-hopping, Charlie and me in mine one night, Meredith and me in theirs another, the two of them in theirs and me sprawled out decadently alone sometimes, too, but that was for sleeping. When it came to fucking, they had the better bed. Not quite big enough for the three of us to sleep in comfortably, at least not for the person who ended up in the middle, but for sex it was perfect.

I loved how easy it was for Meredith and me to push Charlie back against the mattress and strip him naked. To cover him with kisses up one side and down the other, passing each other at his cock, which we both took turns sucking and licking. I loved the flicker of her tongue on mine as our mouths met on Charlie's prick, and I loved the way his hands stroked our hair back from our faces. And the way he murmured encouragement, the hitch in his voice when he reacted to our touching, licking, stroking, sucking.

Meredith didn't notice that I'd paused in my adoration of Charlie's body; she was busy stripping out of her clothes and tossing the extra pillows onto the floor so we'd have enough space for everything else. Charlie noticed, though. He got up on one elbow to cup my cheek with his hand.

He didn't say anything. We could communicate so easily with silence what some people needed an entire dictionary of words to say. I loved that, too.

I moved up his body to reach his lips with my mouth. He was smiling when I kissed him. I toyed with his nipple and trailed tickling fingers along his side, which made him laugh and squirm away. I looked up to see Meredith watching both of us.

"What?" I asked.

She shook her head and shifted closer to run her fingers through Charlie's hair. He turned his head so he could kiss her hand when she pressed it against his face. His fingers closed over it, holding it to his mouth when I grasped his cock, sucking gently, then harder. His hips pushed up, and I laughed softly, gripping it at the base to keep it from choking me.

At the touch of Meredith's hand on top of my head, I looked at her again. She leaned to kiss me. Put my hand between her legs. She was already slick and hot, and I pressed inside her just enough to make her shudder a little. She swallowed my breath when she moaned.

"Lie back," I whispered into her mouth.

Her eyes fluttered open, the pupils wide and dark. I cupped the back of her neck to hold her to my kiss for a few seconds longer, then followed her to the bed when she did as I'd said. Straddling one thigh, I mouthed a trail of kisses along her hip and belly, but unlike ticklish Charlie, Meredith didn't squirm. She threw an arm over her eyes and let her thighs fall open, giving me access to every bit of her.

I looked at Charlie, who'd rolled onto his side to watch. I touched his hair and cupped a hand under his chin to bring his mouth to mine. We kissed as I circled Meredith's clit with my fingertip, but only briefly—I had other intentions for my tongue.

Sex with one person can be complicated if you want to get creative, but it's still possible to sort of just go with the flow. See what happens. Roll around, find the soft parts, see what happens when you rub them against each other. Sex with two other people requires a little more thought. Sometimes diagrams can be helpful.

Sometimes we fucked like a V—both of us pleasuring

Charlie and ourselves. We'd done the daisy chain, Meredith blowing Charlie, who gave me head while I did the same to Meredith. We'd even tried out some of those fancy positions from *The Threesome Handbook*. 'Cuz see, that's the beauty of three, the variations you can't get up to with only two.

Now I settled on my hands and knees between Meredith's legs, my ass in the air, my mouth on her pussy. I kissed her clit, then sucked it more gently than I'd sucked Charlie's cock. Under my tongue and around my fingers, Meredith's pussy was slick and hot. With the reward of her sigh, I smiled and pressed the flat of my tongue to her clit. Lick, lick, lick. Not too fast, maybe just a little too slow. Teasing. I wanted her to come hard, not quick.

Charlie ran a hand down the curve of my back, over my ass. Between my legs from behind to stroke my clit. He pushed a finger inside me, then another, and I closed my eyes. I sank into the sensations of warm woman beneath me and hard male behind me. I pushed back, fucking myself against his fingers.

He got the hint.

The bed moved as Charlie got up on his knees. I heard the mutter of the bedside drawer opening, the tear of the condom wrapper. His cock nudged at me, but I wasn't quite wet enough yet for him to slide all the way inside. I didn't have to worry about Charlie forcing anything, though; he popped the top on the bottle of lube and used a generous amount. His fingers slipped against my clit, then deep inside me, curling against my G-spot.

"Oh, God," I murmured. I had to stop for a few seconds, my fingers moving inside Meredith in an echo of the delicious stroking of Charlie's fingers, but I had to catch my breath.

She made a low noise of protest, her fingers finding my hair and twisting in the short strands. Not quite hard enough to hurt, but definitely enough to let me know I should get back to business. It was difficult to concentrate, though. Charlie's thick cock nudged again at my entrance and I found myself automatically breathing out, opening myself to take him all the way in.

I blinked, biting my bottom lip, then managed to nuzzle against Meredith's clit again. She was so hot, so wet, and her pussy clutched at my fingers as I fucked them inside her—but it was her clit that needed the attention in order for her to get off.

My name broke into two pieces on Charlie's groan. He filled me, pushing in slowly until I couldn't take any more. But he didn't move right away, just put his hands on my hips and held himself in place while I lapped at Meredith's clit. She was shifting under me, lifting her hips. Her arm still covered her eyes, but her mouth was open, lax, her tongue flickering out every once in a while to run against her lips. I caught the briefest glimpse of her face when I stopped to take a breath and acclimate myself to Charlie's cock inside me, and she frowned and tugged at my hair again, pushing me against her.

I smiled against her clit. Charlie had said my name; my goal was to have Meredith not just say it but scream it. I wanted her to let go, the way she did with Charlie.

But then I was having a hard time thinking about anything else, because Charlie started moving. He found my clit with his fingertips, stroking in time to his thrusts, which were slow, steady and amazing. The lube meant his fingers rolled over my clit, never tugging or scraping at my flesh. Smooth. Even when his strokes grew a little ragged as his fucking got faster, it was still fucking gorgeous.

Meredith rolled her hips. Her pussy fluttered around my fingers. I lessened the pressure of my tongue, using the tip instead of the flat and letting her move against me.

Tension coiled tight in my gut. Pleasure, icy hot, trilled through me, in my pussy, down the backs of my legs, into the soles of my feet. I wanted so much for it to spill over, fill me up, break me down. But all I could do was ride it as it built and built.

Meredith came first. The muscles in her pussy bore down on my fingers. Her clit pulsed under my tongue. And she gave me what I wanted—my name, uttered in a hoarse cry. She was thinking of me in those last seconds when orgasm boiled up inside her, and that was enough to push me over into my own climax.

I didn't say anyone's name. I was made voiceless by the pleasure pushing its way through me. I shuddered with it, my fingers digging into the sheets. I gasped. I pressed my face to the inside of Meredith's thigh, found the sweetness of her flesh with my mouth and kissed her there as I came.

Charlie, ever the gentleman, didn't last much longer. He gave a last deep thrust inside me, then a couple shallower ones. Breathing hard, he bent to press himself over my back. I felt the brief brush of his lips on my shoulder blade before he withdrew so I could flop down next to Meredith, whose eyes were closed. She wasn't moving—well, except for her mouth, which was twitching into a smile.

I kissed her shoulder. Charlie joined us on my other side, his arm over my belly so his fingers could rest on his wife's hip. We stayed like that in silence for a few minutes, broken only when Charlie yawned. He stretched. He kissed my neck and got out of bed to pad into the bathroom. The hiss of the shower began.

I was ready to fall asleep, but I didn't want to do it there. I had to work the early shift and knew Charlie would be get-

ting up early, too. Meredith grumbled as I sat up. Her eyes
didn't open.

I kissed her shoulder again, then went into the bathroom
to use the toilet and say good-night to Charlie. He peeked
out the shower door.

"You coming in?"

"Nah, I'll get one in my bathroom." I did meander over
to admire him under the spray, though. "Just came in to say
good-night."

He leaned to kiss me. "'Night. Hey, dinner out tomorrow?
Maybe that new Indian place?"

"I thought Meredith hated Indian food."

"She does." He shrugged, soaping his hair and scrubbing
at it. Suds formed and slid down his face as he tipped it under
the water to wash them away. "But she's got something going
on, some party or something, tomorrow night. It'll just be
you and me."

Just me and Charlie. Why did that make my heart skip in
my chest, as if he was asking me for a date? "I love Indian
food. Sure. Sounds like a plan."

God, he had such a wonderful smile. It lit up his eyes.
"Great! I'll be home regular time."

"I'll be home before you. I'll be ready to go." I braved the
spray to kiss his mouth, then laughed when he pulled me inside with him. "I said I'd take one in my bathroom!"

"You're here already. Why not let me scrub your back?"
Charlie wiggled his eyebrows. The lecher look didn't work for
him; I'd never be able to see him as anything but mannerly.

I turned, though. "Hmm. I guess I can't turn that down."

His soapy hands moved over my skin. With the sex out of
the way, it was still nice to feel his touch. Nicer, in one way,

because both of us knew it wasn't going to lead to fucking. It was just…affection.

I was struck again with emotion. The casual way he turned me to soap my front, standing aside to give me a share of the water. Rinsing me. When he pulled me against him for a hug, my face pressed to his hot, wet skin, Charlie kissed the top of my head and I closed my eyes and willed myself not to burst into emotional tears.

It had been a long time that I'd gone without hugs. Plenty of love, yes. Some sex along the way, sure. But sloppy toddler kisses and grimy-fingered squeezes from Simone and Max aside, I hadn't been with anyone I could just hold on to. Someone I could lean against.

The water would run cold before I wanted to get out of that shower, but that was silliness. I looked up at Charlie, whose back protected me from a faceful of water. I wanted to tell him how I felt, but the words wouldn't come.

I loved him.

The realization of this didn't hurtle into me and shatter, breaking me apart. It seeped inside me, filling all the places I'd never bothered to notice were empty.

How could I tell another woman's husband I loved him? How could I tell just one of the pair? The answer was I couldn't. I kissed him again, instead, and then let myself out of the shower, snagging his towel to dry off with, and handing him a clean one from the shelf. I wrapped the damp one around my hair and wished him another good-night, ready to pad naked through their bedroom and down the hall into my own, where I'd comb out my hair and put on my pajamas.

"Tesla," Charlie said, halting me in the doorway. "Just so you know. I'm not ashamed of you. Of us, or this. It's not about that."

I'd almost forgotten the conversation that had started all this. "I know you're not, Charlie."

In their bedroom, I paused to say good-night to Meredith, but she'd already turned out the light and pulled up the covers. In my own room I stretched out with a luxurious sigh across my bed. For the first time in a long while, though, I thought of Vic as I tried to drift off to sleep. We hadn't spoken since our fight. Right now he might be moving on silent feet through his dark house, checking windows and doors to make sure they were locked. Making sure his family was protected. I missed being part of that.

It took me half an hour of staring at the ceiling and counting endless bleating sheep to realize I wasn't going to fall asleep unless I got out of bed and made the rounds of the house. So I did, because that's what you do for the people you love—you do what you can to settle your mind that they're safe. And then, after I'd made sure the burners were all off, the windows and doors secured, I finally crawled back into my bed and fell asleep.

Chapter
27

"How hot do you want it?" The menu in Charlie's fingers bobbed up and down as he looked it over.

"Hot as you can stand it, son." I winked at him. "How hot is that?"

"Hot." Charlie said it like a challenge. "I'm not sure you can stand it, that's how hot."

I humphed. "You're on. You want to go nuclear? I'm down with that. How about volcanic—can you handle that?"

"Which one's hotter? That's what I want." Charlie sounded dead serious, but he had a twinkle in his blue eyes.

"Let's just tell them to go to ten. And bring lots of yogurt dip."

"I always end up ordering too much food here. I like everything and I want it." He studied the menu some more.

"Didn't your mama ever teach you that having everything

you want isn't always the best thing for you?" I couldn't help teasing him. I was tired after a long day on my feet. I was starving and a little giddy from being out and about with him. Just him.

It seemed a little wrong that this felt so different from the times the three of us went out, or even the few times Charlie and I had been alone at the house. It shouldn't have. I'd spent tons of time alone with Meredith both before and after we'd begun this.

It still felt different.

Maybe it was because I had no doubts about how Charlie felt about me, or if it was okay for me to touch his hand across the table. I didn't have to keep myself from touching him at all. Somehow this meant our fingers twisted together and my toes rubbed along the back of his calf.

"And it's such a waste," Charlie added. "You're right, my mama would be ashamed. I never eat it all and can't take it home."

"Why can't you take it home?" I was in the habit of ordering stuff at a restaurant for the specific purpose of taking half home to eat the next day.

"Meredith doesn't like it."

I could tell my expression had twisted, but I didn't try to smooth it. "Huh? Why should that matter? She doesn't have to eat it."

"She says the smell makes everything else in the fridge reek, and she hates it." Charlie shrugged, his expression not exactly twisting. More like scrunching. The face of a man who knows his wife is being sort of unreasonable, but who isn't willing to bring on a fight.

"Huh. Well. That's just silly. If you wrap it really tight in foil or something, it won't smell at all. So order whatever you want, son, we gon' get our chow on!"

He squeezed my hand. "Great. Your treat, right?"

"Guess again," I told him. "You asked me out, remember?"

"Ah. Yeah. Right. Well, it's a good thing I have a credit card and there's a Home Depot next door."

I laughed. "The credit card I get, but why do you need a Home Depot?"

"For the wheelbarrow," Charlie said serenely.

"Okay, I give. What do you need a wheelbarrow for?"

He didn't even crack a smile, though those eyes once more betrayed him. "To wheel you home after you eat everything we order."

God, how I loved him.

With perfect timing, the waiter came over. True to his word, Charlie ordered too much food. Papadums and curry, lamb rogan josh and tandoori chicken. My stomach groaned just at the thought of it all.

"I'm starving," I told him.

"Good."

"And what we don't eat, we will take home," I added. It was sort of a challenge of my own.

Charlie looked reluctant, but then shrugged. "I do love leftover Indian food."

"God, yeah. Cold lamb rogan josh is…" I kissed my fingertips. "Fucking awesome. And besides, I can help you work it all off later."

He took my other hand, to stroke it with his thumb. "Oh, yeah?"

"Sure. I hear cunnilingus works off two thousand calories an hour." I'd totally just made that up, but was working on Charlie's deadpan delivery.

"What about blow jobs? Maybe I can help you out, too."

"Charlie?"

We both looked up at the same time. The woman standing at our table looked to be in her mid-forties, dark hair, nice dress, nice shoes—I checked, of course. When the man you're with is called out in a restaurant, it's important to assess the threat.

"Ellen. Hi." Charlie's voice sounded normal, but the way he withdrew his hand from mine told me a lot.

I sat up straighter and folded my hands at my place, which somehow made me feel guiltier. Like I'd been caught at something shameful. I sipped water to cover up that feeling.

"Haven't seen you in forever. How's Meredith?" Ellen made no secret of her examination of me before she gave Charlie the stare of death.

Charlie didn't waver in front of it. "She's great."

"Is she still selling Jangle Bangles?" Ellen shifted her weight to one foot, one hip jutting, and crossed her arms. "I never see her at the gym anymore."

"Ah…I think…well, we got a treadmill and some other stuff at home, and I think she exercises there. But yeah, she still sells that stuff."

"She hasn't sent out any newsletters in a while." Ellen sounded accusing, as if it could possibly be Charlie's fault Meredith was ignoring her online. "I guess she's been busy."

"Everyone's busy," I interjected, with a smile as pleasant as I could make it.

"Oh, hi," she said, as if she'd just seen me there. She held out her hand, which I shook. "Ellen Leveau. I'm a good friend of Meredith's. And Charlie's, of course."

I took my hand back, still smiling. "Of course."

"We should really have you over for drinks and game night.

You and Meredith," she added. "I know Jim would love to see you."

"That sounds great. Give Meredith a shout." Charlie didn't have to continue, because the waiter showed up with our appetizers.

Ellen stepped out of the way. "I guess I should let you eat your dinner. It was nice meeting you...."

"Tesla," Charlie said, before I could.

I get a lot of different reactions to my name, so Ellen's raised brows weren't a surprise. Her next question was, though. I mean, some people have no social skills.

"Does Meredith know you're out with...Tesla?"

I wasn't ashamed of what I had with Charlie and Meredith; I'd established that with both of them. But it wasn't my place to out them, either. Besides, while I drew the line at forcing our relationship down the throats of family and friends who might not understand, I kind of liked fucking with random strangers who lacked the manners to know when something wasn't any of their damned business.

"Actually, she doesn't. She had a meeting tonight, so Charlie and I decided we'd come here for dinner because she hates Indian food." I gave Ellen a completely plastic smile. "She'll probably figure it out when she finds the leftovers in the fridge, though. Unless we decide to be super sneaky and not take them home. We haven't decided yet, right, Charlie?"

His lips tipped into a half smile, but he held it back. "Yeah. I think we'll take them home. You're right, they're just as good the next day. We can eat them for breakfast."

Ellen's eyes were flitting back and forth between us, and she looked as if she was trying to smile, but having a hard time of it. It was the look of a woman who knows there's a joke being played but doesn't get it. "So...you're...?"

MEGAN HART

"We live together," I said. "We're roommates, I guess you could say."

"You could say," Charlie added.

Ellen blinked. Her smile got a little more natural. "Oh. Well."

She glanced at the spot where we'd had our hands linked, and appeared a little confused before again looking at Charlie. "I guess that makes sense, then. Tell Meredith I said hi. Tell her to give me a call."

Nodding, she backed away, heading over to her table, where she spoke excitedly to the group of women she was with. They all looked at us. Charlie sighed.

"Ah, shit."

I laughed. "Do you think she'll call Meredith and tell on us?"

"Probably. Meredith used to be pretty close with that group." He laughed then. "They'll pick the whole story apart first. See if they can catch us doing something really naughty. I'm sure Ellen will have Meredith's best interests at heart when she calls to tell her I'm cheating."

I reached across the table for his hand again. I didn't hold on to it for longer than it took to squeeze it, though. "Some people need to mind their own business. That's all."

"We'll have to tell her so she's not blindsided." Charlie dug into the food with a fork. "Meredith would be pissed if Ellen called her, trying to be her friend, and she didn't know in advance what to say."

"So...we tell her. It's no crime we came out to dinner without her." I caught sight of his face and hesitated, suddenly a little more anxious than I wanted to be.

Charlie shook his head. "It shouldn't be."

"But it might be." I broke a papadum into pieces. "That's what you're thinking."

He bit into his lamb, chewed. Swallowed. Drank some water.

"Charlie," I said. "Don't shut up on me. Talk to me."

"She can be moody," was all he said.

"I do lots of stuff with her all the time, without you." Part of my vehemence was that I'd been feeling guilty earlier, and wanted to convince myself there was nothing wrong with what we were doing. I shot an angry glance across the room, blaming Meredith.

"That's different."

I shook my head. "It's not different. Just because I met her first?"

"Because you're both women." Charlie wiped his mouth with his napkin.

I didn't say anything for a few seconds. I concentrated on the food, savoring the flavors and wishing my stomach hadn't started jumping up and down during this conversation. "So?"

"So…it's different, that's all."

"I fuck you both," I told him in a low voice. "To me, that makes you the same. If I can go to dinner with her, go dancing with her, hang out and watch movies alone with her, I can do the same with you. I'm not your side piece, Charlie. You're not cheating on Meredith with me. I'm…I thought I was a part of you both."

"You are," he assured me. He took my hand this time, trapping it between both of us. "Tesla. You are."

"Okay, then. Good." But something still felt off.

Fortunately, the waiter brought the rest of our food, so we could concentrate on eating it instead of talking about anything more serious than work. I didn't have much new to say about that. There was always gossip going on in the Mocha, but since Charlie never came in, he didn't know any of the people and wouldn't understand the stories.

He told me about his class, though. "Something's up with them lately, I don't know what. They won't stop talking. Even the boys. In fact, I think the boys are worse."

"Maybe they just have a lot to say." I pushed away my plate with a sigh. My tongue wanted more saffron rice. My stomach refused.

"Too bad none of it's about the work." Charlie picked slowly at his curry.

"What are you working on with them?" I sipped some tea and sat back in my chair, to surreptitiously unbutton my jeans. "I should've worn elastic-waist pants."

He laughed. "Geography. I know it's not the most exciting subject, but we have to cover a certain amount of information before the standardized tests in the spring. But the kids just won't settle down and pay attention."

I heard the genuine frustration in his voice. "Can you switch things up a little? Change the order of when you're teaching it? Maybe they need some shaking up."

He looked up from the last bite of curry. "You mean try teaching it at a different time?"

"Sure. Can you?"

He took the forkful of food, chewed and swallowed. He wiped his mouth. "Hmm. I might be able to. Just for a few days, anyway. As long as it didn't interfere with any of their special classes."

I shrugged and contemplated another bite of rice, but knew I'd regret it. "When I was a kid, anytime we got bored, my parents said it was because we needed to get out of a rut."

"Geography is a rut," Charlie admitted. "Even for me."

I smiled and let my toes rub the back of his calf the way I had earlier. "You can make it fun for them. I have no doubts."

"Will there be anything else?" The waiter looked hopeful, but we'd both had enough.

He brought us takeout containers and the bill, which Charlie paid with a flourish. I carried the food to the car, and made sure to wrap it up tight in foil and shove it to the back of the fridge when we got home. I stared at it there. A secret we were keeping. It was only leftover Indian food, but I still felt a little guilty.

I didn't have time to dwell on it, though, because Charlie was calling me into the living room and picking out a horror movie for us to watch on Interflix streaming. I toed off my shoes and got under the afghan with him on the sofa. Indian food and snuggling with my sweetie under a blanket while we watched a scary movie? Heaven, in my book.

It wasn't a very scary movie, and I found myself drifting into sleep while we watched. Charlie was solid and warm against me as we shifted around on the couch to get comfortable. The sound of screams and hatchets chopping off limbs tickled the periphery of my consciousness, but I got startled awake only when the overhead light came on.

Blinking and yawning, I sat up to see Meredith in the doorway. "Hey."

Charlie twisted to look back at her. "Hey, honey. How was your party?"

She stared at us for half a minute, taking in the movie and our tangled limbs. "Fine. What are you guys doing?"

I yawned again and stretched. "Apparently I'm sleeping. I should get to bed."

I unwound myself from Charlie's arms and legs and the

blanket, and got off the couch. I bent to kiss his mouth lightly. "'Night."

In the doorway, I leaned to kiss her, too, though she turned her head just the slightest bit at the last moment. I was used to that. I didn't like it, but I wasn't surprised. "'Night, Meredith."

She let me get a step past her before she put an arm around me to pull me back. She kissed me this time, our cheeks pressing together first before I felt the warmth of her mouth there. She pulled back a little to look into my eyes. "Sleep tight."

I smiled. "Are you coming in to the shop tomorrow?"

"Maybe." Her smile took a few seconds longer to cross her mouth, but was totally worth waiting for. "Probably. I should stay here and work, but I like the view there."

I ducked away from her tickling fingers. "Uh-huh. I'm sure Carlos will like to hear that. Oh, wait. You mean Johnny D., right?"

She grabbed at me, pushing me against the wall with her body. "You know who I mean."

I let her push me, and used the chance to put my hands on her hips. "Do I?"

She bumped me with her crotch, then stepped back again to swat my butt. "Go to bed. You'll be grouchy in the morning if you don't."

"I love that you know that about me." The words slipped out quietly, unexpected.

Her lashes fluttered, and she looked away. "Good night, Tesla. See you in the morning."

Another time I might've tugged her closer to me again for a kiss and a nuzzle, maybe tried to woo her into the bedroom with me. But it was late, I was tired, and though I wouldn't have turned down a seduction, I was a little too sleepy to attempt one myself.

Chapter
28

Some days you wake up with a smile on your face, ready to face whatever life throws at you. I was having one of those days, started by a delicious round of oral sex courtesy of Charlie, who I'd surprised in the kitchen while he was making coffee. It had started with a little dance as we'd tried getting around each other, me to the fridge to get my leftover Indian food to take for my lunch, him trying to get the half-and-half.

It had turned into a waltz, a real one. Not a very good one, clumsy and stumbling. It had dissolved into giggles as we conspired over our foil-wrapped packages and early morning silliness. I'd kissed his mouth to keep him from waking Meredith, and the kiss had gone from simple to sizzling in seconds. He got on his knees right there on the tile floor, pushed up my skirt and pulled down my winter-weight tights. Licked me to orgasm in less than two minutes, leaving me breathless. Then he stood, kissed my lips and squeezed my ass, looked at the time and realized he was going to be late.

I'd pay him back.

Unfortunately, not everyone was in the same great mood as me. I was the first one to the Mocha and used my key to unlock the door, but within twenty minutes both Darek and Joy had shown up. Darek was silent, but that was normal for him this early. He didn't usually perk up until about forty minutes after opening.

Joy was characteristically sullen. I hadn't even known she was scheduled to work that morning, which wasn't such a big deal. She often came in to perform unscheduled inspections. Still, I thought I was being funny when I said, "You know, Joy, there's this new thing called a life outside of work. I hear they're on sale this week. Maybe you should pick one up."

Turns out I wasn't as funny as I thought.

Joy had been rearranging a tray of carrot cupcakes in the case. She stood to face me. "Maybe you should mind your own damn business, Tesla."

The bubble of my good mood got pricked, but didn't quite explode. "Sorry."

"You know something? Not everyone is content to just flit around making nothing of themselves. For some people, work's important. Some people take their responsibilities seriously. Some people—"

"Some people need to take a chill pill," Darek said from out in the shop, where he'd been taking the chairs off the tables in prep for opening.

Joy looked across the counter at him. "What did you just say?"

He shrugged, apparently ballsy enough to shoot an undertone insult her way, but not willing to bring the fight to

THE SPACE BETWEEN US

her face. Joy frowned and turned her attention back to me. I didn't want to fight, either.

"I said I was sorry, Joy. I was teasing you."

"Well," she said stiffly, "don't tease."

"Right." Nodding, I stepped back to let her pass me.

Darek and I shared a look across the counter after she'd gone into the back room. He made a whirling motion with one finger at his temple, but I didn't laugh. I didn't think Joy was crazy, just supremely unhappy, and on a day like today, when I was feeling so good myself, that just didn't seem right.

I followed her into the back room, where she had a minuscule office she'd carved out of a former coat closet. It wasn't even large enough to hold her whole desk, which she'd put in sideways, leaving space for the mini fridge where we kept our personal lunches and snacks. When she was sitting at her desk, her chair was pushed back against the wall, leaving just enough space for her to squeeze into the seat. Nobody sat in Joy's chair but Joy.

"Hey," I said quietly.

She looked up from whatever accounting she was doing on the computer. "What?"

"I just wanted to say that I'm really sorry about teasing you. I think it's great that you care so much about your job. I mean, it's good to love what you do."

She gave me a blank look that slowly oozed into derision. "Is that what you really think?"

"I…uh…"

"Really?" She'd have shoved her chair back if there'd been room, but as it was she put her hands on the edge of the desk and pushed at it. "You think I love this fucking job?"

In all the time I'd worked at Morningstar Mocha, I'd seen Joy lose her shit almost on a daily basis. Until this moment, though, I'd never heard her curse with anything stronger than a mild "hell" or "damn." I'd have been less surprised if a toad had dropped from her mouth.

"Guess what, Tesla," she continued. "I don't. In fact, you were right. I'm here all the damn time because I don't have anything else. I have this job. That's it. Because at least while I'm here at work, I don't have to be anywhere else thinking about everything I want but don't have and won't ever have."

We weren't anything like friends. If you'd asked me to make a list of all the people in the world I'd want to spend my time with, Joy wouldn't have been on it. Honestly, I knew I wasn't the only person who felt that way, either, so it was no surprise to me she didn't have much beyond work.

"I'm sorry," was all I could say.

"You're not. You have no idea. You come in here every day with that big grin on your face, like the world's just handed you a big old gift-wrapped box of chocolates and a credit card without a limit. And people love you. They all wait in line, longer than they have to, for you to help them. They ask you how you are, they flirt with you." Joy's voice ground to a halt.

"I'm just nice to them, that's all. Believe me, Joy, I don't love this job every day. Most days I like it, and on the days I don't, I just try to act like I do until…well, until I do again." I shrugged. "It's no great secret philosophy or anything."

She looked bleak, her cheeks and even her mouth paler than usual. Her throat convulsed as she swallowed. "Don't talk to me like I'm stupid. You think I don't know all of that?"

I didn't know what to say. She didn't seem to want comfort or advice or even commiseration. In typical Joy fashion, it seemed she just wanted a fight. "If you know it, why don't you do it then? People don't like talking to you because you're terse, and you grunt."

Her eyes went wide. "What?"

"You heard me," I said. "And you know it's true. I'm sorry, Joy, but you act sort of like a raging bitch most of the time."

She blinked rapidly and sat back in her chair so hard it knocked against the wall. "Get out of here."

I held up my hands. "I came in here to apologize for teasing you, but the fact is, you don't want me to say I'm sorry. You want me to grovel or something, which I won't do. You want to be angry with me for whatever reason. Maybe it's because you're jealous—"

"Jealous! Why should I be jealous of you, Tesla? Because you're funny and cute and people adore you? Because you don't seem to have a care in the world? Is that why I should be jealous?" She spit the words as if she wished she could shoot me with each one.

"Hell if I know." I didn't want to let her rile me up, but my voice rose, anyway. "I like this job, okay? I like my life. No, as a matter of fact, right now I love my life! And I'm not going to pretend I don't just so you don't have to feel like a sorry, sad-sack twat about your own!"

She gasped. I choked myself off before I could say more, already ashamed at what I'd said…but sort of glad, too. She'd pushed me into it.

"And for your information," I added in a softer voice, "my life hasn't been all sparkles shooting out a unicorn's ass. I just try to make the best of things, and they usually turn out okay. Maybe you should try that once in a while."

"Get. Out." She probably wished for a door to slam in my face, but had taken the closet door from its hinges in order to put her desk in there. She twisted in her chair to block the sight of me, and put her hands on the keyboard again, though she didn't type. Her shoulders heaved.

I thought about saying I was sorry again. I'd have meant it. I didn't like saying mean things, even when the other person deserved it, and it seemed over the past few months I'd had to do more than my share of uncomfortable truth-telling. I was sorry I'd been mean, but I wasn't sorry that anything I'd said was true. I got out.

In the meantime, Darek had opened the shop for the first anxious customers. Those who'd be staying awhile had marked their territories with laptops, newspapers and mugs. The ones taking away waited semipatiently in a line that stretched all the way to the front door. I tied on my apron and got to work.

I thought for sure Joy would come out to supervise and find fault with what we were doing, but she kept to herself for most of the morning. It was almost like she wasn't there, and Darek and I fell into our usual routine of joking around and sharing the duties of taking and making orders and cleaning up the tables.

"Morning, Dr. McFancypants." I gestured at Eric's plate, empty but for some crumbs. "Want me to take that for you?"

He looked up from the yellow legal notepad on which he'd been so seriously scribbling. "Hey, Tesla. Sure."

I took the plate and the crumpled napkin and made my best Joker impression. "Why so serious?"

He laughed and looked a little embarrassed. "Oh. I'm working on a query letter. Sort of."

"Oh!" We had so many writers who hung out in the Mocha that I knew all about query letters. Carlos had cursed them, and synopses, too. "Are you writing a book or something?"

He laughed. "No. I guess it's more like an application."

"New job?"

"No. Something else." His brow furrowed as he tapped his pen against the lined paper. He had a box of linen stationery on the table next to him, along with a slim fountain pen still in the gift box. He touched them both briefly before looking up at me. "Rough drafts have to come first, you know?"

"That's what my English teachers always said. Good luck with it. Glad you're not leaving us," I told him with a wink.

He returned it with a grin. "Yeah, like you'd have any trouble finding another butt to put in this seat."

"Hey," I scolded, "don't act like your butt's not special!"

We both laughed at that. So did Sadie, sitting two tables over. I'd missed her coming in, but went to her now as I dumped the garbage in the can.

"Don't even argue with me, I'm totally going to get you your stuff and bring it over. I can't believe you're even out on a day like this." It had dawned gray and now was heavily overcast, the air tingling with the promise of snow.

"It was this or sit home all day watching the game show channel," she confessed. "I took an early maternity leave, and I'm bored out of my mind, Tesla. I've cleaned everything I could clean without bending over, which isn't much when you think about it. And I needed to get out of the house before the weather turns so bad I can't walk here."

I looked past her out the big glass windows. "Yeah, looks like it might snow today."

"I don't like winter," Sadie said flatly, also looking out the window.

"Really? I do. I like being able to bundle up in layers so nobody notices that I'm totally overdosing on hot chocolate and cupcakes. And I like skiing, though I haven't been anyplace but Ski Roundtop in forever. My boyfriend—" I caught myself, thinking of Charlie as my boyfriend. It caused such a delectable, giddy sensation I had to giggle out loud. She gave me a curious look. "He says we might go up to Vermont over

Christmas break. I've never been there. He says it's not quite as good as Colorado but it's cheaper and closer."

"Wear a helmet."

My smile faded a little. "Hmm?"

Sadie's hands rested on her giant belly. She looked sad. "Skiing's dangerous. Wear a helmet, okay?"

"Oh. Sure." I nodded, though I knew I probably wouldn't. I also knew that no matter what a pregnant lady said, especially one as pregnant as Sadie, it was best to agree. "Absolutely."

"Tesla," Joy said from behind me, "Darek seems to be having some issues with remembering the portion sizes for the panini sandwiches. I need you to refresh him."

"Sure," I told her, as agreeable to her as I'd been to Sadie and with as much intent. "No problem."

"Hi, Joy." Sadie smiled.

She smiled, too. "Hi, Sadie. Wow. You're getting close, huh?"

"Another two months. I won't be surprised if we have unexpected twins, the way I'm feeling."

"That would be...wow." Joy cleared her throat.

"Peppermint white-chocolate latte with a chocolate cupcake?" I said to fill the awkward silence Joy had made.

Sadie nodded. "You're awesome, Tesla. Thanks."

At the counter, Joy tugged my elbow with a hiss until I turned. "We don't provide table service, Tesla."

I sighed and pitched my voice low. "You want me to make her waddle up to the counter, or worse, wait in line?"

The line had grown again, thanks to a midmorning rush I could never quite figure out the cause of, but that happened almost every day. It was also a slightly more complicated time, because while it was early for lunch, people did start ordering sandwiches and things in addition to the muffins and bagels. Darek already had the sort of frantic look of being too far behind.

"I want you to do your job," Joy said.

"Here's an idea. Instead of bitching at us," Darek said, "why don't you step in and start ringing up orders? Or, since apparently I don't know how to make a sandwich to your specs, you make some paninis?"

I agreed with him, but didn't have time to say so more tactfully, because Joy whirled on him like an attack dog. I think she even growled. I couldn't see her expression, but it was scary enough to send Darek back a step.

"Why don't you just do. Your. Job!" she shouted.

The almost constant buzz of conversation in the shop stopped. Apparently not caring she had an audience, Joy advanced on Darek. She got right up in his face with a pointing finger he looked ready to bite off.

"If you're going to be such a raging cunt," Darek said, "why don't you just go get fucked?"

I wasn't the only one who gasped aloud at that. I think everyone in the Mocha choked on something when Darek let loose. He pushed past Joy, actually shoving her out of the way when she wouldn't move, then past me.

"I'm so fucking out of here," he told me. "Sorry, Tesla, but I told you if she got in my face again I was quitting. I'm done with this shit."

"Darek—"

"You…you can't quit!" Joy shouted after him.

He paused after rounding the counter, and took in the line of people waiting, every eye on this explosion. "I just did. What, you're going to fire me instead? Fine, fire me. Don't you get it, Joy? I don't fucking care. I'm just so glad to get out of here, away from you. Fire me, I quit, whatever difference, I don't care. I'm gone."

He grabbed his coat from the hook and looked again at everyone watching. "Sorry, folks, show's over. Order your coffee from that bitch up front. She might spit in it when you're not looking, though."

By the disgusted looks I saw, I thought there was more than one person who believed him. Hell, just then I wasn't sure I didn't. We all watched him stalk out of the Mocha, the only sound following him was the jingle of the bell on the door he let swing shut behind him.

Chapter

29

"I hate leaving you here." Meredith pouted and ignored Charlie's pointed look at his watch. "All by your lonesome."

"I told you I'd be fine. I'll go to my brother's, it's not a big deal at all. Seriously." I squeezed her closer for a hug. "But you'd better go. I hear Charlie's sister doesn't like it if anyone's late."

"Oh, God forbid we show up a few minutes off her schedule. I mean, I'm sure we're not even going to be eating right away, but let us show up fifteen minutes after she told us to be there and we'll hear about it for the rest of the day, how they were all waiting for us...." Meredith's lip curled. "Charlie, did you get the pie?"

He lifted the box. "Yes, honey. I got the pie."

She grinned wickedly. "Store-bought. Me? I happen to love

the shit out of Andes chocolate-mint pie, but Susan is really into stuff that's homemade."

Charlie laughed, shaking his head. "She'll eat this."

"Oh, she'll have two pieces while she moans about how she's got to start exercising again, no question. But she'll also make sure to remark how she thought I was going to bring a "handmade" pie. You know she will."

"Of course." Charlie rolled his eyes. "C'mon. Tesla, we'll be back late."

"No worries." I shifted past Meredith to kiss him. "Drive safe. If I'm not here when you get home, text me."

Then, although Meredith was still dragging her feet, they finally got out the door. I heaved a sigh and spun around in the living room with my arms spread out, a real "the hills are alive" sort of moment. I hadn't been alone in weeks.

There hadn't been much alone time in Vic's house, but there at least I'd had privacy. I could close my bedroom door and know that nobody would go in uninvited or without knocking. I could take a shower without someone coming in to use the toilet or the sink or just to chat with me while I shaved my legs.

I loved living here with Meredith and Charlie, but I was seriously craving some time to myself. I put it to good use, too, unpacking some boxes I hadn't yet managed to get through, and arranging some of my framed photos on the shelves in the living room. I hung a print I'd bought from a local artist who frequented the Mocha. I did some seriously dirty laundry and listened to my music at top volume while I danced around the kitchen in my panties.

Suddenly, my plan to hang out at Cap's apartment and eat whatever he pulled from the freezer was totally unappealing. I had so much to be thankful for this year, including the fact

I made it to the grocery store before it closed for the day, that I wanted to celebrate this holiday with more of an effort. I bought a turkey breast and all the trimmings, even the makings for a pumpkin pie. I called my brother, who took little convincing to come to my new place and hang out watching television while I cooked.

I even set Meredith's fancy dining room table with some nice linens and the china she and Charlie had received from their wedding registry but never touched, as evidenced by the dishes still layered in boxes with bubble wrap. They didn't have real silverware, but strangely enough, an unopened package of plastic flatware that looked like real metal. I used that, too.

"Wow. Real napkins." Cap pinched his thumb and forefinger together, the rest of his fingers splayed, and put it to the corner of his mouth. "Fancy."

"Hey. Just because you're uncouth doesn't mean we have to eat like heathens."

My brother laughed. "Stepping up in the world, huh? Fancy new digs, fancy-pants napkins."

"Sit down and eat, you moron," I told him, but fondly.

Not much got between Cap and his food, so the conversation was minimal while we packed away the grub. That was fine with me, too. Meredith talked through every meal, which was probably why she stayed so skinny. She chewed more words than food.

Cap finally sat back from his plate with a loud, long sigh and a resounding belch. "Superb meal."

"Thanks." I wiped my mouth with the fancy napkin and contemplated another few bites of stuffing. "I'm a fine-ass cook, huh?"

"You know it." Cap stretched his long arms and linked his

hands behind his head as he tipped the chair back. "Gimme a few minutes before I'll be ready for pie."

"Help me clear the table. That will help work up an appetite." I laughed at his groan of protest. "Fine. Maybe we can just collapse into a turkey coma on the couch and watch some bad TV for a little bit first."

"Sounds like a plan." Cap grinned.

For just the two of us I hadn't made as much food as I would've for a full group, and we'd eaten most of it, so I had no guilt about leaving what was left on the table for a little while so we could veg out and relax. I was so full and sleepy I wasn't sure I could've managed a full cleanup, anyway. Besides, the pie still needed to cool a little before we could eat it.

In the living room, Cap looked everything over. I knew he was noting the cost of the furniture, the flat-screen, probably even the collection of DVDs and video games. Not that he was judging anything by how expensive it was or not, just that Cap did that sort of thing. Noticed stuff.

"So…that's her, huh?" He was looking at Charlie and Meredith's wedding photo. "Your friend?"

"Yep." I flopped on the couch, sprawling, and dug the remote out of the cushions.

"She was married?"

I paused. I'd been sure Vic would've filled Cap in on the whole sordid story. "She's still married. That's Charlie, her husband."

Cap stared at the picture for a long time. "So…you live with both of them?"

"Well, yeah."

He looked at me, assessing. I could practically hear the gears turning, but in true Cap form he just shrugged and took his place beside me on the couch. No matter what he thought about it, and I knew he thought plenty, he wasn't going to say anything. But to my surprise, he did.

"You should be careful, Tesla."

I could remember times when I'd hated my baby brother. When he broke my stuff or had tantrums to get his own way or just in general had done whatever he could to work my nerves just because he knew he could. The truth was, though, we were closer than a lot of people I knew were with their siblings, and part of the reason was because while I sometimes long ago might've hated him, I genuinely liked Cap.

"Thanks, but it's fine. It's all good." I handed him the remote. "It's not like it was with Mom and Dad, okay? Here, anything but football."

Cap looked disappointed but dutifully clicked channels until he came across some game show that had contestants running through obstacle courses and water hazards. "Even so. They're married. This is their house. It's not like living with Vic and Elaine, right?"

"God. No." I wanted to make that clear. I wasn't sure how much Cap had ever known about what had happened between me and Vic so long ago, but I figured he at least suspected. "Way different."

"So. Just be careful, that's all. And you know if you need someplace, you can always come crash with me."

"Uh-huh. What about Miss Lyndsay?" I poked his side. "Think she'd be down with that?"

Cap stared steadfastly at the television, but I couldn't miss the hint of red flushing his throat and cheeks. I couldn't pass up the chance to grill him about it. Wasn't that what big sisters were for?

"What's going on? Captain?"

At the use of his full name, he shot me a glare. "Nothing."

"C'mon, Cap. I know you're into her. And she's pretty cute. She seems to like you, too. So…"

"So nothing, okay?" He finger-stabbed the remote. "It's not like that. We're roommates."

I had no doubts that's how they'd started out, but I also believed things had become something else, and quite some time ago, too. The question was, which of them was pretending it wasn't more? I had my bets on Lynds, though I wouldn't have put it past Cap to be inadvertently playing hard to get. My brother had a super scary smart brain in the head of a hulking lunk, with hands the size of frying pans. Sometimes the lunk took over the brain. That was never pretty.

"I'm sort of seeing someone, anyway," he said, and I was totally floored.

"What? Who? Since when?"

He shrugged, uncomfortable. "Friend of Elaine's sister."

"Wait a minute. You're dating a friend of Nancy's?" I laughed. Loudly. "Is she like Nancy?"

Cap scowled. "If she was, would I be going out with her?"

"I dunno, Cap, would you?"

He made a face. "Her name's Missy. She's in nursing school. She's…nice."

That didn't sound promising. "Uh-huh. And?"

Another shrug and steadfast glare at the TV. His last stab had turned on the home shopping channel. I knew there was no way he was really watching it. I mean, I love *Torchwood* as much as I love chocolate cake, but watching John Barrowman hawk costume jewelry was totally not Cap's style.

"What does Lynds think about it?" It was the only question I could think to ask. It seemed like an important one.

"What difference does it make what she thinks? She goes out with lots of guys all the time."

"She does?" I hadn't known that, but watching my brother's face as he refused to look at me, I could see he'd known it for a long time. "Cappy, have you ever considered just telling Lyndsay that you love her?"

He groaned and let his head fall against the back of the couch. "Yeah."

His answer surprised me. Cap could talk until your ears fell off about obscure trivia and esoteric philosophies. He could fix cars while talking about higher-level math theorems. But emotions? It seemed hard for him to acknowledge he had any, much less discuss them.

"So, why don't you?"

"Because I'm not stupid."

I patted his shoulder. "I know you're not. So does she. You guys have lived together for what…a year?"

"A year and seven months, actually. And four days," he added. "Not counting the three months of weekends she spent there before she moved in permanently."

"Oh, count those, too."

He smiled a little and finally looked at me. "A long time, okay? Long enough for me to know how I feel."

"So why are you wasting your time with Missy? And her time, too?"

"Because she's nice. Because she likes me. Because Lynds is just my roommate and a buddy and…fuck." Cap frowned and punched a big fist against his knee. "It's just easier to be with Missy, okay? She doesn't expect anything from me but dinner and a movie and maybe a hand job."

I recoiled. It was one thing to assume my baby brother was finger-banging some chick in the front seat of his car after a night out, but it wasn't something I wanted to hear about in detail. "Whoa."

Cap sighed. "Missy's just a girl, that's all. And Lynds…"

"Yeah. I know." I really did. I patted his shoulder again. "But if you don't tell her, how's she supposed to know?"

His expression turned grim. "It doesn't matter."

There was no point in pushing him. I sat back. "Okay. But you know I'm here for you, if you need someone to talk to. I got your back."

He laughed, not quite his usual hearty chortle, but better than the sad face he'd been giving me before. "Right. Same to you."

Impulsively, I hugged him. It had been awhile since I'd spent time alone with just Cap, no Vic or Elaine or the kids, no Lynds, no customers in the shop. Just the two of us hanging out, watching TV, bellies full of good food and no place we had to be. Pretty soon we'd have to haul our fat asses off the couch and clean up, but for now it was lazy time.

"Can I change the channel?" I asked him. "I know you're into cubic zirconium brooches and all, but…"

His laugh sounded better this time. "Uh-huh. Yeah. Let's see what else is on."

We'd just barely settled into some cheesy Syfy Channel monster movie when I heard the rumble of the garage opening. A minute later, the door opened, then footsteps sounded on the tiles of the hall. I couldn't manage to shove myself off the couch before Meredith came through the arch into the living room.

"Sexy pants, where are—oh." She stopped dead.

"Hey, you guys are home early." I got up to greet her. "This is my brother, Cap. Cap, Meredith."

"I thought you were going to his place," she said.

Cap used the remote to turn off the TV, and stood. He

looked extra big all of a sudden, kind of like delicate things would break if he just looked at them. "Hi. Nice to meet you."

"We were," I told her, "but I figured it had been a long time since I'd made Thanksgiving dinner and so I ran to the store and got some things. It was just easier to cook here." I squeezed her, though she didn't give in to my embrace. "How was Susie's house?"

Charlie had sneaked in while we were talking, and he said, "We're back early, is that enough of an answer?"

"Oh, no." To fill Cap in, I said, "Charlie's sister is a little… what would you call her, Charlie?"

"Annoying," he said. "But it was still fun. We bugged out before the board games started, that's all. Dinner was fine."

I'd heard about the board game marathons, which sounded fun in theory but apparently ended up like grudge matches. "So you're both home early, great! I made pie. And we're watching junk TV, but we could play a board game if you want."

Meredith snorted. "Um. No."

"I'll take some pie," Charlie said. Meredith shot him a look. "What? Cap looks like he could put away a slice or two. C'mon, what do you say?"

"Sounds awesome."

The men grinned at each other and became instant friends. Cap followed Charlie to the kitchen, leaving me and Meredith in the living room. She looked around the room, eyes fixing on the framed photo I'd set on the end table, then coming back to me.

"I just didn't expect anyone to be here when we got home," she said.

Charlie might be accustomed to Meredith's "moods," but for me it was still a lot like navigating a minefield that was supposed to have been cleared out. You think it's a field of flowers until you step in the wrong place and get yourself blown up.

"I didn't think it would be a problem, Meredith. Is it?"

She frowned. "I was looking forward to coming home, getting in my comfy clothes and just hanging out."

There was nothing stopping her from doing that as far as I could see. From the kitchen came the raised voices of male laughter, which made me smile. I was glad Charlie and Cap seemed to be getting along. Meredith, however, didn't smile.

"You ate in the dining room."

"It's Thanksgiving," I said. "Listen, if you have a problem with something, you should probably just come out and say so."

I wasn't Charlie. I couldn't pretend to read her mind, and I wasn't interested in playing games. I didn't want to fight with her, but I wasn't going to let her get away with this passive-aggressive bullshit, either.

She didn't seem to know how to take that. "You used my china."

I sighed. There'd be no point in trying to kiss or hug her; she'd only push me away. Not that I felt much like doing either at the moment. "When I moved in here, you told me to act like this was my house, too. Did I misunderstand?"

"No. But…my china," Meredith said in a low voice. "And we never talked about guests. And you left the kitchen a mess, Tesla. That's pretty fucking rude."

This had the flavor of a fight, and it was a taste I didn't like.

"I have every intention of cleaning up after myself. I've never left a mess before, have I? I'd have had it all taken care of before you got home, but you decided to come home early. And really, is it a big deal?" She'd left dishes in the sink overnight more than once. I knew that for a fact.

Meredith's jaw tightened. "I'm just saying, it's shitty to come home and find my house a mess and strangers here I have to entertain."

"You don't have to entertain my brother. Hell, I barely have to entertain him. Cap's just easy that way." More laughter rose in the kitchen. "And it sounds like Charlie's doing it, anyway. And your house won't be a mess in a few hours. Okay?"

I really didn't want to fight with her. I wanted some homemade pumpkin pie with a side of French vanilla ice cream and some chocolate chips on top. I wanted some hot tea. Maybe even a dreaded board game—Uno could be hilarious with Cap, who made up the best unofficial rules.

"Meredith, I either live here or I'm a guest. And if I'm just a guest, then yeah, I guess I'm being kind of rude. But I didn't think I was. I *thought* I lived here as a part of this family. And in that case, you need to get over it."

Charlie never pushed her, so I'm sure it wasn't pleasant for her to be pushed by me. She lifted her chin. "Of course you're not a guest."

"Then get over it," I repeated. "I mean, talk to me about stuff, don't just get pissy about it. If you don't want me to use your china, I won't."

"*I've* never even used it! I think I should've been the first to use it, that's all."

Since she and Charlie had been married for eight years, this argument held little weight with me. Still, I could compromise. "I'm sorry. I didn't know. It's great china. You should break it out more often."

"It's our wedding china. Mine and Charlie's." She puffed out a breath. "So, yeah. I guess I'd prefer if you didn't use our things without asking first."

"Fair enough." I felt bad about the china, but not as bad

as it seemed she wanted me to. "Maybe you need to be more specific about your expectations, Meredith."

"How was I supposed to know you'd just use it?"

I sighed. "Remember when I told you that if we were going to do this it would need a lot of talking? If you wanted me to join you and Charlie, live here, be a part of you, we'd have to make sure to talk about stuff. In advance and when it came up. That's part of the package when you have more than two partners in a relationship. If you don't talk about stuff, then… people get angry. Or hurt."

"Oh, that's right," she said a little coldly. "I forgot. You're the expert."

"So not an expert," I told her. "Also? Not interested in fighting with you about it."

I pushed past her to head for the kitchen. I wasn't mad yet, but I didn't want to get there. In the kitchen, Cap and Charlie had demolished a good portion of the pie. One of them had brought out the chocolate syrup, probably at Cap's suggestion, since that was a Martin family tradition. Also whipped cream, chocolate chips and even some multicolored sprinkles.

"It's like a sundae on pie," Charlie said. "Killer pie, by the way."

I kissed him. "Thanks. Did you leave any for me? I can't tell under the wasteland of all the toppings."

"Plenty left." Cap held up his plate, mouth full, and mumbled, "Pie. Is. Awesome."

"Here, I'll grab you a piece." Charlie put his plate on the counter, but I shook my head.

"I'll get it. You enjoy yours. Anyone want coffee?" Normally I didn't drink coffee at home, since I lived and breathed it at work, but something about pie and ice cream screamed for caffeine.

Cap swallowed and licked his mouth. "Me."

"Me, too." Charlie forked up more pie. "God. So good. I can make the—"

"Hush," I told him with a nudge against his hip as I moved past him to pull the coffee from the cupboard. "I can do it. Eat your pie."

That's how Meredith found us. The men, plates in hand, leaning against the counter, wearing matching mustaches of whipped cream and chocolate. Me laughing at them as I tried in vain to get the coffeepot working, unable not because it was too complicated but because Charlie kept stepping in front of me every time I moved, trying to kiss me with his whipped-cream-covered mouth. I'd just given in and let him.

"You're making coffee?" Meredith said. She had her hands full of plates from the table. "I'll have some."

"Sure." I licked whipped cream from my top lip. "If your husband ever gets his ass out of the way so I can."

"He likes to get his ass in the way." Meredith motioned for both of us to move so she could put the plates in the dishwasher.

I stepped in front of her when she turned with empty hands, the way Charlie had done to me, but Meredith didn't laugh. I put my palms on her hips, shifting them a little, trying to get her to dance with me. She shot a glance over my shoulder toward Cap and frowned. I let her go.

"I really want to get the dining room cleared away," she said.

"I'll help you. Just let me finish with the coffee. And you can have some pie," I wheedled. "It's really good."

I caught the twitch of a smile from her. It was something, anyway. In the dining room, I found her studying the china plate in her hand as if she'd discovered it in an ancient Egyptian tomb. She looked up when I came in.

"I couldn't decide what I wanted," she said. "For the registry. I mean, my mother told me we should pick a china pattern, right? So everyone could buy us pieces. Because everyone does that. I didn't know what I wanted to live with for the rest of my life. So I picked this."

She held up a bread plate, which we hadn't used, so it was still clean. It was white with a design of roses around the rim. Not what I'd have picked, if I were ever so fortunate as to get hitched and have a wedding registry. But it was pretty.

"I think you did a nice job," I said.

She tilted the plate in her hands so it caught the light, and looked at me. "You know why I've never used these plates?"

I shrugged as I moved around the table to stack dishes and gather the used plasticware. "Because most people don't ever eat dinner in the dining room except for a few times a year?"

"Because I don't like them," Meredith said.

I looked up. She stared at the plate in her hands, tipping it, turning it. She traced the gold-plated rim with her thumb and glanced at me again.

"I feel like I got shoved into picking something because it was what people expected, and now I'm stuck with it. And we got a shit ton of this stuff, Tesla. Dinner plates, salad plates, bread plates. A gravy boat." She laughed bitterly. "Really? A fucking gravy boat. A soup tureen. Who ever uses that shit?"

"People who like gravy. And soup." I moved around the table to take the plate from her and put it on the table. "Hey. What's going on?"

"You're mad at me." She crossed her arms.

"*You* were mad at *me*," I pointed out. I rubbed her upper arms, gently squeezing. "Ooh, your sweater's soft."

Sorry wasn't Meredith's style. With nobody else in the room, though, I guess she deemed it okay to snuggle a little closer to me. "I wish we'd stayed here all day. Charlie's sister's dinner was s-o-o-o bad."

"Pie will make everything better. I promise. And we could play Uno. I'm not kidding you, it'll be fun."

She nodded, leaning into me for a second or two before pulling away. We made short work of the dishes on the table, though the platters and serving dishes of food would take a second trip. Meredith paused in the archway and looked at the plates in her hands.

"It's good you used them," she said. "Someone should."

Chapter
30

Joy had wasted no time in hiring someone to replace Darek. Brandy was a little older than me, but proudly told me she'd been working in coffee shops since she was in high school. She named a few of them.

"They're all closed now," she said around a mouthful of gum. "Hopefully this place stays in business longer, you know what I mean?"

She laughed; I didn't.

I wasn't happy that Darek had quit or been fired, whichever it was. I didn't like that Joy had hired this gum-cracking, hair-whipping chick to take his place without even asking me to be part of the hiring process. And though Joy herself had backed way, way off of me since the day Darek walked out, that wasn't really what I wanted, either. Not if it meant that coming to work felt like going to prison. In some ways, dealing with her grouchiness was what I'd grown used to. A habit. With her frosty, frigid attitude to me in direct contrast to her almost ludicrous warmth toward Brandy, Joy was making it pretty painful to be on the job.

Johnny D. noticed. "What's up with the new girl?"

I looked across the room to where Brandy was talking to Carlos. She was supposed to be cleaning up the tables, but seemed to have gotten sidetracked. Carlos was casting longing, shifty glances toward his laptop that Brandy didn't seem to notice or was ignoring.

"Brandy. I don't know. Joy hired her."

"What happened to Darek?"

I frothed some milk for Johnny and added a couple pumps of syrup. "He quit. He and Joy got into it last week, and he just bailed."

"Huh." Johnny shrugged the shoulders of his long black coat. "That's too bad."

"Tell me about it." I handed him the cup and the plate of cheese-stuffed pretzel he'd ordered. "No sweets today?"

"My kid's dropping off my grandson in a few minutes. I'll let him pick. But these looked good." He eyed the pretzel, then looked up at me. "Is it good?"

"Oh…I guess so. I haven't had one yet." I grinned. "Wanna gimme a bite, big guy?"

He laughed, shaking his head. "I'll give you a bite, smart-ass."

"Pffft." I waved a hand. "Bring it. I can handle you."

He turned on the charm, just for an instant, but it was enough to prove to me I probably couldn't handle whatever Johnny D. dished out. "I thought you had a special friend," he said.

"Who told you that?"

He shrugged. "Nobody had to tell me anything. I could see it all over you."

"Like a stain?" I suggested wryly.

"Something like that." Johnny narrowed his eyes at me. "Suits you."

I preened. "Thanks."

The bell jingled; it was Johnny's daughter and his grandson. While the kid ran to him with a squeal, his mom was a little less excited, at least as far as I could tell by her expression. She gave me a half smile, her dad a half hug.

"I'll pick him up about seven tonight, if that's okay. Call me if you need me to get him sooner. Strike that. Have Emm call me when she's ready for me to come get him," she said.

Johnny shook his head, ruffling the boy's hair. "Nah. We got it covered. Right, pal?"

"Right." The kid grinned up at him.

"Don't let him eat too much junk," his mother warned, then looked at me. "One cookie."

"Don't put her in the middle, Kimmy," Johnny said.

She sighed. "Dad. You can't sugar him up and then send him home to be awake half the night."

I left them to their argument and headed out to the main floor to wrangle Brandy back behind the counter. Carlos shot me a grateful look as I told her she needed to get back to work. Brandy only looked surprised.

"What's that supposed to mean?"

"It means," I said, "that I need you in the back prepping sandwiches or even at the counter making drinks."

Brandy gave an insulted sniff. "Fine. I was just cleaning up out here."

I looked around the unusually empty shop. "And you did a great job. I just need some help up front."

The compliment, half-assed and insincere as it was, mollified her. She gave Carlos a smile and went into the back. I rolled my eyes.

"She's gonna drive Joy insane, you know that," he said.

"Might be the only plus to her working here." I pretended to peek at his computer screen. "How bad did she kill your page count?"

"It's been worse." He shrugged. "Some days the words come like a porn star, some days they don't. Hey, so where's Meredith been lately?"

It was a question I'd thought about asking her myself. "I guess she's been busy."

"You guys have a fight or something?"

Surprised, I stepped back. "No. Why?"

"Seems like you were pretty cozy, that's all. And now she hasn't been in for a couple weeks." Carlos gave me a significant look. "Just wondered, that's all."

I frowned, counting back how long it had been since Meredith had been at the Mocha. "She's just had other stuff to do, I guess. Not everyone can sit here all day long, you know."

He laughed at that. "Too bad, right?"

"Yeah." I tapped his shoulder as I passed. "Too bad."

But what he'd said stuck with me. Meredith had come into the Mocha three or four days a week without fail for months. Now that we were...well, doing whatever it was we were doing, she barely came in at all. I saw her at home, of course. And I knew she was still doing all the home parties and other work that had occupied her during her hours in the Mocha's front window. But where was she doing it now?

I didn't have time to dwell on it, because another rush started and I had to get to the front. Brandy, for all her experience working in coffee shops, took forever to make the simplest drinks. She blamed it on the different equipment. I blamed it on her inability to walk and chew gum at the same time.

"My customer," she said during the midst of the rush. She said it under her breath as she passed behind me to get a muffin from the case, so I couldn't be sure I heard her right.

I looked up. "Huh?"

She jerked her chin toward a spot halfway down the line. "Him. My customer."

I scanned the row, some strangers, some regulars, one or two favorites I wasn't about to give up to Brandy. "Who? You mean…Sadie's husband?"

"That guy," she said with a finger point. "Fourth one back, in the suit."

"Yeah. Sadie's husband." I had to think hard for a few seconds to recall his name. "Joe."

"Yeah, Joe!" Brandy whirled to look at me, the muffin nearly skidding off the plate. "He's married? You're kidding me!"

"Um, no, and please serve that muffin before the dude waiting for it decides to reach across the counter and throttle you for it," I advised. "He's hungry and he's been waiting too long."

"Sure, sure." She pushed past me to serve her customer and ring him up, while I helped the woman behind him.

It was not as seamless as when Darek and I worked together, not by a long shot, but at least Brandy was picking up the pace. Except for the fact that as the back-and-forth method of serving went, Sadie's husband was actually my customer, and Brandy was willing to mess up the flow in order to get him.

"Hi, Joe." She leaned across the counter, probably to show

off her tits in her low-cut shirt. "Long time no see, am I right?"

Joe didn't come in here as often as his wife did, but he shot me a smile, anyway. "Hey, Tesla. Hi...?"

"Brandy," she told him, as if he should've already known. "It's me. Brandy."

A slow, dawning look of unease slipped over his face. "...Hi, Brandy."

"From Mary Catherine's coffee shop." Her voice had gone a little high and squeaky. A giggle slipped out.

He looked as if he ought to remember her and knew it, but couldn't quite. "It's good to see you."

"I've lost weight," she said, as if that should explain it all. "Since you saw me last. I used to be bigger."

"What can we get you, Joe?" I figured if this transaction was ever going to get finished, I had to be the one pushing it through. Clearly, Brandy couldn't focus, and Joe was too polite to tell her he had no clue who she was.

"Ah...large special blend to go and a scone." He gave me the smile Brandy wanted, and her a small, sideways glance. "Room for cream and sugar, please."

"I can get it," she insisted.

I wasn't going to fight her for it. We still had four people left in line and most of the tables filled. I got to work and managed to help the next two people while Brandy struggled with Joe's order. Finally, she handed him his to-go coffee and the scone wrapped in paper and a bag. She took his money.

She wasn't ready to let him go, though. "So...you come in here a lot?"

Joe, pocketing his change, looked up. "Uh...no. Not really. Sometimes."

"You live close by?"

"How's Sadie?" I interjected, to give him a break.

He looked relieved, his smile genuine. "Tired. Cranky."

"Won't be long now. Tell her I asked about her, okay?" I handed my customer her coffee and bagel, rang her up and took her money while Brandy stared longingly at Joe.

He nodded, backing up. "Will do. See you, Tesla. And... Brandy."

At the door he paused and glanced over his shoulder. Something like recognition drifted over his face, though it was hard to see that far away. He nodded at her and went out.

She sighed. Since I'd waited on the final customers while she was staring after him, there was nobody waiting when she turned to me with big, wet eyes and a trembling mouth. I braced myself.

"That guy," she said.

"Joe." I washed my hands, something I always did after handling money and before handling food.

"Him," Brandy said.

"Sadie's husband," I said, just to hammer it home. "You know him?"

"He used to come into the shop I worked in before."

"Uh-huh." Drying my hands, I turned. "He's cute."

"Way cute." She perked up, as if maybe we had something in common. "We used to go out."

I found that hard to believe, but didn't want to say so. "Uh-huh."

"Yeah. He's fantastic in bed."

I found that less difficult to believe, but didn't say that, either. Brandy didn't need me to answer. She was still staring out after him, forlorn.

"He's married?"

"Yep. His wife's having a baby any day now."

Brandy whipped around to look at me again. "No! Really? Oh. Shit! Damn. That sucks."

"I doubt they think so," I told her with a frown.

"Why are the good ones always taken?" Brandy huffed.

"I guess because they're the good ones."

She rolled her eyes. "Whatever."

My phone buzzed in my pocket, and because nobody was waiting, I answered it. "Hey, sexy pants."

"Hi, cutie bum." Meredith sounded congested. "What's going on?"

"Work. Same old. Carlos was asking about you." I made sure nobody else had come in and nothing needed my attention before I leaned against the counter. I ignored Brandy's wide-eyed look. "He wants to know why you haven't been in lately."

She coughed. "What's that saying about the cow and the milk?"

"Why buy the cow when you get the milk for free?"

"That one. Why pay for the coffee when I have the coffee girl living with me?" She coughed again. "I feel like shit. I called Charlie, but he didn't answer. Do you think you could pick up some medicine for me?"

"Sure. What do you need?" Reflexively, I thought of the kiss I'd stolen this morning while she was still sleeping. So far I didn't feel sick.

"Something for coughs and headache, fever. Body aches."

"Shit, baby, is it the flu? I told you to get the flu shot."

"I don't know what the hell it is." She sounded annoyed. "Can you just get me the stuff without the lecture?"

"Sorry. Sure. I can stop after work."

Silence. Then a sniffling, snuffling sigh. "I'm sick now, Tesla."

I could hear that. "I'm…it's just me and this new girl in here today, honey. I'm not sure I can get out and run home—"

"I'll be okay." Apparently Brandy had no conception of private conversations, or shame about eavesdropping. "I can handle it."

"Who's that?" Meredith asked with another cough.

"New girl." I looked at the clock. I wasn't due to get out of here until five, when Moira, the part-time chick, came in to relieve me. "I guess I could take my lunch break a little early and use it to run to the store and stuff."

"Could you? I really feel like crap," Meredith said. "Please?"

I knew Charlie wouldn't be able to do it until after school ended, which was earlier than I'd be able to get home from work, but still too late for someone who was sick. I hated running errands on my lunch break. "Of course. Let me make sure everything's under control here and then I'll go out and get your stuff. Okay? Did you drink some juice or hot tea? Maybe take a hot shower, that might help. Did you call the doctor?"

"I don't need a doctor," Meredith said. "I just need some damn cold medicine, okay? Jesus, Tesla."

"I'll be there in an hour." I disconnected the call and found Brandy staring at me. "What?"

"I can handle things here while you go get stuff for your boyfriend," she said.

"It wasn't my boyfriend."

"Oh. It sounded like your boyfriend." A lightbulb went on in her formerly dark attic. "Oh! Friend with bennies? I got it."

"She's my girlfriend," I said deliberately, to mess with her.

Brandy recoiled. "Oh." She recovered, barely, enough to add, "That's cool. That's totally cool with me."

"Really? Good. I'm so glad it's cool with you."

THE SPACE BETWEEN US   273

Sarcasm didn't seem to be her strong point. "Yeah, it's fine. It's all good. No hate, right?"

I sighed. "Brandy. Whatever. I need to run out, but I'll be back in a couple hours. Can you handle things here, really? Because I can see if Moira can come in…"

"No! I mean, is that her name? Your girlfriend?"

I wanted to shake her. "Moira is the girl who works the evening shift. She is not my girlfriend."

"Oh. Okay. Phew." Brandy's nervous giggle was even more annoying than her general one, something I hadn't thought was possible. "No, really. I'm fine for a couple hours. It's not even busy in here."

But it could be at any moment. I looked at the clock again. We usually had another rush between three and four. I should be back by then, no problem. If Joy was here she'd never have let me go, and I was sure if she found out about it I'd never hear the end of it, but I couldn't ask Brandy to keep it a secret. And did it matter? I was going whether I had to face Joy's wrath or not.

It took me half an hour in the pharmacy to pick out what I thought Meredith would need and another ten minutes to get it home. I carried the bags up to her bedroom, which was dim. She was in bed with the TV on. I climbed on top of the comforter to lay out what I'd brought.

She sniffled and shifted higher on the pillows. "Thanks."

I held up a bottle. "Coughs, cold, fever, body aches. This other one is for nighttime. This one is for cough suppression. I didn't know which you needed—expectorant or whatever."

She made a face. "Gross. I need something to make this headache go away and for a sore throat."

I rustled in the bags and pulled out more bottles. We settled on a combination of liquids and pills, which I served her along with some water and orange juice I'd also picked up. I pulled out a couple cans of soup, too.

"Hungry? I can make this for you before I head back."

"Canned soup?" Meredith made another face. "Fat and sodium in dead chicken juice, no thanks."

"It's supposed to make you feel better. Sorry I don't have time to make you some fresh," I told her. "Maybe when I get home tonight."

She frowned and grabbed tissues from a box, holding them to her nose. Despite her complaints she didn't seem that sick to me. A little sniffly, a little hoarse, but that was it. Without her makeup on she did look wan, with faint circles under her eyes she'd never have allowed had she been feeling better.

"I have to get back," I said.

"No!" She clung to my arm. "No, stay, can't you stay for a little bit?"

It would take me another twenty minutes to get back to work, if I didn't hit any traffic. "I can't. I have to get to the Mocha. This new girl's there, and she's sort of a nightmare."

Meredith frowned and gave a shaky sigh. "Tesla...c'mon."

"The medicine should work soon. You'll feel better." I leaned over to kiss her forehead while holding my breath, trying not to breathe in any germs.

"I hate being sick!"

"I don't think anybody likes it." I tried to extricate myself, but she had me held tight. I settled against the pillows next to her. "Take a nap."

"Not tired." She turned to face me. "Hang out with me, Tesla. We never get to just hang out. I don't see you at all anymore."

That was far from true. "You could come into the shop more often. You used to be in there all the time."

"So? It's not like you can sit with me and just talk."

"No, but...you used to come in all the time, and now you don't. No wonder it feels like you never see me." I pressed the back of my hand to her forehead. "I don't think you have a fever. That's good."

"I have one, I took my temperature. It was a hundred."

"Barely a fever," I told her. "Get some rest, that's the best thing for you."

"You could be more sympathetic," she said sullenly.

I sighed. "Meredith, I'm sorry you're sick, but really, you're going to be fine. And I have to get back to work. I get off at five. Charlie will be home by four. I'll make us some dinner. We can all watch a movie. Hang out."

"It's not the same," she muttered.

"What's not the same?"

"It's not just you and me. Girl time."

I laughed, trying to make her smile. "Maybe we'll get lucky and Charlie will decide he needs to grade papers or something."

She shrugged, turning away to focus on the television again. "You make time for Charlie when he wants it. Just Charlie."

Sometimes it's possible to feel guiltier about things that aren't true. I withdrew, saying nothing. I put all the bottles and boxes and blister packs of pills back in the bags, but left them close to her on the bed in case she needed them. She didn't look at me until just as I was leaving, and then she did so reluctantly, as if I'd called her name, though I hadn't.

"Thanks for the medicine."

"I hope you feel better," I told her. "Being sick sucks."

"Yeah." She sniffled and used the remote to change the channel.

I was dismissed.

I wasn't in the best mood when I got back to the shop. Seeing the line stretching nearly out the door, and in fact winding around on itself, tables filthy with crumb-covered plates, and Brandy moving at half speed didn't help. I pushed through the crowd, apologizing, quickly washed my hands and put my apron on.

"I thought you'd be okay," I said to Brandy, who gave me a dumb look. I was coming to realize they were common with her.

"I'm fine. What's the problem?"

I pointed at the long line of grumbling customers.

She looked confused. "You said there's always a rush about now."

"Yeah, but—" I bit off my response. "Never mind. Let's just get this moving."

Things didn't get better when half an hour later Moira called in sick. Since she never did that, I didn't give her a hard time about it. But there was no way I was going to leave Brandy here by herself. I didn't care so much about her sinking, but I did care about my evening regulars. It wouldn't be the first time I'd had to stay from open to close, and with Christmas nearly upon us, the addition to my paycheck would make it easier to buy some last-minute things.

I was dead tired, though, and in no mood for chit-chat. When the bell jingled about ten minutes before we closed, I seriously thought about snarling—until I saw who it was.

"Charlie!" I'd missed my dinner break, and he looked good enough to eat. Well, he always did.

"Hey." Grinning, he leaned across the counter to kiss me. "You almost done?"

I'd sent Brandy in back to take care of the closing stuff and prep for the next day. Shit work I normally would've helped with, except that today I didn't feel like being nice. "Yep. Just have some last-minute things to do, then I can leave. But what are you doing here?"

"Figured I'd come in and see you at work, since I never have." He paused. "Meredith's sick."

"I know. I had to take her some medicine earlier today. She's not feeling any better?"

Charlie shrugged, his mouth twisting sideways. That said it all. I grabbed his tie and tugged him forward for another kiss. That was how Brandy found us.

She stopped with two bags of muffins in her hands. "Um…"

"Hi," Charlie said. "I'm Charlie."

I laughed at her expression, feeling more like what Meredith had called me—wild—than I ever had. "You can put those in the freezer. And go on home, I can finish up."

"Are you…sure?" Brandy couldn't stop staring.

"Yep. Absolutely. Positive." I stroked Charlie's tie with my fingers as he stood up straight, no longer leaning. "You're late shift tomorrow, too, don't forget."

"I know." Brandy backed through the door.

Charlie looked curious. I laughed. "New girl. Joy hired her."

"Joy your boss, the one who's always grouchy."

"Pow, pow." I shot him with my finger-guns. "Right on target."

Charlie nodded as Brandy came out from the back again. She took her coat and scarf from the hook and put them on, giving me a blatantly curious look I ignored by smiling at Charlie. I couldn't help it. Having him there was the perfect antidote to what had been a long and verging on crappy day.

"So…I'll just get out of here, then."

"Nice meeting you, Brandy," Charlie said.

"You, too," she told him as she headed for the front of the shop. "You sure you don't need me to stay?"

"Nope." I gave her barely a glance. "I'll lock up."

I did as soon as she left, turning the lock and the sign from Open to Closed at the same time, then sagging with a huge sigh of relief against the door. Watching from his spot at the front counter, Charlie laughed.

"Long day?"

"You don't even know." I hit the four light switches that covered the front, leaving only the counter lights on. I'd already made Brandy put the chairs up and mop the floor, so all I had to do was ring out the drawer, put the money in the safe in the back and make sure everything else was ready for the morning.

Before that, though, I needed some sugar, and not the kind in the dessert case.

"Mmm," Charlie said when I stood on my tiptoes to kiss him. "If kissing was part of your job description, I think you'd get a raise."

I pressed against him. "If only, right?"

Charlie settled his hands on my hips to kiss me again. Longer this time. Definitely with more heat. He opened for me when I nudged at his mouth, and when I sucked gently at his tongue he slid one hand up my back to cup the back of my head. Perfect, the way his kisses always were.

I sighed, easing out of the kiss to nuzzle at his cheek and neck before stepping back to gaze at his face. "How was your day?"

"Long. Not as long as yours, but long enough."

He looked as tired as I felt. I wanted to go home, take a hot shower, put on my fuzzy pjs and snuggle on the couch, if only I could rouse myself from the comfort of Charlie's hug.

I closed my eyes and put my ear to his chest, listening to the reassuring and steady thump of his heart.

His hand stroked down my back slowly. Then up again. Down. He was petting me, which made me smile.

"Purr, purr," I said.

He laughed. "Nice pussy."

I tipped my face to look at him. "We should get home. Let me just check the back, make sure Brandy didn't leave anything undone. You want to come with me?"

"Sure." Charlie followed me around the counter. "I've always wondered what went on in the back rooms of coffee shops."

"Ooh, all kinds of things." I waggled my fingers at him as I did a quick scan. I'd printed out one of Joy's lists, and Brandy had seemed to hit everything on it, if the checkmarks beside each item were to be believed.

Torn between knowing better than to trust she'd really done everything she was supposed to, and risking the wrath of Joy if we came in tomorrow morning to find something not done to her specifications, I figured I'd better make sure at least most everything had been done. Charlie watched as I looked at the bins and boxes and cartons, and checked the freezer, too.

"You're the queen of your domain," he said.

I twisted to look at him over my shoulder as I put away a box of paper napkins that had been set on the wrong shelf. "You think so?"

He'd been leaning against one of the prep tables, arms crossed. He grinned. "Yep."

I straightened. "Gets you horny, huh?"

He laughed, ducking his head, not quite blushing in that way I loved so much. "Sort of. Yeah."

I sashayed over to him, then did a little strut. "It's the apron, right? Or the scent of chocolate wafting around me? I know, I know. It's the heat from the coffeepots—it's making you crazy."

He laughed harder and reached for me, though I danced just out of reach to shake my ass at him. I twirled and stretched, then stopped to wink at him. He was so beautiful when he laughed that suddenly my heart hurt.

"Tesla?" He moved toward me at once, arms out. "What's the matter?"

I shook my head. "Nothing."

He put a hand to my forehead. "You're not getting sick, are you?"

"No."

"You feel a little warm," he said.

I bumped my pelvis against him. "I guess I got the fever."

"And the only prescription is more cowbell?" Charlie asked, which endeared him to me all the more.

"Or maybe it's just being around you."

He put on a serious face. "Hmmm. What can we do about that?"

I kissed him. He kissed me. It was a beautiful thing, that kiss. Passionate and sweet, just a little sloppy. He broke it first to laugh into my ear, tickling. I put my arms around his neck and jumped up.

Charlie caught me.

No hesitation, no struggle. He caught me just under the edges of my ass so I could wrap my legs around him. He turned to rest my butt on the edge of the prep sink.

It wasn't something we planned, it just happened. It started off silly, and turned sexy in seconds when he kissed me again. When I felt his cock get hard between us. When I pulled him closer with my heels and lifted his shirt from his waistband so I could slip my hands inside.

His warm skin against my palms. The rise and fall of his belly under my touch. The taste of him, the stroke of his tongue on mine. The way he held me so I wouldn't fall.

My fingers found his belt buckle and, seconds after that, the heat and hardness of his dick. Charlie made a small, soft noise into my mouth when I stroked him. Our kiss paused, our mouths still touching.

"Tell me you want me," I breathed against him.

I hadn't meant to say anything, but sometimes feelings make the words come out.

"I want you, Tesla." Charlie pressed his face into the side of my neck, where his hot breath caressed me.

I tilted my head so he could mouth my skin as my hand worked along his length. "Say you want to be inside me."

"I want to be inside you."

"How much?" I gave my palm a twist over the head of his cock.

His voice broke a little when he answered. "So much I can't even tell you how much."

It was good enough for me. My skirt was so short that pulling it up was no problem, but my winter-weight tights were definitely cock-blocking us. I couldn't even tear them with my fingers. We could've pulled them off...but sex makes people crazy. I looked to the wall to my left and the pegboard that stored a lot of different odds and ends. I pulled off a pair of scissors and handed them, handle first, to Charlie, who took them with raised brows.

"Cut my tights."

The rim of the sink was wide and flat enough to hold me, but I gripped it hard as I leaned back and spread my legs to give him access. Charlie held the scissors, brow furrowed, mouth thin in concentration. He looked up at me once more, but when I nodded, he focused on the task in front of him.

I gasped at the touch of metal against my leg, cool even through my tights. Charlie plucked at the fabric with his thumb and forefinger to snip a hole, then slide the blade inside it. Snip, snip, snip, the metal moved along the tender flesh of my inner thigh, cutting the tights and moving dangerously close to my pussy.

I trusted Charlie not to cut me.

He curved the slit he was making across my pussy and down an inch or so on my other thigh, then glanced up at me. Heat flared in his gaze. His hair had fallen over his forehead. The lines at the corners of his eyes crinkled when he grinned.

He put the scissors in the drying rack next to me and then grasped my hips, shifting me closer to the edge. His cock nudged me. I was so wet for him, so ready. I groaned when he pushed inside me, balls deep, the counter at just the perfect height.

He buried his face against my neck again as he filled me. His teeth pressed my skin, and I arched to get him even deeper inside me. When he bit me lightly, I groaned again. It was more than simply what he was doing, it was all of this. Charlie's teeth, his cock, the cutting of my clothes, the way I knew he wouldn't let me fall. All of it turned me on.

"Fuck me," I whispered into his ear. Is there any better way to say it, when that's what you want?

He bit down harder as he fucked into me impossibly deep. I put one hand on the back of his neck while my other still gripped the counter edge. I used my heels to hook around his ass, urging him on. It wasn't going to last long; it couldn't. I was already surging on the way to orgasm, and the shudder of Charlie's breathing told me he was close, too.

I think we both realized at the same time what we were doing, but it was too late to stop. The fact that he was bare inside me only turned me on even harder. Charlie looked at me, his expression tight and familiar. I saw an instant of awareness in his eyes, but there was no way I was going to let him pull out.

"Kiss me," I said.

He did, so hard our teeth clashed. His tongue fought mine. He fucked into me harder, but pushed a hand between us so that his knuckles pressed my clit with every thrust. It was just the right amount of pressure and set me off like the Fourth of July. His name got lost inside my mouth, swallowed by my gasp as I came.

He came a few seconds after me, but in silence. His kiss softened, as did his grip. He moved inside me for another couple of slow thrusts, then pressed deep into me and looked into my eyes.

We didn't say anything.

I wasn't worried about getting pregnant, because I was on the pill. With anyone else I'd have been worried about STDs, but though we'd never specifically exchanged medical reports, I knew Charlie was clean. He'd been married to Meredith for eight years and said he'd never been with anyone else during that time, and I'd believed him. He and Meredith didn't use condoms. In fact, the only reason he and I did was because she'd insisted on it at the first, and we'd never gotten out of the habit.

He was slipping out of me, something we never worried about much at home in a bed, but now I grabbed at a handful of paper towels. Also, I realized how sore my butt was when he pulled away and I hopped off the edge of the counter. We did an awkward shuffle as Charlie pulled his pants up and buckled them, and I used the paper towels.

Still, I laughed as I touched the unraveled ruins of my tights and rearranged the panties he'd pushed aside. I let my skirt fall back down over my thighs. "That's going to be breezy."

"Tesla," he said in a low, uncertain voice.

I hugged him hard. "Don't worry about it."

He held me against him so I felt the puff of his breath on my hair. "Are you…okay?"

In all the time I'd been living with them, I was sure I'd told Charlie I was on the pill. But even though he lived with two women, he'd never seemed that in tune with stuff like periods. "I'm not going to get pregnant, Charlie, don't worry."

His mouth twitched downward, in not quite a frown but the hint of one. Something like sadness passed through his eyes. "If you did…"

"I'm not going to." I squeezed him. "Things are complicated enough. I'm not irresponsible about that sort of thing."

"Nobody ever intends to be."

I kissed him until he kissed me back. "We should get home."

"Yeah." Charlie paused. "I told Meredith I was running out for some groceries."

"But you came here?" I asked in surprise.

"I stopped on the way. I still have to get to the store. We just need a few things." Another pause. "I didn't think…I mean I didn't intend—"

I hushed him with a kiss. "It's fine."

We both knew that if she found out, it wouldn't be. But to say that out loud would make it as wrong as we both suddenly felt it had been. I hated that. We weren't sneaking around, cheating on anyone. We were two parts of three.

To tell him I'd keep it a secret would acknowledge that we had to make it one. Instead, I kissed him again. I patted his ass the way I usually did, to make it all okay.

"You go. I'll finish up here. Meet you at home."

He looked a little relieved. "Yeah. Okay. You need anything at the store?"

"No. I'm fine." I didn't feel like smiling, but did anyway.

And though I wanted to kiss him again before he left, I didn't.

Chapter

31

Instead of going home, I went to Vic and Elaine's. I intended to just do a drive-by, but when I saw only her car in the drive, I pulled in. I'd take my chances if he came home.

I knocked instead of letting myself in, though I still had a key. A nervous-looking Elaine opened the door a crack to peer out, then flung it wide when she saw it was me. She called to the kids as she reached for me.

"What are you doing, knocking?" she cried, enfolding me into her embrace as best she could with the bulk of her belly between us. "Crazy girl. Kids! Look who's here!"

I was attacked from the knees down by one small, frantic warrior who clung to me and demanded to be lifted. "Max. Hey. What are you guys doing up so late?"

"They sleep in longer if they stay up later," Elaine said. "I know, call me Mother of the Year, but I just can't face getting up at six in the morning when it's dark out."

Simone hung back, arms crossed, mouth turned down, eyes suspicious. I'd have to work a little harder on that one. I respected the kid for it, though. I guess I couldn't blame her for being mad.

"Simmy. C'mere and give me a squeeze."

She shook her head. Elaine sighed and closed the door to tug at my sleeve. Max had already begun babbling, a long stream of stuff I didn't understand but nodded over anyway.

"I was having some hot chocolate and popcorn. You want some?" Elaine was already leading me into the kitchen, children trailing behind us. "Kids, give her some space."

Simone had no trouble giving me my space. She took her usual seat at the table and sat with the same frown on her face, not even drinking her cocoa. Elaine rolled her eyes but said nothing.

I understood.

I'd made a promise and broken it. I was anything but proud of that. So when we'd finished our snacks and Elaine had taken Max off to bed, I followed Simone into the bathroom to supervise her brushing her teeth. She did it a lot more vigorously than she used to, scrubbing and scrubbing until I finally sighed.

"C'mon, kiddo, it's bedtime."

She leaned and spat into the sink, then gave me the evil eye in the mirror. "I have to get rid of the plague."

"Uh-huh. That's plaque, and I'm pretty sure you got rid of it. C'mon, I'll read to you if you want. *Anne of Green Gables?*"

She rinsed her mouth and put her toothbrush back. "We finished that already. Daddy read it to me."

"Well, what are you reading now? I could—"

"Daddy won't like it," Simone said, "if we read ahead. Then he won't know what happens."

There was no arguing with her, so I just nodded. "Okay, fine. But let's go get into bed, anyway."

Reluctantly, she let me follow into her bedroom, which had been rearranged and freshly painted. "You got a new bedspread!"

"And pillows!" she cried, running and bouncing on the bed before she remembered she was mad at me. She burrowed under the blankets and turned her face to the wall.

I sat on the edge of the bed. "Simmy. Talk to me."

Her lip trembled, and she drew a heaving sigh I knew wasn't faked. I stroked her hair until she turned to bury her face against my legs. Her small shoulders shook. Tears stung my eyes as I smoothed my hand over her hair, again and again.

"I'm sorry, punkin." I twirled her hair around one finger. "I know you're upset with me, and I don't blame you."

"You said!"

"I know. But sometimes…"

"I know, I know," Simone wept. "Shit happens."

I bit my lip so I wouldn't laugh, even as the stinging tears escaped to slide down my cheeks. I swiped at them hastily, not wanting her to see. "Don't say that."

"That's what Daddy says." She sat up, eyes and nose red, cheeks wet. "That's what he told Mama."

"He wouldn't want you to say it, though." I handed her a tissue, but ended up wiping her face for her.

"Daddy said it wasn't because of me and Max. Or the new baby."

"It wasn't, sweetheart. I'm sorry you ever thought that." I cuddled her close to me and sighed at how I'd done such damage to someone who loved me so much. "I suck. I'm sorry."

Simone breathed a sigh. "Daddy and Mama were fighting a lot."

Shit. "About me leaving?"

She nodded against me. "And about his new job."

"Does Daddy have a new job?" I stroked her hair, then tugged so she'd sit up again. "Not at the garage?"

She shrugged. I shouldn't have expected her to know. I'd have to ask Elaine.

"Why'd you move away?" Simone snuffled again.

"Well…I thought it was time. With the new baby coming, you and Mama and Daddy and Max need more room in the house. And I always knew someday I'd have to move out. I couldn't live in your basement forever."

"That's what Cappy said." She looked up at me with swollen eyes. "He said you had to move out because you wanted to be with other people. More than me and Max and Mama and Daddy?"

"Just different, honey."

"Grown-up stuff." She sounded disgusted.

"Yeah. Grown-up stuff."

Simone fixed me with a stern look. "I know how babies are made, you know. Mama showed me a movie."

Again, I bit back laughter. "Oh, yeah?"

"Are you having a baby, Tesla?"

"Um. No. Not now, anyway." I shook my head and cuddled her again. "But when your new baby arrives, I'll come over and help your mom take care of it the way I did with you and Max."

Simone was silent for a few seconds. "It won't be the same."

Not at all. "Things don't always stay the same, punkin."

"I wish they did," she said.

At that moment, I did, too.

I tucked her tight into bed and read her an old favorite, *The Velveteen Rabbit,* which put her to sleep within the first few pages. I kissed her forehead and listened for a few minutes to the even rise and fall of her breathing. I remembered Simone as an infant, just an hour after she was born. The weight of her. The heat. The way she'd opened her eyes to look into mine when I'd stroked the blond fuzz of her hair.

This was love. I loved this little girl, and I loved her brother. I would love their new sibling, too, I knew. But she was right. It wouldn't be the same. Nothing ever would.

I found Elaine in her bedroom, propped against the headboard with a journal and a pen. She looked up when I knocked on the door frame, and gestured for me to come in. She put the pen and book aside.

"Trying to get caught up," she explained. "They grow so fast. Simone has so much stuff in her baby book, I don't want Max to feel cheated. And as for number three, I guess I'll be lucky if I remember to write down how much he weighs when he's born. Or she."

"Can I see?"

"Sure." She handed me the hardbound book.

I flipped through the pages. She'd written notes on first teeth, first steps. Taped in wisps of hair from first cuts. There were pictures, too, all of us looking so crazy young, though none of them were more than five years old. I studied one of me holding Simone, with Elaine and Vic on either side of me on the couch.

I was crying again. This time it was Elaine who petted my hair as I cuddled next to her on the bed. She didn't say anything, didn't even shush me. She did hand me a tissue, but she didn't wipe my face. I took care of that.

"What's going on?" she asked.

"I miss you guys, that's all." I sat up and blew my nose.

"Nothing's stopping you from coming around, you know."

I choked out a laugh. "Uh, yeah, there is."

"Vic would get over it, Tesla."

"Simone said he has a new job."

Elaine's lips thinned. "Don't act like you didn't know about it."

"I know. I'm sorry. I didn't think it was my place to spill the beans. I told him to talk to you. But he was…" I shrugged, still feeling bad about the whole thing, but wanting to come clean. "I guess he felt I might understand more. Because I knew already."

"He's afraid for me and the kids. All the time. With the new baby coming, he's even more freaked out. He watches too much shit on the news. He sees too much stuff. I try to tell him that nobody can live like that, being afraid…but I guess he thinks if he's on the streets doing something about it, he'll somehow make a difference. Protect us. Or maybe he just wants to be ready to protect us if something happens, I don't know." She sighed. "I tried to tell him that he can't protect us from bad things if he's not actually here, but that didn't seem to sink in. He says he needs to work the weird shifts because he's new, that it will settle down in a few months, and the benefits and extra money are worth it. I'd rather have him, Tesla. We had enough money. We were doing fine."

"I don't think it's really about the money," I told her quietly.

She smiled sadly. "I know."

"Still. He should've talked to you about it first." I blew my nose again and tossed the crumpled tissue in the trash. I couldn't tell if I was stuffed up from crying or from getting a cold.

"Well, if spending a couple weeks on the couch at the garage didn't convince him of that, I guess nothing will."

I looked at her in surprise. "What?"

"Oh, yeah." She nodded. "I kicked his ass out. Told him he'd better get his priorities straight, that if he was going to be a part of this family he had to start acting like it. Let me know when he was going to be here, and then be here. Not keep secrets. I told him we had a new baby on the way, but I was pretty much raising two on my own, and I figured I could make it with three just as well."

"Wow." I was impressed. "Go, you."

She laughed, though without much humor. "My mother raised four kids on her own, Tesla. I'm not saying I thought it would be easy, but a man who's not home isn't any use to a family. I love Vic, but if he thought lying to me was the basis for a strong marriage, he needed some schooling."

"And you gave it to him. Good." My eyes felt hot, swollen with tears, but I felt lighter.

"You know…you can move back in if you want to. Your room's the same. And I won't lie, I'm sure I could use the extra hands. Even though I know where he is and what he's doing now, Vic's still gone a lot."

"Thanks. But…"

Her laugh was more real this time. "I know. A houseful of kids isn't as appealing as one you share with your, um, whatever you call them."

"My boyfriend and his wife. My girlfriend and her husband." I chewed the inside of my cheek for a second or two. "You think it's weird, don't you."

"I think it's unconventional, honey, but when would I ever expect anything less than that from you?"

It had been one thing for Meredith to call me wild, but

hearing Elaine say sort of the same thing was totally different. I frowned. "Why do you say that?"

Elaine looked thoughtful. "Well...honey, you're just...you. You're Tesla. You've always marched to a different beat. It's what makes you special."

"What if I don't want to be special?"

"Everyone is special, whether they want to be or not." She shrugged. "Why don't you want to be special? Don't tell me you want to be normal."

"I don't want to be abnormal."

She chuckled. "You're not abnormal, Tesla. Like I said, you're just you. And if it takes two people to make you happy, well...I guess you're blessed you found them, right?"

"That makes it sound like I'm greedy." Which was probably part of it.

"Having your cake and eating it, too?"

I shrugged. "I like cake."

"Who doesn't?" Elaine smiled. "But just remember. Too much can make you sick."

"So I'm unconventional. They're not." I paused, thinking. "Charlie, especially. He teaches third grade at a private charter school. He doesn't even have a Connex page or anything like that, because some teacher at his school was fired for some stuff she put on hers. Private stuff, set to Private, and still she got in trouble."

"And Meredith?"

I had to be honest. "I think she wants to be wild. Unconventional, I guess."

"But she isn't?"

I thought of the precise ways she needed everything to be arranged, from the clothes in her closets to the food in the fridge. "Not really. No."

"But they both care about you. They invited you to live with them. Be a part of them as a couple." Elaine cleared her throat, sounding a little uncomfortable. "I know growing up you saw that sort of thing all the time, but you do realize that most people wouldn't even think about it, much less do it."

"Yeah," I said wryly. "I know."

She put a hand over her face, laughing. "You living here with me and Vic is totally different, and you know it."

I hesitated. "But you know that Vic and I…"

She peeked at me through her fingers. "I know, honey. That was one of the things he did tell me the truth about—that summer."

I plucked at some of the threads of her quilt. "And it never bothered you? Knowing? I mean, you never said anything about it, and you let me live here. Did you ever…"

"Worry? Get jealous?"

I nodded.

Elaine shook her head. "No, honey. Whatever happened with you two…well, I don't want to hurt your feelings, but it wasn't anything like what Vic and I have."

I laughed. "No hurt feelings. I know that. I was so glad when he started to go out with you, you can't even imagine."

"I can imagine. He was good to you and Cappy. It's one of the things I fell in love with—how generous he'd been to you two. And I knew before he even told me that you two had done some things."

"You did? How?"

Elaine looked serious. "Women always know, don't they?"

I guessed we did. "You know I'd never, ever do anything like that with Vic again, don't you? I'd never get between you that way."

"Honey, if I thought you would, do you think I'd let you in my house, around my kids?"

"I guess not." I rolled onto my back to stare up at her ceiling. "But it's unconventional."

"Oh, I know that. Believe me, my mother had plenty to say about me letting you and Cap live here when I moved in with Vic. Especially about you. But I told her it wasn't any of her business, it was between me and Vic. And if he thought he needed to give you two a home, I wasn't going to be the wicked witch coming in and kicking you out. Besides, that I could see how much he cared about you both showed me what sort of man he was. Loyal and protective. It's what I love about him, even if it's also what makes him such a pain in the ass."

"It's what makes him crazy," I said. "He thinks too much about the world turning to shit."

"And thinks he can protect us from it. I know." She laughed. "Do I love that he's out there on drug cases, dealing with those people? No. But I guess if that's what he has to do, all I can do is support him."

"Even if it drives you crazy?" I rolled over to look at her. "Don't you worry about him?"

"Of course I do. But I just have to hold out hope that everything will be all right. I can't think about the alternatives."

I sighed.

She leaned to stroke a hand over my hair. "You can come back anytime, you know. We love you, Tesla. The kids miss you, and so do I."

I didn't say anything.

"He does, too," Elaine said.

I shrugged. "It was time for me to get out on my own, you know?"

She squeezed my shoulder. "But you didn't, honey. Did you?"

I knew she was right. I'd traded one safe place for another that didn't feel so safe anymore. And all it did was point out to me how much I wanted things to work out with Charlie and Meredith, and how I knew it wasn't going to.

Chapter
32

Charlie and I were playing chess while Meredith flipped through a magazine on the couch. He was kicking my ass, no surprise, since even though I could remember all the moves each piece made, I sucked at strategy. He was trying to help, but I spent more time laughing about my bad moves than really learning anything. At least it made for a quick game.

"We could play Uno or something," I said to her. "Monopoly?"

"Really?" She gave me a look of such disdain I was sorry I'd said anything.

"I just thought…never mind." I turned to Charlie. "How about you?"

"I have papers to grade." He made a sad face. "It would be easier with some popcorn."

I got up as he swept the chess pieces into the box. I kissed the top of his head and worked at the knots in his shoulders for a couple seconds before kissing his cheek. "How about some hot cocoa?"

"Your special homemade?" he asked, sounding hopeful.

"As if I'd give you powdered mix." I pinched his cheek.

Meredith met up with me in the kitchen. She'd pulled her hair on top of her head in a high ponytail that emphasized her cheekbones, the clarity of her skin, the full and silky length of her locks. In contrast to her sleek yoga pants and matching hoodie, I wore an old pair of Charlie's jeans cinched tight with a belt, and one of his oxford shirts over a tank top. I'd washed but not bothered to style my hair, the roots gone dark, and it fell over one eye as I puttered with the milk, cocoa and sugar.

"Want some cocoa?" I held up the milk carton. "Plenty for two. I can make enough for three."

She shook her head and leaned against the counter to watch me work. "It's Saturday night."

I looked at her over my shoulder as I mixed the cocoa powder, sugar and milk in the pot, then set the heat to low. "Yeah. And I don't have to work tomorrow. It's awesome!"

"And we're making cocoa and popcorn and talking about board games."

I loved this gas stove, being able to adjust the heat just so. I bent to eye the flame, but caught sight of her as I straightened. "Yeah? It's great. Totally relaxing."

I needed a night like this, doing nothing. I hadn't been off on a Sunday in forever. I'd worked the early shift today and come straight home, looking forward to the downtime.

Meredith didn't say anything, just watched as I stirred the heating milk. I wanted to make sure it didn't scald. I used a small wire whisk, which made me think of something.

"You know, I was thinking about getting Charlie a milk frother for Christmas. What do you think?"

"Why would Charlie want a milk frother?"

"For cocoa. And coffee. He likes lattes—"

"Charlie drinks his coffee black."

I looked at her. "Sometimes, sure. But he also likes lattes."

"Since when?"

I shrugged. "I don't know. Since I started making them for him? But it would be easier with a milk frother. Faster. He could do it for himself in the mornings."

"Did he say he wanted a milk frother?"

I stirred the bubbling milk slowly and eased it off the heat. "No. But I thought he might like one, anyway. Besides," I offered, "you could use it, too."

"I don't have any interest in making my own lattes."

I paused, then looked at her. "Not everyone has the advantage of being able to come in to the coffee shop and have their lattes made for them, you know."

Not that she'd been lately.

"Charlie barely even likes coffee."

I turned off the burner and put the pot aside. I faced her. "Well, what are you getting him?"

"I haven't decided yet." She shrugged as if it didn't matter, though Christmas was only a couple weeks away.

I grinned. "What are you getting me?"

Meredith sighed. Shrugged again. "What do you want?"

"Hey. What's wrong?" I tried to hug her, but she turned away. "Are you mad about something?"

"I'm mad because it's Saturday night and we're just sitting at home like...like an old married couple!"

"We are an old married couple," Charlie said from the doorway. "How's the cocoa coming?"

"It's done. Haven't made the popcorn yet." I looked at Meredith. "You want to go out?"

She stared at both of us. "We haven't been out together in forever."

She'd been out doing home parties three nights the week before. And I'd been at work on the late shift most of those nights, plus some extra. I knew she and Charlie had gone to some holiday party for his work, something I hadn't attended, of course, and she and I had gone shopping for groceries together. But she was right, the three of us hadn't gone out for fun in a while.

"I figured we'd just hang out here at home," Charlie said.

I'd been hunting in the cupboard for the popcorn, but now I stopped to glance at them both. "Yeah, what's wrong with just hanging out? We haven't done that together in a long time, either."

She sighed. "Fine. Whatever."

She pushed past Charlie, but he caught her by the arms to stop her. "Meredith, wait. If you want to go out…I guess we could. Right, Tesla? What do you want to do, honey? We already had dinner. I guess we could see what's playing at the movies."

"Never mind." She didn't look at either of us. "You two watch a scary movie on Interflix. I'm going upstairs to take a hot bath and read."

"We could join you," Charlie said, his voice trailing off when I shook my head at him.

Meredith didn't even answer him, just left the room. Charlie and I stared at each other. He looked confused.

"Everyone needs some time alone," I told him. "And she's in a mood. You should know better by now."

"I just wanted—"

"Charlie."

He stopped. I went to him, stood on my toes, kissed his mouth gently. "You can't fix her. She's pissy about whatever it is she's pissy about. Anything you say or do right now is going to make her pissier."

He nodded, his hands finding their comfortable resting place on my hips. "Should we go out? She wanted to."

I tried to keep myself from making a face, and didn't quite manage. "Like Mick says, you can't always get what you want, but sometimes you get what you need."

Charlie looked upward at the sound of Meredith's footsteps overhead. "Well...I wish I knew what she needs."

"Me, too, honey," I said with a sigh, and kissed him again. "Me, too."

Chapter
33

Christmas has always been my favorite time of year.

We had a tree, of course. It was a fake one, prestrung with lights. I didn't much like the way it looked, the limbs all perfect. There was no smell. It was pretty yet sort of vacant, not at all like a Christmas tree should be, but I didn't say so because Meredith obviously preferred it that way. At Vic's house we always had a real tree, bought when all of us, Cap included, tramped out through the rows and rows at the Christmas tree farm to pick out the very best. We strung popcorn for it every year, eating more than ended up in the garland, but we also had regular ornaments. Every year Elaine bought all of us a new and special ornament, and I missed them. I missed all of them.

That perfect tree in this perfect house, with Charlie and Meredith the perfect couple…there was only one flawed thing in all of it, and that was me.

In contrast to Meredith's recent snappish attitude, she'd spent the past few days in a giddy, bubbly and utterly charming mood. She was the Meredith I'd first met, sexy and spontaneous, and it should've been even better, since now, instead of mooning over her with a silly crush, I was actually in a relationship with her. I had not one gorgeous and attentive lover, but two.

Why, then, did I feel so alone?

Part of it was the extra hours I'd picked up at the Mocha. Because we were planning to take a trip to Vermont to go skiing during Charlie's school break, I wanted to get in as many hours as I could. It meant long days and nights away from home that I'd formerly spent with Meredith and Charlie. Now, just like they had before inviting me into their life, they spent those evenings alone, most times even going to bed together before I got home.

"Where's your girlfriend?" Carlos asked me from behind his laptop. "Haven't seen her here in forever."

"Oh…" I shrugged. It was funny to hear him call her my girlfriend, even if I knew he was mostly being silly. "She says it's dumb to pay for the coffee when she gets the coffee girl for free."

"Maybe she just heard all the stories she wanted to hear," Carlos said. "She tapped us dry, moved on."

I laughed, though I didn't understand what he was talking about. "Huh?"

Carlos pursed his lips. "Our stories. You know how she always came in and got us talking about stories. Maybe when we didn't have any more, she got tired of us."

The whole shop smelled of cinnamon, spice, gingerbread. Holiday smells that suddenly turned my stomach. "I think she's just been busy."

Carlos opened his mouth. Closed it. Shrugged and turned his attention to his computer. I didn't have time to ask him what he meant, because Sadie came through the door, and I hurried to help him pull out a chair for her. She looked ready to pop.

"What the heck?" I asked, but gently, seeing the look of strain on her face. "Sadie, wow, should you be out and about?"

"I'm going crazy at home," she admitted. "I'm nearly a week overdue. The midwife says she's not ready to induce me yet, and she encouraged me to be active. She said short walks would be good for me."

Sadie managed a smile. "It took me forty-five minutes to heft my bulk over here. I just need some hot cocoa and something sweet, and I'm going to sit here in the corner and read my book and pray this kid comes soon."

I laughed sympathetically. "I'll pray your water doesn't break until you get home. You have a midwife?"

She nodded. "Yep. No home birth, though, that's too scary for me."

"My friend Elaine had a midwife with both her kids. Two home births. She's having a third the same way. It's not so bad," I told her. "Though I'll admit, it's not for me. When I have kids, I want the epidural the second I go into labor."

Sadie laughed softly. "That's sounding better and better. Joe says, why do I want to put myself through something I already know is going to be the worst pain of my life? I can't explain it to him. I guess it's pride or something. My feminine pride."

We both chuckled, and I rubbed her shoulder quickly. "Let me get your cocoa. How about a big fat slice of gingerbread cake with real whipped cream? Fresh this morning."

"Yes, yes and another yes. Thank you." Sadie struggled

out of her scarf and coat to lean back against her chair with a sigh. "Hey, Carlos!"

Leaving them to their greetings, I went back up front. Brandy was working with me today, and as soon as I moved behind the counter, she pounced.

"That's Sadie?"

I pushed past her to make Sadie's cocoa. "Yeah."

"Joe's wife?"

I looked at her impatiently. "Yes. Sadie. Why?"

"No reason. I just wondered what she looked like, that's all."

The phone rang before I could answer her, so I left off the cocoa for the moment to answer, since it was apparent Brandy wasn't going to reach for it. "Morningstar Mocha."

"Tesla, it's me." Joy sounded tired.

I looked at the clock. She was due in to relieve me at two. I was taking off an hour early to do some last-minute shopping. "Hi."

"I can't come in today. You're going to have to stay."

Anger was pointless but unshakable. "What? No. I can't. I told you, I need to get off early today."

"I can't come in," Joy repeated. "And we need a manager there. You can't leave Brandy or Moira alone."

I looked over at Brandy, who, wonder of wonders, had finished the cocoa and sliced up some of the gingerbread cake and taken it over to Sadie. "Jesus, Joy. Really? You can't…I need to…"

I trailed off, sighing. "What if I called Darek to come in?"

"What? No! He doesn't work there anymore!"

Through his Connex status updates, I happened to know that Darek was working two jobs. One at a deli across town that closed at 1:00 p.m., the other part-time managing a bar at night. He could probably use a few extra hours around the holidays, and though he'd never been a full manager at the Mocha, he knew what he was doing.

"But he could handle it, Joy. And if you're not coming in, someone has to. Because I'm out of here at two. I told you that."

Silence stretched. I'd turned my back to the shop, keeping my voice down, but now I glanced around to make sure nobody was waiting for service. Nobody was, but Brandy was still talking to Sadie, her body blocking my view of her.

"Fine," Joy said in a tight voice. "Fine. Whatever. Call in Darek if you have to. But I'll remember this."

"Of course you will," I told her in a voice equally tight. "Just like I'll remember you calling off last-minute after I specifically told you I needed to leave early."

Another long silence. Brandy's hands were gesturing, and I could hear the rise and fall of her voice, punctuated as always by the snap of her gum, but I couldn't quite make out what she was saying. I heard Joy breathing.

"I have to go," I said. "I'm actually working."

"Tesla—"

I paused just before hanging up. "What?"

"Nothing. Call Darek, that's fine. And I'll be in tomorrow."

"Fine." I hung up without another word, just as Brandy came back around the front counter to the tune of the front door jingling.

She looked entirely too smug. When I glanced out into the shop, Sadie's still-steaming cocoa and cake were there, but her chair had been pushed back, and she was gone. I looked again at Brandy.

"What did you do?"

She seemed startled. "What?"

I pointed at the front door. "What did you say to her?"

Brandy donned an expression of such wide-eyed innocence I wanted to smack it off her face. "I didn't say anything. Well, maybe I just asked her how her husband was doing, that's all."

I strained to see through the front windows, catching a glimpse of Sadie's red coat. "That's all, huh?"

"Hey, she asked how I knew him," Brandy said defensively. "Was I supposed to lie?"

More anger burbled up to the surface. "Let me get this straight. You told an enormously pregnant woman you used to fuck her husband?"

Brandy's jaw dropped, but guilt sneaked across her face. "I didn't...I mean, I didn't say..."

"Oh, you pustulant bitch."

Brandy backed up a couple of steps. "Hey!"

"You," I said as I took off my apron and tossed it onto the counter, "are a truly vile piece of trash. You know that? Why would you do it? Never mind. I know why. Because she has a handsome, loving husband and a baby on the way, and you, Brandy, have nothing."

"You can't talk to me like that!" she cried.

"I just did." I pushed past her and grabbed my coat. As I passed Carlos, he gave me a thumbs-up I didn't bother to return. I was out the front door in seconds, moving faster than Sadie could, to catch up to her on the sidewalk. "Hey. Slow down."

I took her arm and she looked at me with red-rimmed eyes, though no tears. She swallowed convulsively, her face pale. Her hair had frizzed around her face where it escaped from her knit hat.

"It's not like I didn't know," she said abruptly. "I mean, I knew about all of it before. But I didn't think I'd ever meet one of them."

I didn't know what she was talking about, but I nodded sympathetically, anyway. The sidewalks were icy, and I tucked her arm firmly in mine to make sure she didn't slip. She didn't protest.

"Let me walk you home, make sure you get in okay." I was glad I'd worn my thick-tread boots instead of slippery soles.

"Thanks." She coughed out a breath of frosty air. "Oh… Tesla, I'm sorry, I didn't even pay for my stuff!"

"Don't worry about it."

She drew in a shuddery breath. "I feel so stupid. But I just didn't want to cry in front of her or anything, and I feel like I cry all the time now at stupid things."

"Um…hello," I said. "Pregnant? Totally allowed. Besides, she was a bitch to even say anything. And honestly, whatever she told you? I'm sure was exaggerated."

"Oh…I know that. She made it out like she and Joe were practically engaged." Sadie's laugh sounded almost normal. "And I know that's not true. But still…when you weigh more than your husband and look like you swallowed a whale, and some young, pretty—"

I scoffed. "Girl, she looks like someone came up and hit her in the face with the ugly shovel."

This time her laugh sounded totally normal. "Oh. That's not nice."

"But it's true. Anyone who takes up shit with a pregnant lady is ugly." I nodded and steered her around a patch of ice. "Where are we going, by the way?"

"Just another block. You really don't have to walk me the whole way."

"Sure I do. What kind of friend would I be if I just let you slip and slide your way home?" I shook my head.

It might've taken her a long time to get to the Mocha, but

it didn't take us nearly as long to get back. She tried to get me to come inside, but I declined; Joy would already have my ass if she found out I'd left Brandy there alone. I dropped Sadie at her door and made sure she got inside.

"I don't expect to see you again until you have a baby with you," I told her. "And then you come in with that beautiful kid and your volcanically hot husband, and you don't let one thing that slitch says upset you. Okay?"

"Thanks." Sadie paused in the doorway. "I knew before I married him he'd had a past."

"That's good, isn't it?" Even with my mittens on, my hands were cold. I rubbed them together, then shoved them in my pockets.

"I'm not sure if it's good or bad, it just is. I know I shouldn't have let her get to me. Thanks for walking me home, Tesla, I appreciate it." She hesitated again. "You know, if you ever need to talk to someone..."

I frowned. "About?"

"Anything. I've been slimming down my practice, but that doesn't mean I'm not available to listen."

"Do I...look like I need to talk to someone?"

Sadie smiled. "Everyone needs to talk to someone sometimes, Tesla. I'm just letting you know I'm here. If you need to."

"Okay. Thanks." I frowned again, uncertain about what had made me seem so much in need of a shoulder to cry on. "You okay now? You good?"

"Fine. Thanks again."

I waited until she'd closed the door before I hopped off her front porch and headed back down the sidewalk. I looked up at the early afternoon sky, turning gray with clouds that promised snow. My cheeks and nose stung from the cold, as did my legs. Today would've been a good one to wear jeans. Fortunately, I was able to reach Darek on his cell, so by the time I made it back to the shop I'd arranged for him to come in and cover me.

The place was empty, something almost unheard of. Brandy looked up with a frown when I came in. She came around the counter to meet me before I was even halfway across the floor.

"You were right. That was a super shitty thing to do," she said abruptly.

Her apology was unexpected and inelegant, and shouldn't have been made to me, anyway. "Yeah. It was. Sadie's a regular, Brandy. And pregnant."

"I know. I know!" She shook her head. For once she wasn't smacking away on a piece of gum like it was her cud. "I was stupid. I just felt like... I dunno. You know how shitty it is when you know you didn't leave an impression on someone who left a really big one on you?"

I eyed her. "Yeah."

She shrugged. "He didn't even remember me. He came into that other shop a few times a week for months, and I waited on him every time. We went out, we had dinner, it was awesome. And the sex was..."

She sighed, looking dreamy, then focused on me. "Joe made me feel beautiful, Tesla. He really made me feel like I was beautiful. But then... I dunno, I was a little too aggressive or something, whatever. And then he didn't even recognize me. I know I lost a lot of weight and stuff, but still."

I knew how much it meant to have someone make you feel beautiful. I could give her credit for admitting she'd been a douchetard, but not a whole lot. "What you did was really dumb and just nasty."

"I know. And when she comes in again, I'll tell her I'm

sorry." Brandy looked contrite. "I mean it. Don't hate me, Tesla, please."

I made a face, grateful we didn't have an audience for the schmoopfest. "I don't hate you."

"You don't like me."

"I hardly know you, that's all." I didn't want to be mean, even though she was right.

Brandy shrugged. "Whatever. But I work here now, and it would be cool if we could get along."

"Have I made you feel like we don't get along?"

"No, but you don't really like me. I can tell."

Great, now I had to worry about hurting her feelings. I didn't have time to hold her hand through this. "I'm sorry if I made you feel that way. Listen, I've got Darek coming in to take over for me when I leave early."

"The guy who got fired?"

"He quit, but yeah. Him."

Brandy frowned. "I can handle things until Moira comes in."

"Joy doesn't want you and Moira here alone. Darek's cool. You'll like him. I promise." I looked at the clock. "Damn, it's empty in here."

She glanced around. "I guess everyone's out shopping and stuff."

"Just what I need to be doing. I have half an hour before Darek gets here, I'm going to go do some prep in the back. Can you handle it out here?"

She gave me a look. "You mean can I handle the total lack of customers? I think so."

Forty minutes passed while I did my prep, trying to get ahead for the next day. Annoyed that Darek was late, I went out front, only to find the place bustling once more with customers and Darek and Brandy casting each other flirtatious glances from either side of the dessert case.

"Hey," I said.

He looked at me. "Hey, I made it. Brandy was just showing me what's new."

The only thing that was new was her, but I didn't point it out. In cartoons, characters with hearts beating out of their chests and flying from their eyes means true love at first sight. Well, it sort of happens like that in real life sometimes, too, minus the cartoon hearts, and with the addition of smoldering glances across refrigerated pastries.

I left them to it. I had a long list of things I wanted to pick up so I could get them in the mail, mostly odds and ends of strange things like the snack foods native to central Pennsylvania that my mother missed out in Cali. I picked up a few bags of groceries for Cap while I was at it. Money well spent as far as I was concerned, since he ate like a rhino. I found some toys for Simone and Max, as well as the cutest little snowman plushie for the new baby.

And then, crossing from one overcrowded store to my car, passing by a shop window I'd never looked in twice, I felt my entire world grind to a shuddering, stuttering stop.

I'd heard of the Green Bean, of course. On the other side of town from the Morningstar Mocha, it wasn't exactly competition, but was probably one of the better known coffee shops in the area. And there in the front window, tapping away at her laptop, sat Meredith.

I stopped in the parking lot, shielded between two cars, my hands loaded with bags that were quickly growing too heavy. She sat alone at her table, but close enough to the other customers that it was obvious she could take part in the conversation. She looked up and laughed as I watched.

She tossed her hair over her shoulders, leaning forward to talk to the man next to her. He gestured broadly, and they laughed together again.

It was the equivalent of finding her naked and sucking some stranger's cock, that's how horrible it felt. Harsh and breath-stealing and painful. She'd told me she was working from home in the cold winter so she didn't have to go outside. That she had the coffee girl at home and didn't need to go out anymore to get her. Meredith had told me a lot of things, and it looked as if at least some of them were lies.

Chapter
34

I didn't tell her what I'd seen.

It would've sounded silly, accusing her of cheating on me with a coffee shop. And who knew, maybe it had been a whim. Maybe like me, she'd been out shopping, and decided just to stop in for something hot to drink. After all, no matter how it felt, it wasn't out of line for her to drink her coffee wherever she wanted to.

She didn't notice that I was quiet, but Charlie did. He didn't ask me why, just pulled me close to press a kiss to my temple and smooth my hair off my forehead. His squeeze comforted me. I leaned into it, breathing in his good, soap-and-water smell. His heat.

"I think we should bag the ski vacation." Meredith tossed this out over the dinner she'd cooked and had ready for us both by the time we got home.

Pasta, sauce, salad, garlic bread. It was the first meal we'd all had together the entire week, but it tasted a little sour to me. It tasted like a bribe.

"What? Why?" Charlie sopped up some sauce with his bread. "I thought you'd already booked something."

"Yeah." Meredith gave him a sideways glance. "Of course you did. Well, it's been hard as fuck trying to find something for three, that's all. Lots of packages for two and four. None for three. We'd have to get two rooms, which is twice the cost."

I had a bite of spaghetti halfway to my mouth and used that as an excuse not to answer with anything more than a shrug. Meredith turned her attention to Charlie again. He was twirling his fork but not eating, and his fork scraped the plate. He didn't say anything at first, then looked at me.

"What about a room with two beds?" he suggested.

Meredith caught his look and frowned. "I'm not paying all that money to sleep crammed up in a double bed."

"You can have your own," he offered. "I'll share with Tesla."

I cringed. "You two go. I'll stay here."

He turned to me. "But you took the time off already, didn't you?"

"It's okay. You two go." I didn't want them to go alone; I didn't want to be left behind. I'd been looking forward to the ski trip. Jacuzzi tubs, a bedroom with a fireplace, the works.

Charlie drank some of the red wine Meredith had poured him. "I guess…"

"No." She shook her head. "I can't get anything now. It's too late."

Charlie put his fork down with a clink. "I thought you were taking care of this, Meredith."

I wanted to leave. I so did not want to be here during the

showdown. But all I could do was stare at my plate and pretend to enjoy the dinner that was now like eating sand.

"I told you. I tried." She frowned. "It's impossible."

"You could've let me know you were having trouble. I'd have helped you. Looked up some stuff online," Charlie began.

"Jesus, Charles, I'm not completely impaired. I told you, I looked up everything, but you do realize that Vermont at Christmastime is booked up pretty far in advance, don't you? What would you like me to do, perform miracles?" She stabbed at her pasta. "I told you, there's nothing reasonable for three. That's just the way it is."

"You don't really need me to go," I said.

She looked at me, her smile fading a little and something dark flittering in her gaze. "No. I guess we don't."

"Of course we do." He turned to me. "I thought you wanted to go."

"No. It's fine." I shrugged and drank some of my own wine. "You two go, if you can get reservations. You should."

Charlie didn't look happy, but he didn't say anything more about it. Later, when I was washing the dishes, Meredith came up behind to slip her arms around me and put her chin on my shoulder.

"Mmm," she murmured into my ear. "You smell so good."

"Did you have a good day?" I asked without turning around. My hands were full of suds.

"Oh. Yeah, it was okay. Kind of slow. I got caught up on my receipts and followed up on all my party leads. Hey, what do you think about me taking on another party business?"

I scrubbed at the pan she'd used to sauté the onions and garlic. "Like what?"

"Oh. Well, there's this really fun adult novelties and toys party company I was thinking of trying out. Under Where?"

"Underwear?"

"Under Where," she said. "Like a question. Under Where?"

Her hands moved in slow circles over my belly, as mine did in the sudsy hot water. "You sell Kitchen Klassics, Wix Alight and Jangle Bangles already. When will you have time?"

Her hands stopped moving. "You don't like the idea."

"What does Charlie say?"

"Haven't asked him. Why should he even care?"

I rinsed the pan and dried my hands, then turned to face her. "For the same reason he cares about everything. Number one, he's your husband. Number two, you probably need money for the start-up kit, right? And three...adult toys? Meredith, that stuff is...well, you know how he is about the school."

She frowned and pushed away from me. "I have plenty of money for the kit. I have parties scheduled every day this week and next, and two on the weekend, plus the orders that come in from my website sales. And I'm so tired of worrying about Charlie's damn school. For fuck's sake, Tesla, he lives with two women. You think it would matter so much if anyone knows his wife sells dildos?"

"I don't know. So do it, then," I said, annoyed. "Why should I care?"

She frowned at my response. "Wow, what's with the bitch face?"

I shrugged.

Her eyes narrowed. "What is up with you? Seriously, Tesla. I'm trying to share something with you that I'm excited about, and you act like I'm kicking a puppy. Is this about the trip?"

I opened my mouth to confront her about the coffee shop, but she stopped my words with a kiss. A long, lingering kiss that took my breath away and made me forget I was upset.

Her tongue stroked mine and her hand slid under my skirt to press between my legs.

"I'm sorry, baby," she said against my lips with that smile that always did me in. "I tried my best, I really did. But next summer we can go on a trip together, the three of us. To someplace sexy. I promise."

It was so hard to resist her, and the truth was, I didn't want to. I let her push her fingers inside my panties to pinch my clit. She bit at my neck as she pushed her fingers lower, inside me.

"Let's go find Charlie," she said. "I think he needs to eat this pussy."

What, was I going to argue? But after, when they'd both fallen asleep, I went to my own bed and lay awake for a very long time.

Chapter
35

It was going to be the first Christmas since Simone and Max were born that I wouldn't be there when they woke up to see what Santa had brought them. Elaine had told me I was welcome to spend the night, in my old room, but since things with me and Vic were still cold, I didn't want to. Whatever had been broken between us was taking an extra long time to fix. I didn't like it, but wasn't sure I was ready to change it.

Cap, to my surprise, was spending Christmas with Missy.

"But what about Lynds?" I handed him the wrench he'd pointed at.

He shrugged and bent over the engine he was working on. Since Vic had taken up undercover detecting again, Cap had been spending more time at the garage. Well, when he wasn't fucking Missy, apparently. It was weird to think of it, not that I spent a lot of time on the details or anything because…gross.

Just that he was with someone other than Lyndsay. I'd always assumed he'd end up with her, if both of them could get their heads out of their butts about how they felt.

"What about her?"

"You've spent Christmas morning with her the past two years."

"Not this year." Cap straightened. "What about you?"

"I'll go over to Vic and Elaine's for dinner, I guess. She wants me. You coming?"

"Vic wants you, too, you know."

I shrugged. Cap rolled his eyes. I sighed.

"Anyway," I said. "I'll be with Meredith and Charlie for the morning, and then they're going to her mother's house. I can't exactly tag along. So."

Cap put the wrench down and wiped his hands on a rag. "So. How long are you going to keep doing this?"

"What? Helping you? I have to be at work by three."

"Not this," Cap said. "What you're doing with them."

My jaw tightened, though it was a question I'd certainly asked myself often enough. "As long as I do it. And it's not a 'this' or a 'what.' It's a relationship. Just like the one you have with what's-her-face."

"Uh, no. Not like the one I have with what's-her-face. There's only one of her and one of me."

"Missy," I said. "Her name's Missy."

"I know what her name is." My brother frowned. "Don't play dumb with me, Tesla. You know what I mean. How long are you going to be the side piece?"

"I'm not the side piece. I'm a part... I'm... We have an agreement. We're... It's not like that." I paused. "It's not like Mom and Dad, either."

"They're married to each other, not you."

I swallowed bitterness, hating that I couldn't argue, hating that I felt like I wanted to lie. "Yeah. Well. Who says I want to get married?"

"You don't ever want to get married?" Cap shook his head. "Shit, Tesla, that's a bunch of crap. I know you do. And you want kids, don't you? Someday?"

"Someday isn't today."

Cap's mouth twisted. "It could be tomorrow. You never know."

"What about you?" I challenged. "You ready to pop the question to Missy? Knock her up? All you really want's a front door?"

Cap, unlike Darek, didn't fail when it came to quoting Adam Ant. "All I really want's a place in the country. Right."

"With Missy?"

He didn't say anything. He didn't really have to. I patted his shoulder.

"So," I asked, "how long are you going to do this?"

"Ahhh, fuck," Cap said.

That about summed it up.

Chapter

36

Everything looks prettier in the light from a Christmas tree. I didn't shake any of the boxes under the tree, but did slip a couple beneath it, surprises in addition to the few I'd put there when Meredith and Charlie placed theirs. Opening gifts on Christmas Eve felt like cheating, but if that's what Meredith wanted…well, Charlie and I were again along for the ride.

"We go in age order," she explained, after our expansive and delicious dinner of roast ham with all the trimmings. "Charlie, then me, and you go last."

I didn't care. It was as much fun to watch them opening their gifts as it would be to get mine. Charlie looked incredibly sexy in the sweater I'd picked out for him, and Meredith oohed and ahhed over the handmade glass jewelry I'd bought her. She said nothing about the milk frother, which Charlie loved, but she had bought him a travel mug set along with some specialty coffee, so our gifts went together really well.

"Your turn, your turn!" Meredith grinned as she handed me a heavy package. "Can't wait to see you open it."

I hefted it. It felt weighty enough to be books. Or tools. Not light enough for clothes. It could've been a pair of new boots…maybe ski boots. Maybe she was going to surprise me, after all. Maybe she'd found a way to make the trip work.

"Open it," Meredith ordered. "The suspense is killing me."

I picked at the tape. They were both rippers, but I liked to ease open a package and save the paper for later, though I never ended up using it. Laughing, Meredith lunged at me until I tore the paper away from the box.

There's always that moment before you open a gift when the possibilities are endless, when it could be anything and you hope it's just what you wanted—no matter what it is. Especially, sometimes, if it's something you're expecting not to get, but desperately want, anyway. Those few seconds when the paper falls away and before you open the box can last forever, and when you finally get the package open and see someone knew you well enough and cared about you enough to get you just the right thing…it's magic.

Or in this case, not.

I stared down at an array of thick, hot pink and purple dildos and vibrators. One was shaped like a butterfly, with a complicated-looking set of straps and a cord running to a remote. A set of metal Ben Wa balls. Some tubes of lube. Some of the items had an unfamiliar logo with a name I recognized—Under Where?

I couldn't speak. Not because I had nothing to say—there were plenty of words working their way up my throat like vomit. Meredith didn't seem to notice, rattling on about the different toys and their uses. This was worse than that episode of *The Simpsons* where Homer buys Marge a bowling ball because he wants one. Worse than getting a dictionary instead of a video game system. Worse even than clothes in the wrong sizes, meant to encourage a diet.

"With all of that, you won't need me anymore," I murmured.

I looked at Charlie, whose smile took away the sharpest part of the edge from Meredith's gift. "Plastic and batteries can't replace you," he stated.

"You don't like it." Meredith's smile soured. She pushed the tissue paper over the toys and sat back. "I thought really hard about which you'd like best, Tesla."

In weeks past I'd have soothed her, told her I loved what she'd picked. Probably even pulled one out to use right there to prove it. I didn't have it in me to do that now. "I know you did."

That was the worst part. I believed she had thought hard about what I'd like…and been wrong. Not just a little wrong, but fantastically, momentously and egregiously wrong.

She put the lid on the box. "Well. I guess it's a good thing I can return everything for credit."

The joke fell flat, but at least it was a joke. I leaned to kiss her, catching her cheek. "Don't do that. They'll be fun."

She shrugged. "It's okay. You can exchange the earrings you got me, right? For a different color?"

Now she was just being a bitch, but that was okay. I could handle that. "Sure. No problem. I can just return them altogether."

Her gaze flickered. She didn't want me to return the earrings; she liked them, I knew. But she shrugged and gave me a tight-lipped smile. "Great. Good."

"I have something for you," Charlie told me, and we both turned to look at him. He held out a small box wrapped in pretty blue-and-silver paper. "Here, honey."

The box was the size of my palm, but had the weight of a promise. I curled my fingers over the top. Something inside shifted.

"Open it," Charlie said.

I did. Nestled inside on a bed of white cotton was a bracelet, a simple band of polished silver in a curving shape, like waves. It was beautiful. It was perfect.

I loved it.

"Thank you!" I took it from the box and slipped it onto my wrist. The metal warmed to my skin within seconds. It was tight enough that it wouldn't get in the way at work, and I twisted my arm back and forth, admiring it.

I shouldn't have thought twice about kissing Charlie for that present, but I did. Meredith had watched him make me come with his tongue, had seen him fuck me until we both collapsed. But having her watch me kiss him now felt somehow wrong.

I kissed him, anyway.

"Jangle Bangles has a matching necklace," she said, even as the kiss lingered. "I'll show it to you in the catalog."

I sat back. I'd never buy something from Jangle Bangles, and I had no doubt the necklace wouldn't really match. "Sure. That would be great."

She stood, looking down at both of us. "I have something else for the two of you. It's a surprise."

Charlie glanced around at the mess we'd made in the living room, paper and ribbons and bows all over, then up at his wife. "What is it?"

"It's not a what, it's a where."

I knew her smile and the gleam in her eyes. I knew the way she slid her tongue across her lips. I could see she was up to something, but I couldn't begin to imagine what it might be.

"C'mon. Let's go." Meredith held out her hands, one to each of us.

Charlie and I each took one, and we followed her.

Chapter
37

"Where are we going, exactly?" Charlie was driving, but Meredith had plugged an address into the GPS, and the monotone voice kept barking out orders.

In the light from the dashboard, her eyes gleamed. She twisted to look at me in the backseat. "It's a club. A special party, for Christmas Eve."

"Dancing?" Charlie made a face. "You know I don't like to dance."

"You don't have to dance. Tesla and I can dance. You can watch." She snuggled up close to him and ran a finger down the buttons of his shirt, then cast me a flirtatious glance. "Or do other stuff."

Charlie laughed. "What other kind of stuff could I do in a club?"

"At this club I want to go to, just about anything you like."

Charlie seemed confused. "Are you talking about something like Spanky's?"

It was a strip club, but not a classy one like Samantha's. Spanky's had peep-show booths and an adult toy store, along with what I'd heard was a pretty skanky club section in the back with dark and private areas and sticky seats. Bleah.

Meredith made a face. "Ew. No. This club is private. You need an invitation."

Charlie still didn't get it. "Like a country club?"

She laughed, low. "Sort of. But not for golf."

"What's it for, then?"

I knew before she said it. "She means for swingers."

"Swingers…" Charlie's brows rose. "What?"

"She wants to go to a sex club." I was talking to him, but looking at her. "Probably at something like a private home, though it's set up like a club. You need an invitation to get in because technically it's a private party. Right?"

"It'll be fun," Meredith said. "I promise."

Even in a swingers' club, there was no real provision for three. Charlie and Meredith would get in without a problem as a couple, something that would've been hard or impossible for him to do as a single guy. And me?

I was a unicorn.

Single, bisexual female available to pair with couples. I was what everyone was looking for, but most people couldn't find. When I told Charlie this in the parking lot, just before we went inside, he laughed in disbelief.

"It's true," Meredith told him. She linked an arm through mine. We'd both changed, dressed to impress, and in my high heels I was finally almost her height. She pressed her chin to my shoulder, holding me close to her side. "Our Tesla's going to be a very popular girl."

"I don't want her to be popular," Charlie said. "And are you sure—"

Meredith kissed him to stop him from speaking. "I know you're worried, but look at it this way. Nobody's going to call the school board. Anyone who sees you here would have to explain what they were doing here, too."

Charlie wasn't totally convinced, I could tell, but I knew she was right. "People keep their sex lives private and secret for a reason, Charlie."

"C'mon. Don't be a spoilsport," Meredith said. "It'll be fun."

"That's what you said." Charlie linked an arm through mine on the other side. "But we don't have to do anything, right? We can just watch."

"Nothing you don't want to," she promised. "C'mon, I'm freezing my ass off out here."

The club was indeed at a private house, a long, low rancher set on a nicely landscaped plot of land surrounded by a fence, and only accessible down a long country road. There was a pool out back, closed for the winter, though three or four hot tubs bubbled and steamed. A couple trailers had also been set up along the open breezeway between the house and what had been a garage, but now looked like a game room. Everything glowed with strings of festive, multicolored lights. A waving Santa and sleigh were on the roof.

"It's an entire complex," Charlie said, as we went up the front steps.

The man who answered the door wore a pair of jeans with no shirt and didn't seem bothered by the cold. With nipples pierced, he gave new meaning to the term "muffin top," and when I caught Charlie's eye I had to fight back laughter at his expression.

"Hi. I called earlier and spoke to Len," Meredith said, as if she did this sort of thing all the time. "Three under the name Smith."

"Sure, c'mon in! I'm Harve. Get in out of the cold." Harve welcomed us into a small living room decorated in early seventies porn chic. Leather couches, tiger-striped carpets, lava lamps. Mud flap silhouettes as art on the wall.

People in all stages of dress, mostly un, lounged or chatted in small clusters.

"Living room," Harve said unnecessarily. "Donation box is right here. Cash only. Suggested donations are listed there on the sign. Kitchen's through there—we have snacks, drinks, just put the cash in the box. If you want bar food, you can hit the bar downstairs. We have a full game room and dance club set up down there, too. Another game room out past the breezeway. Pool's shut down, but the hot tubs are open. Bathing suits optional. 'Cuz this is our holiday party, we're having a bunch of raffles, too. Great prizes. Big-screen TV and stuff. Tickets are five for five bucks."

He gave us a broad, cap-toothed grin and handed us each a brochure. "Rules here. Any trouble, you give me or Len a holler, okay? Make yourselves at home. *Mi casa es su casa,* got it?"

Meredith nodded. "Thanks!"

Charlie and I murmured a thanks, too. He was already perusing his brochure, at least until Meredith nudged him to put it away.

"You'll make us look like total newbs," she hissed. "Jesus, Charlie!"

I linked my arm through his again. "It's okay. I can give you the rundown. I don't see many single guys here, though it's hard to tell. But basically, you might be approached by someone asking to join you or watch. You can say no, and no definitely means no. If you want to join someone or watch, Meredith or I will ask, not you."

Charlie appeared uncomfortable. "You know a lot about this."

I shrugged, looking around. It was more up-front and in-your-face than The Compound had ever been, but then I'd never been allowed into the private adult buildings. "The internet is a wonderful teaching tool, Charlie. What can I say?"

"C'mon, let's get some drinks. Charlie, put the money in the box." Meredith was already moving toward the kitchen, which was just like any normal kitchen except the fridge had a price list on the front and another cash box on the counter.

Charlie thumbed out several bills from his wallet and shoved it in the slot. "Have you done this before, Tesla?"

I shook my head, still gripping his arm as we moved into the kitchen. "Nope."

He paused to look down at me. "You just know?"

I shrugged and gave him a smile. "I know lots of things."

"Because of your parents?"

I nodded. "They kept this stuff sort of distant from me and Cap, but you know. Kids pick things up."

Charlie nodded in turn, looking around the combined kitchen and dining area. Meredith had already cracked the top on a beer and was chatting with a woman in a long red dress. She had huge breasts and nipples that poked out the front. She was gesturing to the man with her. He wore jeans, and like Harve, no shirt, but this guy was far more fit.

"Charlie, baby, you want a beer?" Meredith handed him one. "Tesla?"

"No, thanks." I shook my head. "I'll be the designated driver."

"Good." Meredith made introductions, me and Charlie to Steff and Kirk. She mentioned that Charlie was her husband but said nothing about my affiliation.

Steff's smile crawled all over me and tried to eat me. "Hi."

Charlie pulled me a little closer to him. "Hi."

"First time?" Steff asked.

"You can tell, huh?" Charlie's laugh was too loud.

Steff eyed him. "Oh. Definitely. But don't worry, Charlie, by the end of the night you'll forget you were ever scared."

"I'm not scared." Charlie tipped his beer to his mouth.

Steff's smile was gentler. "Right."

Then she turned her attention to Meredith, leaving me and Charlie to talk to Kirk. It turned out he was Steff's guest, since single guys needed to be sponsored in. It was clear to me by the way she casually and without subtlety caressed his bulging crotch every so often that Steff and Kirk were fucking, but he wasn't her husband or even her boyfriend.

"It's great downstairs. Dancing and some games. And some private rooms," Steff said. "You want to go check it out?"

"Absolutely." Meredith grinned at us over her shoulder as she followed Steff, Kirk close behind.

Charlie hung back at the top of the stairs. His face was serious when he looked at me. The steady thump of a disco beat vibrated beneath our feet, and the stairwell swirled with colored lights. He had to put his mouth close to my ear for me to hear him.

"Tesla, are you sure about this?"

"We're together, Charlie. It's okay. I told you, nobody here will make you do anything you don't want to do. It's etiquette.

I'm sure we're going to see some people fucking or sucking," I said. "But you don't have to do anything you don't like."

"I like fucking," Charlie murmured, his hands roaming over my body. "I like sucking, too."

I laughed and wiggled away from him. "Yeah, I seem to remember that."

Meredith was already dancing when we got to the bottom of the steps. She turned to us, her eyes alight with an excitement I hadn't seen in her for a long time. She gestured, making a face when Charlie hung back.

"Nobody will make me do anything I don't want to do," he said. "Nobody but my wife, anyway."

I pushed him forward. "It's not *So You Think You Can Dance*. Just shuffle your feet back and forth. You're only there for us to grind on, baby."

He grinned at me over his shoulder. "I can manage that."

Meredith greeted us both with beer-flavored kisses. "Dance with me, Charlie."

He gave it his best shot, but there was a reason why he never hit the dance floor. Totally uncoordinated, but endearing, he moved his hips and his feet in opposite directions, while his hands went someplace else. I didn't want to laugh at him, but couldn't help it. Meredith, on the other hand, had turned around to shove her ass against his crotch, bouncing to the music, her beer all gone.

I needed a drink of my own. There was a bar in one corner, with a bartender behind it. He was actually fully clothed, which was a relief, since his cock was at garnish level and I wanted a slice of lime in my diet soda, nothing else.

I took a seat at the bar on a stool shaped like a hand. Very funky. Not very comfortable. It felt as if I might slide off if I wasn't careful, something I fixed by shoving the heel of my shoe against the metal footrest and propping an elbow on the bar.

Charlie and Meredith were having quite a time. He was actually laughing, twirling her out and in again. He dipped her. When she kissed him, he kissed her back. She put her arms around his neck to keep him close. It would've been too much PDA in a public bar, but down here it was tame.

More leather couches like the ones upstairs lined the walls. Open doorways showed glimpses of rooms without any furniture, just mattresses on the floor and mirrors on the walls and ceiling. Closed doors probably had the same thing behind them, with the addition of couples, triples or other combinations getting their freak on.

Not that you had to be behind a closed door to do that. In one corner, lit sporadically by a whirling disco light, I spotted a woman on her knees busily sucking a man's cock, while he slowly jerked the dick of the dude sitting next to him. Another couple fucked, the woman on the man's lap, on a rocking chair in another corner. Most people, though, naked or clothed, weren't doing anything dirtier than making out. Maybe some finger-banging. It wasn't quite an orgy down here, though I had no doubt it could become one.

This was what Meredith wanted. Not satisfied with having both Charlie and me, she'd brought us here to…what? Be voyeurs? Or exhibitionists?

Or just to be unconventional?

"Hi." The woman who took the seat next to me wore a short skirt that showed a lot of thigh, and a corset top, her breasts heaving out above, her belly plumping out a bit below. "I'm Jessica."

"Tesla." I took the hand she offered and shook it.

"Are you here by yourself?" Jessica gestured to the bartender. "Vodka cranberry and another of what she's drinking."

"Um…no, not really. I'm with them." I pointed at Charlie and Meredith, still dancing and kissing. She had her hand on his crotch, rubbing. He didn't look as if he minded.

Jessica's perfectly arched brows rose. "Oh, really? You're in a ménage?"

It sounded so formal when she said it that way. "Yeah. I guess we are."

"Huh." She watched them for a minute, then turned back to me with a smile so friendly and genuine I had to return it. "They look busy. Are you interested in some play with me and my boyfriend? He'd watch, only."

She leaned a little closer. "You're very cute."

"Thanks." It seemed polite to offer her a compliment; the truth was, she'd flustered me a little. Heat flushed my throat and cheeks. "I like your corset. It's very flattering."

She leaned back with a laugh. "New to this, huh?"

"This?" I looked around the basement disco. "Sort of. Not really. Yes."

Jessica giggled again and shifted her hand-stool closer. "That's so cute. But you're not new to kink."

"I guess not." I'd never felt newer to it than just then.

"You like girls?"

"Oh, yes. Sometimes." I looked involuntarily at Meredith. She'd backed Charlie up against one of the support columns. They were barely still dancing. I wondered if he was hard, then knew he had to be.

"So…would you like to go with me and my boyfriend?" Jessica gave a discreet chin jerk toward a guy at the end of the bar chatting with a couple in matching leather outfits. "His name's Carl. Like I said, he'd just watch."

"I…" I didn't know what to say.

In all the talking we'd ever done, the three of us had never spoken about whatever the threesome equivalent of monogamy might be. We'd outlined rules about sharing time and space, but we'd never discussed loyalty. I looked again at Meredith and Charlie.

She was still dancing, but Charlie was laughing and shaking his head. He leaned against the support column as Meredith shimmied in front of him, but it looked as if he'd had enough.

"You want to go ask them, honey?" Jessica said. "We're not really into a group thing, but if you want to check it out with your partners first, I'm cool with that."

"I guess I…yeah." I swallowed some soda to wet my suddenly dry throat. For all my blasé attitude about the rules in a place like this, and how to say no, I suddenly found it hard to just turn her down.

"Not interested?"

"It's not that," I told her. "You're very pretty."

She laughed and leaned close to press her cheek to mine, and squeezed me kindly before sitting back. "Oh, honey. It's okay. You don't have to worry about hurting my feelings. You shouldn't do something that doesn't turn you on, right? That's what all of this is about."

"Thanks. I was flattered to be asked," I told her honestly. "I guess I'm not really into…swinging."

"We have room for all kinds, hon. Me, I'm not so much into any of that dominance and submission stuff, but we get that here, too. Not as much as in some of the bigger clubs down toward Philly. We have mostly just swingers here. But you get some of that other stuff once in a while." Jessica sipped at her drink and looked around for Carl, who was still chatting with the leather-wearing couple. "Bill and Sandy, for example.

They're into three-ways with another guy. Bill likes to suck cock. Carl, he's not into other guys, but he and Bill hit it off. Play golf a couple times a month. They're probably talking about baseball over there."

"You come here a lot?" My stomach was rumbling. I reached for the bar menu, which was pretty standard. Wings, burgers, fries. "Are you hungry? Can I buy you something?"

"No thanks, hon. You go ahead." She shook her head. "We come here just about every weekend. Once a year we go on a vacation with some of our friends, people we met here. Usually we go to Debauchery—it's one of those all-inclusives. Really nice."

I ordered a basket of onion rings. "Every weekend. Wow."

Jessica laughed. "Onion rings? You really aren't interested in hooking up, are you?"

I laughed, too. "I guess not. I only came because Meredith wanted to."

"Uh-huh. That's your lady? She's sort of abandoned your guy."

Meredith had found another partner. Kirk, the guy from upstairs. Of course she had; when had we ever gone out that Meredith danced alone? The difference was that all those other times I'd been the one watching her wiggle up on some strange man, and now Charlie was watching it, too.

I mumbled a goodbye to Jessica and moved across the floor to Charlie. I pushed up on my toes to kiss him. "I found you."

He'd been staring at his wife dancing with the other man; now he looked at me with a small smile. "Was I lost?"

I took his hand. Our fingers linked. "I don't think so. But I'm glad I found you, anyway."

"I'm not a good dancer. I told her she should have fun." Charlie looked again at Meredith, who seemed to be having

a great time. Laughing, eyes flashing, feet moving in time to
the beat.

Kirk put his hands on Meredith's hips, bumping her ass
against his crotch, and Charlie took half a step forward. I
guess he hadn't really noticed I was holding his hand, until
that held him back. He glanced down at our linked fingers,
then brought them to his mouth and kissed my knuckles.

"Looks like she is," he said.

I didn't look at her. I put myself in front of him, not to
block his view but to give him a choice of something else to
see. I placed both my hands on his shoulders, moving close.
Moving against him.

"We'll have fun, too, baby. Dance with me."

"I told you—" Charlie said, but I hushed him with a kiss.

I gazed into his eyes. I put one hand on his hip, keeping
the other at his shoulder, and I backed up a step so that he followed. The music was still thumping, hard-core and fast, but
we didn't have to move like that. Charlie and I moved slowly.
In time with the music, but slow and smooth.

"You can dance with me," I told him. "I don't care if you
step on my toes."

I led him through a basic box step, then another, and though
it didn't match the music, it worked just fine.

"I'm dancing." Charlie's smile lit up the room, even if it
didn't fill his eyes with all its light. He kissed me, nuzzling
softly, then said into my ear, "We're dancing."

Meredith and her partner were on the other side of the
room, with lots of other dancers between us. I could see her
as Charlie spun me in a small circle, but his eyes never left
mine. I knew he saw her, though. Kissing that other man,
letting him rub her all over. And finally, leading her by the
hand toward one of those open doors.

"Hey, hon, I guess I got my answer." Jessica bounced next to us, hand in hand with Carl.

"Yeah, I—"

She smiled and shook her head. "Don't worry about it, hon, it's all good. Though maybe you'd better catch them. Once the door's closed, you're not supposed to knock or anything. But they went in the lookie-loo room. You can peek in on them through the glass, if you want."

Charlie stopped dancing, not caring that we were jostled by the people around us.

"Right. Right. Thanks," I said.

"She just…" Charlie shook his head.

"It's what we came here for, remember?" I didn't like it, or the way Meredith had gone about it, but it was true. "C'mon."

A narrow, dark hall led around the back of the private rooms. We stopped at a small set of steps that led to nowhere, sort of like bleachers, directly across from the panel of clear glass in the wall.

"Look, Charlie."

I already knew what I was going to see. Together we peered through the glass. Because we were higher, we could see everything in the room. The shelves, the mirrors on the walls. The mattress on the floor.

Meredith and Kirk.

His shirt was open, but not off. His pants undone. Meredith had pulled up her skirt, her panties tossed to the side. She straddled his face, her clit pressed to his mouth as she rode his face. She'd pushed her shirt up, her bra down so she could tug and tug at her nipples. Even from this distance I could see how tight they were. How hard. She twisted them, her head thrown back so her hair hung down almost to her ass.

She rocked her pussy against Kirk's face. His erect cock

bobbed, held in one fist as he used his other hand to caress her ass. Once again I was watching her through glass, and I didn't need to hear her to know how she sounded.

Charlie made a small, low noise in the back of his throat and slid closer to me on the step. The only light came from the window in front of us. I felt the touch of his fingertips on my knee, and when I didn't protest, a little higher. I looked at him; he looked at me.

No matter why we'd come here, we were still together.

Meredith ground her clit on the stranger's stroking tongue as her fingers twisted, twisted her nipples. Her mouth opened. Her eyes closed.

The feather touch of fingertips on my thigh. Higher. Urging my legs to part. A soft stroke over the lace of my panties, then another. Nothing pushy or fierce. A touch so slight and unobtrusive I could ignore it if I wanted. Small pressure on my clit. Pressing.

Stroke. Press. Stroke.

I drew in a breath. The air around me smelled of perfume and smoke and sex. The step beneath my ass was hard, unforgiving, not a place to relax, and that was fine because every muscle in my body had gone tight and tense and taut.

Waiting.

I watched as Meredith moved off Kirk's mouth and dropped on her hands and knees, her ass in the air. As he got behind to fuck her, nice and slow and deep and hard. I knew how that felt. She shook, mouth stretched in a cry I couldn't hear but didn't have to. I knew how she sounded when she came.

My body didn't shake or move. I didn't sigh or groan or gasp. I came in silence, bursts of exquisite and torturous pleasure exploding inside me so hard I had to blink away floating specks in my vision. I closed my eyes, and when I opened them, there was Charlie.

He cupped my cheek, his kiss soft. Sweet. He pressed his forehead to mine. "I think it's time to go."

Chapter
38

Charlie was very quiet on the ride home.

Meredith, always chatty but even more so when she was drunk, couldn't shut up. She rattled on and on about "The Ranch," how much fun she'd had, how we should totally go back. She stumbled when she got out of the car, her clothes in perfect order but her lipstick smeared and her hair a mess.

In the house she kicked off her shoes and went straight to the kitchen sink to draw a long glass of water, which she downed right away. Charlie took his time to hang up his coat. Mine, too. He picked up Meredith's shoes and lined them up neatly by the back door. In the kitchen he put his keys into the bowl by the phone where he always left them, and the clink of metal against the porcelain was very loud.

"I don't want to do that again," Charlie said.

I hadn't been drinking booze, but I needed some cold water,

too. Meredith moved out of the way as I went to the sink, but she still stood close enough that I could see the faint lines at the corners of her eyes and a thread or two of silver in her hair. I filled my glass and drank, not looking at her. This wasn't my fight.

But of course, it was.

"Why not?" she demanded.

"I didn't like it," Charlie said.

Meredith's brows knit. She put her glass into the sink, the clink of it on metal much louder than the sound Charlie's keys had made. "Why not?"

"We didn't talk about it beforehand," he said.

"It was supposed to be a surprise."

Charlie smiled without humor. "Yeah. It really was."

I no longer wanted the water, but I took my glass and moved past them both. "I'm going to bed."

"No," Charlie said. "You stay. You need to hear this, too."

Meredith's gaze flickered over me. "Go to bed, Tesla."

"No," he repeated, and it was so unlike him to contradict her that we both looked at him. "She stays. She's a part of this, Meredith. You made her a part of this, so she stays."

What he'd said was true, but I didn't like how he'd said it. Silent, I leaned against the counter, trapped. Meredith tossed her hair over her shoulders, and I saw something about her I'm sure she didn't mean for me to know.

She wasn't as drunk as she was pretending. Oh, sure, she'd had a few drinks, enough to make her giggly. But she wasn't impaired. She knew exactly what she was doing and saying, and she'd known all night long.

She crossed her arms. "Tell me, Charles. What you didn't like about it, when I thought we'd talked about how sexy it would be to try new things. How it would be really hot."

Charlie's shoulders straightened, and he glanced at me, but then focused on her again. "We talked about a lot of things, Meredith, but we also said that if we decided we didn't like something, we wouldn't do it again. I didn't like that place."

"You didn't like me with another guy, Charlie, that's what you didn't like. Why not come out and just tell the truth."

His jaw set. "You're right. That's it. I didn't like watching you with another guy."

Her lip curled, and she turned to me. "But watching you fuck Tesla, that's okay? Watching you eat her pussy, that's fine, too? Wow, Charlie. Talk about a double standard."

"That's totally different, and you know it. She's not some stranger we picked up in a sex club!"

Charlie never shouted, so at the sound of his raised voice, I cringed.

"No," Meredith said, her own voice dripping with derision. "She's some stranger I picked up in a coffee shop."

The world tipped. I didn't want to be there, didn't want to hear the things she was going to say. I put my glass on the counter and moved, but Meredith's next statement snagged me to a stop.

"You didn't complain about that," she said. "Fair's fair, Charlie. You got yours. Why can't I get mine?"

"I'm not something to get!" I cried. I didn't look at either of them. Her words had stung, but the fact Charlie wasn't disagreeing hurt worse.

"Of course you're not," he said, but it was too late.

Meredith laughed. "Oh, honey. Really? Do you know how long we talked about bringing home a girl before I picked you? A long fucking time. It couldn't be just anyone, you know. It had to be someone special. Perfect."

"And you are," Charlie said, though I knew Meredith had been making quite another point.

I stood in the archway between the kitchen and hall, and my hand found the curve in the wall to keep me from stumbling. I turned to face them. "That's not what she means."

She ticked off a list on her fingers. "Not someone we knew really well, in case it didn't work out. Had to be someone we could get rid of with no worries or never see again if we wanted to end it. Right, Charlie?"

He looked pained, his gaze bleak and mouth a grim line, but he nodded.

"Of course, someone hot. Sexy. Someone younger, without kids or a spouse or exes who'd get in the way. Or a family," she said. "Someone without anyone to get freaked out. Someone who didn't have to answer to anyone."

And there it was one more time—envy, that nasty thing. It's not always about what someone else has. Sometimes I guess it can be about what they don't have.

She paused to let the words drop like stones. "Someone wild."

I lost it. I took two steps toward her, my fists clenched, though I had no intentions of hitting her. "I'm not wild! Fuck you, Meredith, you have no idea!"

She blinked rapidly, her cheeks flushing. "I thought about you for a long, long time, Tesla, before I decided you were the right one to ask. So don't tell me I have no idea. Because you did it, didn't you? Without too much thought, even. I asked you to fuck my husband, and you did."

"Because I wanted *you*," I blurted. "But I'm sure you knew that, too, didn't you?"

Her twisted smile said it all, but she looked at Charlie. Then at me. "And now? Don't tell me you don't want him, too."

"Meredith," Charlie warned. "Enough. You're drunk. We're all tired. And we have Christmas tomorrow, a long drive—"

"Oh, fuck Christmas," Meredith spat. "Fuck the drive, fuck all of that. Fuck my stupid family, Charlie. You think I want to get out of bed at the fucking crack of dawn to get over there so my parents can give us another gift certificate to Bob's Big Boy?"

"So we stay home then," he said, sounding a little desperate. "We sleep in. Have Christmas with Tesla."

Her lip curled again, and she looked straight at me. "Tesla has plans."

"She can stay with us if she wants to change them," Charlie said quietly. "Christmas is about being with the people you love."

Meredith drew in a sharp, braying sigh. Her hand slapped my glass off the counter. It crashed on the floor, spraying water and glass chips. The three of us stared at the mess, and she spoke first.

"Jesus Christ, Charlie, would you listen to yourself? Would you? It was never supposed to be like this."

Some delicate thing inside me shriveled and began to die.

"Why did you do it, then?" Glass crunched under my shoe when I stepped toward her, but Meredith didn't move. "Why ask me to fuck Charlie? Why keep asking? Why ask me to move in with you, be a part of you? If this isn't what you wanted, why'd you do any of it?"

She drew in a shuddering breath. "Because I was bored."

Charlie let out a small, low moan of pain. "What?"

She looked at him. Meredith could be charming, giddy, sexy, manipulative, convincing and wickedly funny. She could be soft or hard, loud or quiet, generous or miserly.

THE SPACE BETWEEN US

But this was probably the first time I'd ever seen her be honest.

"I was bored, Charlie. God, I was so fucking..." her breath hitched and she closed her eyes briefly, but then opened them to look at him "...bored."

He shook his head. "I don't...understand. What were you bored with?"

Meredith's eyes glittered with tears, and she swallowed hard. "You, honey. I was bored with you. Everything about you, from the way you combed your hair and wore your ties to how you took so long to make me come. I was just...I was so...bored, Charlie. I'm sorry, but I was tired of fucking you."

"So why not leave me, then?" His throat worked. More glass crunched as he stepped back until he hit the counter. His fists clenched, though I doubt Charlie had any more intention of hitting her than I had.

She gave him a familiar, irritated look. "Because I love you, Charlie, and I don't want to leave you. I just wanted to fuck someone else once in a while. I wanted it...so much." She shuddered, blinking, and silver tears left trails through her makeup. "I thought if you had someone, I could have someone, too. Not forever. Not to take your place. Just once in a while. I just wanted to have some freedom. I wanted to be a little wild sometimes."

Charlie closed his eyes, then covered them with one hand as he turned away. His shoulders twitched. Helplessly, I reached for him, but Meredith's glare froze me in my place.

"You weren't supposed to fall in love with her," she said.

"But I did," Charlie answered, without turning around. "It doesn't mean I don't still love you."

I left them then. Went upstairs to the room they'd given

me, but that had never really felt like mine. I knew she'd follow me, just as I knew Charlie wouldn't.

"And what about you, Tesla?" Meredith asked from my doorway.

"I love Charlie. Yes."

"And me?"

Silence spun out between us until finally I spoke. "Let me tell you another story."

Chapter
39

"It's time for me to go." Vic said this from beneath the hood of some old beater he'd been pretending to work on for the past twenty minutes.

I knew he'd just been pretending because he fiddled a lot with nuts and bolts and wires, but hadn't actually changed anything or even started the car to see how it ran with all the adjustments. He avoided looking at me. I was smart enough to see that.

It scared me.

I went there that day dressed in a short denim skirt, my best panties, a T-shirt clinging to breasts that despite my every wish had not gotten bigger over the summer. I went there prepared to lose my virginity. I hadn't been able to stop thinking about it, or Vic, since the week before, when we'd made out and made each other come on the couch in the back room. Thinking of it, my heart raced and my clit tingled.

But Vic was ignoring me, saying he had to go, and a tidal wave of embarrassment engulfed me. "Where are you going?"

His sigh was so loud I heard it clearly, even though he still had his head buried under the hood. Metal clanged. He pulled back and tugged a dirty hanky from the back pocket of his jeans to wipe his hands. He leaned against the car and looked at me, finally.

"It's time for me to leave, that's all."

"But the summer's not over. We have two weeks left!"

He shook his head and tucked the rag back in his pocket. "Sorry, kid."

My chin went up. "Don't call me that."

"Tesla," he said with a sigh. He pressed the heel of his hand against one eye, then passed his hand over his hair. "Look. I'm sorry."

"For what?" I was bold enough to push him. I wanted to hear him say it, even though I knew it would hurt.

Vic's low laugh surprised me. "You're something else, you know that?"

"What's that supposed to mean?" I put a hand on my cocked hip.

"You're great," he said.

Another wave of emotion swirled through me, this time not embarrassment but satisfaction. I moved closer. When I tried to kiss his mouth, Vic turned his head. Our bodies were touching, but he didn't let me touch his lips with mine. We stayed that way, unmoving, for a second or two—so long I thought the universe had time to grow another planet.

Then he turned his face to mine.

His hands settled on my hips. His mouth took mine, and

the kiss I thought I'd give him became something else. Something stronger, harder. Something I wasn't really prepared for.

I wanted it, though. I wanted his tongue in my mouth, his cock against my belly, his hands on my ass. I wanted Vic so much it made me shameless, and I rubbed myself against him until he stopped, breathing hard, and gripped my upper arms to keep me still.

"You're young," he said.

"You're only five years older than me. My dad's eight years older than my mom. Five years is nothing." I licked my lips, but didn't try to kiss him again.

"I still have to go." Vic pushed me gently to one side and stalked to his office.

I followed. If he didn't want me, he'd have told me to go away, right? I closed the door behind me and studied the way his shoulders slumped. All my big plans vanished with that one small gesture; Vic didn't want to fuck me. I could throw myself at him all I wanted, but I'd only look stupid.

The metal doorknob was cool under my palm, and I was already halfway through the door when he moved behind me. Pushed the door shut. Vic murmured my name, and I turned to face him. He was so close I could feel his breath on my face.

"You're beautiful. You know that?"

I shook my head. Nobody had ever told me I was beautiful. I was too short, tits too small, ass too big. Too smart for boys who didn't know how to talk to girls. Too much of a lot of things, not enough of others.

"Well," Vic said, "you are. And never let anyone make you feel like you're not."

I made some sound of disbelief, wordless because I didn't trust myself to speak.

His kiss was soft and tender. Romantic. It was very sweet and slightly unsatisfactory, all things considered.

"Promise me," Vic said.

"What?" I pushed up on my toes to get closer to his mouth, so my lips moved against his.

"Promise me you'll never let anyone make you feel you're not beautiful. Or not worth something."

I put my arms around his neck. The door was hard against my back, the knob threatening to knuckle into my kidney if I wasn't careful. But I looked into Vic's eyes and saw a lot of truth there. He meant what he said. I nodded.

"Okay. I promise."

He smiled and kissed my forehead. That was not what I wanted. I frowned.

"Vic."

"Yeah?"

"You're making me feel not beautiful."

He laughed and pulled away from me. Took a step back, then another. He held out his hands. "You want me to get into trouble?"

"What trouble?" I demanded. "I'm seventeen, and look around you. Who's going to say anything? They're all too busy fucking with each other to pay any attention to what we're doing."

I sounded bitter, and maybe I was. This had been, aside from that one time last week on that very couch, the worst summer of my life. I had two weeks left to endure before my parents took us home to face a different sort of torture.

I was seventeen and horny, and I already knew how good Vic could make me feel. I was greedy for it, and I didn't really care what anyone else thought. I'd always been good at getting what I wanted. When I saw a flash of desire in Vic's eyes, I moved a little closer. I didn't have much in the way of seductive wiles, but I aimed to use whatever I had.

"Bobby Turner," I said.

Vic's brows lifted. "What about him?"

Bobby Turner was twenty-one, not quite six feet tall, with the wiry body of a terrier and the tenacity of one, too. He'd been coming to The Compound since he was a kid, but his parents had both died in a car accident a few years back. Since then he lived there full-time. He was supposed to be part of the maintenance crew, but he spent most of his time in the greenhouse and in the gardens.

"Bobby Turner," I said, "is trying to get into my pants. Has been since last year."

"You don't let him." Vic didn't sound jealous, just certain.

"He's been fucking Karen Hoffer."

She was a psychologist married to a pharmacist. They had no kids, but they brought their two little yappy dogs with them every year. They didn't stay in the cabins; they had an RV. She was at least fifteen years older than Bobby Turner and also twice his size.

"Mrs. Hoffer?" Vic laughed.

"I saw them together. I saw Bobby Turner on his knees between her legs, eating her pussy." I'd never said that word aloud, and I stuttered a little, but was proud of how it sounded coming out. Strong. Confident. Also a bit sexy. "She was moaning and writhing around, and he was facefirst in it. She was fucking his face so hard I thought she might break his nose. She probably came at least three times."

Vic swallowed, looking awkward. "Wow. Well, good for them, I guess."

"He says he'll eat my pussy until I scream." Actually, Bobby Turner had offered to tongue my clit and finger-fuck me until I turned inside out. But I had a hard enough time saying "pussy."

Vic's laugh sounded uncertain this time. "Does he?"

"I'd rather have you do it." There, I'd said it. It was out there between us, I couldn't take it back, and the worst he could do was say no. Or laugh. That would've been worse.

Vic didn't laugh. He didn't say no. He sighed again and rubbed at his eyes. "Tesla, what we did last week…"

"Was amazing." I moved closer.

He looked at the couch almost as if he couldn't help it, then at the floor. The door. Anyplace but at me.

"You know what my mother told me about sex?" I said.

Vic appeared resigned again. "I can only imagine."

"She said that when the time was right, I'd know it. And that I should make sure to be careful—I'm on the pill, by the way. And that I should pick someone who won't make a mess of it, because there's only one first time."

"Christ. My dad told me to keep it in my pants until I was sure I could do the right thing in case I knocked someone up, and my mother told me she found me under a cabbage leaf." Vic backed up to sit on the desk.

I moved to stand in front of him, though I didn't touch him. "You're the only person who's ever told me I was beautiful."

"That's a damned shame."

"It's true." I shrugged. "I want you, Vic."

Some low, gravelly noise slipped out of him. I put my hands on his knees, then a little higher on his thighs. I didn't push between his legs. I touched him, but didn't move against him even though I wanted to.

"It's you or Bobby Turner."

He barked a laugh. "Shit. No. Not that guy."

"He'll do it," I told him, though I had no intentions of ever

THE SPACE BETWEEN US   355

fucking Bobby Turner, no matter how talented his tongue.
"If you won't."

"I can't."

"You can," I said. "Either you don't want to or you feel
like you shouldn't."

"Both," Vic answered.

I didn't want that to be true. I didn't move. We stared at
each other for another long set of seconds, until at last he put
a hand on my hip and inched me closer, to stand between his
thighs.

"You're a smart girl, Tesla. And you're beautiful even if
nobody's said so before. And you'll find someone to do this
with, I promise you that. But…it shouldn't be Bobby Turner.
Or me."

I was young and horny, but I had my pride. "Fine. I won't
beg."

He hesitated. "Good."

"So tell me what last week was all about, then." I squeezed
his hard thigh muscles through the denim.

His look said I asked a stupid question, but he didn't make
me feel dumb. "I'm a guy."

"You're still a guy," I pointed out, "and you're saying no
now."

"I should've said no then, too."

I bit the inside of my cheek, thinking about that. "So…why
are you leaving? Really?"

Something in his face told me the answer without him having to say a word. Stunned, I stepped back. "You're leaving
because of me?"

"It's not like that."

"What's it like, then? I mean…" I glanced involuntarily toward the couch. "You're leaving because of what we did? But you're not... You won't... You don't have to..."

"I have to," Vic said quietly. "It's my job."

"It's your job to leave?" I blinked away tears.

Then I was in his arms, pressed up against his chest. He smelled good, like clothes dried in the sun and a little tang of sweat and motor oil. His arms around me felt good—better, in a different way, than his tongue in my mouth and his fingers in my panties. With Vic's arms around me I felt as if nothing in the world could hurt me.

Except maybe him.

"No. It's my job... Look. I can't explain. Fuck, I shouldn't even have said anything. Just understand that it's not you."

I pressed my tear-wet face to the soft cotton of his shirt. "Oh, really? It's not me, it's you? That shitty excuse?"

"It's not an excuse." His hand cupped the back of my head. "It's the truth. And I wish I could tell you everything, but I can't."

I had no idea what he was talking about. All I knew was that he was leaving, and I didn't want him to go. I didn't want him to let me go, either. I clung, pride forgotten, and he let me.

"You should get out of here, too," Vic said under his breath. He pushed me back gently and looked into my eyes. "You and Cap. Tell your parents you want to go home. Home's the better place for you. And them. You should get them to leave early."

Suspicion tunneled inside me. "Why?"

Vic traced my eyebrow with his finger, then used his thumbs to wipe the tears from under my eyes. "Just...trust me."

I did trust him, and that's why my parents, Cap and I weren't there three weeks later when federal agents work-ing in conjunction with local undercover officers raided The Compound. In addition to a large number of marijuana plants not so cleverly planted in the woods on the property, they found several fields of opium poppies. Though The Compound members tried to claim the flowers were ornamental only, the purifying and processing equipment set up in one of the old barns was enough to convict twelve of the fifty or so members, including Bobby Turner. During the raid, three people died, including two DEA agents when Karen Hoffer pulled out a shotgun—weapons being clearly against The Compound's philosophy and rules—and shot them before being gunned down herself.

Because of Vic, none of us was hurt. Because of his testimony, my parents were never even implicated in the case. Vic saved us then, and several months later, when my parents' marriage spiraled out of control and I showed up on Vic's doorstep with mascara making raccoon circles of my eyes, Cap at my side, he saved me and my brother in a different way.

I never did forget what he'd told me. To never let anyone make me feel I wasn't beautiful.

"Why are you telling me this?" Meredith asked.

I shrugged. "Because with Charlie I always feel beautiful, Meredith. And with you...I never do."

She drew in a hitching, choking breath. She backed out of the room, closing the door behind her. I heard the rise and fall of their voices, not quite shouts, and though I didn't think I could sleep, at some point exhaustion overtook me and I did.

When I woke in the morning, they were already gone. There was only one thing for me to do. One place to go.

I went home.

Chapter
40

Vic opened the door, his eyes hard when he saw me. He said nothing. I didn't, either. Then he put his arms around me, pulled me close and held me tight. The strong hands that had made a habit of locking doors flattened on my back, his fingertips pressing my shoulder blades.

I cried.

There on the doorstep, with ice under my boots, heat from inside wafting over us, Vic held me while I shook with sobs I stifled against the front of his shirt. He offered no words of advice, no platitudes. The comfort came from his embrace, not his words, and it was exactly what I needed.

"Wipe your face," he said at last, accompanied by a hanky he must've pulled from his back pocket.

"Ew." I shook my head at the thought of wiping my eyes with his snot rag, but it did force back the tears. "No, thanks."

"Come inside." Vic stepped back to let me in. "Everyone's downstairs. You should probably wash your face first. And, Tesla…"

I'd already been heading for the powder room, but paused to look at him. "Yeah?"

"Merry Christmas. It's good to have you here." The sound of excited screams and laughter drifted up from the rec room, and Vic glanced in that direction before looking back at me. "We'll talk later, okay?"

I nodded. Later would be good enough.

The kids were happy to see me, too, even Simone, who begrudgingly forgave me when I showed her the bag of presents I'd brought with her name on them. They fell on the gifts and tore into the wrapping the way kids do, but they also threw themselves onto my lap and covered me with hugs and kisses that smelled of chocolate.

Vic and Elaine were happy with their gifts, too. For Elaine's mom and sister I'd brought gift cards for the Mocha—sort of lame, but something I knew they'd use, and in case they weren't there when I got to Vic's house, something I could just keep for myself. For me there was a wealth of gifts I hadn't expected, and that made me want to cry again, but I held off long enough to get through them all.

Then came dinner, and oh, how nice it was to sit at the table with our familiar china and eat Elaine's traditional Christmas goose with stuffing, mashed potatoes, baked corn, those biscuits from a can that she hated but Vic loved and had taught me to love, too. We laughed and ate, then ate some more. We cleaned up the dishes and then had dessert, then all went back down to the rec room to play with all the new toys.

I managed to creep away to take a peek into my old bedroom, looking empty without my pictures on the wall and clothes in the closet. The bed seemed way too small after so long in a queen-size, but I sat on it anyway and put my hands flat on the bare mattress to feel the places where the springs wanted to poke through.

"It's still yours if you want it," Vic said from the doorway. He came inside and shut the door behind him, then took a seat in the desk chair. "You know that, right?"

I drew in a shaky breath. "I wasn't sure."

"Tesla. You and Cappy...you always have a place here. As long as I have a place, you have one."

It was so good to hear that that I almost cried again. Knowing I could come back was more important than actually moving back in here—something I knew I couldn't do.

"But you won't, huh?" Vic's smile was rueful.

I shook my head.

He sighed and ran his fingers through his short-cropped hair, rumpling it. Even though I knew he'd probably been woken before dawn, he didn't look nearly as tired as he used to. He rubbed his palms against the thighs of his jeans. "Where will you go?"

"I'm sure I can find an apartment. Could I stay here tonight?"

"Of course. You'll have to let me kick your ass at the new Resident Evil, though."

I had a smile for that. "You can try."

Vic grinned, then let it soften. "Tesla...I'm sorry about... whatever happened. I should never have stuck my nose in it."

"You were right, weren't you? Look what happened." I shrugged. "Better it ends now than later, I guess."

"Are you sure it's over?"

I looked at him. "I remembered what you told me."

He didn't ask what that had been. Just nodded. "Well. Then, good for you."

It wasn't good for me, it was awful. It was breaking my heart. It was leaving me alone, and I hated it.

Chapter
41

I didn't expect Meredith to call me, but when my phone rang late Christmas night, I hoped it would be Charlie. He sounded tired, his voice a little muffled. He said my name when I answered, and that was it.

"Is she listening?" I asked.

"No. She's in the shower. She doesn't know I'm calling you."

I was in my old, narrow bed in a sleeping bag, because for some stupid reason I'd taken my comforter and sheets to Charlie and Meredith's house even though I'd known they wouldn't fit the other bed. My phone was cool on my ear, but quickly warmed. I curled into the warmth my breath made in the cave of my covers.

"Then you should hang up," I said.

A beat of silence. "Tesla, I'm sorry."

"For what, exactly?" I wasn't trying to be crappy. Just trying to understand.

"I don't know. What she said, I guess. It's not how I feel. You know that."

"Does it matter, if that's how she feels?"

I wanted him to say yes, it mattered, but Charlie only sighed. "She…booked the trip. She got us a hotel and ski package and everything."

I swallowed a lump the size of my fist. "Good. You go. You should have fun."

"I want you to come."

"I can't, Charlie."

He made a low noise. "I can cancel it."

"You could," I said, tired and heartsore. "But you won't."

"It's not quite a week," he said. "We're leaving tomorrow. Coming back New Year's Eve. We can be together for that, Tesla. We'll just take this little break, get our heads straight. This will all work out. Okay?"

He sounded pleading.

"Okay," I said, but I knew, as he must've, even if he wouldn't admit it, that nothing was going to work out.

Chapter
42

The day after Christmas still felt festive in the Mocha, where we'd keep up all the lights until after the New Year, but I was feeling anything but merry. I wore the new coat Vic had bought me to replace the one I'd torn on the glass, and though I loved it, not even the fresh feeling of new clothes could lift my spirits. I wore Charlie's bracelet, too, which wasn't helping.

"Darek," I said, surprised to see him. "What are you doing here?"

"Came in to see Brandy." He gave me an unabashedly googly grin. "She gets off in twenty minutes. I'm taking her out for dinner."

My brows rose. Darek didn't bother looking defensive, just shrugged. I shook my head and waved him into a seat. When Brandy came out of the back, she squealed and ignored the line of customers waiting for service so she could run over to him. I thought Joy might make something of that, but she only rolled her eyes and stepped up to help me.

"Why don't you leave early," she said across the counter to both of them. It was my turn to raise my brows. Joy shrugged. "It's better than watching them make out."

I couldn't disagree. I watched them, their faces alight with that fresh buzz of new…well, I wasn't sure it was love. On the other hand, what did I know about it? Apparently nothing.

There wasn't much of a rush when Darek and Brandy left, and I fully expected Joy to head for her office to whatever it was she did back there. When she stepped in front of me, looking me in the eye, I stopped. Wary, I took a step back.

"You weren't supposed to come in today," she said.

"I know."

She studied me. "Are you okay?"

It was such a strange question to come out of her mouth that at first I couldn't answer her. Joy looked pale, her generally unsmiling mouth tight in a frown. She'd cut her hair to shoulder length, and it looked good on her.

I shook my head. "Not really."

"Me, neither," she said bluntly. "I've been seeing doctors for months for my endometriosis, and it sucks. It hurts like hell, I have to have embarrassing and expensive procedures, and I'm pretty sure I'll never have kids. Merry fucking Christmas, right?"

"Oh, Joy. I'm sorry." Instinctively, I touched her shoulder, then pulled my hand back right away, but she didn't snap at me.

She sighed. "I am a raging bitch around here. I know it. And I watch you get along with everyone, I see people like Sadie come in here…I see everyone around me having everything I want, and I don't know how to get it. Or worse, know that even if I knew how to get it, I couldn't, anyway."

I didn't know what to say to that.

"I don't want you to quit," Joy said. "We need you here, Tesla."

I coughed. "I don't…I wasn't going to quit. I mean, I'm not planning on it."

"Good." She nodded firmly, her familiar frown easing just a little into something that tried to be a smile. "I'm glad."

"See? You have it in you," I told her. "Let that out a little more often. It gets easier and easier."

Her lip curled and she rolled her eyes, but something about it seemed halfhearted. "Just like meth, right?"

I put my hand on her shoulder again, this time letting it linger long enough to squeeze. "Not really."

She gave me a genuine smile then, the sort she usually reserved for Johnny D. "Let's take down these freaking Christmas lights. They're making my eyes bleed."

I grinned. "Can I change the music station, too?"

"Oh, hell no," Joy said. "I'm not going to be that nice."

Chapter
43

"She's gone."

The words came out of the dark, curling like smoke, and I almost jumped out of my brand-new Christmas boots from Vic and Elaine. I hadn't seen Charlie sitting on the living room couch in the dark. I'd assumed he and Meredith would still be in Vermont. I'd brought some packing boxes and garbage bags, intent on getting my shit out of there before they got back. Even if we did manage to salvage something, I knew it wasn't going to be me living there.

The simple truth was, I didn't want to be a part of them anymore. A part of Charlie, yes. That I couldn't deny. But not a part of the two of them.

I put down my armful of boxes and crossed to him to turn on the light. "Where'd she go? Vermont?"

"No. I don't know." Charlie looked at me, his eyes rimmed

red. A nearly empty bottle of whiskey and an ashtray filled with cigarette butts were both on the coffee table in front of him. He held an empty glass. "I told her I didn't want to go to Vermont without you, that we'd talked about making the trip for three and it didn't feel right with just two."

"Oh. Ouch." I sat next to him, not touching. "Charlie, baby…that was…"

"It was true," he said fiercely. His hair was rumpled, his shirt unbuttoned at the throat. "Dammit, Tesla. It was true."

My heart lifted even as my stomach sank, in a coordinated bit of anatomical talent I'd never have guessed my body capable of. "She just…left? Without telling you where she was going?"

He nodded, then put a hand over his eyes and drew in a long, ragged breath. When he blew it out again to look at me, I smelled the booze and cigarettes on his breath. I was looking at a man undone, and I hadn't been the one to do it. I wasn't really sure I could be the one to put him back together.

But fuck me, I was willing to try.

I took his hand and pulled him closer, our mouths meeting. Tongues stroking. Our teeth bumped, but instead of pulling away, Charlie put his hand on the back of my neck to hold me closer. His low groan pushed my heart into beating faster. His hand between my legs even more so.

Charlie had been shy and sweet and kind and generous with me. He'd been funny and considerate. And now he was desperate.

He pushed me back on the cushions, his kisses bruising and relentless. Delicious. Frantic. He dragged up my skirt and worked at my tights, then opened my thighs to dive between them.

I cried out when he licked me, his lips soft and moving just right against my clit. When he pushed his fingers inside me, he groaned against my pussy. The unaccustomed roughness of his stubble scraped my sensitive flesh in the best of all ways. This was hard and fast, nothing tender about it, and my body responded without hesitation even if my mind and heart were a few steps behind.

His hands fumbled with his belt. His cock pressed against me for a second or two before fucking into me. I cried out again when he filled me, not quite ready for him but embracing the push of him inside me.

Charlie buried his face against my neck. His teeth pressed my skin, then bit. His hands moved under my ass, tilting me against him. The couch protested as we rocked it. Normally I'd have laughed at the sound it made, at how frantically our fucking had begun. All I could do now was rake my fingers down Charlie's back, the material of his shirt keeping my nails from cutting into his skin, and give myself up to him.

This was ending all around me, and all I could do was go along with it.

He said my name when he came. Then again, lower. Softer. He slowed the pace, thrusting once more. Then again. That last press of his pelvis to mine pushed me over the edge into an orgasm brilliantly edged like a diamond, like glass. Beautiful and sharp, and cutting.

Breathing hard, Charlie pressed his forehead to mine. Whiskey breath caressed me. When he pushed himself off me, I ached at the loss, too soon, too sudden. He pulled up his pants and waited until I'd dragged my tights and panties back up my thighs. He poured himself another drink and sipped it, then set the glass heavily on the coffee table and stood. I stood, too.

Charlie's mouth.

That's what I wanted on my body. His hands and mouth. Tongue, teeth, fingers. I wanted the crush of him on top of me, the silken brush of his hair against my flesh, the whisper of his lashes as he closed his eyes against the sight of me.

I wanted Charlie's mouth, and yet something made me turn my face away. His eyes shut, but I couldn't close mine. I had to see every hair and pore, every scar. Every blemish and flaw that made Charlie so perfect.

"If I'd known." His hands were heavy, one on my shoulder, the other on my hip. His breath smelled of whiskey and smoke. He looked like Charlie but didn't smell like him.

Please, Charlie. Please don't tell me you wish you'd missed all of this.

He sighed. "It's just…there's this space between us. This big, wide space. And I don't know what to do with it."

We fill it, I wanted to tell him. But I said nothing. The words wouldn't come. If I couldn't kiss him, how on earth could I possibly tell him that I loved him? That it didn't matter where Meredith had gone or if she was coming back. All we needed was right there. The two of us would find a way to make things work. That it would all be okay.

I could *tell him that,* I thought, as Charlie pulled away. His back was toward me, his shoulders slumped. The jutting lines of his shoulder blades urged me to reach and touch him, but my fingers curled in on themselves instead. I touched myself because I wouldn't touch him.

"I'm sorry," Charlie said again in a low, hoarse voice.

"I'm not," I said finally. "I'm not sorry about any of it, Charlie."

And that, at least, was the truth.

"I love you," I said, and Charlie looked away from me. "I don't regret anything that happened. I'm sorry Meredith couldn't deal with it. I'm sorry if you can't."

He shook his head, just a little. I touched him then, my

hand flat on his back. I stroked my fingers down his shirt, rumpled from our lovemaking. I hooked my fingers in his belt just long enough to tug him the smallest, tiniest amount.

And then…I let him go.

"I came to get my things," was all I said. "I'll pack them up and get out of here."

Charlie sat on the couch again. Poured some more whiskey, but didn't drink it. "She packed it all up. It's in the dining room. I can help you take it out to your car."

This stung me worse than almost anything, that Meredith had already shoved me out of the house she'd invited me into, even though she'd left it herself. Without a word I went upstairs to the room they'd said was mine. It was stripped clean of anything remotely resembling my occupation. I even looked under the bed and found nothing.

In the dining room I discovered the neat stacks of boxes, all sealed with tape. When had she done this? When had she gone? I shook my head, forcing myself not to care, and started taking them to the car. There weren't many, and Charlie helped, though he was a little unsteady on his feet and I did a better job all on my own.

"I want you to know—" he said in the driveway, standing next to my car as we both shivered in the frigid, late December air.

I lifted my chin and put my hand over his mouth to cut off his words. I didn't want to hear him say he loved me, not when I was walking away and he didn't really want to stop me. I stood on my tiptoes and kissed him. Charlie kissed me back.

I stepped away. "Things end, Charlie. It happens. Maybe… maybe she'll get over it and come back to you."

He pulled me close and kissed me, long and lingering, taking his time, but I didn't let myself get lost in it. The kiss broke the way we had, suddenly but not surprisingly. He leaned in, maybe meaning to kiss me again, but again I stepped back.

"Do you have to go?" he asked.

"If you really wanted me to say no," I told him, in a voice only half as bitter as the wind, "you'd have stopped me from taking all this shit out to my car."

He didn't smile.

"Everyone has a story," I murmured, opening my car door and climbing inside. "This is how this one ends."

Chapter
44

Stories end, but life doesn't. Not just because you lose the person you love. Life keeps going. You might cry yourself to sleep every night and wake up in the morning still weeping, but life moves forward in seconds that turn to minutes, minutes to hours, hours to days.

Three weeks after I left Charlie standing in his driveway, I moved into my own apartment. It was within walking distance to the Mocha, a third-floor walk-up in one of the brownstones lining Second Street. It had a minuscule kitchen, a claw-foot tub in the bathroom, two bedrooms just big enough for double beds, and an enormous living room with window seats and built-in bookcases I quickly filled with all the books I'd been stashing in boxes for years at Vic's house.

I'd heard nothing from Meredith, though I'd left her a couple messages telling her I just wanted to talk. I wasn't surprised and could barely be hurt. After all, Carlos had said it—I'd already told her all the stories. There was nothing left to say.

Charlie, on the other hand, called me every day. We never spoke for long. Tentative conversations about work and the weather, carefully avoiding anything that might smack of seriousness. It was nothing like it had been, but I don't think either of us expected it to be.

It took me another week after moving in to unpack everything else. I opened one of the boxes Meredith had sealed up for me. I was looking for an old pair of boots, but what I found was a set of gold-rimmed dishes with roses on them. She'd taken the time to pack them carefully, at least, even if she hadn't labeled the box, and I lifted out one of the dinner plates and held it in my hands, feeling how fragile it was, how breakable if I wasn't careful to keep it safe.

There were other dishes in other boxes. The gravy boat, tucked up tight with bubble wrap. She'd given me the entire set of wedding china.

Someone should use it, she'd said.

They looked just right on the dining room table I'd taken out of storage, the one that had been my mother's before she went to California and left everything behind. I used her linens, too, a lovely old lace tablecloth that had belonged to my grandmother. I set two places. Dinner plate, bread plate, knife, fork, spoon, glass.

I invited Charlie to dinner.

He brought me flowers.

In four weeks, he'd changed. His hair looked mussed, as though he hadn't been bothered to cut or comb it. The faint lines at the corners of his eyes had grown deeper, and ones at the corners of his mouth, too.

He still looked beautiful to me.

We made small talk so strained it hurt my heart. I urged him to sit, and took the spot across from him to serve up the simple pasta dish I'd made. I wasn't hungry, but I forced myself to take a bite.

"She wants to come back," Charlie said, without even picking up his fork.

I put mine down. "I'm sure she does."

"I said no," he told me.

Then he reached across the space between us and took my hand. His fingers squeezed. He kissed my knuckles.

"I love you, Tesla," Charlie said. "And I know I can't expect things to be the way they were before. But I really hope that maybe we can just start over and give this…us…another chance. Because even though we got started wrong, I'd like to try to finish it right."

What, I was going to turn that down? Hell, no. Laughing, I leaned across the table to kiss him, not caring if I dipped my shirt in pasta sauce or squashed my garlic bread.

"All anyone can ever do is try," I said.

Everyone has a story.

This is how this one begins.

★ ★ ★ ★ ★

Acknowledgments

Special acknowledgment to Vicki Vantoch, author of *The Threesome Handbook: A Practical Guide to SLEEPING WITH THREE*, which I found as an invaluable resource while writing *The Space Between Us*.

As always, I could write without listening to music, but I'm so glad I don't have to. Below is a partial playlist of what I listened to while writing this book. Please support the artists through legal means.

Can't Get it Right Today—Joe Purdy
Closer—Joshua Radin
Come Here Boy—Imogene Heap
Early Winter—Gwen Stefani
Ghosts—Christopher Dallman
Glory Box—Portishead
I Think She Knows—Kaki King

Is Your Love Strong Enough—Bryan Ferry
Journey—Jason Manns
Look After You—The Fray
Nicest Thing—Kate Nash
No Ordinary Love—Sade
Reach You—Justin King
She's Got A Way—Billy Joel
Stiff Kittens—Blaqk Audio
Use Somebody—Kings of Leon
Your Song—Jason Manns

★ ★ ★ ★ ★

AWARD-WINNING AUTHOR
MEGAN HART

Liesel Albright dreamed of starting a family with her husband, Chris—not inheriting one already in progress...or one so deeply damaged.

When nineteen-year-old Sunshine and her three children appear on the Albrights' doorstep claiming Chris is Sunshine's father, Liesel offers them temporary shelter. She is stunned to learn that the Family of Superior Bliss, led by a charismatic zealot, has committed mass suicide. Sunny and her children haven't just left the compound—they've been left behind.

For Sunny, however, a lifetime of teachings is not easily unlearned. No matter how hard she tries to forget, an ominous catechism echoes in her mind, urging her to finish what the Family started.

all fall down

Available wherever books are sold.

MEGAN HART

Gilly Soloman has been reduced to a mothering machine,
taking care of everyone except herself. But the machine
has broken down. Burnt out and exhausted, Gilly doesn't
immediately consider the consequences when she's carjacked—
her first thought is that she'll finally get some rest.
Someone can save *her* for a change.

But salvation isn't so forthcoming. Stranded in a remote cabin
with this stranger, time passes and forms a fragile bond between
them. Yet even as their connection begins to foster trust,
Gilly knows she must never forget he's still a man teetering
on the edge. One who just might take her with him.

precious

and

fragile

things

Available wherever books are sold.

MIRA®

www.MIRABooks.com

MMH2924TR